More prai[se for] *[All Other Nights]* rty

IL-9r

"In the slam-bang opening pages of her superb third novel, Dara Horn masterfully establishes both a gripping plot premise and a fascinatingly conflicted protagonist. She sends Jacob roaming across a war-torn land-scape to encounter a marvelous variety of characters, each imagined with empathy and depth. . . . [Horn's] scope is just as ambitious, her talents as prodigious as ever. . . . Horn is too gifted and ambitious an artist to settle for easy reassurances or a facile happy ending; she instead offers her readers the deeper satisfactions of complexity and generosity as she limns a world of agonizing, implacable moral ambiguities and guides her imperfect yet lovable protagonist toward a tentative redemption."

—Wendy Smith, *Washington Post*

"A tale of adventure that weaves the Civil War and the Jews of the North and South together in a web of betrayal and love, dignity and loss, that takes the breath away and makes the heart pound."

—Anne Roiphe, author of *Lovingkindness*

"Riveting . . . written in meticulous but energetic prose . . . *All Other Nights* interrogates and celebrates nationhood and freedom. . . . Conflat-ing Jewish and American history, Horn's third and most accomplished novel portrays Passover, the festival of freedom, amid the carnage caused by slavery. Horn's lively, timely tale extends the range of American Jew-ish literature beyond familiar themes of immigration, assimilation and extermination."

—Steven G. Kellman, *The Forward*

"Would you bump off a relative for a good cause? A really good cause—say, ending slavery? Horn's engrossing third novel forces readers to contemplate such awkward questions. . . . A love story naturally ensues, replete with intercepted letters, fantastic coincidences and miraculous escapes. These implausible twists, in Horn's skillful hands, are not only forgivable—they're delicious. The war supplies the motifs for Horn's themes: the meanings of freedom (not all slaves are physically in chains); the tension between commitment to a cause and allegiance to family."

— Rebecca Tuhus-Dubrow, *New York Times Book Review*

"The richness of the background painted so ably by Dara Horn makes what is a coming-of-age saga a compelling account of one man's development through the horrors of the Civil War.... Dara Horn's skill as a writer and depth of comprehension is fully realized in this remarkable novel."

— Morton Teicher, *Jewish Journal*

"A Civil War spy page-turner meets an exploration of race and religion in 19th-century America in Horn's enthralling latest.... Horn propels the love story at a thriller's pace; the mix of love and loyalty played out in a divided America is sublime."

— *Publishers Weekly*, starred review

"A complex, multilayered, and thoroughly involving historical novel. Horn both unearths a fascinating, relatively unexplored aspect of American history—the role of Jewish Americans in the Civil War—and delivers a novel rich in human emotion and ambiguity. A triumph."

— Bill Ott, *Booklist*, starred review

"Reading Dara Horn's new novel, *All Other Nights*, I felt as if I were traveling on Buster Keaton's locomotive from *The General* through a tunnel into Conrad's heart of darkness—a gorgeous and terrifying ride. This marvelous book consolidates the evidence, for anyone who might still be in doubt, that Horn's talent is quite simply immeasurable."

— Steve Stern, author of *The Angel of Forgetfulness*

"Horn, the award-winning author of *The World to Come*, has written a stunning historical novel that will challenge readers' preconceptions.... Her tale of Confederate Hebrew spies skillfully puts a new spin on a time period that has been researched and written about extensively."

— Marike Zemke, *Library Journal*

"An enjoyably fast-paced amalgam of historical romance, spy novel and political thriller ... a rare and memorable portrait of Jewish life during the Civil War."

— Emily Bingham, *Wall Street Journal*

"Welcome to Dara Horn's stellar third novel. . . . *All Other Nights* has the propulsive, suspenseful narrative of an espionage thriller, but the novel stands out because of the larger moral dilemmas Horn weaves into an epic."   —Sarah Weinman, *New York Post*

"Dara Horn is an astonishing storyteller. One of her greatest talents is for weaving personal tales into the sweeping current of real historical events. . . . Horn employs every method to keep readers irresistibly hooked— from chapter cliffhangers to delicious teasers. . . . But her most effective device is characterisation. Jacob is recognisably human in his self-doubt and vacillation. . . . Perhaps, as Horn seems to suggest in this extraordinary novel, redemption is possible after all—as long as wretches like Jacob are free to make new, and better, choices."

—Ángel Gurría-Quintana, *Financial Times*

"Dara Horn's third novel, *All Other Nights*, shimmers with emotion and historical detail. Set amidst the tumult of the Civil War, Jacob Rappaport is on a quest to find himself. . . . His journey takes him into the bowels of evil, self-loathing and despair; yet there is redemption for him as well as he struggles to make sense of love and duty."

—Sarah Sacha Dollacker, BookBrowse

"*All Other Nights* is such an apparent departure from Dara Horn's previous work that when I learned what Horn was writing, I thought she might not be able to bring it off. I should have known better. . . . [Jacob's] mission, and the idea of bitter-end faithfulness to an extreme, delusional cause, suggest the Joseph Conrad of *The Secret Agent* and *Under Western Eyes*. . . . For a writer as young as Horn to be compared with Conrad shows what kind of league she's playing in. And she plays in it with a skill well beyond her years."   —Jeff Landaw, *Baltimore Sun*

"Part political-and-spy thriller and part love story, this historical novel about Jewish spies during the Civil War offers a fresh look at a well-documented era."   —*Bookmarks*

"The complex world of [Judah] Benjamin and other Jewish Americans during the Civil War is chronicled in Dara Horn's vibrant and compelling third novel, *All Other Nights*, which examines the tenuous relationships of American Jewish spies—between each other, to their religion and to their country—during the Civil War."

—Ruth Andrew Ellenson, Los Angeles Times

"Conflicting values, provocative insights and complex characters are subtly woven into this remarkably ingenious and unpredictable saga of a nation whose races and families are ravaged by the Civil War. Dara Horn has composed a classic page-turner that invites her readers to consider nuances of history, relationships and morality along with what happens next."

—Sidney Offit, Moment

"Horn . . . is one of the finest among the young generation of Jewish writers. . . . [*All Other Nights*] is plot-driven and suspenseful."

—Sandee Brawarsky, Jewish Woman

"[Horn] doesn't shy away from describing the gruesome grit of war and the brutality of slavery. . . . This well-researched book should appeal to Jewish history buffs as well as readers who enjoy an intelligent love story."

—Jewish Book World

"[The book's] ultimate success stems from its religious underpinnings. Its symbolic withdrawals are underwritten by the gold of the biblical narrative. Those resonances—the parallels Horn draws between those slaves and these, between the redeemer of the Old Testament and His manifold successors—give the novel a richness and vigor often lacking in contemporary fiction about this country's bloodiest war."

—Saul Austerlitz, Boston Globe

W. W. NORTON & COMPANY

NEW YORK · LONDON

Dara Horn

ALL OTHER NIGHTS

a novel

All rights reserved
Printed in the United States of America
First published as a Norton paperback 2010

The first chapter originally appeared, in different form,
in the Spring 2007 issue of *Granta* magazine.

For information about permission to reproduce selections from this book,
write to Permissions, W. W. Norton & Company, Inc.
500 Fifth Avenue, New York, NY 10110

For information about special discounts for bulk purchases,
please contact W. W. Norton Special Sales at
specialsales@wwnorton.com or 800-233-4830

Manufacturing by Courier Westford
Book design by Barbara M. Bachman
Production manager: Anna Oler

LIBRARY OF CONGRESS CATALOGING-IN-PUBLICATION DATA

Horn, Dara, 1977–
All other nights : a novel / Dara Horn. — 1st ed.
p. cm.
ISBN 978-0-393-06492-6
1. United States—History—Civil War, 1861–1865—Fiction.
2. Jewish soldiers—Fiction. 3. Jews—United States—Fiction.
4. Life change events—Fiction. 5. Ethics—Fiction. I. Title.
PS3608.O76A45 2009
813'.6—dc22

2008053412

ISBN 978-0-393-33832-4 pbk.

W. W. Norton & Company, Inc.
500 Fifth Avenue, New York, N.Y. 10110
www.wwnorton.com

W. W. Norton & Company Ltd.
Castle House, 75/76 Wells Street, London W1T 3QT

1 2 3 4 5 6 7 8 9 0

For Maya and Ari,

the cause

ALL OTHER NIGHTS

PART ONE

PASSOVER IN NEW ORLEANS

I.

*I*NSIDE A BARREL IN THE BOTTOM OF A BOAT, WITH A CANTEEN OF water wedged between his legs and a packet of poison concealed in his pocket, Jacob Rappaport felt a knot tightening in his stomach—not because he was about to do something dangerous, but because he was about to do something wrong. He was nineteen years old, and he was accustomed to believing that he wasn't responsible for what he did, that there were all sorts of considerations and complications that didn't apply to him. So he had told himself that one knot was the other knot, that there was no distinction between fearing others and fearing oneself. But as he waited through his second endless night with his chin pressed against his knees and his arms pressed against the barrel's wooden sides, listening to the waves slap against the hold of the smuggler's boat that was carrying him to New Orleans, he knew the difference. It had begun on Passover of the previous year, when he first could have said no.

That cold March night in 1861 hung before his eyes like a curtain, the entire evening a hushed held breath of waiting for life to begin. In his parents' townhouse in Madison Square in New York, the long dining table was laden with wine and food, and lined with his father's business associates and their wives and children—and as always, Jacob was seated across from Emma Jonas. Emma was one year younger than Jacob, and utterly homely. At seventeen she was still a child, playing with dolls; it was clear that she suffered from some sort of mental deficiency, but the Rappaports and Jonases were high society, or desperately trying to be, and no one ever mentioned it. After the ritual fourth cup of wine, the conversation returned to the long, dull debate over whether or not a war was imminent, which Jacob pretended to follow so as to avoid Emma's vacant, childish eyes. But he barely heard any of it until Emma's father, who had been silent for most of the evening, suddenly spoke.

"What do you think, Marcus?" David Jonas asked Jacob's father. "I must admit, I've become quite nervous. Shipping is a disaster when you have blockades to worry about."

Jacob watched as his father smiled. Marcus Rappaport was leaning back in his cushioned seat, his full head of blond hair crowning the round boyish face that made him look much younger than he actually was. At that moment Jacob envied his father's happiness, how his father was completely accountable for his own life. Twenty-five years earlier, when he was Jacob's age, he had come from Bavaria as a human pack mule, and walked from farm to farm across New Jersey with a hundred pounds of fabric on his back to sell to the farmers' wives. By the time his only son was born, he was the founder of Rappaport Mercantile Import–Export. For years Jacob worshiped him. Later he became ashamed of him: embarrassed by his father's accent, and, worse, by how his father used him as a showpiece for clients, presenting Jacob with the same pride he displayed when sharing a collection of rare cigars. Jacob was increasingly disturbed by the possibility, which had seeped into his awareness like a very slight but pervasive and lingering smell, that he was nothing more than one of his father's acquisitions, another hard-earned marvel that America, in its infinite bounty, had allowed his father to possess. In the time since he had started working at the firm, Jacob had detected a casual dismissiveness in his father's tone, as though his father somehow sensed Jacob's uncertainties, and disdained them. His father held the maddening conviction that self-doubt was the surest sign of a fool.

"I disagree," Marcus Rappaport said, and turned his smile to David Jonas. "It's all a matter of opportunity. Suppose there's a blockade on shipping from here to the South along the coast. One simply has to rearrange some assets, and become the first to run alternate routes through the Caribbean. Some people might worry about having to adjust so many different accounts, but I'm lucky enough to have Jacob at my disposal. Jacob is brilliant with numbers."

Jacob winced, a gesture he tried to conceal by adjusting his necktie. Across the table, Emma was holding one of the prayer books from the evening's service, cradling it in her stubby, chapped fingers while she lovingly, delicately, and pointlessly folded and unfolded a single page again and again.

"I believe we all agree on Jacob's talents," David Jonas said. Then he turned back to Jacob's father. "And that is why I have an opportunity for you, Marcus."

Now Jacob looked at Emma's father, curious. His face was long and thin, the opposite of his daughter's, his dark eyes quick and alert behind round spectacles, his black hair combed across the protruding peak of his balding head. He was holding out his hand toward Jacob's father, his fingers steady and confident above the wineglasses on the table. "Marcus, I know you've always been interested in my firm," he said. "I've decided that I'd like to sell it to you. At half its value."

Jacob watched as his father raised his eyebrows, his expression just short of a laugh. "You can't do that in good conscience," he said.

"In fact I can," David Jonas replied, "because I would be gaining something else as well." He smiled as the other guests around the table listened. "I propose to give you all of Jonas Mercantile Shipping, at half value, as a wedding gift when Miss Emma Jonas becomes Mrs. Jacob Rappaport."

Jacob's eyes bulged. Surely this was some sort of joke. The service that evening had required everyone to drink four cups of wine; was Emma's father drunk? No, it didn't seem so. David Jonas was leaning forward with both hands braced on the edge of the table, his long, thin face expectant.

Jacob's father laughed. Jacob smiled at him, unspeakably relieved, and was about to laugh himself when he heard his father's answer. "A wonderful, wonderful idea, David," his father announced. "I accept."

Now Jacob stopped breathing. He stared at his father, unable to keep his hands from shaking under the table. Then he looked at Emma, who hadn't even raised her eyes to the company, too absorbed in folding and unfolding the page in her book. His stomach swayed. But now everyone was watching him. His father raised his half-empty glass and leaned toward him, smiling.

. "So, Jacob, to the Union, then?" he asked, with a grin.

Everyone around the table was still watching him, waiting. Jacob swallowed and glanced at Emma once more; she remained preoccupied with the paper between her fingers. He looked at his father, at his mother, at the Jonases, at the table with its prayer books and silver and food, at this astonishing new world that his parents had labored so mightily to bring into being, at the vast promises that had been lavished upon him and the vast obligations required to fulfill them. He looked at Emma again, and understood what was expected of him, what had always been expected. How could he say no?

"To the Union," he said.

His parents and Emma's parents laughed and broke a plate together, an old engagement tradition, and everyone cheered. Jacob Rappaport had been sold.

During the seven weeks before his wedding, he often imagined that he was not one person, but two—one Jacob Rappaport seated in the audience of a theater, quietly fulfilling expectations, while the other Jacob Rappaport stood onstage, about to upend them. He endured night after night of dinners, discussions, arguments, agreements, and then lists of figures that he was asked to disentangle, divining his own purchase price. The ordinary Jacob Rappaport observed the events unfolding before him as he held Emma Jonas's hand, smiled at his father, worked diligently through the figures, stirred sugar into Emma's tea. But on the stage in his mind, the other Jacob Rappaport cursed his father aloud, sent the business into ruin, tipped poison into Emma's cup. He watched these imagined scenes unfold with a fascination that frightened him. On the night before his wedding, he escaped to the 18th Infantry Regiment of New York, unable to understand that he could have said no.

TO JACOB'S ASTONISHMENT, army life suited him. He was surprised by how simple it was to reinvent himself, by how relieved he was when everyone assumed he was just another farmer's or cobbler's or dockworker's son whose reason for enlisting was nothing more than a deep love of country combined with a deep need of cash. That summer and autumn he suffered through several battles, as shocked and silenced by them as everyone else. But one night when spring returned, he was called to the officers' headquarters on an evening when a rumor had spread that the general was visiting the camp. He was certain that he was going to receive a promotion. And when he entered the room on that cold evening and saw the major, the colonel, and the general seated at a table before him, each with a pipe in his mouth, he felt even more certain. He could hardly stifle a smile as he waited for the major to address him, while the general blew a cloud of smoke into the air. But it was the general who spoke.

"Sergeant Mendoza has reported to us that you have relations in New Orleans," he said, resting his pipe in a wooden holder on the table. "Specifically, a Mr. Harris Hyams. Is that correct, Rappaport?"

Jacob paused to breathe, tasting the smoke of the officer's pipe. The mention of Sergeant Mendoza made him slightly uncomfortable. Abraham Mendoza was twenty-one, also from New York City, also a Hebrew, but a sixth-generation American and embarrassingly proud of it. Jacob found him insufferable and assumed the feeling was mutual. Yet one night in the camp, when Jacob was exhausted and lonely and very slightly drunk, he had confided in Mendoza, speaking for the first time about everything he had left behind. Mendoza had been curious, and Jacob had indulged him, grateful for the relief of telling the truth. But then Mendoza had gotten nosy, asking him all about the business, about his father's friends, about his aunts and uncles and cousins—and Jacob, irritated, had finally told Mendoza to leave him alone.

"Yes, sir. Mr. Hyams is my uncle, sir," Jacob said.

"By blood or marriage?" the general asked.

"Marriage, sir. His wife is my mother's sister," Jacob replied, both disappointed and baffled. It seemed unlikely that an announcement of a promotion would commence with a review of his family tree—and with Harry Hyams, of all people. Jacob hadn't seen Harry since he was fourteen years old, but he remembered him as a kind man, one who for years had brought him toys and books and candies from places he had traveled, entertaining him with exotic stories about ghosts who lived in the Louisiana swamps. Now Jacob looked at the officers before him and tried to suppress a shudder. He thought of his parents, and delusion took over: he imagined that his mother had somehow written to her sister to have him sent back home.

The major noticed his trembling, and smiled. "At ease," he said, taking up his pipe.

Jacob put a foot to one side and folded his hands behind his back, but he felt even more uneasy than he had felt before. He grimaced slightly as the general continued.

The officer noticed. "No one is holding you accountable for your relatives south of the Mason–Dixon line, Rappaport," the general said, in an almost fatherly tone. The officer's voice was soothing, comforting, and a familiar relief seeped into Jacob's shoulders. It was a feeling that he had once associated with closing the door to his father's office after a difficult client departed—with being, at last, among family. He breathed as the officer spoke again. "We simply wondered what your opinion might be of this Harris Hyams."

It occurred to Jacob then that perhaps this was a promotion after all, simply preceded by a test that he needed to pass. The illogic of this idea—that a visiting officer would ask him these questions in order to promote him, or that such an examination would require a special visit to the officers' headquarters at such an odd time of day, or that these questions were in any way pertinent to his future in the regiment—did not occur to him. He didn't even think of Harry Hyams; the man himself was irrelevant. Instead he thought of the countless patriotic speeches he had heard in the nine months since he had enlisted, and smartly answered, "Harris Hyams is a slaveowner and a Rebel, sir, and therefore deserving of every disdain."

The three officers smiled. At nineteen, Jacob could not yet tell the difference on strangers' faces between admiration and condescension, and he did not yet know that he ought always to expect the latter. He suppressed a smile of his own, certain that he had triumphed.

Another puff of smoke. "What does he do, this Hyams of yours?"

Jacob winced at the "of yours." Then he felt a memory, the kind that is sensed physically in the body rather than envisioned in the mind. At that moment his body was a small boy's, and Harry's strong hands were reaching down to lift him up. He felt the grip of those hands in his armpits, and the breeze at the nape of his neck as those hands hoisted him high in the air. He pushed the memory aside. "I haven't seen him in years, sir," he answered, still hoping to pass the test. "My father's firm worked with him on occasion. He was a sugar dealer out of New Orleans."

The general chewed on his pipe as the three of them eyed Jacob from what now seemed like a judges' bench. When he spoke again, his voice was slow and deliberate, enunciating each word. "It seems that his professional aspirations have changed since you and he were last in contact," the general said, with a slight smirk. Jacob was disturbed to notice that the two other officers smirked along with him. With deliberate, slow movements, the general placed the pipe back in the holder, letting the smoke weave itself into a smooth veil before Jacob's eyes. Then he looked back at Jacob and said, "Harris Hyams is a Confederate spy."

He might as well have said that Harris Hyams was the king of Scotland. It was preposterous, Jacob thought. "A spy, sir?" Was this another test?

"A very highly placed one, in fact," the major said, and tapped a finger on the table. "With ties to Judah Benjamin."

"What—what ties, sir?" Jacob asked. The name itself had nauseated him: Judah P. Benjamin, the second Hebrew to serve in the United States Senate, and now the first Jewish Cabinet member in history—but one who had chosen to devote his talents to, of all supposed countries on earth, the Confederacy, where he served passionately as the Secretary of State and was the closest confidant of Jefferson Davis himself. Every Hebrew in the Union blanched at his name. As for Jacob, he nearly vomited.

"It seems that Benjamin is his first cousin. But not yours, apparently, your being related through the wife, of course. We're quite pleased about that." He smiled again.

Jacob smiled back. An unexpected ease flowed down into his spine, and he stood taller. He felt a sudden and acute awareness, hovering above the intimate taste of pipe smoke, of his own rightful presence in the room: alive and attuned in every nerve and hair to these officers, pleased by what pleased them, dismayed by what dismayed them, his living body a breathing expression of all of their hatreds and hopes. For a single beautiful instant, he imagined himself as the general's son.

"Hyams has been in and out of the border states in the past few months," the general continued. "As you know, he used to do frequent business in the North, before the war, and has many contacts there." He paused, and looked at Jacob. Jacob couldn't help but look down, dodging the man's eye. Was it a reference to his father? "He has also slipped over the border itself many times, and now we have managed to intercept

his communications with Richmond. Unfortunately he is involved in a
plot." He waited for Jacob, a melodramatic pause that Jacob might have
resented if he weren't so entranced.

"What sort of plot, sir?" Jacob asked.

"An assassination plot. Against President Lincoln."

Lincoln?

"That's—that's not possible, sir," Jacob stammered.

"Why?" the colonel asked.

Jacob saw that the three officers were genuinely interested—certain,
it seemed, that he had something to tell them that they did not already
know. He tried to remember his father's comments about Harry and the
sugar business, but he recalled nothing; the subject had always bored him.
All he could remember were the arguments between the guests at the
Passover table the previous year: how Otto Strauss wouldn't stop arguing that the abolitionists were right, that the slave question wasn't only
a moral problem but an economic one, that no business run on slave
labor would survive the new industrial developments, and how Hermann
Seligman wouldn't stop arguing that Otto was wrong on the business
point even if he was right on the moral point, that as much as he might
agree with Otto in principle, Otto ought to admit he was advocating a
revolution, and revolutions nearly always ended in disaster, as his cousin's
prison sentence in the German states so clearly demonstrated, and anyone heading down that path ought to have a plan quite far in advance
for what he intended to do once the world, however corrupt it had been,
came to an end, and nothing in Otto's argument suggested that he was
even the slightest bit prepared—and then Jacob remembered how his
father had silenced his fighting guests by pointing out, as he did to Jacob
with irritating frequency, that with or without a war, they all ought to
be grateful to God simply for the fact of America, for the astonishing
reality that they could even have this conversation, that they all ought to
stop arguing and accept whatever might happen and be willing to devote
absolutely everything to this country under any circumstances whatsoever, simply out of gratitude for the unimaginable truth that all of them
were here, sitting with their own free children around a Passover table,
with no one to terrify them, and no one to make them ashamed. But
none of it had interested Jacob in the least. He had been busy at the time,

avoiding eye contact with Emma Jonas. "Mr. Hyams is—he's not that sort of man, sir," Jacob finally said.

"We could show you rather convincing evidence to the contrary," the major said, "though we hope that will not be necessary."

"But it's impossible," Jacob insisted. It really was, he knew. It had to be.

"That is precisely what we propose that you ensure," said the general, still smiling, "by assassinating Harris Hyams before the plot can progress."

The three men watched Jacob, grinning at him, as the blood in Jacob's body began draining into his shoes. The room swayed before him. But the men continued to smile.

"Are you suggesting that I kill my uncle, sir," Jacob said slowly. It wasn't a question, of course. The veil of smoke in the air between them parted, dissipated.

"Your actions would do honor to your race," the major said.

"Do—do you mean my country, sir," Jacob stammered, this time trying to make it sound like a question, but without succeeding. In his memory Harry's hands held him under the armpits again, but now his body would not move.

"Both your country and your race, of course," the general said brightly, warming to his theme. "Judah Benjamin and his kin have done your race a great disservice. Every Hebrew in the Union will reward you if you undo what he has done."

The three officers looked Jacob in the eye, and under their gaze, he realized what they saw. While he looked in the mirror and saw a tall, blond, nineteen-year-old American boy, the three men at this table looked at him and saw Judah Benjamin. And Jacob suddenly knew that he would do anything not to be that man. The three officers continued speaking, their words buzzing through Jacob's brain in a blur. But as he listened, he felt himself stepping onto the stage, becoming the other Jacob Rappaport: the Jacob Rappaport whom no one expected, the one who surpassed all expectations, the one who could prove beyond all doubt that his life was entirely his own.

"It is dearly hoped that this is not a death mission for you."

"Though if it should prove to be so, we are confident that you would not refuse the call of duty."

"It is essential that it appear accidental."

"Shooting is no good."

"No one should discover that it was you."

"You will be pleased to know that a plan has been devised."

"Sergeant Mendoza has informed us of a Hebrew holiday several weeks from now."

"The holiday coincides nicely with the navy's plan to take New Orleans."

"You would be a guest at his holiday table."

"A dose of poison would be placed in his drink."

"The effect would be gradual rather than immediate."

"We would provide the lye, or whatever poison is deemed most suitable."

"If you were to be captured, you might consider using the lye yourself."

"You would never consider disgracing yourself by returning without success."

"If you succeed, the entire Union will immortalize you."

"Lincoln himself will thank you, on behalf of your entire race."

"Imagine yourself written up in the history books."

"You would be another Hebrew spy, like in Scripture."

"Cunning."

"Inscrutable."

"Judas Benjamin has done your race a great disservice."

"It can all be corrected with a little lye."

Later Jacob would not recall saying yes. But it did not matter. Their words enveloped him, became him. The curtain rose, and the old Jacob Rappaport disappeared.

2

*I*T WAS MIDNIGHT BEFORE THE EVE OF PASSOVER IN 1862 WHEN the barrel was finally removed from the smuggler's boat and hidden in a stable near a dock in New Orleans. Following instructions, Jacob waited several hours before prying his way out. Through a tiny imperfection in the barrel's lid, he could glimpse the emerging light of a streetlamp nearby. After nearly two days of being entombed in the barrel at the bottom of the boat, he was almost blinded. With his arms numb, it took longer than he had expected to force the barrel open. He emerged, standing on his crimped legs, and crept out of the stable into the empty southern night.

It was a warm night, and very humid, though Jacob was already soaked with sweat. The breeze on that almost-full-mooned night was pure freedom. But his ecstasy at feeling his limbs unfold faded quickly, as he remembered that now the real horror would begin. He hurried out onto the street and past the first stilts of the piers, and climbed down to the riverbank below them. It was a few hours before daybreak, and despite this being cosmopolitan New Orleans, no one but Jacob seemed to be out near the river, not even a drunk. He stripped, buried the filthy rags from inside his trousers under a rock by the edge of the water, and dipped his sweating arms and legs into the Mississippi. The water rushed against his limbs like waves of black ink in the darkness. He felt so dirty that he might have dived right in, if the current hadn't seemed strong enough to drown him. After dressing himself again in a Confederate uniform (borrowed from a corpse who had had the gentility to bleed exclusively onto his hat), he slept for a few hours beneath one of the piers, knowing his nerves would wake him before dawn, and they did. He watched as the first hints of sunlight grayed the air above the river, the sky seething into full daylight as the first few people stepped out onto the docks. He finished off the water he had been so carefully rationing out of his canteen, reached into one of the pockets of the dead man's uniform, and pulled out a paper sign, which he hung around his neck. The sign had been his own brilliant plan. It read:

PLEASE EXCUSE THIS HERO,
WHO HAS BEEN RENDERED
DEAF AND DUMB
BY YANKEE CANNONFIRE,
THO' THE TUNE OF "DIXIE" RINGS IN HIS EARS.

The major had questioned the plausibility of cannonfire rendering someone dumb, but Jacob quickly discovered that the very suggestion rendered those who read it even dumber. Once he had freed himself from bondage, this ingenious sign not only prevented him from becoming involved in awkward conversations with anyone eager to speak to a man in uniform, but it also allowed the Rebels themselves to reimburse a Union spy. By slackening his face into an idiotic smile, pointing to his sign, bowing grandly to the ladies, and holding out his Rebel army cap (collected from a corpse who had been less than punctilious about the blood on the rest of his uniform, but very genteel when it came to his hat), Jacob managed to amass a small fortune in alms—enough Confederate money to provide for whatever needs he might have during his time in the haunted ghost town that was New Orleans.

By midday it was hot. Jacob had never felt humidity like this in his entire life. The whole city was dripping with sweat; there were beaded droplets of moisture on every crooked porch railing of every house in town. And everything drooped. The wooden porches of every house, even the newest ones, sagged in the center, as if giving up on life. Old people sat on these sagging porches, the skin on their frail bodies sagging to match. There were grand mansions here and there, but even the grand mansions looked like abandoned estates, enveloped in cobwebs with bulging, bubbling paint on the walls, the paint itself peeling off in large, hopeless patches in the thick miasma of heat. Low, heavy trees drooped their long branches almost down to the sidewalks. In the streets downtown, where Jacob strolled for some time before heading toward the Garden District, the air was heavy with pipe smoke, sweat, and sloth. Following his memorized mental map, Jacob began the long walk uptown. And it was there, after passing many drooping houses and many elderly men as he walked along his way, that he came across the Hebrew cemetery.

Cemeteries in New Orleans are like small cities of the dead. The ground is too soft and flood-prone for underground graves, so the departed are instead interred in stone mausoleums, some of which are grander than the homes of the living. Hebrew custom demands burial directly in the ground, but because they lived in a swamp, the Jews of New Orleans had developed their own solution, as Jacob discovered as he glanced through the Hebrew cemetery gates. Forced to inter their dead in ground too soft for burial, they had created their own necropolis, where each of the graves consisted of a small elevated mound of mud covered in a layer of grass, tiny raised mausoleums made to look like part of the earth. Each plot was a little grassy plateau marked with a modest stone plaque, forming a city of small truncated mountains: small hopes, small fears, small triumphs and failures, all.

Jacob had never been inside a cemetery. His family was descended from the biblical high priest, and there was a Hebrew law that forbade them any contact with the dead. But it seemed foolish to Jacob to follow such an inane rule now, given what he was about to do. The entire edifice of law and custom dissolved before his eyes. And so he entered, walking among the graves as the sun sank over the drooping trees. He was surprised by how much it disturbed him to stand among the dead, as though he were a child afraid of ghosts. The branches of the low trees around the graveyard's edge swayed in the faint breeze, and each slight movement of the air reminded him that the ground beneath his feet was alive, the earth itself breathing, rising and falling with the most contaminating anguish of both the dead and the living, regret. It wasn't long before he came across the Hyams family plot, under a vine-draped tree. Three generations' worth of Hyamses lay waiting for the messianic age beneath this small piece of soggy land. He paused above them, and began, out of fear, to recite the mourner's prayer. Then he saw the empty space to the side of the most recent grave, blank grassy earth, and he realized that he was the only person in the world who knew precisely who would occupy it.

The words of the prayer left his lips. He glanced up at the sky, where the sun was setting the tops of the trees on fire. If he had been a braver man, or a wiser man, he might have asked God what he was doing, or why he was doing it, or whether the dead around him, eternally burdened with their own remorse, envied him the chance to choose. But instead he looked at the sun and merely saw that the hour was growing late, and that it was time to continue, to do as he was told. He turned away from the disappearing sun, hurried out of the cemetery, and continued on to St. Charles Avenue, remembering to remove his sign just before he reached the large and decrepit wooden mansion that was the home of Harry Hyams.

A SLAVE OPENED the door. Jacob wasn't sure who he was expecting—Harry Hyams himself, perhaps, presenting him with a dagger to insert into his chest?—but this narrow-eyed Negro took him by surprise. The man looked to be about fifty years old, and he was standing with one foot bent to the side. Jacob had wondered at first why a slave this man's age wouldn't be working on a plantation somewhere, but perhaps a cripple had been a discount as a house servant. The slave eyed Jacob's uniform, letting his gaze roll up and down Jacob's chest. Then he looked at Jacob with an expression of astonishing contempt, sweat beading on his forehead. The look on the Negro's face unnerved Jacob. It was the face of a man who was done pretending to please. And Jacob, a novice at pretending, was just starting to accustom himself to absorbing contempt. He narrowed his own eyes, and grinned.

"Mrs. Hyams, please," he said. He didn't know whether Harry Hyams would be home at that hour, and even if he were, Jacob wasn't ready to look him in the eye. Beyond the doorway, he could see an ornate foyer with carved, painted moldings and pale square patches on the walls between the sconces; he wondered if paintings had been sold.

The Negro looked at Jacob again, his gaze crossing Jacob's chest, and for a moment Jacob imagined that the man could see the poison in his pocket. "Who's callin'?" he growled.

For an instant Jacob hesitated, startled to discover that he didn't have an answer. After playing the deaf and dumb war hero, his own real name eluded him, a forgotten line from a script. He paused and glanced down to evade the man's scowl, slipping his left hand into his pocket and fidgeting with the chain of his watch. His skin crawled inside the uniform, the nerves of the dead man alert beneath it as his right hand withered at his side.

"Rappa—Rappa—Rappaport," he stammered. His tongue clung to the roof of his mouth. "Mr. Jacob Rappaport."

The Negro stared again, and for a moment Jacob thought he might be about to spit at his feet. Then he turned his head. "Miz' Hyams!" he shouted. "They's a soldja heah! Mista Rappa!" He grunted and then, as if dismissing Jacob himself, turned and went into the house, letting the door drift closed behind him. Jacob caught the swinging door with his foot and watched the slave progressing down the hall with an agonizing limp, until he could see an enormous blue dress moving into the foyer. As the dress approached, he saw a woman's head affixed to the top of it, hair piled in a tower adorned with shoddy-looking false pearls. Presumably there was also a face somewhere, though the place where it would be was obscured by an enormous fan made of turquoise peacock feathers.

The peacock feathers moved toward Jacob as if the bird itself were strutting in his direction, waving its gaudy tail in a delicate mating dance. "Rappa? Who is Rappa?" a voice behind them asked. The feathers slowly lowered, and Jacob saw her face: the pale green eyes, the full-lipped mouth stretched into a society smile, the guarded greeting and the kindness lurking far beneath it. And then he almost wept, because in the face of Elizabeth Hyams, Jacob saw his own mother standing before him.

It had been several years since he and Elizabeth Hyams had seen each other, and Jacob looked quite different now than he had looked when he was fourteen. But he did resemble his mother. People had always told him so, especially in the year or two before he ran away, when he was still barely able to grow a beard. Elizabeth Hyams must have thought so too, because she didn't even say hello to him. Instead, she looked at his eyes and said, "Dear God." And fainted.

3

"CLEARLY I WASN'T EXPECTING YOU."

Elizabeth had recovered quickly, with Jacob raising her off the ground and the slave limping to the kitchen and back with the smelling salts. Jacob was surprised by how frail her body felt in his arms. Her voice was his mother's, down to the slight German accent. She looked him over. "And in our uniform! But—but you're a Yankee!"

"There was no way to tell you," Jacob said, and tried not to sicken at the words. He then began reciting the story the officers had fed him—the long and tediously sentimental tale of how he had been about to open his own branch of the business in Mobile, Alabama, mere weeks before the war began; how his beloved wife in Mobile, whom he had finally married after corresponding with her for over a year, had died of malaria; how he had been conscripted and had so courageously chosen not to betray her and her family; how he had written to the Hyamses many times but had had the wrong address; how his parents had tried to write too, but of course no one could correspond across the lines; the name and number of his supposed Rebel regiment; the vague imaginary battle where he had lost his comrades in arms; how he had walked all the way to New Orleans; how amazed he was that he had arrived in time for Passover; and on and on and on. Jacob had practiced this monologue so many times, even in the barrel, that he could perform it without the slightest thought. What he wasn't prepared for was giving this speech while being watched by his mother.

"So tell me everything—what you've seen, all of it," Elizabeth said, her eyes full of compassion. She had believed every word.

Jacob looked at Elizabeth and thought of his own mother, of how devastated she must have been when he left, her life's purpose upended. His mother, too, had been one of his father's acquisitions, ordered by mail from his old Jewish town in Bavaria. Her sister Elizabeth, whom

Jacob's mother still called Elisheva, had been similarly exported to New Orleans. Not long after the sisters' departure, the rest of their family in Bavaria had proceeded to die in a cholera epidemic. The two surviving sisters lived in awe of their husbands, whom they regarded as agents of divine rescue; their breathing American children were their evidence of God's presence in the world. For an instant the poison burned in Jacob's pocket against his chest, and he was ashamed to find himself swallowing a sob. Elizabeth mistook his muted sob for a sign of his own painful past rather than her own painful future, and Jacob grimaced as he saw tears gathering in her eyes.

"Oh, you don't have to speak of it," she said, grasping his hands. "It's so cruel of me to ask. It's just that I'm thinking of our boys. Please forgive me."

The knot in Jacob's stomach tightened as her rings dug into his fingers. Again he told himself that it was nerves. And again he knew that it wasn't. He remembered the mesmerizing words of those three men in the officers' headquarters, and he continued his performance as planned. "It will all end soon enough, I assure you," he said.

"I'm delighted to hear it from you," Elizabeth replied with genuine joy. "The newspapers have been so gloomy. Everyone is gloomy, I suppose. Even Harry."

Harry! No, he wouldn't think of him now, Jacob told himself. There was no point in thinking of him now. Luckily Elizabeth was able to distract him. "How are your parents?" she asked.

His parents? Jacob imagined them as he had nearly every night since he had run away—his father enraged, his mother destroyed, both of them unable to comprehend why he had done what he had done. It occurred to him that he was free to hate them. Jacob looked Elizabeth in the eye and imagined, for a brief and liberating instant, that his parents were no longer his parents, that his existence before this moment had been no more than a vanishing cloud, a fleeting dream—that he belonged to no one except the officers of the command. And what was one more lie? "They are well, very well, as I last heard," Jacob told her, and was grateful that the blockade had gone into effect just before he had enlisted; there was no way his mother could have told her that he had run off. "Of course, they were quite concerned about you."

Elizabeth flapped her fan, and Jacob saw her looking at the floor.

"Oh, we are all fine, really," she said, and he heard her first false note. He glanced around the bare, shabby room, then back at her, and noticed a small hole in the toe of her shoe. "Though we're always worried about our boys," she continued. "All four of them are away, of course. Everyone's boys are. For the first time in my life, I've envied those mothers with daughters, the ones who used to envy me." She smiled. "But how glorious to have you here, a fine substitute for our boys! Harry will be so pleased to see you," she told him, fairly chirping. "And in our uniform, too! He already has such admiration for you."

A real man, Jacob had learned during the past year, is one who excels at concealing emotion, succeeding in pretense. He looked down at the hole in Elizabeth's shoe with his lips pursed, in an attitude of what he hoped would come across as modestly hidden pride. He used this opportunity to create a small mental fantasy—an art that he had perfected during his time in the barrel—in which he escaped to the kitchen and delivered the contents of his stomach into the nearest bucket. He reenacted this fantasy in his head several times as Elizabeth spoke of each of her four sons: dear Henry, the brilliant one, whose letters were full of arcane discussions of what was permitted by military law; Richard, the wicked one who was always running into trouble with the ladies, and whose letters consisted of nothing but jokes; Tom, who always saw the world in such a simple and innocent way, and who was now recuperating from some sort of injury to his hand—he hadn't answered her questions about the nature of the wound, but he had sounded so cheerful in his letters that she couldn't imagine it was anything serious; and Charles, the youngest and the sweetest, who never asked anything of anyone—and from whom she hadn't heard since the winter, when he had written to say that he was being stationed somewhere in Virginia. What expert pretenders his cousins were, Jacob thought. Henry and Richard with their letters full of distractions and jokes! And Tom, who was likely hiding the fact that he had lost an arm. And as for Charles, Jacob had been in Virginia that winter too. At one point after a skirmish in Dranesville, he had retreated through a field strewn with enemy corpses, tripping over the bodies of boys. Perhaps he had even killed Charles himself. He tried to think of the mission, of Lincoln, to remind himself that he was about to become a hero, a savior, the one who would, in a single simple gesture, redeem the entire world, tonight. But he couldn't look at Elizabeth's eyes. He was the angel of death.

"Judah will be here, too, I'm sure you shall be pleased to know, though he said in his last letter that he may be late," Jacob heard Elizabeth say. Her words halted Jacob's dark thoughts in their tracks. "I don't believe you've ever met him before. His sister is ill, so he will come alone. His wife and daughter live in France."

"Judah?" Jacob asked. His face showed only gentle curiosity, but he could scarcely believe it. Could it possibly be?

Elizabeth looked at him as though his brains had spilled out onto his uniform. "Why, Judah Benjamin, of course!" she announced. Her cheeks reddened with pride. "He's Harry's first cousin. Oh, I see why you're confused," she said, though Jacob was more astonished than confused. "He married a Catholic, of course," she said, in the low voice that society women use to tell people that someone has had a disease, or an affair. As a Rappaport, Jacob had heard that voice many times. "But that was just for the show of it. Hardly even for the show of it, actually, since he barely shows it. He often comes back to New Orleans for Passover." She beamed.

Jacob found this nearly impossible to believe. What Secretary of State abandons his president in the midst of conflagration, traveling for days on end, just to celebrate a holiday? Benjamin might not have become a Christian, but it was impossible to believe that as a Hebrew he had suddenly become devout. There was another reason for this visit. And Jacob rallied as he understood what it might be.

The smells from the kitchen were now seeping into the parlor, spreading through the room like distant music: old, familiar smells of wet parsley, chopped horseradish, stuffed fish. Suddenly Jacob was a child again, smelling those same smells coming up from the kitchen while he was confined to his bedroom until the preparations were done. He shifted in his stolen uniform and imagined his body becoming the boy he had once been, dressed in a starched shirt and pressed short pants and spotless new shoes, arranging toy soldiers in endless boring rows along his bedroom floor as he inhaled the fresh smells from below, waiting eagerly for the sun to set, for the guests to arrive, for his mother to set him free. The memory lingered in his mouth. Jacob breathed in and wished, for an instant, that time might suddenly stop: that he might remain in this day forever, confined and protected within this room, with this familiar woman and these familiar smells, never released into the strange wilds of the night to come.

He had another thought: that the poison in his pocket might be given to Benjamin instead, surely a more worthy target. But he was too horrified of doing something wrong. The sky in the windows was already growing darker, a heavy blue dusk pressing against the windowpanes. He listened as Elizabeth continued talking about her darling sons and waited for the door of the house to open, dreading the moment when Harry Hyams would come home and join them for the evening meal.

JUST HALF AN hour later, he did. To Jacob's great relief, he came in the door with ten other people in tow, which mitigated Jacob's need to speak with him more than was bearable. Of course, Harry nearly fainted himself when he saw Jacob standing in his foyer. But Jacob was the one holding his breath.

"My dear boy!" Harry exclaimed, doffing his hat in Jacob's direction. "The young Rappaport scion—a real man now! And a Yankee turned Rebel! I never would have guessed it!" Harry was taller than Jacob, over six feet high. The top hat Harry tipped toward him reminded him of his own father's. The similarity in their gestures alarmed him, disturbed him. The collar of the dead man's uniform stuck to his damp neck.

"I never would have guessed it either," he replied. Elizabeth immediately began to babble about the unopened office in Mobile and Jacob's poor dead wife and how he had been conscripted and couldn't bear to betray her and so forth. Jacob was relieved not to have to repeat the story. He had to work hard enough to appear calm, unsure of what to do with his hands. Harry absorbed the lies. He offered his condolences before hiding a grin.

"Tell me, son, do I look older?" he asked.

"Not a bit," Jacob told him. When he dared to look more closely at Harry's face, he was surprised to see that it was true. One always imagines that people are preserved precisely as they looked when one last saw them, but Harry Hyams actually was. The war, which had so clearly aged his wife and nearly everyone else Jacob had crossed paths with in the past year, seemed to have had the opposite effect on Harry Hyams. Unlike everyone else in America, who had become haggard and ill, Harry appeared just as young as when Jacob had last seen him, or even younger. His arms and legs and even his stomach looked lean and muscular. But more than that, the strange reversal of aging showed in Harry's eyes. They gleamed, as though they saw more than they would let on, like a boy playing a prank. When Jacob was a child, that look on Harry's face had intrigued him, making him think of Harry as a boy in man's clothing. But now, as Jacob stood before him in a uniform stolen from a corpse, he saw that gleeful look and felt sickened, sensing, for the first time in his short life, what it might mean to be a boy in man's clothing.

"I must admit, Jacob, I never imagined that we would see each other again. Five years, has it been? How life has changed. How the world has changed."

Jacob smiled at Harry as Harry kissed his cheeks. For an instant he blinked his eyes, and in his mind Harry Hyams became his father: grinning, satisfied, unable to fathom what was about to happen to him. The image emboldened Jacob, making him stand straighter. He thought again of the three officers, of their faith in him, and nodded. "And it continues changing," he added.

An old man standing beside Harry removed his hat. "We're proud of you, son," he said to Jacob. "This isn't the old kind of war. My father was a veteran of the Revolution, and he always spoke of how war should be about principle. I know up north they think it's about principle, but it isn't, son. It's about land. Don't let anyone tell you otherwise."

Never in Jacob's life—his city life, lived in carriages and on cobblestones, with his parents and their friends and their friends' children—had he heard anyone talk about land. No one in his family had owned land for the previous twenty centuries. He had to stop listening. The more he listened, the worse everything would become.

Jacob was grateful when Elizabeth began ushering everyone into the dining room. As he followed the other guests, he saw Harry turn to Elizabeth. He expected to hear a friendly greeting, or even see him kiss her hand. Instead, Jacob heard Harry say, in a voice so harsh it shocked him, "Where is Judah?"

"Late," she whispered back. "He said that he would be late."

"He had better come," Harry said.

Elizabeth smiled. "Oh, he'll be here. Be patient, you old fool," she told him.

Harry grumbled as Elizabeth hurried past him to the table. All of Jacob's memories of Harry were of a cheerful, boyish man who was impossible to annoy. But those were a child's memories. Jacob took a seat toward the end of the table, with a good view of Harry's place at the head, as the service began.

Jacob wondered if there could be anything stranger than sitting down to a Passover seder, the feast of freedom, with every part of the meal served by slaves. But that was exactly what happened at the home of Harry Hyams. It was a good thing that most of the service was in Hebrew, Jacob noticed, because it was far more comfortable without the slaves listening, though there were more than enough awkward passages about freedom that Harry read proudly in English from his seat at the table's head. The limping slave who had answered the door, along with a Negro woman (the cripple's wife, Jacob wondered? Or, he forced himself to imagine, had the cripple's own wife been sold elsewhere, and this woman was a new household purchase, a stranger?), were the ones who carried the platters of matzah and bitter herbs in and out of the dining room while the guests sang the Hebrew hymns thanking God for freeing them from bondage. The others avoided eye contact with the slaves who delivered their food and dishes. But Jacob decided to look at them each time. The woman avoided his gaze, but the man glared back at him, with a look of strange and vicious triumph. It frightened Jacob even more than Harry did. He looked away.

From the beginning Harry Hyams led the service, rising from his seat to raise his first glass of wine and recite the opening prayers. As he sat down and the slaves began to pass around the basin and pitcher for the ritual washing of hands, and then platters of green vegetables, Harry introduced every man at the table, each of whom seemed to be the owner of some plantation or mercantile concern, until he came to Jacob. "And this," he said, raising his glass in Jacob's direction with a wink, "is my nephew, Jacob Rappaport, the greatest turncoat of the century."

Jacob had to force himself to laugh with the company and kept smiling when, a few moments later, Harry addressed him again. "Jacob, as the youngest person at the table, would you do us the honor of asking the Four Questions?"

Jacob tried to hide his grimace beneath a grin. It was the child's part of the service, the part he had recited at his parents' table since he was three years old, but now the nature of the opening question sickened him. Everyone was watching him, and he had no choice.

With a crack in his voice, he began to sing the traditional words, trying not to imagine what they might mean: "How is this night different from all other nights?"

Fortunately he did not have to think about the answer for very long, because a moment later, Judah Benjamin entered the room. Everyone stood.

Every Hebrew in America was fascinated by Judah Benjamin. Southern Hebrews saw him as the messenger of the Messiah, the herald who would proclaim liberty throughout the land to anyone who had ever felt that Jewish fear of power. Northern Hebrews saw him as the beginning of a descent into an American Jewish hell, and whispered at Friday night tables that if the Confederacy were to prevail, the rot of centuries would eat through even the freshness of America and the Jews would be blamed again. After poring over all the information the officers had given him to read in preparation for his mission, Jacob found that his every thought about Judah Benjamin made him ill at ease, and it was only many years later that he was able to understand why.

Judah Benjamin was a clear American genius, one who had achieved nothing through birth and everything through self-transformation. Born on some godforsaken Caribbean island before his family relocated to South Carolina, where his parents sold fruit near the Charleston docks, Benjamin had been admitted to Yale Law School at the age of fourteen, despite his name, lineage, and utter lack of funds. Leaving Yale after being accused (falsely, Jacob was later convinced) of stealing, and unwilling to return to his poverty-stricken parents, he had decamped to New Orleans, where he quickly took advantage of being the cleverest man in town by opening a law practice, getting himself elected to the state legislature, and then graduating to the United States Senate. Along the way he acquired a gorgeous wife from the city's French Catholic elite and later his very own plantation, a fine prelude to becoming the second-in-command of the entire Confederacy. It was American brilliance, plain and simple. His entire life was an elaborate refusal to be the person he had been born to be.

The problem was that it was all a façade. He was a lawyer without ever having finished law school, a planter who knew so little about farming that he traveled to France to learn about seeds, a patriarch of a Catholic family who would never dream of believing that Jesus was a god, a man married into the Southern aristocracy whose wife and child had permanently traded the South for Paris. And everyone who looked at him remarked that they had never seen such a Hebrew face.

He stood in the doorway for a moment without advancing toward his seat. He was short, not much more than five feet tall, with rounded, smooth cheeks like a boy's, dark skin and dark eyes. Jacob had read in newspaper articles about his perpetual mysterious smile, but it was a shock to see it in person. Benjamin's eyes roamed the room, pausing at each face, and the smile on his lips wasn't an invitation to friendship, but a guard against it. It was impossible to guess what he was thinking, and unnerving to try. "It is a pleasure to be here, Harry," he said slowly, as Harry rose to show him to his seat. His voice was careful, articulate, with only a very slight drawl. "It was so gracious of you to include me this evening."

Jacob watched as Harry drew out a chair for him, with a slight bow. The entire company, Jacob saw, avoided Benjamin's penetrating gaze. It was as though they were in the presence of a king. Benjamin took his seat, and it was only when Harry returned to his place and announced the next part of the service that everyone felt free to smile. And Benjamin gave each person his haunting smile back, opened his book, and followed along as Harry continued leading the service, chanting along with the company that they had once been slaves in Egypt until God took them out with a mighty hand. It was extremely strange. Jacob's memories of Harry were of a grand presence, a man who filled a room. But here he saw a different Harry: timid, diffident, waiting for permission. As Harry continued reading the service aloud, he seemed under a spell.

Since it was Jacob's great ambition, at nineteen years old, to achieve the kind of victory that Benjamin had purportedly achieved in becoming an American hero, he observed him across the table for the rest of the evening, looking for clues from the master. He watched him very carefully. And what he saw was that there was something odd about Benjamin, though he couldn't quite place it. It was obvious that Benjamin was fiercely intelligent; everything he said was a sort of aphorism, though

Jacob didn't know whether or not the lines were original. When one of the guests asked him, rather jovially, what new plans Richmond had in terms of strategy, Jacob was disappointed and then frightened when Benjamin looked straight at him and said, as though quoting, "Three can keep a secret if two of them are dead." The company seemed to find this witty, and when everyone laughed, Jacob joined in, hiding his fear. For the rest of the meal Benjamin seemed friendly enough, always smiling. But despite his being a lifelong politician—a former United States senator, and now the second most powerful man in the entire Confederacy—Benjamin had a certain awkwardness about him. He answered questions put to him, but didn't inspire anyone to continue the conversation. It was as if every word he said were carefully parsed out in his mind beforehand, after he had decided whether it was worth saying. While he was silent, he would smile—a strange smile, as if he were laughing at you without your knowing why.

But watching Benjamin was just a distraction for Jacob, an indulgent escape from the riveting personage of Harry Hyams seated before him. Jacob tried to concentrate on the story being told as they chanted the liturgy around the table, describing the anguish of their ancestors, slaves in Egypt, and the vast vindications wrought to liberate them—one of the few moments of Hebrew glory in all of history, perhaps even the only one. But now he imagined how terrible it must have been to live through: the tortures of slavery, and then the horrifying vindication of the angel of death, slaying the firstborn of Egypt so that the Israelites might be set free. And now he wondered: what had the Israelites felt as the great cry went up in Egypt, when there was not a single household where there was not one dead? Victory? Vengeance? Or astonishment at their sheer power, through the will of their God, of determining life and death? Did one of them feel, perhaps, that still, small fear that Jacob felt as he listened to Harry Hyams, with the poison in his pocket?

"In every generation," Harry chanted from the book in his hands, "each person is obligated to see himself as if he personally had come out of Egypt." Harry read with the alacrity and expression of someone who didn't just recite the words, but felt and believed them.

"We ourselves shall come out of Egypt soon enough," Benjamin said when Harry paused. "I have good word of it from Richmond."

The company laughed aloud as the lame Negro—unnoticed by the other guests, glaringly present to Jacob—came to serve the small dishes used for the bitter herbs. "But I thought you said it was all a secret," Elizabeth replied, with a playful air. It was even more painful for Jacob to look at her than it was to look at Harry.

"Victory is no secret, but an inevitability," Benjamin said. "Otherwise we would have been vanquished months ago. It was true in the past, and it remains true now. Every time they rise up to destroy us, Providence rescues us from their hands."

The people around the table cheered. There was something mad about this, Jacob saw, hypnotic. Every person in the company was in Benjamin's power. Soon the meal was served, and the conversation consisted almost entirely of compliments to him, prodding questions about war strategy which he consistently refused to answer, and sad laughter as the women shared stories about their sons who were away, and, though Jacob was the only one at the table who could imagine it, quite possibly dead. The delusion was grand, glorious, and they were all part of it.

4

HE SERVICE WOULD CONTINUE AFTER THE MEAL, BUT FOR THE time being the company had retired to the parlor, to relax and circulate before returning to the table. By then it was quite dark out; the crippled Negro had lit the lights, and a breeze coming through the windows lifted the burden of the day's heavy heat. Jacob tried to chat casually with Elizabeth and some of the other guests, but he positioned himself with his back just in front of Harry. It was then that he noticed Harry moving aside to speak with Judah Benjamin. Jacob kept the small man in the periphery of his vision as he stood beside Elizabeth, letting her babble about her army boys while he listened to the conversation behind him.

"Judah, I know you have abandoned your fathers' faith, but perhaps you would be willing to join me in the drawing room for a discussion about the meaning of freedom," Jacob heard Harry say, his voice low.

Jacob could hear the grin in Benjamin's voice as he replied. "In fact, a good pipe is what I'd prefer."

Harry let out a puff of breath. "Alas, I must report that my wife is a bit more traditional than I, and will not tolerate smoking during the holiday."

"It is only on the Hebrew festival of freedom that one feels more liberated after returning to everyday life," Benjamin proclaimed. "An oppressive tradition if ever there was one. I suppose we shall have to retreat out of doors."

"A brilliant idea."

"Good, then." Benjamin turned, and for a moment he stood looking at Jacob. His expression was a blank; it seemed he hadn't thought he had been heard, or if he did, that he thought nothing of it. He clapped a hand on Jacob's shoulder. "We have great admiration for you, young man," he said. "It's a rare man who sees his kinsman's plight as you do, and comes to his aid. A true loyalty to one's own."

It was a hard compliment to accept, especially coming from Judah Benjamin, Jewish prince of the Confederacy, but Jacob thanked him and shook his hand. It was easier than looking Harry in the eye. Then the two of them excused themselves and headed for the back of the house. Jacob listened a bit more to Elizabeth's pining for her boys and then excused himself in turn, even indulging a slight bow, leaving Elizabeth with three women who had been anxiously awaiting their turn to speak with her. With his curiosity overwhelming any sane sense of risk, he hurried through the halls to the back of the house, following in Harry's footsteps.

THE MOON WAS round, as it always is on Passover, a coin resting on the moist black velvet of the spring night sky. Jacob waited by the house until Harry and Benjamin had rounded the corner of the latrine. Then he proceeded, softly, toward the latrine's open door. It was easy to walk undetected on the soft ground. The drooping tree branches drifted idly in the wind as Jacob entered the latrine without a sound, securing the door behind him and then leaning over the cesspool against the shed's back wall. Benjamin's and Harry's voices came through clearly, over the stink.

"So we've come to discuss the meaning of freedom, then?" Harry asked. Jacob could hear his smile. "I must admit, I find it hard to believe that I am the only reason you are here."

"Don't flatter yourself," Benjamin spat. "Perhaps you haven't heard that the delta is surrounded? All of New Orleans could fall in less than two weeks. Trust me, you are a very minor part of my business here."

Jacob heard a match being struck, then struck again, and then silence. In the fetid shadows of the latrine, he imagined Benjamin's face lit by the sudden flame, his dark eyebrows illuminated from below.

"So here I am, prepared to indulge you," Benjamin added after a few breaths. "I'm afraid you will have to describe your idea in a bit more detail, since I found your previous messages rather shockingly inane."

"I appreciate your attention," Harry replied. At first Jacob assumed that Harry was being sarcastic. But when he spoke again, Jacob knew that he wasn't. "The idea is neither more nor less than it appeared to be. One shot, and he's dead. It's really no more complicated than that."

For the first time, Jacob understood that it actually was true. The bare ground in the latrine was soft, like all the ground in New Orleans. Harry's entire house was built on a swamp.

"Surely it is at least somewhat more complicated than that," Benjamin said.

A pause. "You doubt me," Harry said at last, his voice exacting and composed. "You shouldn't. I've been supplying that camp over the Maryland border with all the rum they could dream of for the past six months, and I don't have to tell you how much information I've collected in the meantime." So he really was a spy, Jacob marveled. It still struck him as impossible to believe. "I shall return there again next week. He visits once or twice a month, and they hold a parade for him. They always warn me when he comes, to make sure I'm not intercepted with goods on hand. I've even gone to the parades, to see where he sits. It's a public parade; the people from town crowd right up to him. Even the officers know me by sight. They're thrilled to see me. They're only concerned about the rum. I know every nineteen-year-old imbecile in that camp. No one will suspect me. For anyone else it would be a death mission."

"And how would you do it, hypothetically?" Benjamin said. His voice was casual, languid, like an adult pretending to listen to a child recounting last night's dream. Jacob thought again of his uncle, of how impressed he had always been by him, and was astonished once more to notice how small Harry had become, a tall man shrunken before the tiny dismissive giant of Judah Benjamin. "Thus far, the details are just as inane as I remember."

Harry panted, eager. "I take my place alongside the seats they have for him. I wait for the part of the parade with the gun salute. I keep the revolver under my cloak even when I draw, and I time my shot to correspond with the salute," he recited, like an obedient child. For a moment Jacob felt ashamed for him. And when he recognized how familiar that obedient voice sounded, he felt ashamed for himself. "No one hears where the shot came from, and before anyone even sees him fall, I slip out of the crowd. It's truly that simple."

The air beyond the wall hissed as one of them lit another match. Jacob breathed through his mouth to avoid inhaling the smell.

"And you genuinely believe that this would serve some sort of positive purpose," Benjamin said, "rather than being a catastrophic miscalculation which we shall all have to pay for in blood." His voice was flat, lifeless.

"You actually believe that this would be, how did you put it? A public service."

"I only regret that I have but one life to give for my country," Harry quoted, with an unmistakably unctuous tone. At that moment, for the first time, Jacob hated him.

So did Benjamin, it seemed. "You aren't the one who would be giving his life," the Secretary snapped. "Or is there some obscure aspect of mar-tyrdom to your proposal, the details of which have escaped my notice?"

The acid tone in Benjamin's voice was unmistakable even through the wall of the latrine. But Harry Hyams apparently chose to ignore it. "If I should be caught," Harry said, "it is something to consider."

Jacob imagined the smoke rising between their faces as Benjamin spoke. "That consideration, Harry, is one of the many weaknesses of your idea," he said. "And quite frankly, it is a weakness in yourself. You are looking for glory. You present this idea as though it were some sort of patriotic sacrifice on your part, but it's clear to me that your motivations are entirely personal."

Harry spoke quickly. "Oh, I'll admit that it's quite personal as well," he said. "We can't live like this anymore. You know that. The slaves all think they know what's coming, and it's dangerous. Elizabeth even told me that she heard them talking about finishing us off. She's certain that they're plotting something. She's terrified."

Was it true? Jacob thought of the old Negro who had answered the door, of the contempt in his eyes, and then he thought of Elizabeth. He tried to picture her, but he found that he could picture no one but his own mother. He pushed the thought aside as Benjamin spoke again.

"That may very well be the case, but it strikes me as a rather con-venient excuse for your own quest for glory," Benjamin said, and Jacob heard how his voice rose slightly, climbing into what must have been his attorney's tone. "Glory isn't for the Jews, Harry. Just think of me. If I am to be remembered at all, even if we are to triumph, it will be only as one who designed the plans that were heroically executed by someone else. We can be slaveowners, we can own whole plantations, but as far as everyone else is concerned, you and I will always be runaway slaves."

Jacob was astonished to hear this from Benjamin, who, as much as Jacob detested him, had certainly appeared to be in a position of glory. But now he knew that what Benjamin said was true. And what was worse, he knew that it also applied to him. He listened as Benjamin continued. "American honor," he said, in his aphoristic way, "the hard unseen labor that raises a country from dust—that can be yours, and you deserve it. But American glory, that belongs to someone else. So I suggest you abandon your expectations."

Was Harry crushed, or defiant? Jacob listened, trying to imagine Harry's boyish face in the fetid darkness, but it was impossible to tell. "I don't expect anything from you," Harry finally said, and now Jacob could hear the gleeful defiance in Harry's voice, the eager, unstoppable boy emerging from the man's clothing. "I don't need your approval. That's the beauty of it, you see. I don't have to be part of your chain of command. I am a free man."

Did he mean it? Surely he meant it, Jacob told himself, and thought of the packet of poison in his pocket. How could he say it without meaning it? He heard the general's voice in his mind: *You would never consider disgracing yourself by returning without success.*

"If I actually believed that, Harry, I would have you locked up for good, to protect the rest of us from your grand ambitions," Jacob heard Benjamin say. "But fortunately I know you better than that." Jacob waited for Harry to speak, but his uncle said nothing as Benjamin continued. "Go have your last cup of wine, and save your dreams of glory for the world to come."

The little packet of poison was burning into Jacob's skin. He imagined Harry's face, and his stomach reeled at he thought of his pathetic, diminished uncle. He pressed his palms against the damp wooden wall and bowed his head, sickened by the smallness of a grown man's dreams and fears.

But now Harry's voice rose with an anger that crept out of his clenched throat. "You have no right to underestimate me," Harry hissed, and then his words escalated, exploding in the thick night air. "I am not confined by your meager expectations. I am a free man, and I will do what I know to be right. I am a free man!"

A loud croak emerged from a corner of the latrine.

Jacob jumped, then leaned back against the wooden wall. In the ink-black darkness, he heard a repulsive liquid noise as something moved across the muddy floor. He held still as the croak repeated, louder this time, and closer to his foot.

"Frogs," he heard Harry mutter. "Can't get rid of them. This year we've even had them in the house."

Jacob heard the two smokers shifting position, settling into the mud, and knew he ought to leave while he could. He carefully stepped toward the latrine door as he heard Benjamin making some reply. When the frog croaked again, Jacob silently pushed open the door and hurried back, unnoticed, into the house. Once he saw that he was alone inside, he leaned against the wall in a foyer by the kitchen, breathing hard as he thought about the two men behind the latrine. The Harry he had observed that night was a completely different Harry from the one he had remembered, in no way related to the person he had last seen five years before. And Jacob imagined himself that night to be completely different too, in no way related to the person he once was: the person who had sat at his father's table on that same night the previous year, the person whom the officers saw as inextricable from the calm, eloquent traitor smoking behind the latrine, the person whose uncle was Harry Hyams. *I am a free man*, he heard Harry repeat in his head. And he knew what he had to do.

While the other guests were still in the parlor, Jacob slipped back into the dining room and looked down at Harry's place at the table. He tore open the packet of poison and poured it into Harry's empty glass, which he then refilled from the decanter of wine, stirring it a bit with Harry's spoon. He was surprised by how simple it was, how little of anything he felt at all. It was as though he were stirring sugar into Emma Jonas's tea. As he replaced the glass, the crippled Negro entered the room. He looked at Jacob with a strange expression that Jacob couldn't quite decipher, as though, perhaps, he were laughing at him. Then he picked up the decanter and began filling the other glasses around the table, humming one of the Hebrew tunes that the guests had been singing. Suddenly and excruciatingly horrified, Jacob retreated to the parlor, just in time for Harry to call the company to return to the dining-room table.

5.

*T*HE SECOND HALF OF THE PASSOVER SEDER IS EITHER TEDIOUS or triumphal, depending on how much one has eaten compared with how much one has drunk. Most years, people drag themselves back to the table tired, sluggish, and ready for the whole evening to be done with. But that night in New Orleans was different. Food wasn't yet scarce, but it had become harder to come by; liquor, on the other hand, had been laid up for years. Even at the genteel table of Harry Hyams, the drink had not quite been balanced by the food, and so the tone that night, after everyone made their way back to the table, was triumphal: most of the guests were more drunk than full, and it showed. The guests sang the grace after meals loudly, with great spirit, the older ones even singing aloud the parts usually chanted to oneself. Afterward, before Harry rose to read the next passage, some of the older guests began laughing about Elijah the prophet, messenger of the Messiah, for whom one opens the door at the end of the evening—joking that perhaps Elijah might arrive this year in the form of a swarm of mosquitoes full of Yankee blood.

Jacob sat at the table in terror, forcing himself to laugh. His head and hands felt light, weightless. In their weightlessness Jacob imagined that his burdens had been lifted, the people around the dining-room table rendered into mere illusions. The room shimmered before him like a lighted box floating in a void. Jacob flipped through the prayer book in his hands, folding the pages back and forth until he reached the page with the questions he had recited earlier in the evening, and for an instant he imagined that it was true: that this night really was different from all other nights, that somehow this dining room had detached itself from the world where the past led to the future and where actions had consequences, that the person he was tonight was an exception, entirely unrelated to the person he had been or the person he would be. He saw the raised glass in Harry's hand, and waited for Harry to bring it to his lips.

Harry pronounced the blessing over his glass of wine, and Jacob stared at him, unable to look away as Harry drank it. When Harry put the glass down, he made a face and leaned back on his cushioned chair, turning to the side where the Negro was waiting.

"Badly decanted, Jim," he called. "Bring another bottle, will you? There's something peculiar about this one."

The Negro muttered something and then wandered off, returning with another bottle that he began to serve around the table. Jacob watched Harry, ridiculously—hadn't the officers told him that the results wouldn't be immediate? He began to feel as though he himself had been poisoned, but Harry showed no signs. Instead, Harry rose to his feet, holding his half-empty glass before him. He was slightly drunk. Steadying himself on the table's edge with one hand and raising the glass with the other, he began to read aloud—in English, this time—the cry of vengeance from the very end of the Passover meal. He drawled out the words slowly, pronouncing them with a firm and terrifying passion:

"Pour out Thy wrath on the nations that do not know Thee, and upon the nations that do not call upon Thy name. For they have devoured Jacob, and laid waste his habitation. Pour out Thine indignation upon them, and let the wrath of Thine anger overtake them. Pursue them with anger, and destroy them from beneath the heavens of the Lord."

At all of the Passovers in his short life, Jacob had heard those biblical words recited dutifully, by happy men with full stomachs who rushed through this passage so as to finally reach the evening's long-awaited end. But in Harry Hyams's voice, Jacob suddenly heard an unexpected tone of actual, frightening rage. Harry looked up from his book and around at the company, and smiled a cruel smile. For an instant, Jacob felt that he was the one who had been devoured.

"I would like to dedicate this fourth cup of wine to the Union," Harry said, in a loud and angry drawl. "May it go the way of all tyrants. May our dear Judah Benjamin lead us as we pursue the Union hosts with anger, and may we destroy them from beneath the heavens of the Lord."

The company broke into applause. Judah Benjamin applauded too, modestly at first. But the applause began to escalate, becoming louder and wilder, until the room roared. Everyone raised their glasses, banging them with their spoons.

Harry's face changed, reddening with passion. "Death to the Union!" he bellowed, his voice louder than Jacob could ever imagine it. Soon everyone took up the chant. It was the drinking, Jacob was sure—or so he believed, until Harry Hyams cried, "Death to Lincoln!"

Judah Benjamin smiled, the same perpetual smile he had worn the entire evening, and in that moment Jacob recognized the sentiment it masked: an awareness of limitations. In the shadow of that smile, in the shimmering gaslight, Jacob saw, with sudden and terrifying clarity, his uncle's powerlessness and also his own—the vast distance between rage and resolve, the crippling need for the approval of others, the fear of freedom that placed even the smallest dreams beyond one's reach. He knew then, without the slightest doubt, that Harry Hyams would never have done it.

Harry's hand was shaking now, quivering in the lighted box of that detached dining room, as his other hand clutched the top of his chair. The rest of the company echoed Harry's cry, man to woman to man, cheering for the angel of death. Jacob banged his glass with them, and in the wave of passion that circled the table, he convinced himself that he had had no choice, that there had been no questions left to ask. When Harry turned to face him, Jacob tried not to flinch, and succeeded.

"My dear boy, Jacob," he said, with the hardened edge still on his drawl as the company's chants died down, "please open the door for Elijah the prophet, may he arrive speedily and in our time."

Jacob forced a smile, stood, bowed to the ladies at the table, and walked toward the door. But when his hand touched the doorknob, he heard a horrid sound, a rattled, muffled gasp. He turned around in his tracks and saw Harry still standing at the table's head, looking straight at him. And at that moment, Harry Hyams poured out his wrath onto the dining-room table.

Jacob had never imagined that it would be so supremely terrible to witness. The commanders must have given him something other than ordinary lye. Harry's eyes rolled back in his head as he vomited black bile onto the silver trays in front of him. He vomited, and vomited, and vomited: his entire life poured out of his mouth before the heavens of the Lord. As the women at the table began to scream, Jacob opened the door, panicked, for the prophet Elijah. But as he rushed back to Harry's side with the other guests, Jacob was the only one who saw the crippled slave—who, it seemed, was no cripple—run out through the open door and into the moonlit southern night.

PART TWO

THE CARNATION OF EVIL

I.

"WHY DIDN'T YOU KILL HIM, TOO?"

It wasn't what Jacob had been hoping to hear. When he left New Orleans—after staying with his aunt and her weeping friends for seven excruciating days, eating tasteless unleavened bread and listening to Elizabeth's animal wail as the cavalrymen reported back to the house again and again on their failure to track down the runaway slave—the journey back was even worse than the journey down. At some point during the long voyage, first in a smuggler's boat and then on a navy gunship, Jacob finally stopped thinking. Harry Hyams no longer existed. Jacob's mind had also erased the faces of everyone else at that seder table. Even New Orleans itself no longer existed. It was an act of sheer will to erase it all, and not an entirely successful one. When he crawled back to the camp and appeared before the three officers at headquarters, what he expected—the only reason he had done what he now wanted to forget—was glory. And at first, the officers did seem pleased. But as Jacob described what had happened that night, their eyes went wide at the mention of one name.

"You had the poison. Why didn't you kill Benjamin?"

The question shocked Jacob, not least because the idea had occurred to him at the time, and he had dismissed it because he was sure that these very people would not approve. He choked, and tried to cover it with a cough. At last he composed himself enough to mumble a reply.

"Those were not my orders, sir," he said. He glanced past the officers, avoiding their eyes. The long, narrow table where the officers sat was scattered with papers, inkwells, pen nibs, and pipe-holders, and anchored on either end by brass spittoons. Outside the windows behind their heads, rain was pouring down in torrents, drenching Jacob's fellow soldiers in their leaking tents. He listened to the rush of rain pounding against the windows and remembered the blind sounds of waves slapping the sides of the smuggler's boat as he crouched inside the barrel, trying to will himself unconscious, paralyzed by what he had done.

"But you might have had the ingenuity to seize the opportunity at hand," the colonel said.

Jacob felt himself beginning to sweat, though the air in the room was cool. "And murder Benjamin, sir?" he asked. Were they serious? Had his murdering of Harry Hyams somehow been insufficiently patriotic? "But they—they consider him a head of state there, sir," he stammered, searching for an excuse. "Even if we know it's all nonsense, wouldn't that have violated some sort of—some sort of rule of war?"

The general laughed. "Judas Iscariot Benjamin is hardly a head of state."

The other two snorted. "He isn't even a figurehead of an imaginary state."

"No one can possibly imagine that that traitor is a head of state."

Dimly aware that he was about to do something foolish, Jacob reached into his breast pocket and removed the Confederate notes that he had collected in honor of his deaf-and-dumbness. Without a word, he peeled off a two-dollar Rebel bill and placed it on the table. The three officers peered down to examine the ragged paper, until all three of them could see the tiny etched lithograph of Judah Benjamin's face, its eerie smile mocking them all. As Jacob watched their faces change from smug to intrigued, he was surprised to feel a twinge of pride. It was the first time a Hebrew face had appeared on currency since the days of ancient Judea. The officers saw him trying to suppress his smile, and frowned.

"So he's a king to you," the general huffed.

"To them, sir," Jacob said quickly.

"But not to you? Then I fail to understand why you did not take action."

Because I am not a murderer, Jacob caught himself thinking, until he remembered that it was no longer true. But surely what he had done was an exception, the moment of pouring the poison into the glass unrelated to the moments before and since. "Sir, I concentrated on fulfilling my mission," he finally said, and came up with an appropriate lie. "If I had divided the poison between two targets, the dose might not have been potent enough to—to achieve the initial goal."

The officers turned to one another and nodded. Jacob breathed, thinking again, as he had thought over and over during those awful seven days, of how he owed his life to Harry Hyams's runaway slave.

"Well, what's done is done," the colonel said. "We are pleased with what you've accomplished, Rappaport." The other two officers grinned.

"Thank you, sir," Jacob mumbled. Was this what he had been waiting for, the justification for the entire mission in his mind? The reason he had poisoned Harry Hyams? For this tiny, worthless phrase, *we are pleased*?

"So pleased, in fact, that we have another opportunity for you," the major said.

Now Jacob listened, standing straighter. A promotion this time. Maybe even a citation or a medal; surely he deserved one.

"You have shown yourself to be quite capable, Rappaport," the general declared.

"We doubted your trustworthiness at first," the major said, with a wave of a hand. "But you have succeeded in putting most of our doubts to rest."

"You are impressively reliable," added the colonel.

"Remarkably dedicated."

"Eminently competent."

"Devoted to the cause."

"There are very few young men who have proven themselves to be as unconditionally devoted as you."

"And of those, it must be said, few are as well-connected as you are."

"Or as . . . cosmopolitan."

"With relations and business partners in so many relevant places."

"Your social liaisons are of a very useful variety, Rappaport."

"You are in a position to render an incomparable service."

"And sophisticated enough to play the role."

"Calculating."

"Clever."

"Convincing."

"Trusted by the enemy."

"It would be a disgrace not to make the utmost use of your abilities."

"Treasonous, even."

"We know we may depend on you for anything the cause may require."

"Absolutely anything."

"With no exceptions."

"Rappaport, are you familiar with the Levy family of New Babylon, Virginia?"

Jacob swallowed. This cannot, he thought, cannot be happening again. "I—I'm not certain, sir," he said.

But he was certain. And the three officers seemed to know it. They glared at him, contempt seeping into their proud faces. "Philip Levy was your father's business associate for more than ten years," the major said, as if he were telling Jacob something he didn't know. "He is the founder of the P.M.L. Shipping Company in Virginia, which was an affiliate of Rappaport Mercantile Import–Export until the war forced the connection to dissolve."

Jacob was perspiring so much by now that he was sure they could see it, dark patches of sweat blossoming under his arms and across his chest. He had no idea what to say. "I had little to do with my father's affairs, sir," he tried.

The colonel glared at him. "Except that you spent the two years before you enlisted working in your father's business, and you received Mr. Levy personally every time he came to New York," he said.

Now Jacob was frightened. This was more detail than he had ever mentioned to Mendoza, or to anyone else he could remember. They had done research this time. Whom had they asked? Were there other rats besides Mendoza? He looked at the eyes of the officers before him and felt himself cornered, trapped. Treason, one of them had mentioned. Had he meant it?

The general blew smoke. "We would like to inquire as to whether you have ever met any of Mr. Levy's offspring," he recited, as if reading from a script.

Jacob's uniform stuck to his skin. "No, sir, I never met anyone in the family other than Mr. Levy," he replied.

He was relieved that this, at least, was true. His memories of Philip Levy were all of meetings with him in his father's offices, Philip always dressed in a stylish suit and top hat, writing down figures as he laughed at how young Jacob was. Jacob had liked him. But he had never come to their home, as far as Jacob remembered, and he had always made his business trips alone. As Jacob racked his mind now, he vaguely remembered Philip once mentioning children his age—as part of his incessant jokes about Jacob's youth, to be sure—but he couldn't remember what he had said. He swallowed and tried to remember even less about him than he already did, terrified to hear what might be coming next.

"Levy is apparently one of those men who produce nothing but daughters," the general said. There was something vaguely rude about this remark, Jacob thought, as though it were some sort of comment on Philip Levy's manhood. It disturbed him, though he could not put his finger on why. "Four of them, actually. Our main concern is with the second one. Eugenia."

Jacob held his breath. A woman?

"Miss Levy, it seems, is an even stauncher Rebel than her parents or sisters. She appears to be at the helm of a spy ring, though it's possible that her sisters are involved as well." He paused. "We managed to hold the city for about a month last year, and during that time we detected suspicious activity in the household. We detained Miss Levy then, but unfortunately we lacked sufficient evidence, and various circumstances forced us to release her after only a few hours. We've managed to move the lines closer to the city this spring, and we hope to take the city again by autumn. In the meantime, there still appears to be a chain of informants in place, and on the other side of the lines, the young lady's guard has likely been lowered. And that is where we hope to rely on you." The general lit his pipe.

"Sir, I won't assassinate a woman," Jacob blurted out.

His words astonished him. If he were capable of refusing to murder a woman, he understood an instant later, shouldn't he have been capable of refusing to murder an uncle? A man? An ostensible head of state? Why one line in the sand, rather than another? Once he had become a murderer, did it make any sense to feel that he was somehow a *better* murderer than other murderers? It did, he believed. He had no choice but to believe it.

The three officers looked at Jacob, then at each other. Suddenly, all three of them laughed. Jacob smiled, confused. At last the major stopped laughing.

"What kind of savages do you think we are?" he asked, with an odd gleam in his eye.

Jacob didn't reply; the truth was that he didn't know. His own failure to answer alarmed him. The general saw his fear, and leaned an elbow on the table. He smiled. This time the smile was a kind one, or so it seemed. "No one is asking you to assassinate a woman," he said, with a warm gentleness in his voice.

Jacob breathed with relief. The three officers heard his breathing, and then all three of them smiled at him. For an instant he thought that they actually understood how he felt.

"Don't worry, Rappaport," the general said. He stood, and leaned over the table until he had clasped Jacob by the shoulder, a gentle, fatherly touch. "We don't want you to murder her." Then he added, still smiling, "We want you to marry her."

2

THE LEVY GIRLS WERE LOONY. JACOB HAD NEVER SEEN WOMEN behave that way in his entire life. Their mother had died eight years prior, while the eldest was still a child. Their father, overwhelmed by the business obligations under which he had buried himself after the death of his wife, had long been at a loss as to how to keep the girls in check. There were four of them, each one a dark-haired, dark-eyed beauty, the older ones gorgeous enough to turn heads in the street. But each one of them was freakish in her own way.

As Jacob quickly learned, the eldest, Charlotte, or Lottie as she was known, had been engaged five times before her twenty-first birthday. Jacob initially assumed she was just a victim of bad luck, until he found out that three of those engagements had taken place simultaneously. During the month when the North had taken the city the previous year, one of her fiancés had been a Union soldier. With him, she had even made it all the way to the wedding canopy, but right at the moment when he had pronounced the wedding formula and tried to put the ring on her finger, she had flung the ring to the floor, shouted, "Nosiree, Bob!" and fled. The second youngest, Phoebe, fifteen years old, was a whittler—a hobby common enough among farm boys, but rather absurd for a girl, let alone a daughter of a businessman. She was actually quite talented, and her detailed carvings of animals and decorative boxes were everywhere in the Levy family's home. The youngest, Rose, a little dark-haired girl of eleven, was some sort of genius at word puzzles. She would often speak in phrases with the letters moved about—or, equally incoherently, in odd strings of words that were the same backwards and forwards, resulting in illogical nonsequiturs like "A dog, a panic, in a pagoda!" and "Do geese see God?"

But none of them was as outrageous as the second eldest, Eugenia. Despite being only nineteen years old—Jacob's age—Eugenia had already had a significant amount of success as an actress before the war, performing all over Virginia and even in Washington. She had been invited to perform in other places too, but her father didn't think it wise to let such a young lady travel so far from home. Later it occurred to Jacob that her father's real concern wasn't what the world might do to Eugenia, but what Eugenia might do to the world. Jeannie, as her sisters called her, wasn't just a talented actress, but also a talented magician who was a master of sleight of hand, as Jacob discovered through several unfortunate situations, including the very first moment he met her. The woman did not seem to adhere to physical laws. Other people walked; she flew.

The Levys' home was a boarding house in New Babylon, a small city in northern Virginia quite near the border of the moment, and not far from where the Confederate camps were set up on the hillsides a few miles past the town limits. There were many people coming and going from the house at all times—including quite a few Northern sympathizers, smugglers and war profiteers—and Jacob needed no outrageous excuse to show up at their door. This time his story was that he was using his business connections to make a profit off the war, by supplying Confederate camps with hard-to-get goods from the North. He arrived one spring evening dressed in an appropriately elegant suit and hat, a great improvement over the dead man's Rebel uniform. He rang the doorbell, sensing a buried, coiled fear rising up within him as he heard someone within approaching. But when the door opened, the person standing behind it was a little girl.

"Good evening," she said, in her high little girl's voice.

Jacob had been expecting a servant or a slave, though he later learned that the Levys, partly due to Philip Levy's recent business problems and partly for quite separate reasons, had not kept a single slave or servant for many years. But it was the height of the person who answered the door that startled him. He couldn't remember how long it had been since he had spoken to a child. Even though his heart was pounding, the sight of her little dark curls brought a smile to his face. "Good evening, miss," he said, and tipped his hat to her. "I would like to speak to Mr. Philip Levy. Is he available at present?"

She curtsied. "Madam, I'm Adam," she said, in a deep, hollow voice. Then she grinned, trying not to laugh.

Jacob had no idea what this meant, but he was hardly about to admit it to an eleven-year-old, not to mention a girl—especially a girl who might soon become his sister-in-law. Instead he smiled, and pretended to follow the joke.

"Adam Levy, I presume?" he asked, intending to humor her.

"I've let a name emanate: Levi," she said, oddly enunciating each word. This time she couldn't hold back, and giggled.

This entire exchange baffled him. It would take several more days in the Levy house before someone explained to him Rose's fondness for anagrams and palindromes. Eager to look like he had understood, he smiled uneasily and replied, "Yes, Levy. I've come for Philip, not Adam, madam. Is he here?"

She curtsied, then turned her back to him in the doorway. "PAPA!" she screamed at the top of her lungs. Then, with an elegant twirl, she turned back to him.

Her scream had knocked the breath out of him. "Name, e, man?" she asked.

The question confused him. Did she want to know his name, or someone else's? It should have been obvious, but somehow it wasn't. He remembered the scowl of the slave at Harry Hyams's door. He was alarmed to find himself opening his mouth and then closing it again, forgetting again, for the briefest of instants, his own name. An image appeared in his mind of the sign outside his father's office, the name painted in large black letters, unassailable, proclaiming where he belonged, who he was meant to be. "Er, Rappaport," he mumbled at last. "Mr. Jacob Rappaport."

The little girl turned around again. "PARROT, PAP!" she screamed. Then she turned back to Jacob, composed her face into a very ladylike smile, and curtsied. A moment later, he at last saw Philip Levy standing behind her.

"My dear Jacob!" he cried.

Jacob looked at Philip Levy and bit his lip, hiding his surprise. He barely recognized him. Unlike Harry Hyams, who had drunk up the war as though it were the fountain of youth, Philip looked dramatically older than Jacob remembered him, even though he had last seen him only about a year and a half before. In less than two years he had become an old man. His hair had thinned, and shone all over with gray; his black mustache and eyebrows looked darker than pitch in comparison, almost comically heavy and thick. His forehead was deeply creased, compressing like a bellows when his black eyebrows rose. The pince-nez on his nose made his face look even thinner and more haggard than it was.

But his energy hadn't diminished. Jacob remembered how he used to bound into their offices as if not a single second of his time in New York could go to waste. Now he reached over the threshold with great alacrity, grabbing Jacob's hand. "One of the people I thought I'd never see again!" he announced. "What brings you here?"

"Oh, all sorts of illegal activities," Jacob said grandly. He was no longer nervous, merely curious. He wasn't going to kill anyone, he reminded himself as Philip escorted him through the doorway of the house. The thought comforted him.

Philip grinned. Clearly he thought he knew exactly what Jacob meant. "Business is business," he said. "I've been trying to specialize in that sort of activity myself." The little girl darted into the house behind her father. "That was Rose," Philip said, waving a hand toward the girl, with a weary sigh. "Don't mind her. Don't mind any of them, in fact. We were just sitting down to supper. It would be wonderful if you could join us. You've picked a lucky night—we have some boarders staying in the house, but none of them are here this evening."

At that moment the little girl darted back, followed by three absolutely stunning girls about Jacob's age, all assembling in a row in the front room behind their father. "I don't believe you've met any of my daughters," he said, then turned to the girls. "Girls, this is Mr. Jacob Rappaport, whose father and I used to work together in New York." He turned back to Jacob. "Of course you've already met Rose," he added. The little girl now stood in front of him, her head level with his chest. "And it's my pleasure to introduce you to her sisters—Charlotte, Eugenia, and Phoebe."

The three older girls curtsied, one at a time at the sound of their names, three dark-haired heads of curls rising and falling before him as they glanced at him with their dark brown eyes. Jacob was awed by all three, unable to believe his astounding luck: they were absolutely spellbinding, and not only because he had barely seen a woman in the previous year. He repeated their names and stepped toward them, bowing grandly to each of them, taking his time with the formalities so as to admire them a little longer. Their dresses were simple, laceless cotton, nothing like the glamorous gowns that the daughters of his father's colleagues wore in New York. They barely wore any face powder, and their shoes were battered and old. But even in their unstylish clothes, Jacob thought, any of the three of them would have made the ladies he had met in New York envious. The three girls smiled at him modestly, one of them even blushing as Rose let out a hiccup. He remembered his mission and stared at them all in disbelief. Was he really looking at a ring of spies? He had expected some sort of hint, in a gesture or a glance—subtle perhaps, but unmistakable enough to erase his doubts—of ambition, calculation, evil. But there was nothing of the sort. These were simply Philip Levy's daughters. And they were beautiful. He swallowed, fighting down fear.

Eugenia was the last in the row. All four girls looked quite a bit alike, even the little one, but Eugenia immediately caught his attention. Her hair was wilder than her sisters', tamped down by at least six pins and ribbons that he could see. The two sisters standing beside her had avoided looking directly at him, but she looked straight at his face, with deep brown eyes so intense that he could not look away even if he had wanted to. She was smiling, but there was something odd about her smile. Her expression puzzled him until he saw that she was trying not to laugh.

Embarrassed, he tried to speak. "The pleasure is mine," he said, in far too loud a voice, and then, stupidly, bowed to Eugenia again.

This time Rose, standing alongside her sisters with her father's hands on her low shoulders, burst into giggles. Jacob turned to look at her, then at the other girls, and watched in bewilderment as all of them but Eugenia began snorting, struggling not to laugh out loud. Several agonizing seconds passed before he caught a glimpse of himself in a mirror on the opposite wall and noticed that he was wearing one of Eugenia's hair ribbons.

He grabbed at it with clumsy hands, his scalp stinging as he pulled it off his head. How on earth had she done it? His face was burning, but he knew that shame was not an option. It was his assignment to be a gentleman at all costs, even if it meant playing the fool. He turned to Eugenia, and forced a smile.

"My dear Miss Levy," he said, as he held the ribbon out to her in the palm of his sweating hand, "I do hope you will accept this small token of my new affection."

He was proud of this reply, and even prouder that her sisters finally laughed out loud. The chorus of female laughter sounded to him like a round of applause. Eugenia smiled back at him, a friendly smile. He looked at her, still encouraged by her sisters' laughter, and felt suddenly at ease.

But his pride couldn't last. Eugenia curtsied again, and spoke. "Gladly, Mr. Rappaport," she sang. Hers was an actress's voice: clear, distinct, presumptuous. "But only if you will allow me to repay you."

She reached into the bosom of her dress. Jacob glanced at her father, who was checking his pocket watch, before allowing himself to admire the shadowed curve of her skin as she slipped her fingers beneath the dress's neckline. He was still captivated by this display when she suddenly withdrew her hand, flourishing it before his eyes. And that was when he saw that she was holding his own wallet.

He stood there flabbergasted as she opened the wallet and removed a two-dollar Rebel bill, which she then dangled in front of his nose so that he was looking at Judah Benjamin's lithographed face. "I suspect you will agree that this is worth far more than that token of your affection, even with the current currency depreciation," she said. "But for your troubles, Mr. Rappaport, I do hope you will accept it."

Jacob was speechless. He looked at Eugenia again, then at her laughing sisters. Eugenia reached toward his stock-still open hand, helped herself to her ribbon, and placed both the bill and the wallet in his frozen palm. "We hope you will join us for supper," she said, and curtsied. Then all of the sisters turned, as if in a choreographed ballet, and followed her out of the room.

For a moment Jacob stood alone with their father, staring at the wallet and the bill in his hand. When he finally looked up, he saw Philip Levy watching him, with a tired grin on his face. "As I said at the door, please don't mind any of them," Philip said. "And do join us, if you are still willing."

Jacob caught his breath, and once again forced himself to smile. "Mr. Levy, it would be an honor to stay with you and your very talented family," he said, and placed the two-dollar bill in Philip's hand.

Philip returned the bill to Jacob. "We can discuss it later," he said. "For now, you are our guest. Please come with me." And the two of them followed the girls into the dining room.

It was a warm night in late May, very humid, and the air in the dining room was thick and full above the long table. Dusk had not quite fallen, but Lottie rose from her seat to light two lamps on either end of the room. The room seemed to gleam in the lamplight against the deepening blue that pressed against the windowpanes, the four girls' faces glowing as they talked and laughed. Jacob watched the family around the table and marveled. He thought of the filthy camps where he had slept and eaten for most of the past year, the mud-coated tents and the vomit-stained blankets on ordinary nights, and then the choking smell of already rotting flesh on those howling twilit evenings when he had clawed his way off of battlefields, the night air riven with the long screams of those not yet dead. It suddenly seemed impossible to him that those places and this room could exist in the same world. He looked around the table at the faces of the chattering Levy daughters and imagined that this room was a sealed compartment in time and space, with an entire world contained within it—an alternative world, independent from reality, where this house with its lights and laughter and beautiful girls had somehow, impossibly, become his home. Phoebe stepped away to the kitchen and returned to pile an impressive heap of food onto his plate, roasted chicken and bright orange sweet potatoes and some sort of awful greens he had never tasted before. Except for the greens, he devoured it all with relish. He noticed Jeannie—as he had just heard her sisters calling her—watching him from across the table. When he glanced up at her, she flashed a smile at him, as though they were sharing a secret. Jacob tried to smile back at her, but didn't quite succeed. Sweat dripped beneath his collar as he put down his fork, wary of what might happen next.

"So I don't imagine you've seen combat, as a supplier to the camps," Philip said, after swallowing a mouthful of potatoes. "A lucky thing."

"Yes, very lucky," Jacob agreed, and wished he had been that lucky. Aside from the heavy odor of the food, the room had a sweet scent, he noticed. It was a smell he associated with girls his age—a slight, aching smell, like fruit not yet ripened. He wondered if a man like Philip, living in a house full of girls, would still notice that smell.

"The wounded are everywhere. They are difficult to ignore, much though we might wish they would disappear," Philip said.

"Did you ever see anyone really injured in the camps, Mr. Rappaport?" Jeannie suddenly asked.

Jacob was still embarrassed to look at her, but he remembered the mission and forced a smile. She leaned forward, and a lock of dark hair fell loose over her forehead, dangling just above her eye like a curtain waiting to be drawn open. His supreme embarrassment did not erase the fact that she was incredibly beautiful.

"Unfortunately, yes," he said, more truthfully than he would have liked.

Jeannie raised her narrow eyebrows, brushing the loose curl aside. "Really quite badly injured?" she asked.

He paused as he watched her, confused. She seemed genuinely interested, though in a rather macabre way. "Yes," he said, "but I don't believe that this is ladies' talk. I suspect your father would agree." He glanced at Philip, hoping for support. But Philip said nothing, helping himself to more potatoes.

Jeannie shimmered with energy. There was something captivating about her, Jacob saw, but he didn't yet know whether it was the compulsion of beauty or the fascination of an imminent train wreck. "Did you ever see anyone who had a broken jaw, for instance?" she asked.

Her younger sisters smirked; the elder one groaned. "Oh, Jeannie, not again!" Lottie wailed.

Jacob hesitated, wondering what new humiliation awaited. Philip, who had been disregarding the whole exchange, finally looked up, his hands frozen in the air above the potatoes. He glared across the table at her. "Eugenia, if you even think about doing that, at the table or anywhere else, you will regret it for many years to come."

But Jeannie clearly hadn't listened to her father in many eons, and her father was apparently resigned to her not listening, along with the rest of the circumstances of his widower's life. She smirked at her father, who merely sighed. Just as Jacob was wondering what on earth Jeannie could possibly be about to do that everyone was dreading, a series of carriage bells rang just outside the front door.

"Oh, is that Major Stoughton again?" Lottie asked, turning in her seat. "Stupid Yankee. He'll never give up on me, will he?"

This was intriguing. Jacob had been briefed on the Levys' policy of taking in Northern smugglers and other undesirables as boarders—out of sheer financial desperation, he had gathered—but he hadn't quite imagined it in reality, especially when that reality involved four phenomenally beautiful girls. Though not a boarder himself, Major Stoughton, as Jacob would later learn, was a Federal officer, decorated in the Indian wars and loyal to his old command, despite his origins in Virginia. His mother, an elderly invalid, still lived in New Babylon, and he knew the border guards well enough that they were satisfied with the passes he produced, and the generous compensation he provided, to cross the lines and tend to her. With this convenient excuse, he was able to pursue his actual goal: courting Philip Levy's eldest daughter. Lottie, Jacob saw, was biting her lip.

"What do you expect when you keep leading him by the nose?" Phoebe asked with a grin. "I suppose you're planning on having him propose to you too!"

Lottie turned back toward Phoebe, and snarled.

"Draw noses onward!" Rose screeched, her voice full of glee.

The bells rang again, and a man's voice outside called, "Lottie, darling? Are you there?"

"Oh, fine, I shall meet him outside," Lottie groaned, and turned to look out the window. Jacob leaned forward in his seat and caught a glimpse of the person coming up the front path—a man in a smart suit and hat, about ten years older than he, strutting impatiently along the flagstones.

At that moment, as Jacob and everyone else turned toward the windows, the room resounded with a loud bodily crack, like a bone being broken.

Jacob spun back toward the table and saw the most ghastly sight. Jeannie was slouched in her chair, almost collapsed onto Rose's little shoulder. But what was horrifying was her face: the entire lower half of it—her lower lip, teeth, cheeks and chin—was grotesquely shifted, as if her jaw had been dislocated by a sudden blow. Her eyes were rolling toward the back of her head. He had never seen anything like it except once in a circus sideshow, and the circus lady had been a freak.

"Miss Levy!" Jacob shouted, and instinctively jumped out of his seat. "Are you all right?" He reached across the table toward her, and then glanced at the others. No one else at the table had even moved. Even Philip continued chewing his potatoes.

The grotesque gargoyle that was Jeannie's face lay limp for another terrible instant against the back of her chair. Then the eyes in the face suddenly rolled back into view, and looked at Jacob. Jacob watched in astonishment as Jeannie raised her arms and somehow, repulsively, snapped her jaw back into place.

"I'm fine, thank you," she replied. Her sisters laughed.

This mission, Jacob realized, was going to be much harder than he had expected.

3

HERE WAS NO QUESTION THAT JEANNIE WAS BEAUTIFUL. IT WAS simply her personality that was utterly repellent. Jacob never felt free to say anything to her, or even near her, without fearing that it might lead to some absurdly embarrassing exchange. And after the incident with his wallet, he guarded his personal belongings ferociously, burning any messages from the command immediately after reading them. His contact in town was the local baker, through whom he and the officers—via a chain of intermediaries—exchanged messages baked into rolls. The coded messages that he sent back through the bakery were simple, optimistic. *ESTABLISHED IN HOUSEHOLD. WILL REPORT AS MATTERS DEVELOP; SITUATION PROMISING.* But it was during the second week of his stay with the Levys that he saw just how difficult his task might become, for entirely different reasons.

That early summer evening, not long after supper but still before dusk, the doorbell rang. Jacob was sitting in the front room at the time, pretending to read a gleeful article in the *New Babylon Intelligencer* about how the Army of the Potomac was sure to be routed within the month, but really watching Lottie, who was sitting quietly opposite him, working on a needlepoint in her lap, and Phoebe, who was whittling something out of a dowel of wood. Their father had gone out right after supper, and Jacob was hoping to get to know the sisters, or at least to make them accustomed to his presence in their home. He had tried to think of some way to speak to them, but neither of them would even glance up from her work. Jeannie, unfortunately, had escaped to her bedroom immediately after supper. Rose had also disappeared. The doorbell rang again, this time twice. Phoebe, groaning, rose and answered the door.

"I've come to call on Miss Eugenia," Jacob heard a man's voice say. The voice was unctuous, presuming, like an actor's in the theater. "Is she home at present?"

"JEANNIE! IT'S MR. WILLIAMS!" Phoebe screamed toward the stairs. Screaming, Jacob had noticed, was the normal procedure for announcing callers at the house. The room froze for a moment, a tableau vivant, everyone awaiting some sound from upstairs. When none came, Phoebe once again groaned aloud. "I'll fetch her," she said. Lottie didn't even look up from her needlepoint as Phoebe bounded up the stairs.

Jacob had stood when the door opened, out of habit, and now he had a clear view of the visitor standing across the room. The man was perhaps five years older than Jacob, and he wore an impeccably clean and stylish suit and hat. He was taller than Jacob too, with a pushed-up nose and a sandy blond mustache. He seemed to be making a deliberate effort to look past Jacob, surely searching for Jeannie coming down the stairs over Jacob's shoulder.

Jacob knew that he ought to sit back down and return to his Rebel newspaper. But he was curious, and anxious. He glanced at Lottie, who hadn't looked up from her needlepoint, and then at the visitor, who was still eyeing the stairs behind him, and decided to speak.

"Pardon my prying," he announced, "but what is your relation to the Levys, Mr. Williams?"

Williams took off his hat and twirled it in one hand, revealing a tall forehead and closely cropped blond hair. He looked Jacob up and down, with ill-disguised disdain. Something in his gaze reminded Jacob of the panel of officers, the painful knowledge that what they were seeing was nothing like what he thought he saw when he looked in the mirror. He winced as Williams watched him.

"And who might you be?" Williams asked, without even pretending to answer Jacob's question.

If he were as coy as Williams was, he would get nothing out of him. He stepped toward the visitor until he was at arm's length. "Jacob Rappaport," he announced, and offered his hand. "An old business associate of Mr. Levy's, though now merely a boarder."

"A pleasure, Mr. Rappaport," Williams said, in a voice rich with displeasure. He took Jacob's hand limply in his, as though he were appalled to have to touch him.

Jacob dropped his hand quickly. There was something about the visitor's presumptuous tone that made him want to imitate it. Partly for his own amusement, he did. "Please, call me Jacob," he cooed.

"In that case, please call me William," said Williams.

Jacob knew he shouldn't say anything, but the visitor's condescension had made him bold. "Your name is William Williams?" he asked, trying to keep his face in a serious frown.

"Indeed," said William Williams. "The Third, in fact." His face radiated contempt.

The idea that there was not merely one person in the world named William Williams, but three, pushed Jacob to the brink of hilarity. He struggled to keep himself from laughing out loud. "I don't suppose you have a middle name," Jacob said.

"Wilhelm," William replied.

Jacob tried very, very hard not to laugh, and did not quite succeed. Perhaps the Levy sisters were affecting him; he had abandoned completely any notion of decorum. He pretended to cough, and pursed his lips until he managed to compose himself. "You never did answer my question, William, about your connection to the Levys," he finally said.

William Wilhelm Williams the Third smiled, but said nothing. The silence itself struck Jacob as patronizing, as though the visitor were above answering questions from the likes of him. The pause lasted a long time before a voice emerged from the other side of the room.

"He's Jeannie's beau," Lottie said, dryly.

William Wilhelm Williams the Third looked at Jacob and Lottie with an enormous smile spread across his face, proud as could be. Then they heard the inelegant thumping behind them as a newly powdered and curled Jeannie galloped down the stairs.

"William, how perfectly lovely," Jeannie sang. Her arrival at the foot of the stairs was dramatic, as her childlike galloping dissolved, in an instant, into a lady's remarkable poise. She crossed from the stairs to the doorway in controlled, graceful motions, as though she were stepping onto a stage, her plain dark dress transformed into an elegant gown as she flowed across the room. Jacob watched her as she offered William her hand, which William loudly kissed. He glanced away for a moment, listening to the sound of William's lips against Jeannie's fingers.

William turned and bowed to Lottie, and then to Jacob. "My friends, please excuse us," he bellowed, his voice ridiculously grand. The two of them exited through the front door.

Jacob tried to listen to them heading toward the street, but that soon became unnecessary. They turned just outside the door and stood chatting on the veranda, clearly visible through the window. Jacob couldn't hear what they were saying, but he saw Jeannie tossing her dark curls. Then he watched as they took their seats. He had hoped, unrealistically, to see them sitting face to face, on separate chairs, but to his dismay they were cuddled together on the wicker bench. He saw the back of Jeannie's curly-haired head as she rested it on William's shoulder, then saw William's lips moving as he whispered in her ear.

Jacob looked across the room and saw Lottie still sitting like a mechanical doll, putting stitch after stitch into her needlepoint. Phoebe hadn't returned. He cleared his throat, but Lottie didn't look up.

"Miss Levy, I wondered if you might entertain a young man with a personal question," Jacob said, lowering his voice.

Lottie still didn't look at him, but he could see that she was making a special effort not to do so. She made a stitch in her needlepoint, and immediately took it out.

"I am always pleased to entertain young men with personal questions, Mr. Rappaport," she finally said. Her voice was curt, unpleasant. "One could say that I am perhaps far too pleased to do so."

Jacob decided to be direct. "How long has that gentleman been courting Miss Eugenia?" he asked.

He saw Lottie stiffen. "Mr. Williams? Oh, a few months or so," she said. He could hear how she was pretending to sound uninterested, even bored. "But they've known each other for years. He was an actor in the theater with her. They met doing a play before the war. He was in the army, of course, but his right arm was slightly injured. No one can tell, looking at it, but he can't aim properly anymore. Now he's an entertainer for the troops."

"A rather enduring friendship," Jacob said blandly. *I can act just as bored as you*, he thought. He paused before prying even more openly. "Does he intend to propose?" he asked. He worked hard to make his tone dull, temperate, as though he were asking if she thought it might rain.

"Imminently, I'm sure," said Lottie, with just as much studied nonchalance. She jabbed at the pattern in her lap. "It doesn't matter, though. Jeannie would have to run off with him, and she would never do that. She'd never see us again if she did, and she's far too attached to us. And Papa would never let her marry him."

This was reassuring, at least. What might he have that William Wilhelm Williams the Third lacked, Jacob wondered, besides a perfectly functional right arm? "Because he isn't Jewish?" he asked.

"No, not that," Lottie said. "Papa would be appalled to have me admit it, but frankly Jeannie is so hopeless that he would probably even tolerate that. Papa has become a master of toleration."

One would have to be, Jacob supposed, living with these girls. He leaned forward, listening.

"But Mr. Williams doesn't get along with Papa very well," Lottie continued. "He barely even speaks to Papa, even though he's practically married to Jeannie already, and when he does, he's unbearably rude. Most people here have the sense at least to be polite in person, no matter how vicious they are behind someone's back. Papa's parents came from Prussia, and he says they always just accepted that kind of treatment, but he vowed he never would. He's a very proud man." Lottie was a fountain of information, Jacob thought. It was as if she knew, in that vague way that women know things, what he was after. "And Papa doesn't like how Jeannie acts around Mr. Williams, holding hands and so forth. He thinks it's unseemly," Lottie added as she took a new spool of thread from the basket on her lap. "Of course, Jeannie herself is rather unseemly, as you've noticed," she said.

Jacob blushed. One always tries to convince oneself that others will forget one's most humiliating moments. They never do.

"It's much worse than you think, though," Lottie said. "She's even kissed men on stage. Papa has already given up on her. He knows that no suitable man in his right mind would marry someone like her."

The image of Jeannie kissing a stranger on a stage—or even, perhaps, kissing William Williams—had an electrifying effect on Jacob. He put his hands in his lap, and attempted to compose himself. "Unseemliness doesn't bother everyone," he said. He tried to speak confidently, like an actor reciting well-rehearsed lines. "What's unseemly to one person may be quite attractive to another."

Lottie finally looked up. Jacob couldn't help but grin. After days of being terrified of saying something wrong, he thought of Jeannie and felt ready to act.

"What might be required, do you suppose, for one of you ladies to get married?" he asked.

Lottie blanched, then grimaced. The pause before she answered lasted far too long, and Jacob became nervous again. "That would depend which one of us you mean," she said at last. "Personally, I must admit that I'm not terribly interested at the moment."

She glanced at him with an expression of mild disdain as she returned her eyes to her lap, and he was surprised to feel slightly insulted. But he puffed up his chest, taking a deep breath of self-approval. He had other plans.

"What about your sisters?" he asked.

"I think you will agree, Mr. Rappaport, that Rose and Phoebe are both a bit young to entertain any proposals at present."

Now she was making it hard for him. "Excluding Rose and Phoebe, then," he parried.

Lottie looked at him. "It is my impression that Jeannie would not mind your attentions, if that is what you mean," she said, her voice strangely cold.

Success, he thought. Or was it? "It seems as if she wouldn't mind anyone's attentions," he replied.

"Including yours," Lottie said.

At that moment, Jeannie returned, with an absurdly loud goodbye to William on the doorstep. Jacob observed her gestures as she curtsied in front of William, watching the curve of her long fingers around the edges of her skirt. More hand-kissing ensued, followed by William honoring Jacob with yet another contemptuous look. Jeannie hurried upstairs, and Lottie quickly joined her. But just as she rounded the stairs out of sight, Lottie flashed Jacob the very slightest of smiles. And Jacob saw that there was hope.

4.

AT FIRST DURING THE DAYS JACOB WOULD DISAPPEAR FROM the house, ostensibly to his undisclosed business in supplying the camps, but usually to his contact at the local bakery and then to odd circuits around the town, which he tried to vary daily. New Babylon was a small city—large enough to have been a rather busy railroad junction before the war, which was why Philip Levy's business was based there, but no longer large enough for Jacob to lounge in taverns for hours on end without eventually arousing suspicion. After the first two weeks, he began implying to Philip that his business had dried up and that it wasn't safe for him to return home. Soon thereafter Philip took him on as a bookkeeper and manager. It seemed like an impossible stroke of luck, but Jacob quickly discovered that in fact Philip needed him desperately: his finances were in a shambles. His attempts to move his shipping business to other parts of the South had largely failed, since the number of railroads available was quite limited and transport by boat had become almost impossibly risky. He admitted to Jacob that he had started taking in boarders at the house out of desperation, and by now they constituted most of his income. Jacob did his best to cut Philip's losses by rearranging certain debts and credits, and was proud of how much he managed to salvage. He refused to accept payment from Philip; the command was smuggling money to him anyway, baked into the rolls that he picked up at the bakery. In exchange, Philip let him stay at the house for free.

In the evenings Jacob situated himself in the house's front room, which seemed to be the best place to speak with the girls after supper. Philip usually spent his evenings going out to taverns, desperately trying to drum up business, or else buried in papers in his study a few rooms away. He seemed to avoid the girls deliberately once supper had ended, and Jacob took up the habit of sitting in the front room with them, pretending to read. Usually the older two were waiting for their gentleman callers—Major Stoughton for Lottie, and William Wilhelm Williams the Third for Jeannie. They came to the house with eerie regularity, and never at the same time—often, in fact, on alternating days, as if the sisters themselves had timed it, and after a few weeks Jacob began to suspect that they had. He watched as the couples left for an evening stroll, or took their turns sitting on the veranda, sometimes for hours on end, the men stroking the young ladies' dark curls. Afterward, when the summer evening at last began to darken, whichever sister had been out would hurry back inside, and the other would accompany her upstairs. The younger two sometimes followed; on other nights, they remained in the front room with Jacob, absorbed in their bizarre work.

One night during Jacob's early weeks at the Levy house, Phoebe came into the front room after washing the dishes to continue whittling a wide wooden dowel, sitting down on a chair in the corner as she carved a design around the outside of the wood. Lottie, fresh from cleaning the boarders' rooms upstairs, was out on the veranda with Major Stoughton. Rose was still sweeping the dining room; Jeannie was in the kitchen, where Jacob could hear her scrubbing the floor. He had noticed that in lieu of keeping actual servants, Philip Levy had judiciously employed his daughters instead.

"Would you do me the honor of showing me what you're making?" Jacob asked Phoebe. "I've seen you carving, and I am quite intrigued."

Phoebe smiled, slightly, and handed the piece to him. The wood was carved nearly all around with birds flying in formation, layered over a semblance of clouds in the background. Now Jacob was able to see how intricate the work on it was—and also to notice that the inside had been hollowed out almost completely, making the exterior design even more delicate, and even more impressive.

"It's a handle for a riding crop," Phoebe said, before he asked. "Jeannie asked me to make it."

The family did not own any horses; Jacob had never seen any of them riding anywhere, even on a hired horse. "For Mr. Williams?" he asked.

"Of course. Who else?"

Jacob passed the piece back to her, his heart pounding. "It's lovely," he said. "Your work is better than any boy's I've ever seen." She took the piece and shyly looked back down at it, avoiding Jacob's eyes as she returned to work. But he could see that she was pleased.

Rose entered the room, ignoring them both as she sat down next to the wooden secretary desk. She helped herself to a charcoal pencil and sheet of paper from the desk, and immediately began scribbling something. Jacob turned back to Phoebe, wondering what more he might be able to learn.

"Do you make things for Miss Charlotte's gentleman too?" he asked.

"You mean Major Stoughton?" Phoebe grinned. "Oh, no. I couldn't possibly do it for a Yankee." She continued whittling.

"Yankee," Rose muttered from her seat across the room. "Eek, nay!"

Phoebe was clearly accustomed to ignoring Rose's odd outbursts, and carved without interruption. But Jacob decided to press further. "Doesn't Miss Charlotte—well, doesn't she cater to Major Stoughton's attentions herself?" he pried. He had Phoebe flattered now; he needed to use his chance. "It seems unfair to make something for Mr. Williams but not for Major Stoughton."

"Who knows what Lottie wants?" Phoebe said, in a tone that made it clear that she herself knew, quite well. Phoebe lacked Jeannie's acting talent, Jacob noticed. She blew some sawdust off the wood. "Probably not Major Stoughton," she added, and grinned.

This half-candor was intriguing, but Jacob's thoughts were soon interrupted by Rose. "Major Tough Tons," Rose announced, scribbling furiously with her pencil, then scratching something out. "Major sought not. Majors ought not."

He turned toward where Rose was scribbling. As she continued scribbling, he pictured her nonsense words in his head. All of them spelled *Stoughton*, he noticed, with the letters rearranged. The girl was a freak of nature. But his goal, he reminded himself, was to win the whole family's affections; every effort had to be made, even if it meant indulging the inanities of a freakish eleven-year-old girl. "Are you making some sort of puzzle?" he asked innocently.

"Major to gunshot," Rose replied, without looking up. "Major to shotgun."

Jacob perceived that this line of inquiry was useless. Phoebe groaned.

At that moment Jeannie entered the room, holding a stocking and some darning thread. When she saw Jacob, she paused, just barely, and then glared at Phoebe. Phoebe rose quickly as Jeannie sat down in a chair next to his.

"I'm going upstairs now," Phoebe said loudly. "Rose, please join me."

"Majors ought not," Rose answered. But she did stand up, carefully rolling up her piece of paper and taking it with her as she followed her sister upstairs. For the first time, Jeannie and Jacob were alone.

"Good evening, Miss Levy," he said carefully, and allowed himself to admire her. She had been working hard in the kitchen, and it had given her face an almost radiant gleam. He looked at her dress and immediately noticed how the bones of her corset pushed against the worn dark fabric, drawing his eyes up from her waist. The coiled fear in his stomach tightened again, an animal thrill that coursed through his limbs. It was all, he reminded himself, for the cause.

"Good evening, Mr. Rappaport," she replied, her tone bland, uninviting. "How is business?" she asked.

He wondered what she meant. "Unfortunately it has been much better in the past," he said delicately. "But your father is a very dedicated man."

Jeannie threaded her needle and began stitching. "That would be one way to put it," she said.

The air in the room suddenly felt very warm to him, his chest becoming damp under his shirt and vest as he tried to think of a reply. She seemed to sense him watching her, and she took her time pulling the thread through the fabric. This gave him time to observe her at close range, imagining the wonders hidden beneath her dress. In the days since he had met her, she seemed only to become more stunning. Her lips, he saw, were perfect. But then she spoke again.

"We are all rather curious about you, Mr. Rappaport," she announced, still stitching. "Tell me: why aren't you still in New York?"

The question alarmed him. He bit his lip, admiring the curve of her body as she leaned over the stocking in her lap. She hadn't looked up at him. "What do you mean?" he finally asked.

"Well," she replied, "you are clearly a gentleman with many opportunities. Papa says that you are brilliant with numbers." The phrase settled into Jacob's gut like stale bread. "You've apparently saved us from imminent bankruptcy."

Was it true? Jacob thought of the financial disaster he had discovered in Philip's office and knew that he had done nothing more than bail some water out of a sinking ship. Yet he saw no reason to disabuse her of the idea. "I did what I could," he said, trying to sound modest. "But your father deserves most of the credit."

She glanced at him, skeptical, then looked back at her needle. "Papa also says that your father is one of the most brilliant businessmen he's ever met, and that he's fabulously successful. Hobnobbing with British bankers and so forth," she said. "Supposedly you all live in grand style over there. And without any armies at your doorstep either." She said this last sentence with great contempt, as though Jacob personally embodied an army at her doorstep. He understood that he did. "I'm sure that in New York you spend all your nights at glamorous balls, and that beautiful young ladies are tripping over each other to marry you. Even if you wanted to have some sort of adventure as a smuggler or a speculator, your father probably could have bought you a whole plantation here for a pittance. Certainly you had no need to stay in a boarding house. Especially an inelegant one like ours, without a single slave. None of us can make head or tail of why you're here."

This frightened him. Did she somehow suspect him? He thought carefully and chose to tell the truth, or at least something close to it. He braced a hand against his knee.

"My father and I are no longer on speaking terms," he said.

She looked up at him, startled. Her brown eyes focused on him, and for the first time he saw her seeing him, instead of waiting to be seen. When she spoke, her voice was different, more natural, its arrogance dissipated into the warm air in the room. "Why not?" she asked.

"We had a disagreement," he said.

Now she was interested, he saw. She put down her needle and leaned toward him in a remarkably unladylike posture, planting her palms against her knees. His own mother would have considered her crass, he thought. But he was enchanted. As she leaned forward, he caught a glimpse, beneath the neckline of her dress, of the upper edge of her corset, and the sweet slender ache of a shadow between her breasts. "What sort of disagreement?" she asked.

"About a—a lady," he answered. "He wanted me to marry her."

"I see," she said, leaning back. The shadow disappeared. "And you said no."

"Not exactly. I just left."

She considered him, twirling a dark lock of hair around a finger. "Why didn't you simply say no?" she asked. "Then you could have stayed there, and continued hobnobbing with British bankers and the like."

"It wasn't a choice," he replied. "It was a matter of obligation."

She drew her thin eyebrows together, as if trying to solve a puzzle. "Obligation to whom?" she asked. He was amazed by how interested she was, how the pretense had drained from her voice. "To your father, or to the lady?"

"To everyone."

"To everyone but yourself," she said.

An unease crept into Jacob's body. He had never allowed himself to think of it that way. But Jeannie was still curious. "Did your mother want you to marry her, too?" she asked.

This was more than Jacob wanted to think. Picturing his mother meant picturing Elizabeth Hyams. But Jeannie was watching him, her dark eyes on his. He imagined leaning toward her, taking hold of her waist, her hair, her breasts. "I suppose she did," he said.

"But did she say so?"

Her boldness took him by surprise, and so did the question. His mother rarely said anything in the presence of his father. She had been only seventeen years old when his father imported her from Bavaria, and she had known no one in America but him. It pained her to have produced only one child who lived past infancy. In lieu of worrying about children she didn't have, she worried about the business, about the house, about their friends, about doing her very best to ensure that everyone was enjoying all of their hard-earned bounty as much as possible. His father spoke to her lovingly in front of other people, but Jacob had heard him shout at her in private. With his father she was deferential, diffident, at his mercy. More than once, Jacob had discovered her hiding in some obscure corner of the house, her carefully powdered face blotched and streaked with tears. Each time she told him that soot was irritating her eyes, that something must be done about the chimneys.

"No," he answered. "But I never heard my mother say no to my father."

Jeannie laughed. "I never heard my father say no to my mother," she said. "She always acted quite ladylike in public, but there was no question of who was in charge."

Jacob laughed along with her, marveling at how honest she seemed, how willing to talk and to listen. In her laughter he heard something close to friendship, the first friendliness he had encountered since his talk with Mendoza the previous year, on that lonely night. He decided to encourage her candor.

"Surely you've had disagreements with your father too, from time to time," he said.

Now Jeannie hesitated. She picked up the stocking again, and blinked. Several long seconds passed before she spoke.

"My father and I disagree about nearly everything," she said.

He saw how her eyes turned away from him, and wondered how he could bring them back. "He's always seemed rather accommodating to me," he tried.

"Of course," she replied, her voice arching into a slight sneer. "Philip Mordecai Levy would never dream of upsetting an important merchant from New York. It's only his own daughters he can't speak to."

Jacob watched as she rethreaded the needle, moistening the end of the thread with the tip of her tongue. She slipped the wet thread through the needle's eye. His body shuddered, plucked like a string on a harp.

"Papa was one of the last people in town to stop doing business with the North," she said. "My sisters and I found it rather revolting, considering what happened to our mother."

Jacob sensed that he shouldn't ask anything more. But he couldn't help himself. "What do you mean?"

Now she looked back at him, her sneer vanished. Her voice dropped. "You mean you don't know?" she asked.

Jacob looked at her, confused. "I suppose I don't."

She glanced at him once more, then looked back down at the stocking. A long moment passed before she spoke. "We used to keep slaves in the house," she finally said, her voice strangely still. "One of them was an old woman who took care of my sisters and me when we were small." She put the stocking down on her lap, though she continued looking at it, rather than at him. "One day she went out to tend to the garden, and she came back into this room holding Papa's shotgun. She started cursing some tribe that had sold her mother in Africa, and then she screamed that our parents were devils—the 'carnation of evil.' That was what she said." Jeannie paused. "If you look at the south side of the room by the door, you can see where we patched the wall. Papa was barely able to get the gun away from her before she killed anyone else."

Jacob glanced at the wall next to the door and noticed a small swath of paint that was a slightly darker shade of green than the wall around it. He stared at it in disbelief. Jeannie would have been eleven years old at the time. Surely she had misremembered it somehow, or was recalling it secondhand. But Jeannie wasn't finished.

"And Papa freed them," she said, with the slightest quaver in her voice. "Can you imagine? The old woman was hanged, but there were two other slaves in the house who knew all about what she was planning. They must have. Papa didn't even sell them off. He just set them free. Lottie was thirteen then, and she hasn't respected him since."

Jacob breathed in. Against every element of his upbringing, he didn't offer his condolences, or even try to say anything comforting. Instead he glanced again at the patch on the wall across the room and asked her, "Did you see it happen?"

She looked at him, and for the first time he saw she was serious. Without her laughter, her eyes had a firm and terrifying power.

"All of us saw it," she said.

And then Lottie came in, and the two sisters hurried upstairs.

5

JACOB BEGAN TO NOTICE THAT HE AND JEANNIE WERE BEING LEFT alone more often by her sisters, particularly when their father was out. At first it appeared to be coincidence: Jacob would enter the front room in the evening, and Phoebe and Rose would immediately remember that they had some cooking for the next day to be done in the kitchen that couldn't possibly wait. On other nights it was Lottie who vacated the room, announcing that she had forgotten to refill the lamps upstairs or to take the laundry in from outside when it looked like it might rain. Jeannie and Lottie still had their little cabals, of course, racing up the stairs together after William Williams or Major Stoughton had departed, but on evenings when neither appeared, Jacob found himself alone with Jeannie again and again. Each time she was curious, eager, asking him questions about his life in New York, speaking to him more than any woman had ever spoken to him before. He answered her, startled by the warmth of her words, by how welcoming she was, by how, for the first time in years, he suddenly felt at home.

"Did you often go to the theater in New York, Mr. Rappaport?" she asked one evening, after Philip and Lottie had gone out and Rose and Phoebe had hurried upstairs.

"Of course," he replied, though the memory was unpleasant. Each time his parents had brought him to the theater, he had the distinct sense that they were there not to see the plays, but to be seen by the other people in the audience, as though they themselves were the ones onstage. Yet there was something about speaking with Jeannie now that set him at ease, as though his entire former life were nothing more than a vaguely remembered dream. He continued to search her words and gestures for some sign that would reveal her inherent evil. Instead, to his astonishment, he had found a friend.

"What was the best performance you ever saw?" she asked.

Jacob hesitated. Surely he ought to name something by Shakespeare, if he were to impress her. But instead he found himself telling the truth. "A hypnotist," he said.

Jeannie glanced at him, her smile descending into a smirk. "I saw one of those a few years ago," she said. "It seemed quite clear to me that the volunteers were all arranged in advance."

"My father felt the same way, and he wanted to prove that it was all a trick," Jacob said. "But he was afraid that the hypnotist would mock his accent in front of everyone if he were to volunteer, so he told me to volunteer instead."

Jeannie watched him. Her fingers moved along the armrest of her chair, and for an instant Jacob wondered if she wanted to reach for his hand. "How old were you?" she asked.

"Fourteen," he replied. "I raised my hand, because I was sure I wouldn't be chosen. But before I knew it, I was onstage."

"So was it real?" Jeannie asked. Her tone was genuine; he saw how her eyebrows rose, her body angled gently toward his.

"Well, I decided that I would pretend to be hypnotized, just to prove my father wrong," he said. Jeannie smiled, and he felt emboldened, honest. "My father doubts everyone, you see. He reserves his faith for God. He's never trusted another person."

"My father is like that too," Jeannie said. "At least, he's never trusted me."

Jacob considered this remark, and wondered what it might mean. But her hair was coming loose again, and with a brush of her hand across her exquisite forehead, his thoughts of her father dissolved. "My father's lack of faith is quite extreme," he said. "He always assumes that everyone is trying to exploit him or humiliate him, or even to destroy him. I suppose that was what happened to him before he came to America, and he never changed. I wanted to make him believe in something."

"By deceiving him yourself," Jeannie said with a grin.

"Yes," Jacob admitted. The air was cool in the room that evening, cleansed and fresh from the afternoon's gentle rain. "But the strange thing was that it turned out to be quite real. The man really did hypnotize me."

Jeannie squinted at him, skeptical. "How do you know?"

"Because he made me sing onstage, and I never would have sung in public out of my own free will."

"What did you sing?"

"'The Star-Spangled Banner.'"

Jeannie laughed. But Jacob remembered that night and felt a swell of strange pride. His plan had failed twice over, he had discovered when he returned to his seat in the audience: his father didn't believe he had been hypnotized, and assumed Jacob had simply played along. But to his astonishment, his father was proud of him. For months afterward, he heard his father boasting of how his son had stood up in front of hundreds of real American strangers to sing the national anthem. And Jacob was secretly proud of it too: thrilled by how he had been freed, for that fleeting moment onstage and away from his parents' accents, from any reason to be ashamed. The memory of it made him feel lighter than air, his limbs cool and weightless as he admired Jeannie's body in the chair beside his. He listened as Jeannie launched into stories from her acting career, and caught himself feeling happier than he had felt in years.

But the next day the message from the bakery demanded to know how long the command would have to wait for a wedding, or at least more definitive information. And when Jeannie was alone with him again in the front room that night, telling him how she once ran off to Richmond for a week to play the lead in *Romeo and Juliet*, he knew he could no longer wait.

"Mr. Williams had arranged for me to take the role there, and I told Papa I was visiting a friend in the next town," she was telling him, her smile radiant. "But Papa saw the review of the performance in the newspaper. It was a wonderful review, too. Apparently I was quite convincing in my portrayal of the dead maiden in Act Five. Of course Papa had no appreciation at all. He told everyone he knew that he was ready to strangle Mr. Williams, and after that he barely let me leave the house. But a month later he went to New York—to meet with you, I suppose—and Mr. Williams and I performed an illusionist show in Petersburg. Fortunately Papa was still in New York when they printed the review."

She laughed, and Jacob tried to laugh with her. But he couldn't. Instead he coughed, and watched as she waited for him, her laughter fading. She saw that something had changed.

"Miss Levy," he said abruptly, "I hope you will forgive my prying, but I have been mad with curiosity. What are your intentions with Mr. Williams?"

To Jacob's surprise, Jeannie did not seem at all caught off guard. She paused, then ran a hand through a curl along her ear, and smiled. He wondered if it were his imagination that made her seem relieved.

"Why do you ask?" Jeannie replied, perfectly calm.

He swallowed. "Well, it seems to me that a gentleman in his position ought to be more eager to propose," he said. He fidgeted with the chain of his watch, unable to control his nerves. He thought of the latest note from the bakery: *YOUR PROGRESS IS ESSENTIAL TO VICTORY,* he had been grandly reminded. *THE LIVES OF YOUR FELLOW SOLDIERS ARE IN YOUR HANDS.* But somehow the officers' vague threats seemed secondary now, irrelevant to the presence of this woman before him. To hide his nervousness, he stood up and took a few steps toward the corner of the room, pretending to straighten a picture on the wall.

"You'd like to know my intentions with Mr. Williams?" Jeannie asked. He had turned back to face her now, from his spot near the corner. For an agonizing moment, she twisted a lock of hair around her finger, refusing to reply. Then, just as he was about to shrivel into the wall, she laughed out loud. "Oh, please!" she said, after a breath. "Mr. Williams is just—just—well, Mr. Williams, I suppose. He cares for me quite a bit more than I would ever care for him."

Jacob didn't know whether to believe this. She had followed him a bit when he got up, moving from where she was sitting toward a tall ladderback chair just a few feet away from where he stood in the corner, and now she settled down on the chair. Immediately he noticed that the skirt of her dress had gotten caught on the knob on the edge of her seat, which hitched her skirt up so completely that it revealed her leg to the knee.

Jacob looked away, and coughed, watching her out of the corner of his eye and waiting for her to notice and pull the skirt back down. But he was shocked, and shaking. She wasn't wearing any stockings. He hadn't seen a woman's leg since he was a child. Jeannie's skin was silk-like, gleaming, surely never once exposed to the sun. He allowed himself a glimpse, and couldn't look anywhere else. Her skin shone in the room's dim lamplight.

"Miss Levy, pardon me—but your—your—oh—" he stammered. It was only then that he understood that she had done it on purpose.

She rested a hand on her bare knee. "Forgive me, Jacob. It's so stifling here," she said. "You can't imagine what it's like to have to be under all these skirts all the time. A lady can hardly stand it."

Jacob had never before heard her say his name, except as "Mr. Rappaport." His eyes bulged.

She noticed. "Of course," she said, "it's not nearly as hot here as it is on the stage. Do you know how many lights are used on a theater set?"

"N—no," he mumbled. Her leg seemed to stretch on infinitely. He envisioned it continuing well beyond her hand, up and back and underneath.

"Almost a hundred. They have gas lamps set up along the edge of the stage, and on the ceiling too, and there's no breeze at all," Jeannie was saying. "One can't allow any kind of breeze, actually, because then the lights might dim and the audience couldn't see a thing. You can't imagine how sweltering it is to be surrounded by those lights, and with everyone watching you, too. And doing all sorts of things onstage, and pretending to mean them all."

Jacob's eyes were still glued to her leg. She stood up, and the skirt fell back down to her foot. "William was even jealous when I once kissed an actor on stage. Just because it wasn't him. Isn't that ridiculous? It was the theater, the theater's all make-believe. How absurd can he be?"

"I—I don't know," Jacob mumbled, mourning the covered leg. Her reference to William, by his first name, irritated him. Then he noticed that he was missing a chance to denigrate him, and tried to recover. "I mean, absurd, you're right," he said loudly. He wasn't making sense, he knew. But he had taken one step toward her, then another. He couldn't help it.

"Please don't think whatever you're thinking about William," she said. "He's nothing to me, really. Truly nothing. I can't explain it to you now, but someday I shall."

This was astonishing, Jacob thought—though not nearly as astonishing as her spectacular leg. Her eyes seemed filmy, distant. He had only seen her look like that once before, when she had told him about her mother. For no reason, and for every reason, he believed her.

"I haven't been in a play since before the war," she said, in a voice softer than he had ever heard her speak. She was standing just inches from him now. "I know it's wrong to complain about it—the war's been hard on everyone, and this is such a silly thing. I know no one has a right to complain until they lose an eye or something like that. But I miss it. I really, really miss it."

"I would be pleased to remind you of it," he said softly.

Everyone reassures the young that they will know what to do when the time comes. It isn't true. Jacob hadn't the faintest clue what to do when he found Jeannie's astounding delicious lips suddenly pressed against his own. Fortunately, Jeannie did. And he didn't regret that he had more than one kiss to give for his country.

"MR. LEVY, I HAVE a question for you," Jacob said to Philip one Saturday morning. "It's about Miss Eugenia."

Jacob had by then endured many nights of savage kisses from Jeannie after her sisters had gone upstairs, ones that drove him insane by never going as far as he desperately needed. The woman's sleight of hand was absolutely maddening. One night she would reveal a leg; the next, her dress's neckline would be off-kilter, stretched almost to the point of revealing her breast before she would laugh and shift it back into place. In the meantime, while his eyes popped, she would have somehow managed to grab his pipe out of his pocket, or his handkerchief, or once—to his horror—a coded letter (luckily sealed) that he was about to send to his contact, which he convinced her was a business receipt. From then on he buried his unsent messages in the lining of his hat. And still her kisses left him reeling for days. She would invariably excuse herself and retire to her room, insisting that her father might return home and catch them, at precisely the moment when he felt he could never let her go. She was right, too; the tavern closed at ten o'clock, and Philip invariably returned within moments of Jeannie's escape up the stairs, leaving Jacob only seconds to compose his sweating, stirring body into that of a bored gentleman reading a newspaper. He stopped sleeping; he was burning alive. On other nights she was tender, resting her head on his chest almost innocently and telling him things about her mother and sisters. He told her everything he could about his family, relieved to live without fear. He was surprised how much was left of his life that he still could freely tell her. The little smiles from her sisters made it clear that there were no secrets among the women of the house. Lottie laughed aloud whenever she saw him. Rose sent him scraps of scrambled verse, "from Jeannie," then giggled when he begged her to translate them; she never complied. Phoebe even whittled a snuff box for him, "from Jeannie," in the shape of a heart. He was on his knees.

Some things had failed to change. William Wilhelm Williams the Third still came to call quite regularly, and Jeannie still enraged Jacob every time she went out to the veranda with him. She assured Jacob again and again that she was merely letting William down gently, that she was certain that if she told him straight out, he would return to the house with a shotgun and a grudge. Jacob had no choice but to accept what she said, though his face burned every time he heard William's unctuous voice at the door. He even began thinking about ways to kill him, though he could not determine whether these thoughts were serious. They felt serious to him. His ultimate mission loomed in the back of his mind, but he managed to hide it well behind the vast pillars of desire that had become his reason for living. He sometimes ignored the messages that came through the bakery insisting on updates, replying only to one out of two or three with something vague about how everything was progressing as planned. Except for the fervid meetings between Jeannie and Lottie after Major Stoughton or William Williams departed—which he had of course reported, though the girls were far too cautious for his eavesdropping to succeed—he had almost no proof; in the way of concrete evidence he had collected nil. He still allowed himself to dream that Jeannie might be perfectly innocent, that they could live an actual life together, that his initial intentions would become irrelevant, that someday soon the war would end and no one would ever have to know that it hadn't always been real.

It was a sunny Saturday morning, and he and Philip were returning from the synagogue—or more accurately, from the little rented house near the bakery that served as one. Philip was hardly the sort to attend services regularly, but that week it was the anniversary of his wife's death. The entire household seemed to droop. Even the girls had curbed their usual exuberance, their movements and chatter in the front room limited, quieter, as if they were aware of another person seated in the room with them, watching and judging. When Philip mentioned where he would be going that morning, Jacob offered to join him, and was delighted to see Philip actually smile at the prospect. During the service Philip seemed cheered by his presence, though the entire morning was difficult for him. Jacob listened as he stammered through the mourner's prayer.

But now they were on their way home, and Jacob's attempts at small talk had failed. In the silence, he had finally dared to broach the subject.

"About Eugenia?" Philip asked. He looked up at Jacob briefly, then continued walking. "Don't tell me she's been embarrassing you."

"What do you mean?" Jacob asked, as innocently as he could.

"I suspect you've noticed by now that Eugenia has a certain fondness for embarrassing everyone in sight," Philip said, his voice fierce. "Me in particular, of course. No one has any idea how much I've done for those girls. And Eugenia is completely intent on destroying everything I've ever tried to do for her." He was walking with his hands low at his sides, but Jacob saw how he had balled his fingers into fists.

Jacob thought of what Jeannie had said, how her father had never trusted her, how she and he disagreed about everything. But he had to proceed. He swallowed, and dared. "Then perhaps you would be pleased to know that I would like to take her off your hands," he announced. "Mr. Levy, I would be honored to have your permission to marry Miss Eugenia."

Philip was stunned. He stopped walking, and turned to face Jacob. "You—you can't possibly be serious," he stammered.

"Of course I am," Jacob replied.

Philip turned red. "You must be out of your mind."

This was not exactly the reply Jacob was hoping for. He paused, thinking it through. It had not occurred to him that a strategy would be required. But nothing at the Levy house had gone as he had expected. "It seems that I have approached this with a somewhat different perspective," he said delicately.

"Do you intend to get behind that other fellow, William William Williams the Ninth?" Philip spat.

"Oh, Eugenia isn't interested in him," Jacob said, with a smile.

Now Philip paused. "You think she's merely leading him along somehow," he said, eyeing Jacob. "Rather unlikely, if you ask me. Though I suppose a young man is entitled to his delusions."

"No, I don't think she's merely leading him along," Jacob said brightly.
"I *know* she's merely leading him along. She's made that quite clear
to me."

Philip's back straightened, almost imperceptibly so. Jacob saw his
opportunity, and seized it. "Mr. Levy, I think that your daughter Eugenia
is a beautiful, bright, talented young lady," he said, "and I hope that I may
be privileged to take her as my wife."

"You're mad," Philip said, and kept walking. But Jacob could see,
creeping through his blushing face, the tiniest of smiles.

Jacob kept pace beside him. "Mr. Levy, if there is something about me
that displeases you, I hope you will be forthright enough to tell me so,"
he said. In a moment of sudden panic, he wondered if Philip somehow
knew.

"Other than the insanity of your plans, no," Philip huffed. "Frankly, I
just think you need to know what you'd be involving yourself in. Eugenia
is not an ordinary lady."

"I am quite aware of that," Jacob said. Then he added, at considerable
risk, "And I hope you don't believe that I am an ordinary man."

Philip pushed his pince-nez back up on his nose, then stopped walking again. He looked up at Jacob, considering him. The pause was long,
almost unbearable. At last he spoke.

"The real shame," he said, "with this awful war, is that your parents
won't be able to come to the wedding."

Jacob was quite surprised to find tears gathering in his eyes. Philip
took him by the shoulders and kissed his cheeks. Philip's own face had
become wet with tears.

"I don't know if my wife would have loved what has become of Eugenia," Philip said, "but I know that she would have loved you."

Jacob ought to have been disgusted with himself then. But at that
moment, he persuaded himself that it was true.

6

*T*HE WEDDING PLANS SOON TOOK ON A LIFE OF THEIR OWN. THE officers would have preferred that the marriage be immediate, but Jacob had proposed in the thick of summer—days, for Hebrews, of mourning the destruction of ancient Jerusalem; there were three whole weeks when the wedding was forbidden to take place. The girls were thrilled about the delay; it gave them more time to gossip, to plan, and to add names to their father's list of invited guests. But Jacob grew more and more nervous.

The messages from the bakery since his betrothal had been pleased, but expectant. *FAILURE IS TREASON*, he was reminded. In his head he heard the three officers endlessly repeating: *We doubted your trustworthiness at first. But you are impressively reliable, Rappaport. Clever. Convincing. Devoted to the cause. We know we may depend on you for anything. With no exceptions.* He heard their smug laughter behind him each time he touched her. And theirs was not the only presence he sensed. When he sat beside her in the front room, he imagined that he saw her mother watching him, immobile and silent, beside the patched wall near the door. His nights became exquisite, repulsive, fear and desire dissolving together into liquid dream. In his dreams he would pull a bridal veil back from her face like a curtain and reveal, to his revulsion, the face of Harry Hyams, vomiting black bile. He dreamt of their wedding night, of trying to remove her gown, his hands unsteady between her shoulderblades as he undid an excessively complicated series of buttons, panting as he freed her body from its bonds. But when the dress loosened, her flesh finally visible and shimmering in lamplight, he saw papers dropping from beneath her skirt like molted skin. He crouched on the floor to retrieve them and found that they were his own letters from the command, still damp with her sweet sweat. He woke as she laughed in his face.

One day during those three weeks, Philip sent Jacob back to the house in the middle of the day for some important papers he had left behind in his study. At first as Jacob walked toward the house, he anticipated a visit with Jeannie, his blood humming within him. Only as he stepped into the silent house did he remember that the girls had gone off to the dressmaker to find patterns for Jeannie's wedding gown. The boarders were out as well. He was in the Levy house alone.

It occurred to him to search the sisters' rooms for evidence, but he had done that several times and had discovered nothing but novels, magazines, pots of face powder, clutches of hairpins, innocuous letters from cousins somewhere in Mississippi—and the far more haunting and delectable evidence of petticoats, stockings, garters, girdles, knickers, corsets. If the sisters had secrets more intriguing than their undergarments, they had hidden them beyond his reach. Instead he hurried through the front door and on to Philip's study. Then he noticed something resting in the corner of the front room, the corner that Jeannie had consecrated with their first kiss. It was a riding crop, with a delicate carved handle, and something about it looked familiar to him. Then he recognized it: it was the wooden handle Phoebe had made, for William Williams.

The cur, of course, had not dared approach the house while Jacob was home since Jeannie's engagement; at least he had the sense for that. But the mere presence of this object in the house alarmed Jacob, enraged him—and his heart pounded as he understood that William must have left it in the house deliberately, when no one was home, as some sort of sign for Jeannie.

He looked around the room, considering. The girls had planned to visit the dressmaker at noon; at the moment it was only a quarter past. Looking around once more to be sure no one was home, he hurried into the corner and took the riding crop in his hand. Carefully he unscrewed the handle. There, in the hollowed-out space that Phoebe had whittled, he found precisely what he expected—a rolled-up piece of paper, a letter, for Jeannie. He read it through:

To my dearest Eugenia,

> The rules of decorum compel me to offer my most profound and most sincere congratulations upon your recent betrothal, and to wish you nothing but the deepest joy in your forthcoming

marriage. But you know that I have never been a man to follow the rules, and certainly not when those rules contradicted the ruling of my own heart.

Surely there is no way to convey to you the pain and agony I have suffered upon the occasion of your engagement. Oh, Eugenia, beloved, I am sickened, sickened! To think of you in the arms of another man—oh, my darling, it is as though you have run me through with the enemy's spear! And to lose you to one of your own race, when you were so close to seeing the light of salvation I presented to you! Oh, Eugenia, to know how near you came to evading the dread fires reserved for sinners, and then to see you wander back into the wretchedness you were born into— oh, it is agony even to envision it. You yourself cannot even conceive of the torments your soul came so close to escaping, the everlasting torture decreed for your race, before I promised I would rescue you. It would disgust me if I didn't adore you so. The image of the anguish you will endure in Eternal Tarnation will never be erased from my mind for as long as I live, and I shall forever suffer from that awful vision.

But oh, Eugenia, it is no use. I know you cannot change your mind; it is a prison you live in, a prison built by your family, your race, and your vengeful God. Eugenia, my dearest, I would beg you to reconsider this tragic choice if I thought it would do the slightest bit of good. Alas, I know better, and can only stanch my flowing tears with the hope that the comfort you might find in your family's acceptance will somehow, impossibly, make you as happy as I would have made you. I, for one, am certain that it never will.

> *With all my undying love,*
> *William Wm. Williams, III*
> *A parrot's pappy*

The entire letter unnerved him. The man was a rather awful correspondent, for one thing. Jacob was nineteen years old and had never written a love letter of his own, but if he were writing one to Jeannie, he liked to think that he would have had the dignity to congratulate her and be done with it, without sobbing all over the page and dragging in her vengeful God. The idea of "Eternal Tarnation" almost made him laugh out loud, and he suspected that Jeannie would find it rather amusing too. If she and he and the rest of the unconverted Hebrews were really going to hell, he thought, at least they would know a lot of people there.

But what disturbed him most was the very last phrase after William's signature, "A parrot's pappy." Clearly it was some sort of private pet name. The idea of the two of them sharing pet names with each other nauseated him. He was about to tear the letter to shreds when he looked at it again.

A scrap of paper was sitting on the secretary desk in the front room, with one of Rose's charcoal pencils beside it. He sat down in the chair by the desk, seized the pencil in his hand, and printed across the paper, in large block letters:

A PARROT'S PAPPY

He looked at the words for a moment. Then he began moving the letters around, recording every attempt at a recognizable word below the phrase:

STOP, PAPA, OR, PRY, APART, PARTY, TRAP, ROT, PAY, TOP, STORY, TRY . . .

He kept trying, and came up with quite a few possibilities, but it quickly became tedious. It occurred to him that he needed Rose's help, though he could hardly ask for it. Then he remembered Rose once screaming something, a lifetime ago, the moment he first arrived at the Levys' house.

He crossed out the words he had scribbled at the top of the page and wrote out:

RAPPAPORT

Then he looked at the letters that were left. He didn't need to try all the possibilities this time. The answer glared at him like Jeannie had the very first time he saw her. He wrote the remaining four letters slowly, until their meaning sliced the page open like a gleaming knife:

RAPPAPORT A SPY.

His heart stopped.

When he regained his senses, he considered his options. The wedding was still ten days away. Clearly he needed to flee. But for reasons he didn't allow himself to understand, he knew that he wouldn't. Instead he held the letter in his hands, along with his page of scribbled words, and walked, slowly, as if in a trance, toward the kitchen.

The worn rugs on the impeccably swept wooden floor gave way to splashed bare boards and rutted red bricks beneath his feet. He had almost never been in the kitchen before. It was the Levy girls' domain, and he could sense their recent presence there, the room's surfaces moist and expectant. As he crossed the threshold and stepped onto the wet floorboards, he breathed in the smell of them, the sweet ripe scent that rose in delicate threads through the air, laced through the odors of stove polish and soot.

He struck a match from his pocket and incinerated the page of scribbled words at the back of the stove. Then, holding the letter, he moved, hypnotized, toward a wooden tub resting on a bench in the corner, filled with a thin skein of clear water. He dipped a finger into the water and held it above the letter like an ancient high priest sprinkling blood, watching as the drops fell on the words beneath the signature of William Wm. Williams, III. He rubbed the water gently into the paper until the script beneath the signature dissolved, transformed into a stain of tears shed by William for his beloved lost Jewish girl. He placed the letter back inside the handle of the riding crop, gathered the requested papers from Philip's study, left the house, and hurried back to the office, where the father of his bride was waiting for him.

PART THREE

JACOB'S FIRST WAR

I.

IN THE HOURS AND DAYS THAT FOLLOWED, JACOB'S VAGUE SENSE of dread crystallized into a pure animal terror. William Wilhelm Williams the Third held his death warrant. It occurred to Jacob that he needed the man dead. But how? He didn't even know where William lived, and he certainly couldn't ask. In the meantime there was Jeannie. Since their betrothal she had become almost motherly toward Jacob: withholding all but the most familial touches, replenishing his plate at the table, greeting him in the morning and asking after his dreams. It comforted him, and frightened him. In the front room of the house he once again sensed her murdered mother's presence, the ghost's disdain poisoning every word between them. He felt the dead woman's eyes on him each time he approached her daughter. Her gaze was unforgiving, fierce with the knowledge of the future bestowed upon the dead.

"Something seems different about you tonight," Jeannie said to him as they sat on the veranda together, on the evening of the day he discovered William's letter. He had been grateful to leave the front room, where, he had noticed upon returning home from the office, the riding crop had disappeared. Outside the house darkness had fallen, and the floorboards of the porch groaned slightly beneath them. The house, Jeannie had once told him, had been built fifty years earlier by her mother's father, who had run it as an inn. The floorboards near the threshold seemed to exude a bitter triumph about returning to their original purpose, welcoming strangers. They creaked as Jacob waited for Jeannie to sit down on the old wicker bench. Taking his seat on the bench beside her, Jacob listened to the crickets and rustling leaves and felt a profound unease seeping into his body, surrounded by wild and primal darkness. Before he left New York, he had never known that a summer evening could be so devoid of the clop of horses' hooves, so bereft of human voices, so ink-black, so terrifying. Without thinking, he slid closer to Jeannie, his trousers pressed against her skirt. As his leg touched hers, he sensed his fears receding, the warmth of her body against his spreading over him like a peaceful shelter.

"What is it?" Jeannie asked.

He watched her brush a curl behind her ear. For an instant he imagined revealing everything to her, falling on his knees and begging for her forgiveness. The image lingered in his mind like a perverse fantasy, seared with desire and longing. He wanted to confess to her almost more than he wanted to peel off her dress. Instead he straightened on the bench and resumed his role. "Only nerves, I suppose," he said. "I am getting married, after all."

"Who are you afraid of? Me?" She laughed. "I'm not any more frightening now than I shall be in ten days."

Jacob swallowed, and attempted a joke. "On the contrary," he told her. "Every good man lives in fear of his wife."

"In that case, you have nothing to be concerned about," she said, and smiled.

He tried to laugh, and failed. But she was still waiting for him to say more. He felt the tug of confession again, and fought hard to resist it. "I suppose that everyone who gets married is concerned about—about becoming trapped somehow," he said. He had meant it as a distraction, but as the words came out he pictured his own parents standing before him: his mother's hand caught in the crook of his father's elbow, unable to move except through his will.

"I wouldn't think that would worry you at all, considering how you ran away from that poor lady in New York," Jeannie said. He thought it was an insult, but she laughed again, a friendly laugh. "It seems to me that I ought to be the one concerned about being trapped."

Sweat gathered under his arms. Sometimes he was sure she knew who he was. But her generosity seemed genuine, her friendship real. She was smiling at him now, her hands open on her lap, offering kindness.

"That was different," he said softly. "It was a business arrangement, for my father's benefit. The lady was an imbecile. It had nothing to do with her wishes or mine."

A light seemed to pass across Jeannie's eyes, genuine empathy. She winced, and tried to hide it with a grin. "Surely I ought to be worried about you fleeing nonetheless," she insisted. Her voice sounded playful this time, a laugh made of words. But she spoke more quickly, her spirited tone edged with fear. "At some point you are bound to become homesick for New York, and to leave me behind for the British bankers' daughters and their elegant balls."

Jacob pictured the house where he had grown up, and noticed that the image meant nothing to him. Everything that had happened in his father's house meant nothing to him. He looked down at the floorboards of the veranda, hearing them creak as he shifted on the bench. "I feel more at home here than I ever felt at home," he said.

She glanced at him, incredulous. "Here, in Virginia?"

"Here, with you."

For the first time, in the dim lamplight on the veranda, he saw Jeannie blush. She looked down at her lap, her lips pursed as her face reddened, vulnerable. The evil of what he ultimately planned to do shadowed him, the dark summer night tightening around his throat. He tried to distract her. "You must be at least a bit anxious about the wedding, too. Aren't you?" he asked.

The distraction worked. She looked back at him with a slight smile, and then sat straighter, brushing a dark curl behind her ear. A long moment passed before she spoke. "I don't think I ever told you that I've performed as an escape artist," she said at last. "I was in a show in Petersburg where I pried myself out of coffins and that sort of thing. It's a talent I developed out of necessity. My father was always trying to keep me in the house."

Jacob tried once more to smile, wondering if she were changing the subject. But then she took his hand in hers. "You shall never be trapped with me, Jacob. I promise you that," she said. "Because I can get us out of anything." Then she held up her other hand, revealing a metallic glint of something in her palm: his key to the house. Jacob touched the pocket of his own vest, where he kept his key. It was empty, of course. He finally laughed.

He felt her fingers on his neck, creeping up into his hair. "Please, Jacob, please trust me," she said. Her voice was honest, her breath hushed in his ear. "I want someone to trust me. It's all I've ever wanted."

"I trust you," he said. As he kissed her, dark liquid beauty spilling between his lips, he believed that it wasn't a lie.

THERE IS A HEBREW custom of separating the bride and groom during the week before the wedding—to heighten the anticipation, Jacob supposed, though his heart was racing enough already. Every day he searched the streets for William Williams, keeping watch, making contingency plans, ciphering optimistic messages for the command. *WEDDING DATE APPROACHING; FURTHER CONFIDENCES IMMINENT*, he wrote, and wondered whether he would make it to his wedding day alive. It was with great trepidation that he was shepherded out of the Levy house to the home of one of Philip's former colleagues, an old Hebrew widower named Solomon Isaacs.

Jacob had met Isaacs a few times; apparently he had been a friend of Philip's father, years ago. He was a tiny elderly man, a traditional sort who always seemed to be reading an old book and who always kept his head covered, even in the house. He had a thin face and thin hands, and he wore the same black suit every day, along with a monocle tucked beneath one of his enormous white eyebrows. He lived alone, his children having all moved to Washington or to Richmond, and he seemed worn down by life. Jacob saw him and imagined Philip Levy in twenty years.

During most of that week, he and Isaacs saw each other little. By day Jacob was at the office, and in the evenings he roamed the neighborhood, watching for William Williams and his minions on their hunt for him. But the night before the wedding, Jacob returned to the widower's home at suppertime, where Isaacs had been dining alone. He seemed delighted to have Jacob join him. Their conversation was awkward throughout the meal, until he invited Jacob to have some ale with him in the parlor. As Jacob sat down with him, tankard in hand, Isaacs asked him if he spoke German, and Jacob said yes.

Speaking German felt to Jacob like a relief, as though he had been unburdened of a great secret. He hadn't spoken German to his parents since he was a boy; after he turned thirteen, he had insisted on answering them in English. In German he was a child, protected and innocent. The old man's personality was different in German, too. In English he had been formal, stiff. But in German he embraced Jacob like a father embracing a son, his words rich with advice and love.

"Jacob, I cannot tell you how blessed your arrival here has been," Isaacs told him as they drank. "Philip's father, Joseph, and I were friends since we were boys. Ever since Joseph passed away, I have felt as though Philip has been my own child. And these past eight years have been so very painful for him. Nothing has caused Philip more heartache than trying to care for those girls after their mother died, and as the girls have gotten older, his heartache has only grown worse."

He paused, took a sip of ale. He was one of those old Jewish men, Jacob noticed, who grow harder and sturdier as they get older, becoming more solid, their remorse and sadness steadying them, rooting them like trees. "There is simply no one suitable here for them to marry," he continued. "There are so few Jews here, and even fewer young men, and since the war started, almost none. In Prussia we had other problems, but finding a match for a young lady—well, it was nothing! Believe me, if Philip were in Koenigsburg with those beautiful girls, every one of them would have ten young men lined up at the door for her, and Philip's only trouble would be choosing the best among the best." Jacob thought of Lottie's engagements, and wondered how much Isaacs knew. Very little, he suspected. But even very little was surely too much. "Living here is like living in the wilderness, with no pillar of fire to lead us." He leaned toward Jacob, and put his hand on his. "You may not know it, Jacob, but you were sent here by God."

Jacob thought of the three officers at the table at headquarters, pipe smoke smoldering between his eyes and theirs. He was the only one who saw the pillar of fire coming. But the old man was expecting him to reply.

"I—I feel blessed to have found Jeannie," Jacob stammered.

"The blessing is hers, and Philip's," Isaacs said, and returned his hand to his own lap. "I only pray that God will provide for her sisters as well."

Jacob took another sip of ale, wondering if he dared to say what he needed to say. He looked up, and for an instant he thought he saw something of his own father in the way Isaacs smiled at him as he raised his glass again. It was how his father had looked to him when he was a child: a person to respect, to aspire to. And he decided to speak.

"Herr Isaacs," he said, "I must tell someone this. I am very worried about—about tomorrow. Almost afraid."

Isaacs put down his drink, still smiling. "It's good that you are nervous," he said. "It means that you are honest. Just be kind to her. And patient."

Jacob could hardly bear to listen to this, but Isaacs wasn't done; there was more to endure.

"Be patient with her, during the day as well as at night. Christian men think that when they marry, they are buying a slave—someone to love them, honor them, obey them," Isaacs said. "But you've read the marriage contract for tomorrow. You know that you are the slave, not she. Remember that. You have to let her rule you, guide you. It's the secret of every happy Jewish family for the past three thousand years. There is nothing more manly in the world than serving her. You will be the better for it, and so will your children."

Jacob drank more ale, but it didn't help. The thought of actually marrying Jeannie, of living with her the way Isaacs assumed he would, was too painful. Aware of the risks, he changed the subject, too afraid to go on with the charade.

"Herr Isaacs, it isn't that," he said, his voice low. "Well, it is, of course, I'm sure it is for everyone, but it's something else too that worries me."

Isaacs squinted at him through his monocle. "Money, then," he guessed. "Philip tells me you're a talented businessman, even at your age. Give it time."

"No, that's not what I mean either." Jacob swallowed. "Herr Isaacs, have you ever—have you ever been afraid for your life?"

Isaacs looked at him for a long time. Then he took a breath, and spoke. "Young man," he said slowly, "this is not my first war."

Jacob watched as Isaacs coughed, then drank more ale. For a long time neither of them spoke. Just when Jacob was about to stammer out some platitude, Isaacs spoke again. "I was married once before I came here, in East Prussia. When I was your age the Russians burned through the town as they defeated Napoleon. That was my first war," he said. He paused again. Jacob fidgeted with his watch chain, glancing around at the bare painted walls, until Isaacs continued. "Some soldiers made a game of capturing Jewish girls and taking them as slaves. My wife and I had just gotten married then, and they took her and her sister. I—I pleaded with them to release her, I begged them on my knees, I offered them everything I owned, but—well, it was a comedy to them. Her sister endured it, and later she was set free, pregnant. She told me how my wife took her own life instead." He stared at the back of his hand for a long time before returning to look at Jacob again. "Wars come and go, young man. They come and go, and you come and go with them. It's like the weather, like a storm or a drought. All you can do is take shelter and wait for them to pass."

Jacob saw then that they were speaking across oceans, across centuries. There was simply no way to tell him, no way to make him understand that in this new wilderness, wars were no longer like the weather—that he and Jeannie weren't victims but perpetrators, that they were causing it, that the very battle he feared the most would be taking place in bed with his new bride, tomorrow night, if he made it through the wedding day. But tonight, Solomon Isaacs, man of the past, was his only shelter.

"Thank you, Herr Isaacs," Jacob said, and bowed his head.

"You ought to go and get some sleep," the old man replied, stifling a yawn. "You'll want to be at your best tomorrow morning."

Jacob agreed politely, and excused himself upstairs. He undressed with slow movements, his brain dulled by ale, and climbed into bed, feeling vaguely protected by the presence of old Isaacs downstairs, and by the ghosts of other worlds who accompanied him, lost with him in America. But many hours passed before Jacob fell asleep.

2.

On the morning of his wedding Jacob woke to the sound of rain. Through the warped glass of the bedroom window, he saw shivering ribbons of water spilling down from a lead sky, the grass and trees glowing the brilliant green of a wet summer day. He thought of the rain outside the windows of the officers' headquarters, wondering for a moment where he was. Then he remembered, and he looked at the clock. It was late; if he were to escape, there was no time left but now. But as he rose from the bed, his body would only move slowly, as if in a trance. He stepped to the washbasin in the corner of the room and splashed water on his face, his skin still tender from the barber's blade the day before. As he patted his cheeks dry, he glanced in the mirror and was surprised by his own expression. The man in the mirror appeared proud, confident: it was the Jacob Rappaport he had always imagined becoming. He grinned and ran a comb through his hair, amazed by how independent he was of past and future, a grown man's satisfied smile reflecting back at him. Then he recognized the face in the mirror. He looked exactly like his father.

He spat in the basin and looked away, turning to the window. This time he saw a man under a canvas umbrella approaching the house. He panicked, thinking of William, until the man shifted the umbrella and he saw who it was: the rabbi. For a final instant he fantasized about running away. But he thought of Jeannie, remembering the evening on the veranda, her fingers on his neck, her words warm and alive in his ear. He dressed quickly, put on his top hat and hurried down the stairs. When he arrived, old Isaacs and the rabbi had already set the marriage contract on the dining-room table. In minutes it was signed, witnessed, completed: the bride legally acquired, his obligations to her inscribed in ink, binding. They escorted him through the rain to the Levys' house, where he crossed the threshold and saw his bride.

The sisters had draped the entire front room with garlands of white flowers, which he knew Rose and Phoebe must have spent days collecting in the woods outside. Two boys Phoebe's age—sons, Jacob remembered, of one of Philip's colleagues—were standing in the corner, playing a pair of fiddles. Guests lined the room, a parade of shabby suits, dresses and top hats. But Jacob saw only Jeannie, who sat on a chair in the middle of the room in a simple white gown. Her face was radiant, as though she were made of pure light. It seemed impossible that she was real.

Jacob lowered her veil over her face, wincing as he remembered his dream of Harry Hyams, and then they were led under a canopy of branches and flowers that the girls had built by the front-room window. He was so captivated by Jeannie that he spilled the wine on his suit when the rabbi passed the cup to him. Then he tried to stammer out the Hebrew wedding formula, and had to repeat it over and over, even with the rabbi's prompting, before he got it exactly right. The guests were laughing at him, but Jacob barely heard them. His chest tightened as he held up Jeannie's mother's wedding ring. He thought of Lottie and was suddenly certain that this was all an elaborate joke, that Jeannie was about to laugh in his face, throw it down and flee. He was amazed when she allowed him to put it on her finger, and for the rest of the ceremony he kept waiting for her to fling it to the floor. Even after he smashed a glass under his foot (which also required three or four tries) and everyone shouted their congratulations, he still could not quite believe it. It was only when he and Jeannie retreated to Philip's study, with the door guarded by the rabbi and old Isaacs, and she leapt into his arms, that he made himself believe that it was real.

When they returned to the front room a few moments later, the house seemed to spin with happiness. The fiddlers were playing, and the women had begun to dance as the men passed around the drinks. Philip rushed to them and embraced them both, his face washed with tears. A line of guests waited behind him, anxious to greet them, and Philip quickly disappeared into the crowd. Jacob had expected to feel that knot in his stomach, the sinking sickness of shame and fear, but to his astonishment he felt nothing but joy. Jeannie was at his side, clutching his hand, her mother's wedding ring digging into his skin. Jacob was talking with Jeannie's aunt from Richmond and blinking back tears of his own when, in between the notes of the fiddle music, he heard an innocuous sound, like a child entering a noisy room. It was the doorbell.

At first no one answered the door. Out of the corner of his eye, Jacob saw Phoebe excuse herself from a conversation, stepping aside to glance out the front-room window. Then the door resounded with a loud and terrifying thump, and burst open. On the threshold stood William Wilhelm Williams the Third, dripping with rain, holding a raised shotgun in his hands.

For a few moments the fiddlers continued playing, and it took a surprisingly long time for everyone to turn toward the figure in the doorway. There was a fraction of an instant when Jacob had seen him but Jeannie still hadn't, and his first impulse was to clutch her hand and turn her away from the door: if everyone ignored him, Jacob insanely believed for that second, then perhaps he would simply disappear. But one of the fiddles stopped mid-note, then squawked as the musician clutched the bow. The second fiddler glanced at the first, and both of them turned toward the door. As the music ceased, the conversations around the room trickled into silence until everyone was looking in the same direction. And then Rose screamed.

William stood still in the doorway as the room slowly transformed into a theater, with every last person present watching him before he spoke.

"Good day, everyone," he announced, with an enormous smile on his face. The guests scurried like insects against the walls. Only Jacob and Jeannie remained frozen in the middle of the room.

For an instant time stopped, and Jacob was paralyzed, waiting for death. But it soon became clear that William wouldn't begin firing immediately. He was a man who loved being onstage, and for this performance he clearly planned to follow his script to the letter. As he stepped across the threshold, he even took a bow, as though he expected the guests to applaud.

"I'm so sorry I missed the ceremony," he continued. "It must have been lovely. Of course, I'd be curious to know how you people get married. Did the bride and groom get to drink from a cup of blood?"

"William," Jeannie said softly.

Jacob looked at her, then at William. William took three grand steps toward them, entering the room.

"Dearest Eugenia," William said, and bowed deeply to her, his gun raised above his shoulder as his head swept down nearly to his knees. "Please, do forgive me for my lack of punctuality. I'm sure my invitation was lost in the post. The post is so unreliable these days."

Jacob was shaking, but when he turned to glance at Jeannie, he saw that she was perfectly poised. "William," she said, her voice steady and clear, "I know you have a weakness for the dramatic denouement, but this isn't one of your plays. I suggest that you leave."

Her calm amazed Jacob. For a moment he wondered whether she had somehow planned this, or if perhaps she had some magic up her sleeve that would allow her to steal away his shotgun the way she had stolen Jacob's wallet. But he felt her hand trembling in his.

"Did you read my letter, Eugenia?" William asked.

"What on earth are you talking about?" Jeannie replied, in her laughing voice. She dropped Jacob's hand. "William, do stop being ridiculous." She seemed remarkably composed, as though the gun were merely a stage prop. But she was turning pale.

"Lying wench. I know you read it."

For an instant Jacob thought of old Isaacs crouching somewhere in the room behind him, of Isaacs's first war, and he pushed Jeannie behind him so that he could stand between her and the gun. "Jeannie, please go upstairs for a moment," he said loudly. His voice was quaking, but he continued. "Mr. Williams and I will discuss this outside." He had noticed a knife lying on one of the buffet tables alongside the door; perhaps he could grab it on his way out.

William leveled the gun at Jacob. "I have nothing to discuss with you," he said.

Jeannie stepped out from behind Jacob's back. "William, I read your letter," she said. "Your letter was very kind. I did appreciate your concern for—for my soul. Truly I did. But please, let's be civil," she said, her voice reeking sweetness.

William glared at her, his eyes cold. "I meant it, Eugenia. I meant every word of that letter. Particularly the ending."

Jacob waited for William to announce his guilt, or for Jeannie at least to ask what he meant. But William wasn't even looking at Jacob now. "Every word out of your mouth is a lie, Eugenia," he said. "The kiss of Judas, that's what you gave me. But you shall be paid back. His kisses are worse than yours. You'll see." William was imagining himself onstage, Jacob saw; he spoke as though he were reciting lines.

"William, you've misunderstood," Jeannie said. To Jacob's shock, his bold bride took several steps forward, moving toward the man with the gun.

"Jeannie, stop!" Jacob shouted, and jumped in front of her. But he wasn't quick enough. William, still holding the shotgun in one hand, had already stepped toward her and grabbed her arm. She drew back, but he had caught her too tightly: he pulled her toward him and threw her to the floor, splayed at his feet.

Jacob rushed toward her, but now William had his grip back on his shotgun. He planted a foot on the skirt of Jeannie's dress, and as Jacob reached for her, William butted him away with the gun, slamming the barrel against Jacob's head three times, until Jacob fell to the floor at Jeannie's side. Then he hoisted Jeannie to her feet with one hand, her skirt still caught under his foot. Her dress tore. She stood by herself for a moment as William returned his hand to the trigger, before looking down at her bared legs. Jacob was on all fours, struggling to stand again while attempting to keep the room from moving in his swaying field of vision, when he saw Jeannie try to cover herself, shrinking back down to her knees.

William rested a foot on her hand, then looked up at the crowd and grinned. "Ladies and gentlemen, you all will be reading about Miss Levy in the newspapers soon enough. But allow me to be the first to inform you that this charming young lady is a Union whore."

Suddenly, in the tiny corner of rationality Jacob retreated to in his brain as he reeled on the floor, he understood what William was thinking. Jeannie hadn't responded to William's letter, or, rather, had responded by not responding, by marrying Jacob regardless. So William had then concluded that she was actually a double agent—working with Jacob! It occurred to Jacob that there must be some sort of posse outside the house, waiting to arrest them both. He glanced past William through the open door, but he saw no one, not even a horse. Apparently William had decided that he could take care of both of them himself. As Jacob looked up at the shotgun, he knew that he could.

"Mr. Williams," someone said behind them.

When Jacob managed to turn around, he saw Philip standing at the back of the room, just outside the door of his study, in his top hat and tails. His hands were raised in front of him and clasped together high, as if in some sort of ecstatic Christian prayer. It was another long second before Jacob saw that Philip was holding a revolver, pointed at William Wilhelm Williams the Third.

"This is my daughter's wedding, and you are not invited," Philip said. His voice was calm, even, utterly without fear. The revolver was steady in his hands. "Now please get out of my house."

The guests remained plastered along the walls, the women clinging to the men as everyone crouched at the edges of the room. Jeannie, apparently forgetting her dress, tried to stand again, but Jacob pulled her back down to the floor. William was startled, but now he leveled his gun again, at Philip.

"Philip Mordecai Levy. The Shylock of the Old Dominion. Greetings, sir. I'm so sorry I can't offer you a pound of my flesh, but perhaps you might accept a pound of Rappaport's instead."

In his top hat, Philip blazed like a pillar of fire. He spoke slowly, carefully. "No one else in my family is going to die in this room."

William cocked back the gun, and smirked. "Levy, your confidence is impressive. In that case, I challenge you to a duel. Rappaport can be your second, and Eugenia can be mine." He looked straight at Philip's pistol, and kept grinning. "Obviously, Levy, you've never been in a duel before. If you had, you wouldn't be here at all."

Philip did not move. "Williams, I am only going to warn you one more time. Get out of my house."

William laughed out loud. It was a long laugh, five long descending notes that plummeted into a growl. Then he aimed the gun carefully at Philip, and fired.

The guests hit the floor as William pulled the trigger. But as Jacob watched William, he saw the most amazing sight: as William fired, his right arm suddenly snapped inward in a frantic spasm, recoiling toward his shoulder so that the barrel of the gun flailed madly toward the ceiling as the shot rang out.

The plaster hadn't even begun to fall from the bullet hole in the ceiling when a second shot screamed through the room. William staggered backward and fell to the floor, blood flowing gently from his head onto the threshold of the house. The battlefield injury that had made him into an entertainer for the troops had ensured that crippled William Wilhelm Williams the Third would never again win a duel.

And contrary to all of Jacob's expectations for his wedding day, it was Philip Mordecai Levy who spent Jacob's wedding night in jail.

3

"JACOB, NOW THAT I'VE BECOME YOUR WIFE, THERE IS SOMETHING I have to tell you."

One of the guests had sneaked out of the house to fetch the police when William first appeared, though by the time the police arrived, there was nothing left for them to do but cart the body away and arrest Philip. Rose had screamed like a baby, clinging to Philip's legs until the constable had to pry her off of him in order to escort him to the county jail. The guests had departed in a daze; the sisters had surrounded Jacob and an alarmingly stoic Jeannie, and sobbed. It wasn't until many hours later that Jeannie and Jacob found themselves alone in Jeannie's bedroom, which Lottie had permanently vacated to share with Rose and Phoebe, and to which Philip had donated his own four-poster double bed. The sisters had strewn white flowers all over the bedspread. But when they were finally alone, Jeannie sat on the bed and at last began to cry herself.

"Jacob, you must know that I didn't love William. I did once, a few years ago, when I was only a girl and had never met anyone else, but I haven't now for ages. Really," she said when she had regained her breath. Her face was red, swollen with crying. "He loved me, of course he did, but I didn't love him. Please believe me."

This wasn't the conversation Jacob had hoped to have on his wedding night, but nothing had gone as expected. He found himself remembering old Isaacs's advice, and took her gently in his arms. "I believe you," he said softly.

She sobbed some more as Jacob held her. Jacob thought of old Isaacs and tried to be as patient as he could, tried not to expect anything at all, as he waited for her to speak again.

She slowly stopped crying, and breathed. "Really, it's true. I didn't love him," she repeated.

"I believe you, Jeannie," Jacob started to say again. Before he could get the words out, she continued.

"I didn't love him, but I needed him," she said. "Papa didn't know it, but William was my contact."

Jacob held his breath. Could it possibly be? "Your—your what?"

"My contact. He was sending messages for me to the commanders in the camps."

Jacob knew he had to play the fool. It wasn't difficult; he was flabbergasted already, by the events of the day and by everything else. And by this time, he was as good a performer as Jeannie. "Messages? What messages?"

"Information about Yankee troops. When they would be coming, where they would be coming from, how many at a time, which generals, where the headquarters were, what kind of armaments, that sort of thing."

Jacob stammered, feigning shock. "But—but—but how could you know—"

"Lottie," she said. "Major Stoughton is in love with her, and he's as pompous as they come. Worse than William, even. He loves to brag. He tells her everything, just to impress her. It never occurs to him that ladies also have brains." She smiled, with wet cheeks. "Phoebe carved the compartments whenever we needed to hide the messages, and Rose put them into code."

Jacob was silent for a while, letting his mouth hang open. He hadn't known these details; he had certainly suspected them at first, but at some point after Jeannie revealed her leg to him, he had stopped suspecting. Now he wondered whose sham this marriage was: his, or hers? His mind raced with possibilities, and suddenly he knew he had to keep up his guard.

"But—but how could you take the risk?" he stuttered, and prayed that his shock was convincing. "Were they—was someone paying you?"

"No one was paying us at the beginning," she said. "It started this past winter, when the Yankees took the city. William suggested it at first, and then we—we simply did it, because how could we not? With all these people in the house, and with what happened to our mother—really, anyone would have done the same thing."

Jacob thought of William helping her escape from her father's house to play Juliet in Richmond, escorting her to another world where she could step onto a stage and prove that she was someone else entirely. He wondered if William had been her equivalent of the three officers, if William had used the same sort of shaming to wear her down. And William had had his own dream too, just as Jacob's commanders did: conquest.

"The Yankees even arrested me then, but I managed to convince them that it was all a misunderstanding. It's remarkable what gentlemen will believe when they see a lady's legs." Jacob glanced away, his eyes on the bedspread. "Recently they started paying us," she continued. "I tried to give the money to Papa. I told him it was from needlework I sold to the dressmaker. But he didn't believe me. He thought I had found another acting job somewhere, with William."

"He was right."

"He was furious. He was convinced I was going to run off with William. That's why he was so excited when you arrived. For a time I thought he had planned it, as if there were some grand scheme to bring you down here just to marry me."

"Your father didn't plan anything," Jacob said quickly. He winced at just how close she came to knowing the truth, and suddenly wondered if, perhaps, she did really know.

"But then I didn't care how you came here, I was just so glad that you had come," she said. "I hadn't known how unhappy I was, how terrible I felt with William always expecting what I would never give him, how awful it was pretending for him all the time, until I met you."

He should have felt ashamed, he knew. Instead he was overwhelmed with joy. "Jeannie," he panted. She rested her head on his shoulder, and he stroked her hair, just as he had seen William do it, a lifetime ago, through the front-room window. Her hair spilled onto his hands, liquid warmth flowing between his fingers. A curl wound its way around his thumb, binding him to her.

"Now we have no contact, no one," she continued. "Papa's too proud to admit it, but we need the money. Especially now. They aren't going to let Papa out of jail."

"Jeannie, of course they will," he said, and thought of old Isaacs again. "There were dozens of witnesses in the house today. The court will set bail for him, he'll have a trial—"

"The trial is what I'm afraid of. Papa has a lot of enemies in town. And William was a popular actor. He's a hero around here, especially since he was wounded," she said. "I've been thinking about this for the past few hours, and I keep remembering all the times Papa told people how much he hated William. A jury would be a catastrophe for Papa, and the judge won't be better. Even bail would be dangerous for him. He would have to find somewhere to hide. I don't think the court will hang him, but it will be a long, long time before he comes home."

For the first time that day, Jacob's shock softened into sadness. *No one knows*, Jacob remembered Philip saying, *how much I've done for those girls*. No, Jacob thought, and no one ever will.

"I—I can run the business for him," he stammered. But that, he knew, wasn't the point.

"The business is ruined already," Jeannie said. "You know that. It's just the boarding house now. And—and our own business, if one can call it that, but now that's ruined too. We can't do this sort of thing without contacts who trust us completely. There isn't any way to continue it."

Now Jacob's heart raced. The moment had arrived. *FAILURE IS TREA-SON*, he remembered. He forced himself to think of where he would have been tonight if he hadn't been sent to the magical time capsule that was the Levys' house: sleeping in the mud, then rising at daybreak to move again, chased through the forest like an animal by the enemy, guessing when or whom the next bullet would hit, wondering whether he would live to see nightfall. He thought of the first corpse he had ever seen while retreating through the Virginia woods: a blue-uniformed boy, slumped against a tree, whom Jacob had mistaken for living until he noticed the flies crawling across the boy's still-open eyes. He thought of standing before the officers, of what he had promised, of what needed to be done. *We know we may depend on you for anything. With no exceptions.* He unwound her curls from his fingers, and spoke.

"There is a way," he said. "I can become your new contact."

The words were scarcely out of his mouth when he wished he had never said them. But it was too late. Jeannie turned to face him.

"You?" she asked.

"Yes," he said, and steeled himself. There was no going back. "I know people in the camps." He thought of Harry Hyams. "I was bringing them rum for months. They all remember me."

Her face lit up. She was beautiful that way, even more so than before. "Do you know General Jackson?" she asked. "He was William's contact." Her voice was full of hope.

Stonewall Jackson! Now Jacob was frightened. He had pictured her passing minor messages to some twenty-year-old sergeant who took the credit for himself. He had never imagined her doing anything at that high a level. How many people had died because of what she had done?

"No, but I know one of his deputies," he lied, praying that she wouldn't ask him to name anyone. She didn't. Instead she listened. "I could explain the situation to him, and pass the messages along for you."

She looked at him, and suddenly smiled. Her face glowed. "Thank you, Jacob," she whispered.

Her torn wedding dress was gleaming in the lamplight, darkness luring him beneath her ripped skirt. He reached behind her curls to her neck and back, tracing her skin with his finger, following the line of her spine down to the buttons of her dress. She kissed him, and pulled him down with her onto the flowers her sisters had picked for them. For the rest of that night, Jacob was able to forget his first war.

JEANNIE WAS RIGHT about Philip. The judge denied him bail, and didn't even bother to set a date for a trial. Other than his lawyer— someone who used to work for the company, whom Jacob had managed to track down—Philip was barely allowed any visitors. His family was forbidden to him completely, because women weren't permitted to visit the jail. When Jacob at last managed to see him, more than a week after the wedding, he was astonished to find him in a tiny cell without even a bed or a stool in it, only a floor covered with straw and mouse droppings, which he was sharing with a Negro who lay sleeping in the opposite corner. The sleeping Negro surprised Jacob even more than the cell itself. He couldn't imagine why they had been put there together. Perhaps the jail was already full; either that, or Jeannie was right about the judge.

The warden shackled Philip, removed him from the cell, and led them both into a locked room with two benches in it. On one of the benches, an old fat guard was sitting, eyes drooping. The room stank of liquor. When the warden closed the door and Philip and Jacob sat down on the bench on the opposite side of the room, the guard glanced at both of them, then slumped down against the wall. In minutes he was snoring.

Philip sat beside Jacob for a moment in silence. Jacob had noticed slaves being transported in shackles around town from time to time, but he had always turned away from them. He had never before been this close to a man in chains. Philip's hands were locked together and absurdly posed at his groin, like a man about to urinate. His knees knocked against each other from the weight of the irons on his legs. Jacob thought of him as he had seen him just two years ago, at a business meeting in his father's office in New York, and struggled not to weep.

But Philip, while weary, didn't seem ashamed. "Thank you for coming," he said. "I want you to know that I thank God every hour that you are with the girls."

Jacob didn't know what to say. "I—I'm so sorry," he tried.

Philip shook his head. "It's better that I'm here," he said. "Williams has quite a following. If the judge had let me out on bail, I would have already been lynched."

Jacob started to laugh, then stopped when he noticed Philip's face. Until he saw Philip looking down at his knees, Jacob had thought he meant it as a joke. When Philip spoke again, his voice was low and bare. "Jacob, this place is a wilderness," he said slowly. "I don't mean the jail. I mean the entire South."

Philip turned to face Jacob, and squinted. He wasn't wearing his pince-nez; Jacob wondered if it had been confiscated, if Philip were not only imprisoned but blinded as well. "It's like the book of Judges: 'There was no king in Israel, and everyone did as he pleased,'" Philip quoted, in his slight drawl. He tried to gesture with one hand, but the irons were too heavy for him, and his hands sank back into his lap. "It was like that before, but since the secession it's been made institutional. Savagery is a way of life. Tell me, Jacob, has any civilized person in New York ever settled a score with a duel?"

"Alexander Hamilton," Jacob said, after a moment. "Fifty years ago. Across the river, on the Jersey side." He forced a grin. "The more common custom in New York is to bankrupt someone first, then slander him in the newspapers, and then allow him time to despair until he kills himself."

Philip tried to laugh, a tired, burdened laugh, before giving up. He let out a little groan.

"You should know that when my wife and I first married, I wanted to move north," Philip said. He moved his knees apart, then let them fall back together again. "To Philadelphia, I was hoping. My brother lives in Philadelphia. But my wife refused." Jacob smelled sweat and filth on Philip's clothes, and tried not to breathe in. "Her family had been here since the Revolution. She said she couldn't abandon their graves. I told her how many graves my parents left behind in Prussia, but she insisted that this was different, that this was hers." He twisted a wrist inside the shackles. "She was a wonderful person, but she was wrong. She died because of where we lived." He glanced at Jacob. "I'm sure you heard the story from the girls."

Jacob nodded, and looked down at his lap. The last thing he wanted was to hear it again. "The girls have always blamed the slave, of course," Philip said. "Of course the slave did it, and of course that's what the girls saw, and I know they were too young to think of it any other way. They still are. But I know better. And I blame myself."

Jacob tried to make his voice firm. "Mr. Levy, that's absurd," he said.

"No, it isn't. It's true. I've been thinking about this for eight long years." Philip turned to him. "You saw my cellmate," he said.

"The Negro?" Jacob asked. He couldn't imagine what Philip wanted to talk about. Just being reminded of the cell made him uneasy.

"His name is Caleb," Philip said. "He's very well-educated. You would be shocked to hear him speak—he sounds like he could be a man working in our office. Apparently his master's son is an abolitionist, and has been helping him for years. He's here now because his master was ruined. He has to stay here until someone buys him, so his master can pay back the debt." His voice dropped to a whisper. "No one has guessed it, but he's working for the North." The guard on the bench across from them let out a loud snore.

Jacob was astounded—not merely by the information, but by the fact that Philip had shared it with him, and had assumed him to be sympathetic. What else did Philip know? He heard the guard shift on the bench, his snores growing louder. The smell of stale liquor seeped across the room.

"I challenge you to show me a Prussian prison where the guards are asleep," Philip said. To Jacob's relief, he was smiling. "Now tell me how the girls are. And don't lie to me."

Philip tried to lift his hand to rest it on Jacob's, but the shackles made his movements ridiculous. Jacob flinched, and looked away.

"Everyone is managing well, under the circumstances," Jacob told him. "Even Rose isn't crying anymore. Please don't worry. I—I can't tell you how grateful I am to you for what you did for me, and for Eugenia."

Philip looked down at his shackles. "I know what Eugenia has been doing," he said softly.

For a moment Jacob wondered what he meant, and hesitated. But soon the pause became too long. "She hasn't been in any plays, if that's what you mean," he said quickly. "She told me you thought she had been working again in the theater somehow."

Philip looked at him, leaning toward him so that his unaided eyes focused on Jacob's. "I'm not nearly the old fool you all imagine me to be," Philip said. "Do you think I don't know what happens in my own house?"

Jacob froze in his seat.

"Jacob, I am relying on you to make her stop. She'll find a way, even without that bastard Williams. This isn't a game. Part of the reason I let you marry her was because I needed someone to stop her. I couldn't do it myself." Jacob listened, astonished. "You must convince her to stop, before anything worse happens. Believe me, the wedding was nothing compared to what might be coming next. She'll get you both killed."

Jacob felt himself turning pale. "I—I don't know that I can do anything about it," he stammered.

"You have to, Jacob. It isn't a choice. You have to turn her around. Or else you'll both be dead."

A key turned in the lock, and the sleeping guard suddenly opened his eyes and straightened in his seat, his hand on the pistol at his hip as the warden came in.

"Come back," Philip said to Jacob as the warden escorted him back to his cell.

"I shall," Jacob promised, and wondered if he ever could.

4

*T*HREE WEEKS AFTER THE WEDDING—THREE WEEKS OF JACOB AND the Levy girls making every petition they could think of to hasten Philip's release, and three weeks of failing—Major Stoughton returned from behind the lines, his carriage bells ringing outside the Levy house one evening in the deadening summer heat. Lottie went with him eagerly, climbing into his carriage for an evening tour of the town. Philip would never have let her ride in the carriage with him, Jacob was sure, but no one remained to say no. Jacob was the man of the house now. Rose and Phoebe went up to their bedroom while he and Jeannie waited in the front room for Lottie to return. When she did, instead of the two sisters running upstairs, they remained in the front room with Jacob.

"What did you hear?" Jeannie asked.

Lottie eyed Jacob cautiously. She and Jeannie looked very much alike, Jacob had long noticed, but Lottie rarely smiled. When she did, there was something of Judah Benjamin's perpetual smile in her expression: aloof, defiant, calmly and maddeningly aware of the limitations of others. She gave the impression that she already knew what everyone else was thinking before they themselves did, and that she already disdained it. During his time with the Levys, Jacob had often thought of Lottie as an alternate version of Jeannie—the version that sat in the audience, coolly observing everything around her, while the real Jeannie performed onstage on her behalf. Lottie hesitated before she spoke. The cabal was different now, and Jacob sensed that she didn't accept it.

"He told me something quite significant this time," she finally said. "The Yankee retreat in June was just a ruse. The Federal navy is going to massively increase its forces at Norfolk, and then they expect to send fifty thousand troops back toward Richmond. Under McClellan again, but this time he's really going to move. They're going to cut all the rail lines and burn everything in their way."

This was astonishing to Jacob, but Jeannie remained surprisingly composed. "When?" she asked.

"Two weeks," Lottie answered. "We have to get the message out immediately."

Jeannie took Jacob's hand. "Jacob can do it."

Jacob had dreaded this moment, but now he almost enjoyed it. He squeezed Jeannie's hand in his.

Lottie nodded, then looked away. Something seemed odd about her, though perhaps it was just that Jacob was seeing her honestly for the first time. When she looked back at him, he saw that she was close to tears. "Jacob, I don't know how much longer I can continue with Major Stoughton," she said.

"But Lottie, you've been marvelous," he murmured, unsure of what she meant. Was she testing him?

"He's right. You always have been," Jeannie added. "Why, Lottie? He doesn't suspect, does he?"

Lottie looked down at her lap. "No, but—oh, I can barely say it. He—he put his hand up under my dress."

Jacob was both amazed and ashamed to hear this; surely this sort of detail ought to have been for her sisters' ears alone. Or did she expect him to defend her somehow, now that her father couldn't? Jacob's opinion of Lottie had been painfully low: he wouldn't even have thought that something like this would trouble a girl who had been duping men for months and even seemed to relish it. Both Jeannie and Lottie looked at him, waiting for him to respond. *Draw noses onward*, he thought.

"It will be worth it," he told her. "I promise you."

An instant later he saw that he had said the wrong thing, that he was merely reassuring her of her high price as a Rebel whore. Lottie refused to look him in the eye.

"Lottie, think of what you've accomplished already," Jeannie said. "If you don't wish to continue with him, don't. He won't be the last."

"No, he won't be," Lottie said simply. Finally she looked up and smiled at Jacob, an odd, cold smile. "Thank you, Jacob, for everything," she said. She kissed his cheek, and walked upstairs.

When they heard her bedroom door thump closed above them, Jeannie turned to Jacob, taking him by the hands. "You can't even imagine what this means to us, Jacob," she said, her voice hushed. "It was always so difficult with William. He was only happy if I complied with everything he said, exactly as he said it. He wouldn't even deliver the messages for us if he didn't find me cooperative enough." For a moment Jacob wondered what she meant by this, before deciding that he did not want to know. "I was always expecting him to turn on me in a rage."

"It seems he surpassed your expectations," Jacob said. "But that was my fault." He bit his lip, tripping on the edge of truth.

Jeannie shook her head. "It had nothing to do with you. He would have turned on me regardless. I always expected it," she told him. "I've always expected it from everyone, I suppose. Ever since what happened to our mother, I've felt like I have to look over my shoulder all the time. All of us have." She was gripping his fingers tighter now, he noticed, thin blue veins rising on the backs of her talented hands. "But I'm so grateful to be with you, Jacob. I—I've never felt so free before. Like I have nothing to be ashamed of."

On another night, Jacob might have taken the time to be ashamed of himself. But that night he cast every hesitation from his mind. All he could think of was that he and Jeannie were now absolutely alone in the front room of the house, sitting side by side, with no prospect whatsoever of being interrupted by Philip on his way home.

ROSE GAVE JACOB the message the following morning, rendered into code. Jacob was alarmed to notice that the message wasn't written in one of her silly anagrams, but actually in a genuine Rebel cipher, the Vicksburg Square. The commanders had briefed him about it before he left, a lifetime ago. It was a surprisingly simple code that one deciphered with a square made of ordinary alphabets laid out along the horizontal and vertical axes, so that the letters lined up in a diagonal pattern, and one simply had to trace one's finger along the opposite axis to decipher the letters in the message. The code used key-phrases for further encryption, but there were only three key-phrases—*complete victory*, *come retribution*, and *Manchester Bluff*—and to decipher that layer of the code, one only needed to try each of the three. The key-phrase here, he could tell, was *come retribution*, and by using it, he managed to decipher enough of the first few words to convince himself that what Rose had given him wasn't a joke. It would have taken many, many hours to decipher all of it, so he didn't try.

The larger dilemma, he knew, was that the paper he now held in his hands was what he had been waiting for, the entire purpose of his venture into the land of the Levys: evidence.

He went to Philip's office that morning and sat at Philip's desk, looking at the paper in Rose's neat handwriting. The jumbled letters seemed to rise from the page, flying free in the air, forming words he had heard before. *We doubted your trustworthiness at first, Rappaport, but you have succeeded in putting our doubts to rest. Please, Jacob, please trust me. It's all I've ever wanted.* He sat for a long time with his eyes fixed on the message, immobile as a corpse. There was nothing to do at the office, of course. He left, and paced the streets, trying to think.

New Babylon was a wretched place for thinking. The only businesses that were still running well were the slave auctions. In Jacob's wanderings around town, he passed, as usual, a storefront with a broadside proclaiming AUCTIONS AND NEGRO SALES, where a steady stream of people was moving inside. He had never been inside before, and he had no intention of going inside at that point either, and certainly no reason to do so. But that day, with Rose's message burning in his breast pocket, he stopped on the sidewalk in front of it, hesitating about fifteen feet from the door.

Alongside the storefront was a sort of gated alleyway which he had passed many times on his way through town. In the alleyway was a row of iron doors with bolts on them, each spaced about eight feet apart. Jacob had always assumed that these were horse stables, though presumably for very valuable racehorses or thoroughbreds. But as he stood by the alleyway that morning, dragging his heavy mind through town along with Rose's coded message, he saw something he had never happened to see before. A man in a smart suit came out of the storefront and rounded his way to the alley gate, which he unlocked with a key from a large ring on his belt. Jacob was standing just a few feet away, and out of embarrassment he pulled out his pocket watch, pretending to wind it so as to have a reason to remain there on the sidewalk. The man approached one of the iron doors and unlocked it, yelling something that Jacob couldn't hear. Instead of horses, Jacob saw a row of slaves, chained to each other and wrapped in ragged blankets, shuffling out of the cell. He backed across the street, nearly getting himself run down by a carriage, as the man led the group out of the alleyway and into the storefront. Jacob stood there for at least five minutes, watching men in suits proceeding inside, until, without thinking at all, he crossed the street again and walked through the open door.

What shocked him most was that they were naked. On the platform at the front of the room stood eight Negroes—at first he counted seven, but as he edged his way up toward the front of the room, he saw that the platform simply wasn't high enough, and he hadn't been able to see the head of the two-year-old girl above the crowd. Other than the child, there were four men and three women, the men stripped to the waist and the women, to Jacob's astonishment, stripped completely, their skin strangely shining in the daylight from the windows. The women stood with their arms crossed in front of them until buyers began climbing up onto the platform to squeeze and pinch their arms and not very accidentally brush against their breasts, all before pulling open their mouths to inspect their teeth. Jacob moved toward the platform, almost unconsciously. As he moved closer he saw that both the men's and women's torsos were slicked heavily with grease, to hide their scars. The soft shine this gave their bodies made the entire scene even more compelling. Jacob had never been inside a brothel, but many of his fellow soldiers in the camp had brought dirty pictures with them, and in the long dull months before he was sent to New Orleans he had naturally stared at them all. The greased naked women on the platform, and the men squeezing and pinching them, gave him a feeling familiar from seeing those pictures: a thin, weak veneer of shame barely hiding a terrifying core of animal thrill. He shuddered, trying to control it. In his first conscious movement since he had seen the auctioneer lead the slaves out of the alleyway, he slunk toward the back of the room as the auction itself began.

The first chattel on the block was "Dabney, field hand," who, when his name was called, stepped forward, almost to the platform's edge, and immediately began pacing the platform and even jumping up and down at the auctioneer's command. Apparently he had done this before. He looked to be about Jacob's age, though with a muscular body that Jacob's office work had never afforded him. The auctioneer read off a brief description of Dabney, which mainly seemed to consist of how many bushels of tobacco he was able to carry and how far he could carry them, along with a brief mention of his history of good behavior and his lack of attempts at escape. The bidding went quickly, until the price reached a thousand fifty dollars—sold.

The winner was a man about ten years older than Jacob, wearing a linen suit and a large pocket-watch chain across his vest. He stepped up onto the platform to hand some sort of ticket to the auctioneer. But he had barely done so when Dabney took a step toward him, head bowed.

"Young mas'r," Dabney suddenly said.

Jacob was struck by how odd it was to hear his voice; a voice somehow seemed utterly alien coming from one of these greased naked beings on the platform. But what was even more unexpected was what he began to say.

"Young mas'r, I—I loves Dorrie, young mas'r," he said, and pointed toward one of the naked women in the row behind him.

The woman he pointed at was tall, almost Jacob's height and Dabney's, and about their age as well. She hugged herself, and bowed her head. Among the three women on the platform, she was by far the youngest and also the prettiest; she had been the one who had attracted the most buyers to check her teeth.

"I loves her well an' true; de good Lord knows I loves her better than I loves anyone in de wide world," Dabney continued. His voice was trembling now, and Jacob saw that Dorrie was trembling too. "Please buy Dorrie, young mas'r. We'll be married right soon, and de chillun will be healthy an' strong, an'—an'—Young mas'r, Dorrie prime woman. Dorrie, come show how strong you is."

To Jacob's surprise, no one interrupted this display. When Jacob glanced at the auctioneer, the man even seemed to smile; presumably it was in his interest to sell off the whole platform as efficiently as possible, and this sort of drama might somehow drive up a price. The winner turned, following Dabney's pointing finger.

Dorrie stepped forward, shivering, and slowly unfolded her arms, stretching them out in front of the winner's face. This proved to be a colossal mistake, for the result of it was to expose her breasts once more, and dramatically, to the entire crowd. Jacob's own throat throbbed as he felt the animal thrill surge again within him. Her body was phenomenal.

Dorrie folded her arms back over herself as the auctioneer began reading her description, something involving field work and breeding years, but it no longer mattered. The bidding for her began, and the price quickly went through the roof; soon she was more expensive than Dabney. The previous winner's face fell as the price moved past twelve hundred. As a businessman, Jacob had long learned to tell when someone is bluffing, and he could see that the winner wasn't. To his credit, he tried.

"Young mas'r, please buy Dorrie," Dabney called, from the back of the platform this time, but his new owner simply shook his head, with a pained expression on his face.

The bidding slowed, and soon the auctioneer was calling for a final price. Suddenly Dabney moved forward and dropped to his knees beside Dorrie. "Young mas'r, please," he said one more time, and Dorrie knelt down beside him. Jacob saw him try to take her hand, but her arms were wrapped tightly around herself, her eyes fixed on the floor. The gavel fell, and it was over.

The image of the two of them, naked on their knees, burned itself into Jacob's body. He left the building and circled the town madly, trying desperately to erase it from his field of vision. After a while he turned down an alley and stepped into an actual horses' stable, retching wildly. He forced himself to think of Harry Hyams, willing the dark bile within him to pour itself out, but he could not vomit it away. It was branded onto his gut forever.

With Rose's message in his pocket, he proceeded to the bakery.

5

JACOB STOOD IN FRONT OF THE BAKERY, THE IMAGE OF DORRIE AND Dabney on their knees seared into his stomach. He glanced at his reflection in the door's window and reached for the doorknob. But just before pulling the door open, he paused. The naked women on the platform burned in his mind's eye, and suddenly he pictured the only other woman he had ever seen without clothes. In his memory he saw Jeannie as she had been just the previous night: lying naked on their bed as he unbuckled his belt, her bare body breathing before him in the dim candlelight, waiting for him. He understood what he was selling. His hand slid from the doorknob, and he walked away.

He hurried back toward Philip's office as he tried to justify his choice. At least, he told himself, he might already be serving his country simply by not delivering the message to Jackson as he had promised. If the Federals really were about to march on Richmond again, imagine the devastation to them that he would be preventing just by keeping Rose's message safely in his own hands! If that were the case, then he had already saved thousands of Union lives—even, perhaps, the lives of his own fellow soldiers from the 18th New York. Besides, he reasoned, might he be even more useful to his country by simply *accumulating* more evidence of this type? After all, if Jeannie and Lottie were to be arrested, some other chain of spies would surely spring up in their place. But here he was stopping the damage at the source, like the little Dutch boy who saved his country with a single finger in the dike. Why not let Lottie and Jeannie continue passing their information to him, so that he could *continue* stopping them? Yes, he decided, that was the best approach. He retreated to the office and quickly buried Rose's message in the lining of his hat. He sat down at Philip's desk and composed a vague message in code for the bakery: ACTIVITY DETECTED IN HOUSEHOLD; CURRENTLY INTER-

CEPTING ENEMY COMMUNICATION; ESSENTIAL NOT TO INTER-
RUPT MISSION AT THIS TIME. When he was finished, he went back to
the bakery to deliver the goods.

Jacob's contact at the bakery had the ridiculous name of Achilles Fogg,
and his surname suggested the atmosphere in his shop on that humid
afternoon. The air in the bakery was thick, heavy with flour and heat.
Jacob found it difficult to breathe.

Fogg was used to it. He was an old man—fat, as any good baker ought
to be, with a thick mustache and a perpetually reddened face, his fore-
arms scarred and singed from too many accidents by the ovens. Jacob
often wished that he could really speak to him, if only to alleviate the
sheer loneliness of what he had been doing for these past months, but
also to find out what it was about him that made him do what he had
agreed to do. Jacob assumed that he was motivated by some sort of ide-
alism, imagining that he must be a secret abolitionist hiding runaway
slaves in his cellar, or a practical philosopher who believed that union
was the only path to peace, or a pious Christian who wanted nothing
more than to help the needy and serve his God. Or it might just as easily have been the money. Jacob would have loved to ask him, but he had
been instructed never to speak with him more than necessary, and Fogg
had apparently been taught the same. The baker was the only person in
the shop when Jacob finally entered, though there was always a risk that
another customer might appear at any moment; they usually said little
to each other, almost nothing at all. Fogg saw Jacob through the heated
haze, and grinned.

"Thought you'd be comin' before," he said. "Saw you out there 'bout
a quarter past."

"Oh, yes," Jacob stammered. "I was about to come in, but I—I left
something behind at the office."

"Not much business these days, I reckon," he said. The phrase was a
code, a reprimand from the commanders. Roughly deciphered, it meant:
RAPPAPORT, WHERE IN HELL HAVE YOU BEEN?

"No," Jacob replied, and then thought he would test him. "It seems
like the auction house is the only success left in town."

This wasn't part of their script. The baker smiled again, but Jacob
couldn't read anything in his expression. Something told Jacob that the

baker wouldn't say anything more; he was far better at this than Jacob would ever be. Perhaps, Jacob thought while watching the man's creased red face, this wasn't his first war.

"What'll it be today?" Fogg asked, and rubbed his thick hands together.

"The usual, thank you," Jacob said.

"I got it all ready for you," Fogg replied. "Good you don't come in before. Ellis only jes' deliver 'em." Ellis was a Negro boy about Rose's age who ran deliveries of flour and other supplies to the bakery. Of course, Ellis must have been working for them too.

Achilles Fogg brought out a small sack filled with rolls, exactly as he always did. "That'll be seven cents," he said. "Sorry we done raised the price. Money's gone way down these days."

Jacob reached into his pocket and passed him his message, along with a handful of pennies. The paper disappeared into the baker's thick, sweating palm. "Thank you," Jacob murmured, and quickly turned to leave.

"We'll be expectin' y'all agin soon," the baker called as the door swung shut behind him.

That meant the commanders needed more than Jacob was giving them, and were getting impatient. Well, Jacob thought, they would have to keep waiting. He returned to the office, where he shut himself up in Philip's private study before picking and eating his way through several of the rolls. The rolls, as always, contained what Jacob expected—and what Jeannie and her sisters needed. When the day wore thin, Jacob went back to the Levy house, filled with an intense feeling of happiness. For the first time in his life, he would be feeding his family, all on his own.

SUPPER AT THE Levys' house since Philip's imprisonment had become even more stultifying than before. The girls refused to speak to the boarders, and Jacob couldn't manage to make conversation with them the way Philip always had, not with the four sisters watching him. That evening the meal limped along until everyone was done eating, at which point Lottie loudly announced that she was embarking on a new project to sew socks and shirts for needy Rebel soldiers, which she would be working on upstairs, and excused herself. The three boarders of the moment blushed darkly—war profiteers, all, who seemed to welcome Jacob's presence, and particularly his accent, at the head of the table in the Levys' house. But in the wake of Philip's departure, Lottie was making it clear that the girls would stand on their own, their pride and contempt intact. The boarders looked to Jacob for sympathy, but he avoided their eyes. They quickly left, heading for the tavern. Once they had cleared the table, Phoebe and Rose hurried upstairs to join Lottie, leaving Jacob and Jeannie in the front room, alone.

Jeannie rushed toward him as soon as they were by themselves. "Did you give them the message?" she asked.

"Of course," he lied. To his surprise, the lie was easy to tell. He knew he had saved her, and that was enough.

"Oh, Jacob, thank you!" she cried, and threw her arms around him. Her soft cheek against his was enough to erase his doubts.

"And this is what they gave me," Jacob said, and presented her with his snuff box. It was the one that Phoebe had carved for him, "from Jeannie."

Jeannie took it in her hands, knowing immediately what Jacob meant. She opened the lid, dipped a finger in to push the snuff aside, and carefully lifted the floor of the box until she could reach the secret compartment. Out of it she withdrew a single bill, folded into a tiny rectangle. It was still moist from the bakery roll from which Jacob had extracted it that afternoon, but when she unfolded it, it was legible enough.

"*A hundred dollars?*" she asked.

"Quite deserved," Jacob replied. But his stomach fluttered. The currency, he knew, was depreciating by the day; should there have been more?

He watched as Jeannie shook her head. "This is much more than they ever gave us before. Twenty at a time, maybe. Never this much."

Jacob had simply thought of it as Rebel money, which was worthless as far as he was concerned. But no one in Virginia saw it that way then, not yet. And now he was worried.

"Did they mention anything about it when they gave it to you?" she asked.

Jacob maintained his actor's face: straight, candid. "No, nothing in particular," he said.

"How odd," she said, running a finger over the box's carved lid. She gave the box back to Jacob as she examined the bill in her other hand. "When William paid us, there was never more than—"

Suddenly she stopped speaking and looked up, eyeing Jacob. Jacob watched as she screwed her face into a sneer. "What a fool I've been," she announced.

Now it was over. In another instant Jacob would have fallen at her feet, begging her to save his life. But just as he was about to open his mouth, she said, "William must have been keeping the rest for himself all this time. Papa was right. He was pure scum." Then she smiled. "I can't thank you enough."

Jacob sucked in his breath, trying to hold back a gasp of relief. "I only did what you asked of me," he said. The lie was harder this time, but still not painful. The jealous triumph over William made him unaccountably proud, though Philip deserved the credit. And Jacob knew what he had really done for her, even if she never would.

"Jacob, you don't know how good you are," Jeannie said with a sigh. She tucked the money into her dress, and enfolded him in her arms.

If he were a better person, he would have turned away, excused himself, told her he couldn't hold her now, that it would have to be another time, or another life; he would have vanished from the world entirely, poisoned forever with dirt and shame. But instead he started kissing her, and soon he found himself reaching up under her dress. He had every right. He had paid in full.

6

PHILIP LOOKED BETTER THE SECOND TIME JACOB SAW HIM. IT was just over two weeks since Jacob had decided not to turn in his evidence when he was finally granted permission to return to the jail for another visit. This time he was brought to a different room, one with a table and stools instead of benches, and a chair along the wall for the guard. It was the same guard from his first visit, the old drunk. But this time he was awake, if inattentive, yawning over a copy of the *New Babylon Intelligencer*. And someone—Philip's lawyer?—must have alerted the jail to the bad impression Philip's cell had made, because instead of showing Jacob to Philip's cell, the warden brought Philip directly into the room where Jacob was waiting. Philip was still shackled, but he seemed to wear his chains more lightly now. When he first saw Jacob, he almost smiled.

They spoke for a time with a merciful lack of passion. Philip told him what the lawyer had said about his chances with the judge, which the lawyer apparently did not find as dire as Jeannie had predicted, though Jacob suspected that Philip was merely making the picture rosier for his sake. And Jacob in turn briefed him carefully about the business, lying even more than usual. He saw no reason to damage Philip's good mood. Things were practically jovial between them until Philip suddenly leaned his shackled hands across the table toward Jacob and frowned.

"Jacob, I have a favor to ask of you. A large one," he said.

Jacob glanced at the guard, who was lighting a pipe. It must be something about the lawyer, he guessed. With the guard ten feet away, there was a limit to what else Philip could possibly ask. "You know I would do anything for you," he said.

Philip looked at him. "I'd like you to buy Caleb. Bill my account."

At first Jacob had no idea what he meant. His initial thought was that this was some elaborate delusion about the business; perhaps Philip's time in the jail was driving him mad. Jacob spoke slowly, as if to an imbecile, and asked, "You'd like me to buy what?"

"Caleb, my cellmate. If you give the warden seven hundred dollars, he's yours."

Now Jacob was certain that Philip had gone mad. "Why? What for?"

"I know it sounds like a lot, but trust me, he's a bargain," Philip said loudly, in response to no question Jacob had asked. "At auction he would be over a thousand dollars. But this is a foreclosure sale. It would make an excellent investment." Philip paused, and watched Jacob.

Now Jacob saw that Philip was speaking for the benefit of the guard. "I mentioned him to you last time," Philip said, emphasizing each word. "Do you remember?"

Suddenly Jacob understood, though he found it almost impossible to believe. "Yes, I remember," he said slowly. "I shall consider it."

"Don't consider it," Philip told him. "Come back with the money and do it. As soon as possible. Today or tomorrow, if you can." His voice was even, but urgent. "Use my account. This is a business opportunity that you must not miss."

The guard had actually been listening, it seemed. He chuckled, a snorting sound, and as Jacob looked at him, he looked away and shook his head. "Always money, money, money," he muttered, ostensibly to himself. "Even in jail, they still tryin' to make a buck."

Philip blinked twice, then glanced at the guard. The guard was still grinning, but now he was pretending to ignore them, looking down at his newspaper and deliberately rustling its pages. Then Philip turned back to Jacob, and smiled.

He raised his shackled wrists and wiped his eyes, awkwardly moving one thumb and then one wrist along the edge of the other wrist's shirt cuff. Then he rubbed at his shirt cuff a bit more, wiping his eye with his other fingers. Jacob almost offered to help him, but before he could decide whether Philip would appreciate his help or be ashamed of it, Philip lowered his hands back to the table, the irons clanging on the wood. A second later he clutched Jacob's hand firmly and quickly let go. Jacob felt something small and light, a tiny bit of cloth, folded into his fist.

Jacob nearly unfolded his fingers to look, before he thought better of it. Instead he slipped whatever it was into his pocket. Then he looked up at Philip again, and he saw for the first time that his smile was strikingly, beautifully familiar. Jacob couldn't help but laugh. Apparently Jeannie had inherited her talent for sleight of hand.

"That's the sort of thing the baker would appreciate," Philip said as Jacob laughed.

"The baker?" Jacob nearly swallowed the words.

"Jacob, don't be tiresome," Philip said. "I've known Achilles for years, though he has never respected me much."

How much did Philip know? Jacob was still speechless when Philip finally spoke again. "Of course, by now I hope you know that respect isn't in the cards for us," he said. "But you can make your way through life without it. All you can hope for is a bit of honor now and then—private honor. No one will ever give it to you, no one will ever congratulate you for it, no one will ever even know you have it, but you earn it, and it's yours."

The last time Jacob had heard this was from the mouth of the Confederate Secretary of State, as he stood behind a latrine in a swamp. Now he was hearing it from a man in chains, and this time he already knew it was true. He could say nothing; there was nothing left to say.

"Are the girls all right?" Philip asked.

Jacob started to ramble about Rose and Phoebe ignoring the boarders, and about Lottie knitting socks for the troops, but Philip drummed his fingers once on the table and glared. Jacob knew what he really wanted to know. "I'm keeping Eugenia under control," he finally said.

"I am depending on you," Philip said softly. "Please protect her. I know you have the ability to protect her." The voices of the officers echoed through Jacob's mind: *We know we may depend on you. With no exceptions.* "It will be very dangerous for her. And for you, too. If she doesn't turn around, she'll be shot in the back."

Jacob didn't know whether or not this was a metaphor, and he didn't care to find out. But now he was torn, and terrified. "I am already doing more than I can," he said, almost pleading. "What else can I possibly do?"

"Buy Caleb," Philip said.

Then the warden came in, and took Philip away.

JACOB LEFT THE JAILHOUSE and made his way toward the office. The day soon grew long, deadened with sorting through fruitless accounting, correspondence about canceled plans, and the growing pile of notices of debt. After too many hours of watching him pretend to work, Jacob even sent the secretary home, wondering how soon he might have to let him go. Alone at last, he pulled the rag of paper out of his pocket.

It was a little square of cotton cloth that must have been cut from a shirt, covered with words written out in block letters. The words were written in an odd, brownish-looking ink. Only after quite some time did Jacob realize it must have been blood. It read:

HOME MORNING RIGHT MOVING FOR VENUS EIGHT TO GLORY LOVE HILLCREST MILO ASHTON MARS LIZA TOMORROW TRUTH.

As soon as Jacob saw the word *HOME*, he froze in Philip's chair. Could it possibly be?

He wouldn't, couldn't believe it until he tried. He took out a piece of paper and a charcoal pencil and set to work.

The word *HOME* meant four columns with four words in each, routed from bottom to top in odd-numbered columns and top to bottom in even-numbered ones. He reassembled the words after *HOME* according to the route, in a way that had become commonplace to him from deciphering the command's messages during the past few months:

1	2	3	4
FOR	VENUS	ASHTON	MARS
MOVING	EIGHT	MILO	LIZA
RIGHT	TO	HILLCREST	TOMORROW
MORNING	GLORY	LOVE	TRUTH

Now, reading horizontally from left to right, some sense emerged. VENUS was a code word for "Colonel," MARS was General Longstreet, MILO meant "thousand," LIZA meant "troops," and RIGHT meant "east"—this much Jacob had already filed in his memory. The last three words, GLORY, LOVE, and TRUTH, were column-fillers. As he had long suspected, they meant nothing at all. Which left:

FOR COLONEL ASHTON. LONGSTREET MOVING EIGHT THOUSAND TROOPS EAST TO HILLCREST TOMORROW MORNING.

This was almost unfathomable. Jacob sat rereading the words for a long time, unable to understand. How on earth could Philip's cellmate have known any of it? Perhaps it was a ruse, but it was difficult to imagine what incentive the slave would have to lie. No, Jacob was confident it was true; the slave had gotten the information legitimately, even if the information itself was somehow fraudulent or imprecise. But how had he found out? Hadn't he been sitting in jail? If Philip had hardly been allowed any visitors, surely a slave wouldn't have had any at all. Through what magic had he done it? Still pondering, Jacob read it again, until the last two words jumped out at him. He stopped thinking, pocketed the bloodstained scrap again, along with a few coins, and ran to the bakery as fast as he could. Once he had slipped the message into the baker's fat hand, he ran back to the office to see what more could be done.

He consulted the account books and went to the safe, where he removed seven hundred dollars in Rebel cash for the following day's purchase. He would have gone back to do it that day, if it weren't already so late. The investment, he saw, was worthwhile; there was no time to waste. He was nearly frantic as he walked back to the Levy house, wondering how he would ever be able to face the sisters that night. Then on his way home, he remembered something else, and bought a newspaper.

He scanned the headlines, but there was nothing but the regular carnage and body counts, and the lists of casualties by name on the inside pages, as usual. One blessing of living in New Babylon was that the newspapers did not report the names of casualties for the Union. If everyone Jacob knew had already been killed, he did not want to know. But despite the ordinariness that had bled itself out of what used to be horror, that day's paper was something strange indeed.

He flipped back to the front page, reading the headlines again, and looked once more at the date, calculating in his head. Exactly two weeks and one day had passed since Lottie's rendezvous with Major Stoughton. Yet even when he read through the entire paper, and bought every other paper available, Jacob could not find a single word about the Federal navy increasing its force at Norfolk.

7

*T*HAT EVENING AND THE FOLLOWING MORNING, THE LEVY HOUSE
seemed unusually tense. Instead of leaving Jacob alone with Jeannie after
the boarders had gone out for the evening, Lottie, Phoebe, and Rose sat
down in the front room with them as Jacob told them about his visit
to Philip. The girls were eager for every last detail of how he seemed
to be faring, and as he had after his first visit, Jacob continued to lie as
much as possible. They didn't hear a word about his cell, or the guard, or
his shackles, or anything about the business proposition he had made to
Jacob. Instead, Jacob talked about Philip's happy mood, and how well he
looked as they discussed some business matters. By the time Jacob was
done, the sisters must have pictured the two of them having a meeting
over a few fine cigars.

Even after that conversation had exhausted itself, something about
the way Lottie looked at Jacob still left him too embarrassed to retreat
with Jeannie upstairs. Instead he remained in Philip's old chair with Jeannie in the seat beside him, reading one of the newspapers he had bought
on his way home. Rose was scribbling earnestly on a piece of paper, while
Phoebe was whittling a new box; Lottie was knitting socks for the Rebel
army. The clicking of knitting needles in the chair opposite Jacob's made
him unaccountably nervous. Jeannie was occupying herself with a needlepoint, and he couldn't help but wonder why Jeannie hadn't joined in Lottie's knitting spree. Not long after Jacob had begun pretending to read
the newspaper, Lottie put down her sock and looked right at him. For a
while he gazed at his paper, trying to withstand her eyes, but soon he had
to give in. When he finally looked up, she was grinning at him.

"What's the news today?" Lottie asked.

"News?" Jacob asked stupidly.

"Yes, the news," she said, and laughed out loud. "You have about five newspapers there. Surely I wouldn't be remiss to expect you to be well-informed this evening."

Jacob glanced at Jeannie, hoping for help. Jeannie barely looked up. The sisters had had some sort of fight, it seemed. "Oh, the news, of course," he replied, and then improvised. "I was interested because the statehouse was supposed to pass a new tariff bill today. It could be good for the business, if it goes through. But it seems they postponed the vote."

"Star comedy by Democrats," Rose remarked. Her sisters ignored her.

"What about the front?" Lottie asked.

"The usual murder and mayhem," he said, with a theatrical sigh. "But one just has to accept that by now."

"One doesn't have to accept anything," Lottie said icily.

"Live not on evil!" Rose proclaimed.

Jeannie suddenly stirred, putting a hand on Jacob's arm. He looked at her and saw that she had just understood what Lottie was asking about. "Jacob, is there any news about the Federal navy?" she asked.

"Federal navy," Jacob mumbled, and began rustling the newspapers, just as he had seen the guard in the jailhouse rustle his when he went to visit Philip. "Federal navy," he repeated, turning pages.

"And fear Levy," Rose announced.

Ignoring Rose, he flipped more pages in the paper before returning Lottie's glare. "No, nothing about the Federal Levy—I mean, the Federal navy," he stammered. Rose giggled.

"That's a good thing, isn't it?" said Phoebe. "I'd heard a rumor that the Yankees were planning an attack." Phoebe, he had noticed earlier, was the most honest of the sisters: the most loyal, and the worst liar. Lottie narrowed her eyes at her, but she simply kept whittling, with a growing smile on her face. "Thank goodness for that. I suppose anybody who was thinking about attacking us heard the Rebel yell, and turned back."

"Belly reel," Rose said. "Won't lovers revolt now?"

Clearly, Phoebe thought the girls' own Rebel yell had sent the forces away. Jacob wondered if perhaps he could convince Lottie and Jeannie of the same. While he thought of how best to try, he decided to change the subject. "Have you girls ever heard it?"

"Heard what?" asked Phoebe.

"A real Rebel yell," he said.

"William did it for me once," Jeannie said, then blushed as Jacob turned to her. Hearing William's name still enraged him, and she knew it. She took his hand. "He tried to teach me how, but I couldn't ever do it myself. Of course, I couldn't do a lot of things he wanted me to do." She smiled. Jacob squeezed her fingers as they curled around his hand, and felt at home.

"I've never heard it before," Phoebe said. She put her box down in her lap. "What does it sound like?"

"I don't think I could imitate it, or even describe it," Jacob said truthfully. "It's like—well, imagine someone scraping a nail across an anvil. Or a chicken shrieking just before you chop off its head."

Rose and Phoebe both laughed. Lottie sat straight in her seat, with a calm smile on her face. But Jacob no longer cared about Lottie; the laughter in the room was what he needed.

Jeannie leaned forward. "I think there's more of a bellow to it," she insisted.

"Imagine if you took a screaming man, strung him up by his feet, and whirled him around and around a maypole," Jacob said.

"But louder," Jeannie said. "Like a dying whale."

"Or an elephant giving birth," he said. "To triplets."

Jeannie, Rose, and Phoebe laughed out loud, and Jacob couldn't help laughing with them. It was the happiest he had felt in weeks. And that was when Lottie opened her mouth and screamed.

It was a Rebel yell. A real one. No one who had been in any battle in that war could ever forget it. The first time Jacob heard it, he was in the third advancing line, and it was louder than the cannonfire that followed it, the sky breaking open with the thundering screams of five thousand men. They were advancing then, but when he heard it he stopped in his tracks, paralyzed. Ten feet ahead of him, a seventeen-year-old private was shot in the head and fell to the earth, precisely where Jacob would have been standing if he hadn't stopped.

Lottie's Rebel yell shook the house, an animal sound that vibrated through the walls and churned Jacob's blood. Her sisters turned pale. Then she stopped, and smiled at Jacob.

A long silent moment passed under Lottie's eerie smile, until Jeannie finally opened her mouth. "I have a horrid headache," Jeannie announced. Her own smile had vanished. She turned to Jacob. "Jacob, won't you please join me upstairs."

It was a command, not a request. He was pleased to obey it. He didn't look back as Jeannie pulled him up the stairs and into their bedroom.

She closed the door and sat down on the bed, pulling off her shoes as he sat beside her awkwardly. Outside the window, a hushed rustle of leaves announced a sudden rainfall. The rain poured down in heavy, angry waves, streaming across the windowpanes and pounding on the roof. He watched as she took the ribbons out of her hair, and waited for her to speak. At last she did.

"Jacob, I don't like being at home anymore," she said.

He paused, trying to decide what she meant. "Would you like to go somewhere?" he asked, though he knew this was impossible.

"I don't know, Jacob. It's just that this isn't really home now."

"Jeannie, of course it is," he said. There was no way he could justify taking her anywhere else, even if he had somewhere to take her.

"No, it isn't. I miss my parents," she said. "I miss—I miss both of them. But I didn't expect to miss my father this much."

It occurred to Jacob that Philip would be surprised to hear this, and honored—his private honor. He wished he could somehow tell him. Jeannie must have wished it too.

"Would you hold me, Jacob? Just hold me."

For the rest of that night, he did.

JACOB LEFT THE LEVY house in a hurry the following morning. Lottie had been strangely friendly to him at breakfast, asking what his plans were for the day. He had told a vague lie about meeting one of her father's clients at the office at nine; she seemed pleased with that, and offered him a larger breakfast than usual. He barely ate. Instead, he said good-bye to the sisters and rushed off in the direction of the office. But as he neared the main street in town, he turned, and headed toward the jail.

"I'd like to see the warden, please," he announced to the old drunken guard. The guard was seated at the desk by the door, smoking a pipe.

The guard looked up at Jacob and sneered. "Warden ain't in today. Today, I'm all y'all got. But you ain't got no more visitin' time 'til next month. So you ain't got no business here. Have a git day," he said, and blew smoke in Jacob's face.

The guard watched Jacob, waiting for him to turn around and leave. But Jacob stood still. "I haven't come for Mr. Levy," he said. "I've come to buy the slave."

"The nigger?"

"Yes," Jacob replied, and felt his face growing hot. "Must I wait until the warden returns, or may I buy him now?"

The guard smiled. "If you gonna buy him today, then you givin' that money to me."

"Fine, then," Jacob said. Now he was certain that the slave's owner would never see a cent of it—that Philip's hard-earned money was going straight into the guard's pocket. But he did not care. "How much?" Jacob wondered if, in the warden's absence, the guard would raise the price.

Fortunately the guard was no businessman. "Seb'm hundert," he said. "You got it?"

"Yes," Jacob said, and began to take out his wallet. But then he thought of something. "May I come in?" he asked. "I would like to see him first before I buy." It would be another chance to exchange a word with Philip.

But the guard saw through him. "You ain't lookin' at nothin'. You's buyin' him, I know it. Y'all got yer business proposition," he snorted. "An' I already says, you ain't got no more visitin' time. You jes' stay right there with all that money," he said. Then he turned and headed around the corner of the hall, announcing to no one, "Suckin' our blood."

Jacob waited in the hallway for about a quarter of an hour, wondering whether he could summon the courage to yell something to Philip. But he knew he needed the guard on his side if he ever wanted to come back. Soon the guard returned, with the Negro in chains. Unlike Philip, he was shackled not only at the wrists and ankles, but also at the neck. Jacob hadn't gotten a good look at him before, when he was sleeping in the straw in Philip's cell, but now he saw that the slave was about thirty years old, and very tall, despite the irons pulling on his neck. He was wearing a pair of dark trousers and a torn gray shirt. His bare feet were large, callused almost into hooves. A curled beard covered his jaw. He had a large forehead, his hair receding slightly from it, and a rounded welt of a scar on one temple. He glanced at Jacob, his eyes bloodshot and blank.

"The money," the guard said, and tapped a foot.

Jacob took out his wallet and began peeling off bills. The guard's eyes bulged as he removed each note. At first Jacob placed them on the guard's desk, but then the guard grabbed them right from Jacob's hands, stuffing each one in his pocket as Jacob offered it.

"Sold," the guard announced. Then he took out his key ring, and removed one of the smaller keys. "This one's for them chains," he said, and threw it at Jacob. It nearly hit Jacob's face before he grabbed it out of the air. "I sugges' you keep'm in 'em 'til you git home. Now git out."

"Thank you," Jacob said, and offered him a sweeping bow. Jacob was smiling; he couldn't help it. The Negro looked at him. Jacob was about to take him by the hand or the arm before he saw that he was supposed to take him by the chain attached to his neck. The two of them walked out the jailhouse door.

Jacob led him, walking around the building until they were on the other side of the jail, facing the landscape at the town's edge, the wooded foothills opening before them. Much farther away, on a low-slung mountainside in the distance, Jacob could see the Confederate camps set up, and a large house on a hilltop that must have been the generals' headquarters. Long lines of colorful laundry flapped in the wind beside the house. He glanced around, saw no one, and proceeded into the woods until he could no longer see the jailhouse behind them. Then he stopped and turned to the Negro, unsure of what to say. "Caleb?" he asked.

"Thank you, Jacob," the chained man said.

"Let me open these," he told him, and set to work on unlocking the shackles, first on the man's neck, and then on the wrists before continuing on to the ankles. It took much longer than it should have. Jacob had never seen it done before, and his hands struggled with the locks. It wasn't merely the unlocking that was difficult for him. For a moment he wished he were Philip, who had at least had a conversation with a Negro before; Jacob felt painfully awkward, and didn't know what to say. As he fumbled with the ankle lock, Caleb laughed out loud, bending down and taking the key out of Jacob's hand. He freed himself.

"How nice to meet you," he said once all the chains were off, and shook Jacob's hand. Caleb's hand was cold and dry, the palm almost comically large. "I am a great admirer of your father-in-law."

Philip was right; his voice didn't sound at all like Jacob had expected.

But nothing had been as expected. "I—I brought your message to the bakery," Jacob said.

"So I heard," Caleb replied, with a gentle smile. "Thank you."

"I don't understand how you could have—"

Caleb looked him in the eye. "I can't tell you now," he said. "I have to hurry to the house."

"All right," Jacob replied, though he was disappointed. What house, he wondered?

"Your father-in-law suggested that you may need to come there too," he said. "If you do, it's the caretaker's shack outside the cemetery by the woods. Knock on the cellar door. Do you know the password for the Legal League?"

The Legal League was a network of Negro spies that funneled people and information northward—in legend only, as far as Jacob had believed. He had never before even considered that it might actually be real. "No," Jacob said.

"'Friends of Uncle Abe,'" Caleb quoted quickly, under his breath. "'Light and loyalty.'" He craned his neck backward and opened his mouth, as if drinking in the sky. "I hope we shall meet again in this world," he said, looking back at Jacob. "If we don't, you have earned a place in heaven. May I be privileged to meet you there someday."

He had no idea how wrong he was, Jacob thought, remembering the murder at the Passover table that spring. Eternal Tarnation was already waiting for him. But before he could reply, Caleb ran. Jacob watched his long legs flying into the woods. In seconds he was out of sight, leaving nothing but a pile of chains in the mud. Jacob turned around and retraced his steps through the forest until he had returned to the back side of the jailhouse. He made his way around the building, heading through an alley behind the jail to the street leading to the center of town. On the other end of the alleyway, Jacob saw his wife.

SHE WAS LEANING against the gray stone building on the other side of the alley. She couldn't have seen him with Caleb on the opposite side of the jailhouse, he understood with relief; she must have just spotted him heading toward the jail, and waited there in the alleyway for him. He hurried toward her.

"Jeannie, how—how did you know I was here?" he asked. "You know that you aren't allowed to visit the jail."

He glanced around the alleyway; no one else was nearby. She looked beautiful there, standing alone against a stone wall still glistening and dripping from the previous night's rain. He leaned in to kiss her, and saw that her face was gleaming with sweat. She didn't kiss him back.

"I followed you," she said.

"You followed me?" He thought of their conversation the night before, and smiled. Did she want him to run away with her? "Well, the jailhouse isn't any better than your own house, trust me. I thought I would try to see your father again, though I'm sorry to say I didn't succeed." Lying had become natural to him; he didn't even think about it. As for why Jeannie was waiting for him in the alley, he was barely curious. It seemed clear that this was some sort of girlish fantasy of hers, following him into town. Maybe she had had an argument with her sisters. Of course he didn't mind her company. "I must go to the office now; the secretary is going to wonder where I've been. You may walk me there, if you'd like," he said.

She was silent. He turned to walk toward the main road, holding her hand. But she refused to move, and pulled him back. At last he faced her. "Jeannie, is everything all right?"

"Jacob, don't go to the office," she said. "They're waiting for you there."

Now he was baffled. "Who's waiting?" he asked.

"Lottie is having you arrested."

He stood still, and choked. "What?"

"She told me she was sending a posse for you. She's had enough."

He could barely breathe. "Enough of what?"

"Jacob, let's end this charade. Lottie and I both know that you're a Yankee spy."

He clenched his fists, feeling the blood drain out of his head. "What on earth are you talking about?" he asked. "Jeannie, don't be ridiculous." But his voice was too loud, and he instantly knew that the words weren't right. It was what Jeannie had said to William when he walked into their wedding reception with his shotgun.

Jeannie smiled. "You are a terrible actor, Jacob. And besides, I found where you hid Rose's message in the lining of your hat."

He gasped for air, then grabbed his hat off his head. It couldn't possibly be true. He turned it over and started running his hands desperately under the lining. Nothing.

"I found the other messages there too, before you sent them out."

"What—what messages?" he spat, though it was already useless. He was still standing, but she had knocked him to his knees.

"The messages you've been sending north. I've been pulling them out of your hat and putting them back in for weeks." She grinned at him. "Sometimes I even refolded them differently, just to test you. Of course you never noticed."

He glanced at the inside of his hat, then at Jeannie, then at the hat again. There had to be some mistake.

"Don't worry, Jacob," she said. "The Yankee cipher is much better than we expected. Even Rose couldn't decipher it."

Jacob dropped his hat. It seemed to fall slowly, slowly to the ground, landing in a mud puddle that filled a missing cobblestone.

"The message Lottie gave you about the Federal navy was pure invention. Major Stoughton didn't tell her anything that time. If you had really sent the message on to Jackson, he would have known it was impossible. You never would have been paid. And even if someone had believed it, no one on our side would have paid you that much."

"But Jeannie, how could you—how did you—" He didn't even know what he wanted to ask.

"Jacob, I didn't want you to be caught. Lottie did."

He remembered the scene in the front room the night before, and started breathing again. Lottie?

"She wondered if you would still continue after you were married to me, if you were really that low. She even made up the story about Major Stoughton behaving despicably to her, just to see if you would be a gentleman and defend her. According to her, a real gentleman who heard something like that from his sister-in-law wouldn't have hesitated to challenge him to a duel, considering that we don't have any brothers and Papa is in jail. Only the worst Yankee scum would treat a lady like trash the way you did."

Jacob bit his lip and tasted the metallic flavor of blood in his mouth. He thought of his visit to Philip, of everything Philip had said, and was petrified by a shameful fear. *Savagery is a way of life*, he heard Philip say in his head.

"A *duel?*" he asked, trying to steady his voice. "After what happened with William? But Stoughton didn't really—she couldn't possibly—"

"Lottie says only a coward would have responded the way you did, and that you didn't even defend me at our wedding. You aren't even enough of a man to serve in your own army."

He decided to use his very last defense for his life as a man. "I *am* in the army," he said. "I'm in the 18th Infantry Regiment of New York."

This seemed to surprise her; her arrogant poise dissolved as he spoke. "I'm many things, Jeannie, but I'm not a coward," he said, and winced. It sounded weak, staged, and of course it was, if not downright false. But what else could he say? "And the wedding—Jeannie, you don't really think—I wanted you to leave, Jeannie, so that I could confront him. I saw where I could take a knife from the buffet, and I—I told you to leave, Jeannie. I tried, Jeannie, but you wouldn't—Jeannie, you can't possibly believe her," he stammered. "You can't possibly think that I would—"

But Jeannie was barely listening. "I tried to convince Lottie not to arrest you," she said. "I tried to tell her that I could talk you out of it. But she didn't care in the least. Lottie only wants to win. She thinks it would be retribution for our mother. I once thought that too, but not like Lottie. Nothing else matters to her. She hasn't been happy since then, and she doesn't want me to be happy either."

Jacob heard her words, bewildered. In the midst of his amazement, he was suddenly honored. He had made her happy.

"Lottie was certain you were going to have me captured," she continued, and her voice dropped. "I was sure of it too."

Lottie's yell was still ringing in Jacob's ears. He imagined her screaming in the front room, watching Jeannie and Phoebe and Rose turn pale.

"But you didn't, Jacob. You didn't. It's true that you didn't send the message, but you didn't have me captured either. I was waiting for that. But you didn't do it. Why didn't you do it? Don't you know that it's treason for you? Don't you know you could be hanged?"

Jacob thought again of that afternoon with Rose's message in his pocket, of almost going to the bakery, of the slave auction, of the bakery again. He thought of Phoebe's snuffbox, of Rose's non sequiturs, of Philip in chains, and then of Jeannie putting her ribbon in his hair, of Jeannie lying naked on the bed before him, of Jeannie sitting beside him on a frightening summer night, of the only thing she asked of him.

"I couldn't do it," he said.

He was surprised to see tears in her eyes. She tried to hide them, blinking as she looked down at the ground. When she looked up again, her face was blank, rigid. But she had turned pale.

"They will start searching for you soon," she said. Her tone was someone else's now: firm and grave. But he could hear the slightest quaver in her voice. "I am going to stand right here until I can't see you anymore."

He opened his mouth to speak, but no words came out. The stone wall surfaces on either side of the alleyway gleamed with runoff from the previous night's rain, rising like walls of water on his right and on his left. She pointed to the end of the alleyway, the outlet to the woods.

"Go, Jacob. Now, while you still can. Run."

For a moment he stood still, lifeless, unable to move. And then he ran, looking back over his shoulder as Jeannie disappeared.

PART FOUR

COME RETRIBUTION

I.

AT FIRST JACOB HID IN THE WOODS TO THE EAST OF THE town. He had nothing with him except what was in his pockets—which after buying Caleb wasn't much in the way of money, and nothing at all in the way of food. It was mid-September, and for the first time since his arrival in Virginia, the air had turned cool. Once in the woods, he wandered all day long, trying to maintain a straight path to steer himself farther away from town. Soon he saw that he was running in circles. Every sound in the woods—a twig falling, a squirrel running over dried leaves on the ground, a bird rustling the branches above him—forced him to freeze in his tracks. As he stumbled through the woods, he recalled the encounter with Jeannie and felt an unexpected elation. At last he allowed himself to think it: *Jeannie set me free.* He came to a small clearing in the woods where he could see the town in the valley below. The river curled between the brick and stone and wooden buildings, winding its way past the town between clusters of trees that gathered like handfuls of dark, soft hair. The air tasted clean and rich in his mouth. For the first time, he saw that Virginia was beautiful. The whole world was beautiful.

Before he enlisted, Jacob had never seen a forest except through the windows of a train. He remembered a story his Hebrew tutor once told him: that when the Jews first came to German Poland, they found the entire Talmud carved into the bark of the trees of the forest, waiting for them. Soon he found himself absurdly examining the tree trunks, hoping for a sign. He saw nothing but bark and mud, lichens and moss. After a few hours, during which he began to recognize certain trees and clearings and understood that he had barely progressed at all, hunger and exhaustion and the recent weeks of sleepless nights wore him down. He paused for a moment and at last gave in, lowering himself down onto the roots of a large tree. *She set me free*, he thought once more. Before he knew it, he had fallen asleep in the afternoon light.

It was a tormented sleep. With his legs wallowing in mud, his body remembered the last time he had tried to sleep outdoors: on a retreat a few weeks before he was sent to New Orleans, the first skirmishes of the spring. The dead and the dying were just beyond the forest from where he had retreated, and all night he had listened to the wounded screaming for help, for water, for mercy, the sound of their shrieking following him in and out of dreams. Now he rolled in the mud again, tumbling into sleep, unsure whether waking or sleeping was worse. In his dreams he was running from Lottie. She was followed by hundreds of soldiers, their Rebel yells reverberating through his skull. He ran through the woods, always only a turn or two ahead of them, then tripped over a body. He glanced at the corpse and saw that it was Abraham Mendoza, his dark eyes still open, his olive-skinned face bloated with death. As he paused over Mendoza's face, Lottie raised a rifle and fired at him, laughing. He was falling to the earth, covered with wet blood, when he woke up.

He woke with a jolt and found himself lying on his stomach on the forest floor, his face and hands and suit covered with mud. The light in the woods had grown dim. He began walking again, wondering how much longer it would be possible to evade the search party, whether he would be able to walk all the way to Washington, how he would feed himself in the forest on the way, what he would do when darkness descended. Then, through what he could only think of as the providence of God, he came upon the cemetery.

He had wondered what Caleb meant when he had mentioned a cemetery outside of town. The only cemetery he knew of in New Babylon was the one beside the church across from Philip's office, a little local graveyard full of dead patriots who had donated their lives to better wars. But here, beneath a grove of willows on the edge of the woods, at the end of a narrow dirt path leading up from the valley, he had come to a small patch of earth layered with soft, long grass and brown slabs of stone. The sun had just set over the trees. In the fading daylight, Jacob thought at first that the stones were the ruins of an abandoned house. The air had turned quiet, as it does in the first weeks of fall when the days begin to shrink and vanish, rattled slightly by the nervous shivering of crickets. Brushing aside a drooping curtain of willow branches, he stood at the edge of what was clearly a little graveyard. The slabs of stone and beds of grass came sharply into focus in the twilight, and he saw, as his ancestors had once seen on the tree trunks of Europe, the Hebrew letters engraved into the stones.

He had never been to a cemetery before New Orleans—because of his priestly descent, but also for a much simpler reason. His own grand-parents were buried somewhere in Bavaria; any cemetery containing anyone his family cared about was half a world away. As far as he knew, a Rappaport had yet to die on American soil. He had grown up in a world without graves—and in a land, he now knew, that wasn't yet fully his, unsanctified by death.

This little graveyard was much smaller than the one in New Orleans, but the sixty or so stones in it were all quite close together, and nearly all of the graves—each labeled in both Hebrew and English—had one of only four last names: Cohen, Cardozo, Noah, and Gratz. Jacob stepped forward and onto the sleeping generations of Cohens, Cardozos, Noahs, and Gratzes who lay beneath the damp grassy soil, awaiting their resurrection from their native land at the end of days.

For a moment he glanced about for a Levy grave, but he soon gave up. The Gratzes and Cardozos fairly owned the place; even the Noahs and the Cohens had only a toehold of three or four plots each. Gratzes in particular held dominion. The oldest grave he saw at first was a small slab of greenish stone, leaning back in its place almost to the ground. He squatted down to read the faded inscription in Hebrew and in Eng-lish: RAPHAEL GRATZ. The birthdate was too covered in lichens to read, but the death date was clear: *1796.* Then he noticed an even older grave, belonging to SARAH GRATZ, evidently Raphael's BELOVED WIFE, who had died in *1784.* His own grandparents likely hadn't even been born by then, Jacob reflected in the strange quiet of the cool evening. But for Jacob, the notion of grandparents was an abstract one, contained not in people living or dead but rather in a phrase or two that his parents would occasionally mention, anecdotes that were invariably cut short and tinged with regret. He remembered his old Hebrew tutor in New York going over a passage from the Bible with him, something about Abraham buying a place to bury Sarah, her grave becoming the first piece of the promised land that the Hebrews ever owned. He pictured Raphael Gratz seventy-five years ago—a little man, he imagined, wearing ridiculous white stockings and a white powdered wig—negotiating with some farmer to buy a grave for his own Sarah in this new wilderness that had become his home. This little plot of land belonged to the Gratzes in a way that New York didn't belong to Jacob, and perhaps never would.

He backed away from Sarah Gratz's grave, following the progress of half a century of Gratzes who rested in a long row under the willow trees. He came to the very last grave, a clean, upright stone at the little cemetery's edge:

DEBORAH LEVY
(NEE GRATZ)
1821–1854

He looked at the stone, then at the ground below it, and knew who it was. Below her name were four Hebrew words, a quote from Proverbs, followed by a translation:

WHO CAN FIND
A WOMAN OF VALOR?

Jacob looked at the stone for a long time. The wind blew, a gentle twilight breeze that barely stirred the fallen leaves at his feet. He read the words again and again: A WOMAN OF VALOR. At that moment he understood everything: Jeannie's deceptions, Rose and Phoebe's endless loyalty to their older sisters, Philip's broken heart, and most of all, Lottie's passion, her determination, her—yes, it was the right word—glory. Lottie was burning with glory, the first Hebrew glory since ancient times. It was the glory of her mother, buried in her beloved Virginia, and the glory of all of the other Gratzes, the glory of their finally finding their own promised land.

The graveyard had darkened, the native-born dead drinking in the evening dusk. Remembering the custom his tutor had taught him, he found a pebble on the ground and placed it carefully on the grave marker, stone upon stone. Then he noticed the wooden shed at the edge of the cemetery, and saw, through a crack in a plank close to the ground, a tiny shining light.

He watched the light, wondering if it might not simply be a reflection of something, or some sort of optical illusion, anything that did not involve a living person watching him from the shed—until he understood who it might be. He stepped carefully forward, crushing dead leaves in the cool evening air until he reached the side of the shed, where a tiny, awkward cellar door leaned against the bottom of the wall. He squatted down and pulled at the handle, but it was chained from the inside. He knocked.

"Who's there?" a voice asked.

The voice didn't sound like Caleb's. It was higher, perhaps a woman's, or a child's. It reminded Jacob of when he had first arrived at the Levy house, many lifetimes ago, of his surprise when little Rose opened the door. But now he had to remember what to say next. He paused, racking his brain. It had only been hours earlier that he had bought Caleb and set him free. Was it really just a single day?

"Friends of Uncle Abe," Jacob said.

"What do you want?"

Was there more? Yes, Caleb had said something more. But what? Jacob tried to remember. Something about light.

"Light and—" he said, and paused. Light and what? *Light and liberty*, surely. He almost said it, but he hesitated. No, of course not: it was something much better than that, and much harder to find.

"Light and loyalty," he finished, and held his breath. A chain rattled as someone unlocked the door, someone more experienced than Jacob would ever be at handling chains.

2

THE PERSON WHO OPENED THE DOOR WAS ELLIS, THE NEGRO BOY who made deliveries for the bakery. He was about Rose's height, but bone thin. He had short cropped hair and enormous dark eyes, and wore a pair of ragged gray overalls with no shirt, though the day had been cool. His feet were bare on the wooden steps that rose up from the cellar. He held a lit candle in one hand, and as Jacob took hold of the open door, he quickly lowered his other hand around it to shelter the flame, peering out into the darkening graveyard.

"Come in," he mumbled.

Jacob followed the boy down the steps. As he closed the door behind him, he imagined himself dropping down below the Gratzes, burrowing into the earth.

The boy returned the candle to a small lamp resting on a wooden crate, in the corner of a small and mostly empty room. There was a straw pallet and a blanket on the floor near the wall on the right, and four small wooden crates arranged around a larger crate on the opposite side. The large crate had a cloth draped over it, and sitting on top of it was another lampstand and a book. There was a small barrel in one corner, corked closed, and on top of the barrel were two dented tin cups and two tin bowls, one half-filled with dark yellow mush. The floor was dirt. As he looked down, he saw his own expensive mud-covered leather shoes, and the boy's bare feet.

The boy took a seat on one of the wooden crates next to the make-shift table and folded his arms, looking at Jacob, waiting. Something in the narrowness of his eyes reminded Jacob of Harry Hyams's slave. Now the boy's narrow eyes were roaming across Jacob's chest, evaluating his watch chain, his vest, his mud-encrusted suit. Jacob felt as though he were standing across from the three officers in Washington, waiting to be judged.

"I'm so sorry to disturb you," he finally said. "You're—you're Ellis, aren't you."

"Yes, Mis'r Rapp'port," the boy said.

Ellis must have heard his name from Fogg. The boy continued glaring at him, an unnerving gaze that made Jacob feel accused. He found himself thinking again of Rose, of her greeting him at the Levys' door, and he felt extremely old. What a horrid world, he thought, that we are giving to these children. How will they ever build it up again?

"Please, call me Jacob," he said at last, then winced. He remembered the last time he had said it: a lifetime ago, to William Williams the Third.

"Yes, Jac'b Rapp'port," the boy replied.

Jacob waited for the boy to say more, but it was clear that Ellis had no intention of making this conversation easy for him. "I'm so sorry to disturb you," Jacob said again, then remembered he had already said that. His face grew hot. *If I were a Negro,* Jacob thought, absurdly, *I would be invincible: no one would ever see me blush.* He cleared his throat.

"Caleb Johnson told me I might come here, if I needed to," he said quickly. "I cannot thank you enough for taking me in. I assure you I wouldn't have come unless the need were urgent. I hope you will forgive me for arriving unannounced, and accept my gratitude for your hospitality. I would like to offer you some compensation for your kindness, though I'm afraid I left town rather hastily today, without much in the way of funds."

He fumbled at his dirty pockets, trying to find his wallet. At last he pulled it out and opened it. There was nothing in it but a crumpled two-dollar Rebel bill. He took the bill out and placed it on the table next to the book. Now he was close enough to see the cross emblazoned on the book's cover. Judah Benjamin's lithographed face gazed up at him beside it.

"We don't want your money," Ellis said.

Jacob paused, humiliated. He was cowering, he knew, the old Isaacs within him seeping out again, pushing him to his knees. "Well, then, thank you again, then," he stammered. "If Caleb—if Caleb Johnson is expected here, he—"

The boy was still watching him. "My father'll be here soon," he said.

Now Jacob was startled. "Caleb is your father?"

Ellis smiled. "I hadn't seen 'm since he'd been locked up. I jus' saw 'm today." He picked up the two-dollar bill on the table, stood, and returned the bill to Jacob's hand. "I heard what you paid this mornin'. Seems like plenty to me," he said.

Jacob stared at Ellis, searching for his father's features. He vaguely remembered the dark mark on the side of Caleb's forehead, and glanced at the corresponding spot on Ellis's head. Then he noticed a long, raised scar along the side of Ellis's cheek, streaking down to his neck and shoulder. It occurred to Jacob that neither this nor Caleb's scar were birthmarks.

"Have some cornmeal," Ellis said, stepping toward the barrel. "I 'ready ate some." He uncorked the barrel and filled one of the metal cups with water. He put the cup and the half-filled bowl on the table, and waved a hand at Jacob to sit down.

"Thank you," Jacob said. He was still blushing as he sat on one of the crates. The cornmeal smelled disgusting, even worse than what he remembered of army food. The boy offered no fork or spoon. Jacob didn't care. His hands were filthy, but he plunged his fingers into the gruel and ate.

Ellis kept staring at him, then suddenly spoke. "My father tol' me I gotta read while I wait for 'm. He's gonna be mad if I don't finish before he's back. Pardon," he said. Then he opened the Bible on the table to a page marked with a ribbon. He bowed his head down toward the book, squinting, mouthing the words very slowly as he read.

The boy could read? Jacob nodded at him, relieved not to have to speak to him while he ate, and even more relieved that the boy wouldn't continue watching him as he stuffed his mouth with his dirty hands. But he finished the food quickly, and it soon became awkward to watch Ellis struggling with the words.

"What are you reading?" Jacob finally asked. Only after he had said it did he realize what a ridiculous question it was.

"Word o' the Lord," Ellis said, without looking up.

"So I see," Jacob replied. He decided not to ask more. He had met more than his share of soldiers who had tried to persuade him to abandon his apparent fate of Eternal Tarnation; the persuasion process had always involved reading aloud to him about Jesus, and had never ended well. But Ellis's Bible was opened to a place quite close to the beginning, nowhere near the second half. "Whereabouts?" Jacob asked.

"Moses singin' at the Red Sea. I gotta read the whole song." Ellis looked up, then back down to where his finger rested on the text. "'I will sing unto the Lord, for He hath proudly triumphed,'" he read aloud, his voice halting agonizingly before almost every word. He pronounced "proudly" as "proodly," and "triumphed" as "tree-oomped." A bead of sweat formed at his temple. "'The horse and his rider hath He hoo—hoor—hurled into the sea.'"

Jacob sat up, recognizing the words. It was the portion he had chanted at his bar mitzvah service, years ago. He remembered memorizing the passage and the translation, and recalled how he had thought at the time that there was something vaguely ridiculous about what he was reading. In the moment immediately after the Israelites escaped Egypt via the miraculous upending of the sea, the song barely even mentioned the parting of the water, or even the fact of liberation. Instead, all of the praise of God was for drowning the Egyptian army. He had never understood it before. He thought of the message Rose had given him, ciphered with the key-phrase *come retribution.* Everyone on every side was waiting for it.

"Pharaoh's chariots done drowned in the sea. All that," Ellis mumbled, half to himself. "It ain't much fun, readin' a song nobody can sing. My father says there ain't nobody now that knows how they used to sing it."

Jacob remembered his time in the barrel on the way to New Orleans, the parting of the sea of memory. "I can sing it," he said.

Now Ellis looked at him again. "You can?"

"Only in Hebrew," Jacob added, then shrugged. He regretted mentioning it.

"That's how Moses would've done it," Ellis said. "Sing it for me."

Jacob wondered if he really remembered it. But when he began to sing it, it was as if a different person had borrowed his voice—a person he used to be, long ago. The words flowed out in a wave of triumph, one after another, until he ended on the full crescendo: "Until Your people has passed over . . . to the sanctuary, O Lord, that Your hand has established—The Lord shall reign forever and ever!"

The song ended, and the person he used to be ended along with it. The world shrank down to the size of the small dark room. Avoiding Ellis's eyes, he looked at the scar on Ellis's neck.

"A nice song," Ellis conceded. Jacob finally looked him in the eye, and ventured a smile. Ellis smiled back, and added, "But your singin' is awful."

There was a knock at the cellar door. Jacob froze in terror, but Ellis laughed. "Light and loyalty," a man's voice called through the locked door. Ellis got up, still laughing, and let his father in.

"SO MY REDEEMER has arrived," Caleb announced with a smile.

Jacob looked up at him from his seat on the wooden crate. Caleb was so tall that he couldn't stand straight in the little room. He hunched his shoulders, his towering head shadowing the room like a reigning giant. He reached out his hands and, to Jacob's surprise, bent down and kissed Jacob's dirty cheeks.

"I'm so sorry to impose," Jacob said softly, feeling his face warming again. "I found myself in a rather urgent situation today. Your son has been very gracious."

He waited for Caleb to ask why he had come, but he didn't. Clearly he had been trained, as Achilles Fogg had been, to ask as little as possible.

"You are always welcome here," Caleb said. "I only regret that I wasn't here to greet you. But I had an opportunity this evening to arrange a meeting with my wife. She was very grateful to you for passing her message along."

Jacob was confused. "The message about the troop movements?" he asked.

Ellis poured Caleb a cup of water from the barrel. Caleb sat down on one of the crates, took the cup, and brought it to his lips. He continued drinking for a long time, making Jacob wait and watch as the Adam's apple on his long thin neck bobbed up and down. A scar along the side of Caleb's neck throbbed as he swallowed.

"My wife is one of General Longstreet's slaves at his headquarters," Caleb said. "The officers discuss everything in front of her, as though she weren't there."

Was the whole Confederacy littered with spies, in the form of slaves? Even if it were, what Caleb was saying still struck him as impossible. "I don't understand," he finally admitted. "The message was from you, not from her. You were in jail."

Caleb was grinning now, along with Ellis. "Headquarters is on the hilltop outside of town," Caleb said. "My wife does the officers' laundry at headquarters, and every day she hangs different shirts on the laundry lines. Most of the time she uses the lines in the back, where nobody in the valley can see them, but if she uses the lines on the edge of the hill, then it's a message. The number of shirts she puts out is the number of troops that are moving, in thousands. She pins them to certain parts of the line, depending on the direction the troops are moving. When the shirts are all on the left, facing the valley, that means west; all on the right means east; both sides with an empty space between them means north; and grouped in the middle means south." Caleb grinned. "Of course she didn't expect me to see it. She only hoped it would be noticed by someone in the League. But as it happened, our cell faced the right direction. The warden took away your father-in-law's spectacles, but he only needs them for seeing things nearby, not for distance. He climbed onto my shoulders to look out the window, and I borrowed his eyes." Caleb took another sip of water. "Thank you for delivering the message."

Everything about this man cast Jacob into a state of awe. Caleb was leaning toward him now, still smiling. "Now please tell me how we can best serve you here," he said.

The word "serve" made Jacob's stomach sway. He glanced at Ellis and then at Caleb, his eyes running along their scars. "I don't need anything," he said quickly. "I don't mean to trouble you."

"You forget that you are my personal Moses," Caleb said. "Now is not the time to be polite."

Jacob sat straighter. "Really," he said. "I—" Then he paused. There was no choice; he was trapped. He felt like flinging himself at Caleb's feet. "I need to go back north," he said, barely breathing. "As soon as possible."

He was relieved when Caleb's posture didn't change. "That was what I needed to know," Caleb said. "The League has sent people back over the lines many times. I can't say it's simple, but it can be done." He took another long drink of water. "I would advise waiting here for two weeks, until everyone is convinced that you've already left. After that I can arrange your passage to Washington. You have reunited me with my family. It is the least I can do to welcome you here, and to reunite you with yours."

"Thank you," Jacob mumbled, though he barely understood the words. His family? Who was his family now?

"I shall put the message through that we will arrange for your return,"

Caleb was saying. "Ellis will deliver it to the bakery tomorrow. Is there anything else urgent that you need to include in the message?"

Jacob thought of Jeannie stopping him in the alleyway. But he had to do it. "Yes, there is," he said.

"Write it here," Caleb told him. He reached into the pocket of his baggy trousers, pulling out a charcoal pencil and a swath of old newspaper and passing them to Jacob. "Don't worry about the code. I can cipher it for you before I send it. Unless you would prefer that I not see it, of course."

"That's all right," Jacob said. There was some empty space along the top of the paper, above the masthead. He began scribbling words, trying to minimize the message as he always did to make the coding easier, and this time to fit the entire message in the space before the newsprint began. He wrote quickly, pushing the pencil hard onto the thin paper, entering the words that had been burning in his brain:

MISSION COMPROMISED BY CONFIRMED CONFEDERATE AGENT CHARLOTTE LEVY. REQUEST CAPTURE OF CHARLOTTE LEVY AS SOON AS POSSIBLE.

As he wrote out the words, he felt himself burning with glory. He read it over once, then handed it back to Caleb.

Caleb looked at the page, reading slowly, mouthing the words the way his son had read the Bible, like someone who only learned to read poorly, or late. Then he looked back at Jacob. His face was grave.

"Charlotte Levy?" he asked. "She isn't Philip's daughter, is she?"

The question surprised Jacob. The idea of Lottie as Philip's daughter, rather than merely Jeannie's sister, seemed strange to him now. He thought of his first evening in Philip's house, of meeting the Levy sisters, how they had all lined up before him next to their father, a row of beautiful dark curls. "Yes, she is," he said.

"Your wife?" Caleb asked.

"No, no," he said quickly, and looked back at Caleb again. "Philip has four daughters."

"I remember," said Caleb, in a measured, careful tone. His voice filled Jacob with unease.

"My wife is named Eugenia. Charlotte is her older sister," Jacob said. He looked back at Caleb, anticipating relief.

But it didn't come. The scar on Caleb's neck throbbed. "She's Philip's daughter. Your wife's sister," Caleb said slowly. "Your own sister, in effect. And you are handing her over." He kept his eyes on the paper in his hand.

Jacob swallowed. "She's a danger to the Union," he heard himself say.

Caleb pursed his lips, then let out a breath. "You know that this will break Philip's heart all over again."

Jacob thought for a moment of defending himself, of reciting for Caleb an entire litany of Lottie's betrayals, but he knew it didn't matter. He looked at the bare dirt floor.

"It isn't a choice," he said.

Caleb frowned. "There are always choices."

Jacob was silent.

Caleb looked at the message one more time, and finally shook his head. He folded it carefully and placed it in his pocket. "We are supposed to envy the white men for their freedom," he said. "But I have to say that I will never, ever envy you."

3

*J*ACOB'S TIME IN THE BASEMENT ROOM PASSED IN A SLOW AGONY. Caleb and Ellis were free men now, or at least freed by the assumptions of others, none of whom imagined the immense liberty of will that the two of them enjoyed. With the help of a friend of his former master's son, Caleb had gotten himself placed cleaning latrines in Longstreet's encampment, conveniently reunited with his wife, while Ellis was still ostensibly the property of the baker Achilles Fogg, delivering goods of various kinds to and from headquarters as well. Occasionally Caleb came back too, ostensibly on some errand for his masters. But now it was Jacob who was the fugitive, imprisoned in the little underground tomb on the graveyard's edge, with nothing to do but read Ellis's Bible and alternately anticipate and dread his return. Sometimes Ellis would return at night, bringing food from the bakery, though not nearly often enough. Jacob was famished, his empty stomach aggravating his frayed nerves. At last the day arrived when Caleb would come, at midnight, to help him escape. The taste of forthcoming freedom was so intense that Jacob almost clawed at the walls of the basement room.

As the endless day wore on, he perched on a crate and peered out through the crack in the planks that gave him a view just above the ground level. There he could see a little sliver of the graveyard outside, the daylight fading over the graves. He had done this for many hours during his imprisonment, and not once had he seen a single living creature, except an occasional squirrel. But as the daylight drained into dusk, he squinted through the planks and saw a small figure moving toward the graveyard, one that eventually resolved into a person, and then into a woman, a dark-haired woman in a long dark dress.

His heart pounded. For an instant he was sure he was about to be discovered. Then he saw the woman crouch next to one of the last graves in the row, touching a pebble that had been perched on the gravestone.

"Jeannie!" he shouted.

She jumped, startled, as she turned toward where he was hidden. But she didn't run away. He scrambled down from the crate and rushed to the door, struggling to unlock the chain that held it closed. When he finally pushed open the door and emerged from the ground, Jeannie was standing before him.

He was close enough to touch her now. In those dark two weeks in his graveyard cell, he had forgotten the smell of her, the deep sweet smell of the side of her neck, like overripe fruit. He watched her, breathing in. Something in her demeanor made him hesitate to reach for her. Instead he followed her, like an obedient child, as she led him a few steps from the open cellar door to sit with her in the weedy grass beside her mother's grave.

"Jeannie," he said. "How did you find me?"

She swallowed before she spoke. "The lawyer brought me a message from Papa," she answered, slowly. "It said you might be here."

Her face was severe, solemn, as though she had aged in merely two weeks. For a moment he wondered whether something awful had happened, more awful than she could ever tell him. "I didn't believe it, but I came anyhow," she said. "I saw the stone on the grave, and I knew you had been here."

She took him in her arms, and he devoured her, unable to stop kissing her. Then he pulled back, glancing around the graveyard in the graying daylight.

"Jeannie, how could you come here on your own?" he asked. He tried not to sound suspicious, but he couldn't help glancing over his shoulder, searching for Lottie's posse in the late afternoon shadows. Or had Lottie already been captured? "Do your sisters know you're here?"

"No, I didn't tell any of them," she said.

So no one had yet come for Lottie. That meant he was still in danger. Was Jeannie here as a lure, to draw him into a trap? He searched her face; her eyes were still on his. He decided, for no reason and for every reason, to believe her.

"They all think I'm in the house," she added.

This confused him. "But—but aren't they at home?" Usually at least Rose and Phoebe would be home at this hour, even if Lottie was out with some unsuspecting suitor. Had Rose and Phoebe now taken on gentleman callers too, for the cause?

"No, they went to the synagogue," she said. "I told them I was feeling too sick to go. It will be another two hours before they come back, maybe more."

"Synagogue?" He was baffled. He had never seen the girls go to synagogue during all the time he had lived with them. He hadn't even seen Philip go, except on the anniversary of his wife's death. Had someone else died?

"Jacob, you've forgotten everything," Jeannie said. "How could you not know that tonight is Yom Kippur?"

The Day of Atonement, of all things. The late afternoon light was fading, long shadows stretching across the soft yellowed grass. Jacob hadn't been outside in two weeks, and now even the dying light terrified him. He imagined men waiting to capture him behind the trees just past the graveyard, rustling footsteps in the woods. "Jeannie, I can't stay here with you," he told her. "I have to go back inside."

Her fingernails dug into his hands. "Please don't make me go home," she said. "I want to stay with you."

He looked down at the grass. "It's impossible," he said. "I'm leaving tonight."

She clutched his hands, pleading: "Take me with you."

For one brief, delusional moment, he considered it. He imagined bringing her into the little cellar room below the graves, telling Caleb that he needed to arrange for her passage, meeting her in a few days somewhere across the lines, and then somehow living out his life with her as if none of the events of the past year had ever occurred, as if he had simply met a daughter of one of his father's business associates and married her like a normal human being, as if there had been no war.

"I can't."

Now her face changed. She released his hands, looking at her mother's grave. When she spoke, her voice was perfectly even, flat, cold. "You told them about me and Lottie, didn't you," she said.

It wasn't a question. He tried to lie, but to his astonishment he couldn't. "I told them about Lottie," he said, finally. "Only about Lottie."

Jeannie's face turned pale. She looked down at her lap, and he saw her mother's wedding ring glimmering in the fading light. "Anyone who comes to capture Lottie will take me too."

He shook his head, desperate. "That isn't necessarily—"

"Please, Jacob. Save us, even if we don't deserve it." Jeannie said, her eyes still on her hands. She was begging now, turning into her own version of old Isaacs, pleading on her knees. "I'm not asking for myself. I'm asking for Rose and Phoebe. Even if they weren't taken too, they can't run the house alone. They're—they're children."

Jacob avoided her eyes. "I had to tell them about Lottie," he said. "She tried to have me hanged."

"I know, and she should have," Jeannie said. "It was the right thing for her to do."

He understood then, with staggering clarity, that his dream of living a real life with Jeannie had been only that, a dream. They lived in different countries now. "You can't stay here with me, Jeannie," he told her. "I wish you could, but you can't."

She clutched his hands again. "I haven't been well since you left," she said. "I feel so ill that I have to leave the table at meals, so that I don't become sick in front of the boarders."

He could feel how cold her fingers were. "You—you've been ill?"

"Yes," she said. "Because of our baby."

Or at least that was what he thought she said. "Because of what?"

"Our baby," she repeated, and smiled.

This should not have been unfathomable, yet it was. "You—you can't be serious," he stammered. A baby?

"Of course I am. I'm your wife."

She was! "Jeannie," he gasped. It was impossible, but it was true. Everything could be rebuilt. "Did you tell your family?" he asked. The question was giddy, delirious—as though they were living in some other realm where reality didn't apply, where her mother hadn't been murdered, where her father wasn't in jail, where her sister wasn't trying to have him hanged, where there was nothing but family and love.

"Jacob, don't be cruel."

The graveyard was dark now, generations of Gratzes sleeping underground, with the weight of two more generations seated just above them. Jeannie sat rooted to the earth, her dark dress spilling over the soft shadowed grass. When she spoke again, her voice quivered in the darkness: "What are we going to do?"

Jacob's vision reeled, overwhelmed by everything and everyone to whom his life was owed. He made a decision. He stood, and Jeannie rose beside him, watching.

"Some—some people have been hiding me here," he told her, afraid to say more, and pointed to the shed. He could barely make it out now in the shadows. He put his arm around Jeannie's waist, clasping her against him in the dark. "They've arranged to take me back to Washington tonight at midnight. Perhaps they can take us both. If they can't, then at least you might hide here until they could arrange it. Once we cross the lines, I will find you."

In the dark he heard her breathe. "Thank you," she whispered.

He held her in his arms and imagined the child suspended within her. "Come with me," he said. He began moving toward the shed, with Jeannie beside him. He held her tight, cleaving to her, his skin electric with unexpected joy.

For a few steps she walked with him, her arm threaded around his waist. But then she stopped. In the darkness, her hand slipping from his back made him lose his footing for a moment, unsupported, falling through space.

"I must go home first," she said.

"Why?"

There was the briefest of pauses before she answered. "There's evidence in the house that I need to destroy," she said, her voice an odd whisper. "It won't take long."

He jolted, wounded. Then he understood why she was going back: to warn Lottie. "Jeannie, stay here," he told her.

But she had already removed her hand from his. "I will come back in an hour. I promise," she said. "Consider it a vow, for Yom Kippur." She kissed him, so briefly that he barely had a chance to feel her lips against his. And she ran.

"Jeannie!" he shouted.

He started to run after her, but he couldn't keep up with her; his legs were crimped and crippled from two weeks of being buried alive in the little cellar room. He gasped, feeling like a fool.

"I'll come back," Jeannie called over her shoulder, and hurried onto the path down to the valley.

He stood in the graveyard, watching her shadow vanish in the dark toward the dim lights of the town. He ought to have returned immediately to the cellar. But instead he remained beside her mother's grave. The cemetery had become a small dark room, walled in by blackened tree trunks. The only light came from the fat curve of the moon rising above the trees, the looming white smile of Yom Kippur eve. Although the night was cool, there were still many fireflies in the graveyard, their tiny greenish lights buzzing on and off in subtle rhythms, as though the dead below the earth were sending up telegraph signals to the living. He watched the sparks in the darkness, and for the first time in months he was liberated from shame. He stood in front of Jeannie's mother's grave and asked for her blessing for her daughter, and for the child. Then he returned to the cellar room, and waited for Jeannie.

He waited an hour, then two, then three, then four. Then it was midnight, and Caleb came for him. Jeannie never came back.

4

"CONGRATULATIONS, RAPPAPORT. YOUR MISSION WAS A GREAT success."

The journey over the lines had happened in a matter of hours. After all his time in the Confederacy that summer and fall, it was astounding to Jacob how short the trip was back into the Union, how little time was required to travel between two worlds. He rode in the back of a cart, folded into a locked steamer trunk, and then another member of the Legal League—one whose voice he heard from inside the trunk, but whose face he never saw—took the trunk aboard a makeshift raft and floated him up the Potomac in the dark. At daybreak, he was in Washington, where a Negro boy Ellis's age opened the trunk, helped him out of it, and ran away before Jacob could thank him. He made his way to the camp alone.

He spent those hours in shock. When Caleb arrived to take him, he was afraid to tell him about Jeannie. Instead he told him that he had seen someone in Confederate uniform come by the graveyard that afternoon, and that the hideout might be compromised. During the long night of Yom Kippur, with his body folded into the trunk, he thought through thousands of improbable possibilities in order to avoid thinking the truth: that despite him, despite the baby, despite everything, Jeannie had realized where she belonged. Every route through his maze of thoughts led to that same inevitable end. In desperation he recited as much as he could remember of the Yom Kippur evening prayers, begging God to forgive him, sending his prayers up into an imagined night sky just past the lid of the trunk, pleading for absolution when daylight arrived. By noon on Yom Kippur, he was standing in the officers' headquarters in front of the same three men who had sent him to the Levys, in the same filthy suit he had been wearing that morning a lifetime ago when he had first freed Caleb from the jail, and in every buried moment since. He was a corpse dragged out of the ground, awaiting judgment.

The officers' headquarters was precisely as it had been the very first time Jacob had stood inside it: the same wooden tables and chairs arranged exactly the same way around the room, the same large boards with maps full of metal pins against the walls, the same spotless planks on the floor, the same three officers still seated before him at the same long table with its brass spittoons on either end, the table still littered with papers, ink-wells, pen nibs, pipe-holders, and trays full of ash. It was as if this room had been exempt from the passage of time. The three officers were still sitting precisely as before, straight and unbroken, their brass buttons and decorations gleaming in the shining daylight from the windows, a divine tribunal hovering over a sinning world. Only Jacob had changed.

"Our most sincere congratulations," the general repeated. He looked at Jacob's filthy suit and smirked. "Of course, there was no need for you to dress for the occasion."

The officers on either side of him chuckled, waiting for Jacob to laugh, or at least to smile. Jacob looked at them, his face blank.

They stopped laughing. The general turned to the colonel, who passed him a sheet of paper. He glanced down at the paper, then back at Jacob. "You will be pleased to know that as of this morning, we have the Levy sisters in custody here in Washington." On either side of him, the colonel and the major nodded and grinned, their beards flecked with ashes from their pipes.

Jacob was still staring blankly, his body bedraggled from the long pain-ful night, but as the words registered in his brain, his stomach lurched to life. "The Levy *sisters*, sir?"

"Two of them, that is," he said, consulting the paper in front of him. "Miss Charlotte and Miss Eugenia."

Jeannie?

"Regrettably, the younger ones managed to escape," the general said. Jacob was shaking now, bracing his feet against the floor. "A loss, to be sure. But Pinkerton is confident that the younger ones are useless with-out the older ones. The spy ring has been broken. And the return of Caleb Johnson to the field is valuable to us as well." The general refilled his pipe, then lit it again. "Congratulations, Rappaport. We are pleased with what you've accomplished."

There it was again, the phrase that had apparently provided Jacob's entire motivation for murdering Harry Hyams, and now for destroying the lives of the Levys: *We are pleased.* But Jeannie! Could she really be here, in Washington?

"Not only are we pleased, but we would also like to offer you a promotion in recognition of your service. As of today, your new rank is sergeant," the colonel added.

Jacob remembered how he had longed for this very announcement a lifetime ago, how he had come before this same tribunal as an arrogant boy, awaiting what he thought was his due. But now the concept was repulsive. The words condensed in the air in front of him, gathering on his filthy suit like congealed tar.

The three officers looked at him, waiting for his gratitude. He held his breath. Then, as they watched him, he heard himself say, "I only requested the capture of Charlotte Levy, sir, not Eugenia."

The general waved a hand. "Accept the credit, Rappaport. You deserve it."

The major cleared his throat. "We have the report that arrived by telegraph of their capture. Perhaps you'd like to hear it."

"Yes, sir, yes, I would, sir," Jacob stammered, nearly biting his own tongue.

The major passed the paper to the general, who looked down at it carefully, scanning it for details before reading aloud.

"'Miss Charlotte Levy was successfully apprehended by Federal cavalry squad on 2 October at nine o'clock in the evening, at the entrance of the rented house used as a place of worship by Congregation Shanga—Shangar—'"

"Sha'arey Tzedek," Jacob said.

The general shook his head. "It says here 'Shangarai Zedeck,'" he said, following the words on the paper with his finger.

"It's just the way it's spelled in English, sir," Jacob muttered, then wished he hadn't spoken at all. They had taken them from the synagogue? On Yom Kippur?

The general continued reading. "'Miss Charlotte Levy was apprehended as worshipers departed the building at the conclusion of prayers. Miss Eugenia Levy was apprehended in the family residence approximately a quarter-hour later, as she prepared to depart the house in an apparent attempt at flight.'"

She had tried to come with him after all! He listened, momentarily exultant. Then he saw the general's smug smile as he continued with further details of the cavalry's successful evasion of local militia and its arrival in Washington, and he thought of how Jeannie was likely arrested in the front room of the house—the room where she had first kissed him, where they had gotten married, where Philip had killed William, where Jeannie's mother had been murdered, and where now the cavalry had dragged Jeannie off to prison, for the cause.

"We congratulate you on the successful capture of two lady spies, Rappaport. It will be noted on your record that you brought about the downfall of two enemy agents, Charlotte and Eugenia Levy."

Jacob heard himself speak. "My wife's name is Eugenia Rappaport, sir."

The general snorted, a sound that was almost a laugh. He glanced at the colonel and the major, exchanging smiles with them, and then looked back at Jacob, apparently waiting for him to smile back. When he didn't, the general laughed out loud.

"You may relax now, Rappaport," he said. "We appreciate that you have become rather accustomed to this performance during the past few months, but now you may finally feel free to return to reality. That lady is no more your wife than I'm the emperor of China."

Jacob looked the general in the eye. The general continued to smile, though he did stop laughing. "Really, it is quite honorable of you, Rappaport. Your chivalry is to be admired by all." He struck a match, wedging his pipe between his lips. "But you may be confident that we can annul any legal status the marriage might have, should that be necessary. If for some reason that should prove inadequate for your future needs, rest assured that we shall make whatever provisions may be required to facilitate your divorce." He smiled again, puffing on his pipe.

His divorce? Jacob thought of Jeannie, pregnant and in prison, less than ten miles from where he was standing at that very moment, and could hardly breathe. He longed to ask if he might visit the prison, but it was too obvious that that would be absurd; even he knew that he would have to be kept as far from her as possible while she awaited trial. And what the general said next made it even more impossible yet.

"Meanwhile, we do feel that it is too dangerous for you to continue serving in the Virginia theater at this time," he said. The theater, Jacob thought. The colonel and the major both nodded. "We have reassigned you to the western campaign until we have further need of your services."

"The western campaign?" Jacob repeated. The west—Tennessee, Missouri, Mississippi, other improbable, uncivilized places—loomed in his mind like a wide empty wilderness. They were getting rid of him.

"It ought to be a more rewarding assignment for you than combat in Virginia," the colonel said brightly. "General Grant is expected to cut off the upper Mississippi soon. Your services were already quite useful at the delta this past spring. We expect you will excel anywhere. You are scheduled to depart by train tomorrow morning for the Department of the Tennessee."

"Congratulations again, Sergeant Rappaport," the general said, slapping a hand on the table. "We look forward to engaging your services in the future, should the need arise. Unless there is anything else you would like to discuss with us, you are dismissed."

That was all? An entire family destroyed, his own life a burning wreckage, and he was dismissed?

The officers sat filling their pipes, waiting for him to leave. But Jacob did not move. Instead, he said, with his voice as steady as he could make it, "I would like to ask for clemency, sir."

The three men paused, each holding his pipe in midair, a tableau vivant in the bright noon light streaming through the windows. "Clemency for whom?" the general finally asked.

"For—" Jacob paused. He had almost said "Eugenia Rappaport" again. "For Miss Eugenia Levy, sir."

The general grunted. "On what grounds should we offer her clemency?"

"Miss Levy enabled me to escape, sir," Jacob said, at last. "She warned me that her sister planned to have me arrested. I would have been captured if it weren't for her. She saved me, sir. Surely one must consider that to be a service to the Union."

The three officers looked at each other, their pipes still levitating in air. The major spoke. "Surely that was only because she hoped you might return the favor, precisely as you are attempting to do now."

Jacob did not reply. The general leaned forward, twirling his pipe in his fingers. "There is a possibility that her sentence will be lenient, particularly as it appears that her sister bore most of the responsibility," he said thoughtfully. "But she will have to be held for six months at least, so that any information she might still have would become useless to the other side."

Six months! He imagined Jeannie growing rounder, with guards insulting her changing shape in prison. Six months *at least*? Who would deliver the baby behind bars?

"After that, depending on her case, she might be traded for one of our own agents behind the lines, although fortunately none of our agents are being held by the enemy at the moment."

Somewhere deep in Jacob's brain, crawling out of the ruins of his thoughts, something emerged that might be called a plan. "Sir, in exchange for my services, may I make a request?" he asked.

The general grunted again. "You've already received a great deal for your services, Rappaport."

The well of goodwill had apparently run dry. But Jacob needed to try, at least. "I would like to request a particular prisoner exchange, sir, based on my time in the field."

"You may request it, though that doesn't mean we will honor it."

He held his breath before he spoke. "I would like to suggest that Miss Eugenia Levy be exchanged for her father, sir."

The general's eyes narrowed. "Her father?"

"Mr. Philip Levy, sir. He's being held there in the county jail."

Three pipes entered their respective mouths, and three pairs of lungs simultaneously inhaled. Three wisps of smoke filtered the air, drawing thin curtains over the light that poured through the windows between their eyes and his.

"We aren't in the business of granting favors, Rappaport," the general finally said. His tone was harsh now, almost angry. "If Miss Levy's father is a criminal under Virginia law, that is not our concern. We don't hand out free passes for scoundrels."

Jacob watched him through the veil of smoke. "By that reasoning, sir, Caleb Johnson ought to be returned to jail behind the lines," he said, surprising even himself. "He was being held quite legitimately according to Virginia law."

The veil of smoke parted, and the general spoke again, stung. "I believe we can all confidently distinguish between Federal agents and common criminals, Rappaport."

Jacob could see the general's hand rising, about to wave him out the door. "Sir, Mr. Levy has already served independently as a Union agent," he said, trying to keep the desperation out of his voice. "He was the one who arranged for me to free Caleb Johnson. He is currently in jail for killing a Rebel agent who was part of his daughter's espionage ring, one who had attempted to kill me. Mr. Levy is responsible for my return as well as Agent Johnson's, and at least as responsible as I am for the dissolution of the ring. Without his efforts, Agent Johnson would still be incarcerated, and I would have been killed."

This interested them. Three pipes returned to their respective mouths, and once again the veil of smoke fell. At last the general removed his pipe. "Does Agent Johnson know this?" he asked.

"Yes, sir," Jacob said.

The three of them looked at each other again, though Jacob could read nothing in their faces. Finally the general spoke. "We shall consider it," he said, his tone blank. "Is there anything else we ought to discuss?"

We shall consider it. As recompense for the destruction of his life, it wasn't much better than *We are pleased.* He knew they wouldn't give him anything more. But he still needed to ask.

"Could you please tell Miss Eugenia Levy that I am alive, sir?" he said, his voice almost a whisper. "Just that I am alive."

He expected them to laugh again, but this time they didn't. The general looked at him, and for the first time Jacob saw mercy in his eyes. "We shall," he said. Then he stiffened, embarrassed. "And now you are dismissed."

The colonel took a piece of paper and scribbled something on it, to which he then affixed a seal. He handed the paper to Jacob. "Congratulations on your promotion, Sergeant Rappaport. Report to the quartermaster for your uniform and supplies. You will be escorted to the train tomorrow morning at eight o'clock."

"Thank you, sir," Jacob murmured, and left. There were no more choices to be made.

5.

LATE THAT AFTERNOON, AS THE DAY WANED INTO DUSK, JACOB
returned to the infantry tents, hoping, in the remaining moments before
his departure, to find some of the men he remembered from the time
before the last few months. But it was as though he had fallen asleep,
only to wake up and find the entire world replaced. He walked through the
camp again and again, and each time he recognized no one. Even in
the barracks where his own company had slept, he saw no one he knew.
The camp was the same, but occupied by new regiments: the soldiers
were all strangers to him, and young ones at that, even younger than he
was, like a new crop of students arriving at school in the fall. He looked
at the faces of the soldiers around the camp—lounging on the grass,
smoking, playing cards, drinking moonshine out of their canteens—and
was shocked to see that they were nothing more than boys. He walked
among them like a ghost.

Outside the mess hall was a large wall of boards where, Jacob remembered from another life, men used to post notices of card games and stolen socks. Now someone had almost entirely covered it with tacked-up
pages torn from a newspaper. Jacob had seen his share of casualty lists,
but this one was much longer than any he had ever seen before: pages
upon pages from a full-sized newspaper, with names by the thousands
in the tiniest of print. He proceeded toward it in a trance, the words on
the pages sliding into focus as if under a lens. The headlines had been
ripped away, but at the top of the first page, someone had scrawled the
words *ANTIETAM LIST*. Regiments followed in order below it. He traced
a finger along the columns until he found the 18th New York.

The battle had taken place the previous week, it seemed, while he
was trapped in the basement room. Jacob read through the names and
recognized almost all of them. An entire world had disappeared. Halfway
down the list, he saw the name that made him stop reading:

Mendoza, Sgt. Abraham. 22 years old, New York City.

He read the words again, unsurprised, and stricken. After six generations in America, Mendoza had been the last. But Jacob was the first, and now there would be a second. For that, he wished he could thank Abraham Mendoza.

JACOB BOARDED THE train the following morning. Many of the people on the train were in uniform, and almost everyone on board, civilians and soldiers alike, smiled at him as he found his way to his seat. But their smiles passed through him, as though the other passengers were merely figures in a strange and vivid dream. He settled down on a wicker seat beside a window, rudely ignoring the elderly man who sat down beside him. Instead he turned to the window, watching trees and meadows and farms blur before his eyes.

As he watched the smear of the world race by, he became more and more convinced that everything would be resolved for the best in some way he couldn't yet fathom, that he would somehow see Jeannie again. Jeannie, after all, was someone to whom the rules of reality had never applied. He reminded himself that the war might end soon, in a matter of months or even weeks; when it did, he imagined, she and he would return to one another as if they both had been wiped clean of all their sins. He was already thinking of names, dreaming that the baby would be a boy.

An hour later, the train reached the first stop, and the old man seated beside Jacob disembarked. As the man made his way out of the car, Jacob saw that he had left a newspaper on the seat, the *Washington Daily Chronicle* from that very morning. Jacob picked it up and began to read.

He avoided even glancing at the front page; war news no longer interested him. Instead he flipped through the paper in a perfect imitation of a man without a care, hoping to find some irrelevant story to stimulate idle thoughts. But then he saw a short article on the second page, just below the paper's masthead:

REBEL LADY SPIES CAPTURED!

Hebrew Sisters Sold Secrets to Jackson, Lee

*

YANKEE PLOT SUCCEEDS:
HEBREW AGENT OFFERS
"MARRIAGE OF INCONVENIENCE"

*

YOUNGER SPY SISTER DIES IN PRISON

*

PINKERTON CLAIMS "PROVIDENCE"

Jacob read the fourth headline over and over. It had to be a mistake. For a moment he thought of putting down the paper, pretending he had never seen it; he imagined that if he had never seen the headline, it might be even less likely to be true. Then he decided that if he read the article, he might be able to confirm that it was a mistake. Perhaps there was some other pair of captured Hebrew sister spies somewhere, a parallel world whose similarities to his own situation were merely coincidental. He read on:

> Two young lady Rebel spies were captured by Federal cavalrymen this past Friday in New Babylon, Virginia. The Secret Service announced that the sisters, Miss Charlotte and Miss Eugenia Levy, had been selling information concerning Federal troop movements to Gens. Jackson and Lee for more than nine months, commencing last winter when the city was held by Federal forces. The ladies were incarcerated in the Old Capitol Prison in Washington, where the younger of the two, Miss Eugenia Levy, suffered an apoplectic stroke and perished.
>
> The lady spies were captured after a most unusual Yankee plot. A Hebrew agent from New York City, whose name the Secret Service has declined to disclose, was sent to live as a boarder at the home of the Levys, Hebrews with whom he had been acquainted through business liaisons prior to the war. According to Secret Service Chief Allan Pinkerton, his mission was to marry Miss

Eugenia Levy, whom the Secret Service suspected as the head of a ring of Rebel spies, and then to report on her activities. "Surely it was an enviable mission for any young man," Mr. Pinkerton said. "For the young lady, however, it can only be described as a marriage of inconvenience."

The agent performed his task in a superior fashion, marrying Miss Levy according to the Hebrew rite and quickly entering into the confidence of both his wife and his sister-in-law, Miss Charlotte Levy. He was soon able to intercept communications that the ladies had directed to Gen. Jackson's headquarters. The ladies' capture by Union cavalry forces swiftly followed suit, along with the safe return of the Hebrew agent home.

Miss Eugenia Levy suffered a severe attack of hysteria within hours of her imprisonment, followed by a fatal stroke of apoplexy. Attendant doctors declared the young lady deceased.

Mr. Pinkerton was adamant in his belief that the younger Miss Levy's demise expresses the justice of the Union cause. "One cannot but see the hand of Providence in the fate of the lady spy," Mr. Pinkerton said. "As it is written in Scripture, 'The judgments of the Lord are true and righteous altogether.'"

Jacob read the article once, then twice, and then fifteen times more. Each time he read it he told himself that it had to be a mistake; each time he read it he knew that it wasn't. After an eternity of pressing his forehead against the glass that separated him from the smear of horror that had become the world, he recited the prayer for the dead.

PART FIVE

THE WITCH OF HOLLY SPRINGS

I.

JACOB DID NOT KILL HIMSELF ONCE HE ARRIVED IN TENNESSEE, but that wasn't for lack of trying. Assigned to join the 23rd Ohio as they trudged their way south from Grand Junction to somewhere in Mississippi called Holly Springs, he put his own pistol to his head almost every night. But each night he decided that being forced to remain alive was a much truer punishment than death would have been, closer to what he deserved. He avoided speaking to anyone except to give and receive commands—ostensibly in obedience to his orders not to discuss the missions he had served, but really because he could not bear to face his fellow men. Along with his new post, he had also been given a new name, Sergeant Jacob Samuels, that everyone but the higher officers believed to be real; often enough, when someone addressed him, he didn't recognize it and failed to respond. Among his fellow soldiers he quickly acquired the nickname "the Hebrew Ghost."

It came about quite innocently. When the train that brought him to Tennessee stopped in Cincinnati, Jacob had bought himself a Hebrew prayer book from a Jewish book peddler there. Once he arrived at his new post, he began reading it regularly, not because he had suddenly become devout, but rather the opposite: it was a way of occupying himself with something supposedly lofty so as to avoid his fellow soldiers. It worked, at first.

Since he had been imported from the east, rumors about him abounded, and his silence reinforced them. In the evening hours, after Jacob retired early to face down the barrel of his gun, he often heard the men joking outside the tents about how Sergeant Samuels had actually died at Antietam Creek after personally disemboweling hundreds of Rebels; according to the most popular legend, his victims' comrades had subsequently captured him and flayed him alive. His ghost had then returned and relocated to Grant's campaign, as a warning to anyone arrogant enough to believe that real victory was within sight. The men saw Jacob reading his little leatherbound book and assumed it to be the Gospels; soon they were referring to him as Lazarus. And Lazarus he remained until one cool October evening in a forest in northern Mississippi—officially Grant's territory, in the Federal Department of the Tennessee—when Elijah Dodge, an eighteen-year-old private, approached him with a question and noticed the letters on the book's binding. That night Jacob listened from inside the tent as Dodge lounged with about a dozen other soldiers around a fire outdoors, spitting tobacco into the woods. Jacob was conducting yet another pantomime with the barrel of his gun when he heard Dodge mention his new name.

"Sergeant Samuels isn't just any ghost," Dodge said, to what Jacob guessed to be about a dozen men sitting outside. "He's a Hebrew ghost."

"I thought he might be," replied another voice. Jacob recognized it as Edwin McAllister, a sergeant like himself, though a popular one who socialized easily with the men. He was a twenty-two-year-old bookbinder from Cincinnati and, even Jacob had noticed, a comedian of the kind every regiment hopes for, the sort of person who turns the worst boredom into a stage for his own entertaining act. Most nights he recruited his fellow soldiers to perform in outrageous impromptu skits that he made up himself, mocking whomever in the regiment most deserved it. But that night he was lazy, at least at first. "It's a good sign for us," McAllister added.

"Why?" someone else asked. It sounded like Charles Hoff—nineteen, a farmer from just outside Cincinnati, and in fast competition with McAllister for the role of company comedian, though unlikely ever to win.

Someone spat a wad of tobacco on the ground before McAllister replied. "Living Hebrews are good luck," he said. "They're evidence of the kingdom of the Lord on earth."

Jacob assumed this was some sort of joke. He waited for the punchline, but none came. The others waited with him, until finally Hoff snorted. "Says who?"

McAllister didn't have a chance to offer a retort before Dodge butted in. "It's true," Dodge said. "My father's a pastor. He says that living Hebrews are messengers of God."

Jacob had never heard that before. The other men were as skeptical as he was. He listened as they laughed. "In that case, dead Hebrews are definitely bad luck," Hoff grunted. "And Samuels is a dead messenger at best."

"Like the original Samuel," Dodge said.

"Like who?" someone else asked.

"The ghost of the prophet Samuel, from Scripture," Dodge volunteered, then took a breath, apparently about to launch into a lecture. "Don't you remember? The Israelite King Saul was meeting the Philistines in battle, and he wanted advice from the prophet who had died. So he asked a lady who could raise the dead—a witch, the Witch of Endor—to call up the dead prophet Samuel to advise him. It was a bit hypocritical, I suppose, since King Saul himself had outlawed witches in his kingdom, so I suppose one has to imagine how terrible things must have already been for him to have to inquire of a witch. But I suppose King Saul was never a particularly admirable sort, and I suppose one has to imagine that at this point he was a bit mentally disturbed as well. So of course he went to find the Witch of Endor, and then the witch summoned up the prophet Samuel's ghost, and then the ghost of the prophet told him that he was doomed, doomed, absolutely doomed, and I suppose one has to imagine what poor King Saul must have felt when he had gone and broken his own laws just to learn that his entire kingdom was doomed, though I suppose that one also has to imagine that—"

"Dodge, you're boring everyone to tears," McAllister interrupted. "Let's give them a contemporary version. Instead of King Saul, I'll be General Grant, and Hoff will be the Witch of Holly Springs. And Dodge, you can be the dead prophet Samuels. Now let's show them all how it goes."

The nightly McAllister pageant was about to begin, though such productions had never before featured Jacob as a character. This was significantly more interesting than the barrel of his gun. Jacob was sitting near a loose tent flap, and he gently lifted it until he could duck beneath it. The men's backs were to him; everyone's attention was focused on the three men who had just secreted themselves behind a clump of pines beyond the fire. Jacob took a seat along the edge of the tent, well behind the group, still holding his pistol in his lap. No one noticed him as McAllister and Hoff emerged from behind the trees.

McAllister had draped his jacket over his shoulders like a cape, and wore a crown of brambles on his head. He staggered out of the woods as if drunk, swilling imaginary liquor from his canteen. Hoff, meanwhile, had covered his own hair with a wig of dangling ferns. He was wearing his shirt as a skirt tied around his legs, his trousers apparently rolled up beneath it, exposing his bare feet in the mud. He had stuffed his socks into his exposed undershirt as makeshift breasts. The audience roared.

"Pray help me, dearest Witch of Holly Springs, for I am in utter despair," McAllister groaned, then mock-swigged from his canteen, belching aloud.

"O noble King Grant, wherefore despaireth thou?" Hoff squeaked. "Thou hast every pair of testicles in the Union conscripted to thy service!"

McAllister waited for the laughter to die down before answering. "Nay, the testicles at my disposal are insufficient for my needs," he huffed. "Recall, dear witch, that each one of these sorry testicles must be rolled through two hundred miles of swamp, and then shot out of cannons at the Rebel citadel until it falls. Dear witch, I need your help!"

"Your majesty, such largesse is beyond my means," Hoff squeaked.

McAllister swilled more water from the canteen, which he spat at Hoff. "Alas, then I must content myself with the advice of withered remains. Witch, I implore you, bring me a desiccated corpse!"

"Whose flaccid form shall I raise up on thy behalf?" inquired Hoff, with an obscene gesture. The performance, Jacob reflected, was amusing only if one were extremely bored, or somewhat drunk. Fortunately the audience was both.

"Resurrect the deceased Sergeant Samuels, the Holy Martyr of Antietam," McAllister bellowed. "I implore you, raise up his dry bones!"

"Yes, sir!" Hoff squealed, then turned toward the woods. "SAMUELS!" he yodeled. "Raise up thy flaccid form, in honor of the King!" He reached into his shirt, pulled out one of his balled breast-socks, and threw it into the trees behind him, to the delight of the crowd. Then Dodge emerged from the woods.

His face was catatonic, slack-jawed, and he had striped his skin with thick layers of black soot. He stood still for a moment between the trees, gazing into space, and then stepped in a strict march toward McAllister, raising his rifle. At first he leveled it at McAllister, who shrieked and swooned. Then, as if noticing an error, he turned it toward his own face, his bulging eyes peering down the barrel of his own gun. Jacob swallowed a gasp; they had seen him. Dodge paused for an inordinately long time, peering down the barrel as if searching for something, while the crowd laughed harder and harder. Then, with a shrug, he dropped the gun to the ground. The audience guffawed.

"Grant," he roared, "how dare you raise me from my slumber?"

McAllister tripped over his own feet, then fell to his knees, pressing his face to the ground just before Dodge's boots. "O, great Hebrew prophet of yore!" he proclaimed. "My attempts to rout the Rebel citadel at Vicksburg hath failed mightily of late. Tell me, O prophet, what size balls will be required in order for my men to win?"

Dodge stared into space for a long time as the laughter continued, until Hoff threw his other breast at him. Then he jolted, and spoke. "Your majesty," he intoned, "having been flayed alive myself, I must inform you that no balls in the world are large enough for your needs." The audience laughed once more. Dodge paused, wiping some of the soot from his face, and spoke again, his voice low and deep. "Hurl thousands of men into the flames, and you just may succeed. Then your entire nation shall become like me, a withered husk walking the earth."

The laughter faded, and Jacob watched the men before him shift uncomfortably in their seats on the muddy ground, waiting for a joke that didn't come. No one was expecting this rather serious turn in the burlesque. McAllister and Hoff quickly tried to set things right. Hoff, all out of breasts, took the fern wig off his head and set it on Dodge's. "Thank you, my dear," he crooned, and kissed Dodge loudly on the cheek. "Your optimism will inspire us all. And now, please feel free to go to hell."

McAllister scrambled to his feet and swallowed another swig from his canteen. "There's nothing like a dead Hebrew to make one appreciate the finer spirits," he announced, before turning back to Dodge. "If you ever require assistance with your weapons, I should be pleased to provide it."

The crowd began to laugh again, with uneasy relief, as Dodge started backing himself into the woods. Then Dodge's eye caught Jacob's. McAllister and Hoff followed his gaze until all three of them were looking at him. The crowd turned around, until every man present was staring.

"Sergeant Samuels," McAllister stuttered.

Jacob looked at him, then at the others, watching as the blood drained from each of their faces. Then he slowly rose, turned around and retreated to the tent, leaving behind a silent quorum of withered husks of men.

LATE THAT NIGHT, after the others had gone to sleep, Jacob went outside to smoke, using a cheap corncob pipe that his parents would have been ashamed to see between his lips. He sat down on a tree stump outside the tent and watched the stars. It occurred to him that many people look up at the stars and believe that they are witnessing the divine presence, or remnants of the past, or prophecies of the future. When he looked up, he saw nothing but a cold night sky.

"I owe you a drink, Samuels."

Jacob looked down from the stars and saw McAllister standing beside him. McAllister squatted to sit on the dirt beside the stump, a supplicant at Jacob's knees. "I do mean it," he said as he sat down. "I hope you will accept."

Jacob glanced down at him. He was a short man, with fair hair like Jacob's and a constellation of freckles across his nose. In this pose he seemed to Jacob like a little boy, ghostly and pale in the starlight. McAllister sat at his feet, waiting for him to speak. After a small eternity, he did.

"I can't tell anyone where I was before I came here," Jacob finally said. It was the most he had spoken since he had boarded the train that had taken him to the underworld where he now lived. "But in the end I might have preferred Antietam."

McAllister sat still for a moment, puzzling over what Jacob had said. Jacob glanced at his face and noted the moment when he gave up trying to understand, or thought he understood enough. McAllister pulled out a pipe of his own and lit it, releasing a small breath of smoke before speaking again.

"This past spring the regiment was at Shiloh," he said.

Jacob understood then that McAllister had assumed his silence to be something quite different from what it was: not guilt, but pure grief. The assumption that he was suffering innocently shamed him even more. "Some men manage it by turning philosophical, but most of us just drink and make jokes," McAllister said. "When it's no longer possible to be happy, it's usually good enough to pretend."

McAllister waited a moment for Jacob to reply, but Jacob said nothing. Even the silence felt like a lie; there was nothing Jacob could say to relieve it. Friendship was impossible. He ought to be grateful simply to be able to fool others into believing he was still a man. Finally McAllister spoke again. "When we arrive in the next town, I'll take you somewhere worthy, to repay you for my idiocy," he said. "Would that be acceptable?"

To satisfy him, Jacob nodded, and they both fell silent. After a long time smoking in the darkness, they both went back into the tent, returning to their respective nightmares. Two weeks later, when McAllister finally made good on his promise, he introduced Jacob to the Witch of Holly Springs.

2

HOLLY SPRINGS WAS A SMALL TOWN IN NORTHERN MISSISSIPPI—
now officially part of the Federal Department of the Tennessee—
surrounded by beautiful forests and blessed with an impressive share
of castle-like estates, along with an even more impressive share of well-
stocked saloons. It was a stop on the railroad line to Jackson and New
Orleans, the hometown of the founder of the Mississippi Railroad,
whose enormous mansion General Grant had promptly commandeered
to house his own wife. The people in the town—women, children, old
men, and the occasional amputee—loathed the soldiers, of course. Little
boys threw rocks at them as they walked by. Since the Union advance, the
place had been flooded with war profiteers; the town held huge stores of
cotton that no one had need of in the Confederacy, and now unscrupulous speculators were apparently making a killing buying them up and
selling just about anything to the desperate residents in exchange. As a
result, the town was experiencing quite a boom under the new occupa-
tion, with a flourishing underworld of profiteers, which apparently irked
Grant as he attempted to use as much of the town as he could as a place
to stockpile his own supplies. The taverns and saloons were doing great
business since they had arrived; new ones seemed to spring up every day.
So it happened, one tired afternoon after their arrival, that Sergeant
McAllister and the supposed Sergeant Samuels made their way toward
town in search of a drink.

Jacob had not been looking forward to this. Their regiment, one of
the last reinforcements to arrive, had been camped just outside of town,
engaged in rather low-level work repairing some damaged railroad tracks
and otherwise guarding the supply line, for almost two weeks before
McAllister remembered his offer and felt guilty enough to fulfill it. He
was apparently no more excited than Jacob about their little outing, but
he was cheerful in his attempt to make a go of it. When he met Jacob on

the main road toward town, Jacob saw that he had brought Hoff with him, which to Jacob was a relief; it meant that he still wouldn't need to speak.

"Where to?" Hoff asked.

"I have an excellent destination for us," McAllister announced. "A tavern just down the road from the depot. I found it last night."

Hoff groaned. Like most of the others, he had spent the previous two weeks becoming a connoisseur of the local scene, and was already bored by it. "I'm sick of trying new places," Hoff said. "They're all the same. We already know the whiskey is best at Smith's."

"Ah, my friend," said McAllister, raising a finger, "but the best thing about this place isn't the whiskey."

"Then why bother?"

McAllister grinned. "The tavernkeeper there is a young lady," he said. "Not a bad-looking one, either."

"A lady tavernkeeper?" asked Hoff. "I don't believe it."

"Believe it," McAllister said. "Apparently it was her father's place until he died."

"Poor thing," Hoff said, with mock pity. "Surely she is in need of some masculine companionship."

"That's what I was hoping," McAllister said, with a theatrical sigh. "But she's a lady sphinx. Won't indulge anyone who can't solve her little riddles. Trust me, I tried. I thought it would only be honorable to give you both an opportunity to try as well."

They both glanced at Jacob, dutifully waiting until he shrugged.

"Capital idea," said Hoff. "At least I won't face much competition from the ghost."

McAllister led them about half a mile off the main road, on a dirt track leading toward a few houses just a short way from the center of town. It was November, and even though it was early afternoon, the day was already fading. The dirt track they were following was turning gray under the orange sky. Dead leaves swirled in little circles on the wind before them as they walked, crunching beneath their boots. Hoff and McAllister began talking about various adventures they had had with the local "ladies" while off duty in Memphis, but Jacob soon stopped listening. He looked up and saw a thin streak of cloud turn deep purple, a war wound gashing the sky. It reminded him of standing in the Hebrew cemetery in New Orleans, of seeing the sky change color over the trees just before he continued toward the home of Harry Hyams. He forced the memory from his mind.

As they turned a corner on the road, Jacob saw a long wooden house emerge before them—or, rather, he saw what might have been a house, if it hadn't been hidden behind a lawn of tall grass, with its roof and walls grown over with a tangle of brambles. It was as if the place had been abandoned years ago; the idea that living people still occupied it was enough to stir a hint of hesitation into his breath. Beneath its thick layer of thorns, the house might just as easily have been a cave, or the lair of some mysterious beast. As they approached, Jacob saw a weathered gray wooden sign hanging beside the open door. Though most of the paint had worn away, he could make out enough of the carved red letters to read what it had once clearly said: SOLOMON'S INN.

Inside the tavern, there was little to dispel his impression that it was more lair than room. The windows were few and small, and even though it was still late afternoon, candles had been lit, making the faces of the few patrons there gleam from below like hovering ghosts. The tables—about four or five long ones, plain planks with plain plank benches—were mostly occupied by officers much older than they were, along with a few old civilian men taking an early supper. Two boys were ferrying food and drinks from the kitchen to the tables. The three of them entered and took seats at the bare wooden bar, the other side of which was occupied only by a rack of tin tankards hanging by their handles, a few shelves lined with bottles of mostly unlabeled liquor, and a well-stoked fire with an enormous old pot dangling over it, a cast-iron cauldron steaming with something that smelled like cabbage soup.

"I see we have arrived in high society," Hoff sneered.

"Trust me just this once," McAllister whispered. At that moment, a young woman burst through a door behind the bar.

She was tall, just a few inches shorter than Jacob, with dark eyes and dark curly hair. She wore a plain black dress and a canvas apron that made her hips flare out, an effect that was soon obscured by the bar itself. Her neck was long and pale under her dark curls, one of which hung just above her eye, having escaped from the bonds of a red ribbon in her hair. Jacob watched as she stuck out her broad lower lip, puffing a stream of air expertly at the errant curl until it fluttered back behind her temple.

She glanced in Jacob's direction, and smiled. Her smile unnerved him. It was the first time a woman had smiled at him since the last time he saw Jeannie. He looked down at the counter, running a finger uneasily along a scar in the wood.

"Miss Abigail!" McAllister announced with a grin. "Do you remember me?"

Jacob glanced up again and watched as the woman's smile changed, becoming more ordinary, polite, dutiful. The curl fell back down over her eye; this time she pushed it behind her ear with a pale, thin hand that she quickly returned to her hip. Her dark eyes blinked, fluttering with either indulgence or annoyance, or both. Though she was almost too thin, there was nonetheless something solid about her, as though she were a pillar in the room, rooted to the ground as she held up the sky. Another man might find her beautiful, he reflected. But as he watched her, an excruciating thought seeped into his consciousness, an eternal pollutant to his soul: no one in the world would ever again be Jeannie.

"Of course, Sergeant McAllister," she said. Her voice had a bit of a drawl, but a controlled one, perhaps because she was addressing three men in blue uniforms. "How could I forget you?" Her eyes darted back to Jacob again. He once again avoided her glance, looking at his own hands as they rested on the bar. His wrists were thin and pale, bristling with blond hair. For some reason that he could not name, he was afraid.

"This time I've brought some friends," he heard McAllister say. "This is Corporal Charles Hoff, and this is Sergeant Jacob Samuels. Gentlemen, meet the proprietress."

"I'm Abigail," she said, and curtsied. "Charmed."

Jacob bowed to her quickly, allowing himself to stand up straight again for a better look. He watched her smile at him, letting the sound of her voice saying her name echo in his ears. Then he realized something, an impression he hadn't allowed himself to register when he saw the sign outside the door, and bowed to her again. As he straightened, he watched as she scanned his face and saw her thinking, puzzling. She was about to say something to him, but before she could bring out the words, McAllister slapped the bar.

"My colleagues and I would each like to ask the young lady if she might be inclined to go out for a promenade tomorrow afternoon, privately of course. But she says there's a riddle we need to solve first," he said, in his most charming voice. "Only the gentleman who knows the answer to the riddle gets to escort the young lady. Am I remembering that correctly, miss?"

Abigail smiled again, the dutiful smile this time. "Yes. And meanwhile, will it be whiskey all around?"

McAllister nodded eagerly as she took down three small tin cups from the rack behind her and began filling them. One of the two boys who had been serving the tables came up to the bar, moved around to the back, and stood on a stool behind it as he reached for something on a shelf. "Here, let me get it for you," Abigail said, and took down a bottle of brandy, passing it to the boy. The boy climbed down from the stool and paused at the bar, facing them. His head only came up to the young lady's chin. For an instant Jacob thought of the other children his age he had seen in recent months—Ellis, Rose, the boys throwing rocks in the streets of Holly Springs—and felt a surge of shame at the horrid world the adults were leaving behind. The boy's hair and eyes were dark like Abigail's, but his shoulders were stooped, and his face was locked in a sneer. His expression seemed oddly familiar to Jacob, though it took him a moment to place it. It was the way that Harry Hyams's slave had glared at him when he arrived at the Hyams house in his stolen Rebel uniform: a look of unconditional, unparalleled contempt. To see it on the face of a child was nothing short of terrifying.

Jacob's companions failed to notice. "The young scion of the establishment, I presume?" McAllister asked with a grin.

Abigail put a hand on the boy's shoulder. "Yes, this is my brother Frank," she said.

Frank contemplated the three of them for a moment, eyeing their uniforms. Then, rather suddenly, he razzed his lips and spat, a drop of spittle landing on the bar just short of McAllister's hand. Jacob watched as McAllister turned bright red.

Abigail slapped the boy's arm, though the slap, like her smile, seemed more dutiful than meant. "We don't spit at the patrons, Frank," she said, then added, in a loud whisper, "even if they deserve it." She slapped him again as he departed with the bottle of brandy. "My apologies, gentlemen," she said, in a tired voice that suggested this had happened before. "His father died at Shiloh."

Her father too, it would seem from her expression. Suddenly Jacob was ashamed of the sniggering conversation on the road about how the young lady had inherited the tavern. He thought of how McAllister had mentioned that the regiment had been at Shiloh; surely McAllister and Hoff had both seen their friends killed there. Perhaps one of them had killed her father himself; who could know? But sentiment was a weakness now, as it always is among young men. If the word "Shiloh" evoked anything in either McAllister or Hoff, neither would let on. There was an uncomfortable pause as the three of them drank their whiskey, looking down into their tin cups as the young lady pulled a rag out of her apron and wiped the spittle off the bar.

After Abigail refilled their drinks, Hoff regained the confidence to speak. "So what's the riddle?" he asked. "I'm a certified genius, miss. If I can't answer it, no one can."

"I very much doubt that," she said, and glanced again at Jacob. Her eyes on his made him inexplicably nervous. He looked away.

McAllister raised a hand. "I know I gave the wrong answer last night. But may I try again?"

Abigail turned back to McAllister, and laughed. "You may try, but you've already lost."

"So what's the riddle?" Hoff called, banging a fist on the bar.

Abigail smiled. The three of them watched her, their attention rapt. "It's simple, really. Here it is: What is the opposite of meat?"

Jacob watched as Hoff frowned and McAllister smirked. But Jacob smiled to himself, a quiet, secret smile, and gave himself permission to continue staring at the woman behind the bar. And then she saw him smiling, and knew.

"Don't guess vegetables," McAllister warned, waving a finger in the air at Jacob and Hoff. "I already tried that, and I paid the price. Now I'm going to guess bones." He turned to Abigail. "That's my new answer, miss. The opposite of meat is bones. Bare bones. Well?"

Abigail grinned. "I told you, you've already lost," she said. She glanced at Jacob, and paused. He picked up his cup and swallowed down the whiskey, peering at her as he drank. The air between them was electric. The other two men failed to notice.

"But am I right?" McAllister begged.

Abigail looked back at McAllister. Then she leaned on the bar on her elbows as she gazed into McAllister's face, close enough to kiss him. He smiled, until she said, "No."

"Oh, I am slain!" McAllister groaned, and threw himself on the bar in an absurd swoon, splashing out a few drops of whiskey in the process. "I am slain on the enemy's sword! Oh, someone please bury my poor meatless bones!"

Hoff grinned. "Is it my turn yet?"

Jacob glanced down again, then looked back as Abigail planted her elbows back on the bar, inches from Hoff's face. "Yes, sir," she said, flicking her hand against her forehead in a mock salute. "Your answer, Corporal Hoff?"

He leaned back, his grin even wider. "I see I've won already," he announced.

"If you're the winner, then what's the answer?" Abigail asked, her voice teasing the narrow gulf of air between their faces.

"It's very simple," Hoff said. "Feed."

"What?" McAllister asked. Like Jacob, he was a city boy through and through.

"Cattle feed," Hoff said, grinning. "Feed is what keeps a bull alive, and meat is a dead bull. So feed is the opposite of meat. See? I win!"

"Congratulations," Abigail said, and leaned even closer to him. For an instant, Hoff closed his eyes and leaned forward in a comic pose, as if waiting for a kiss. As a result, he didn't see her back away, turning to stir the pot behind her. "You have won the right to escort Sergeant McAllister around town tomorrow afternoon."

Hoff blinked his eyes, then gaped in genuine astonishment. After a moment he recovered in order to collapse theatrically on the bar, but he was less graceful than McAllister, and knocked his skull against the wooden counter. "Damn!" he yelped, then clutched his head with his hand. Apparently he had really hurt himself. "Pardon, miss," he grunted.

McAllister laughed out loud. "Fallen in the line of duty," he announced, placing his newly emptied cup on top of Hoff's head. "The gentleman regrets that he had but one life to give for his country and his meat." He turned to Jacob. "Samuels, would you like to venture a guess?"

Hoff raised his head, pressing the heel of one hand against his temple. "Miss, don't bother with him," he said, jerking his other thumb toward

Jacob as he finally sat upright. "No one's ever seen him open his mouth. The whole company calls him the ghost."

Abigail's lips spread into a slow smile. "This is Mississippi," she said. "Even the dead are entitled to their opinions." She turned to Jacob, and asked, "What is the opposite of meat?"

The candle on the bar between them lit her face and body from below. For one unimaginably precious instant, Jacob imagined Jeannie standing before him, risen from the dead, with a baby at her breast.

"Milk," he said.

"That's right," Abigail replied in a whisper. The possibility of some-one actually answering her had been too remote to be real. Her hands had been fidgeting with the strings of her apron, but now they were still. When she looked up, the blood had drained from her cheeks. Her face was the color of chilled white milk.

"No, not the ghost!" McAllister wailed.

"Miss, you can't waste your affections on him!" Hoff screeched. "He's a walking corpse!"

McAllister banged the counter with his fist. "And what kind of answer is that? *Milk*? Where's the sense in that?"

"Who says that milk is the opposite of meat?" Hoff whined. "Where is it written?"

Abigail smiled. "I shall be honored to meet you tomorrow in the square at one o'clock, Sergeant Samuels," she said to Jacob, and curtsied behind the bar.

"Of course," Jacob stammered. "The honor is mine." His voice sounded unfamiliar even to him.

"And you may escort your friends back to the barracks now," she added, gathering their empty cups and depositing them somewhere beneath the bar. "We will be closing in a few minutes."

"Closing?" Hoff gasped. "But it's Friday afternoon!"

Jacob turned slightly and saw the two boys gathering dishes and hur-rying them back to the kitchen, collecting money from the tables. He almost laughed.

"Yes, it's Friday afternoon," Abigail said. "We shall be open again tomorrow night. If you would prefer not to return to the camp, I've heard the whiskey is quite good at Smith's."

McAllister groaned as he reached into his pocket, plunking a few coins onto the bar. Abigail took them, curtsied once more, and disappeared through the door behind her.

Outside, as they left the tavern, the sun had just dropped behind the trees. The sky was purple above them as they walked down the road away from Solomon's Inn. A quiet had descended from the branches on either side of the road, flowing down from the clouds and draining the world of worry and regret.

"How did you know that, Samuels?" McAllister asked at last. "Why is milk the opposite of meat?"

For a moment Jacob thought of trying to explain it—the biblical law against cooking a goat in its mother's milk, the extension of the law into never mixing milk and meat, the prohibition on consuming any meal that blended birth with death—but he saw that there was no point in trying; in the end it would have explained nothing at all. And at that moment he suspected that the law itself was in fact nothing but a magic spell, inscribed into the tradition thousands of years ago for the sole purpose of being called up for duty on this Sabbath eve in Holly Springs, Mississippi, to bring him face to face with a woman who could raise the dead.

"I suppose it's just my good luck," he replied.

"You bastard," McAllister said, and slapped his arm, hard enough to hurt.

"I say we go to Smith's," Hoff announced.

They did. But Jacob did not join them. Instead he sat down on a tree stump on the side of the road and stayed there for a long time, watching the sunlight disappear, taking the past week, the past month, the past year, and slipping them into the archive of life. When he returned to the camp that night, he fell asleep without raising his gun to his head.

3.

THE NEXT DAY JACOB WENT TO LOOK FOR ABIGAIL IN FRONT OF the post office in town, where he almost had trouble spotting her among the dozens of women who were gathered to sell what looked like the entire inventory of their homes to whatever men in blue happened to be passing by. Cartloads of books, trinkets, and especially men's clothing were for sale. The square was crowded: Jacob's fellow soldiers were buying up cotton socks and shirts and undergarments by the sack from the closets of the deceased. It was a cool November afternoon, bright enough to fool one into believing that spring was on the way, that this was part of the trajectory of days leading up to the brilliance of summer, when clothing and care could be sold off at a profit.

Abigail wasn't the sort to be fooled. She was wearing a coat, though a thin one, a dark cotton cloak that was hanging open, with buttons missing. Jacob saw her leaning against the side of the post office building. She was standing with her arms folded in front of her in a very unladylike posture, which she barely bothered to adjust once he arrived. It occurred to him that there probably hadn't been any men in town for over a year, except for slaves; all the ladies had long given up their airs, and were hardly going to return to them for the sake of the enemy invaders. Abigail had her hood pulled up over her hair, though the same errant curl still hung in front of one of her eyes. When she spotted him, she stepped away from the wall and threw back her head until the hood fell to her shoulders. As she raised her head again, she blew a puff of air up at the loose curl again until it cleared her eyebrow, freeing her face. Jacob watched this ballet of gestures and was entranced by the power it revealed: a bold woman's casual disregard for what anyone else thought of who she was.

He bowed to her, a shallow bow that was little more than a nod, feeling strangely embarrassed by the gesture. She smiled and curtsied, stooping so low as to be ridiculous—a winking acknowledgment that their meeting itself was a kind of joke, a parody of courtship, in a town square that was a parody of a town square, in a country that was a parody of a country, in a world that was a parody of a world. Everything about her movements rendered the present situation absurd. The only way to avoid being shamed by her was to know that she was right.

He offered her his arm, and she slipped her hand into the curve of his elbow. His skin tingled as her fingers touched his sleeve. He glanced at her sideways as they began walking and saw that she was avoiding his eyes, which made him want to watch her more. Despite his enchantment, there was something repulsive about her, as if her body were ringed by an impenetrable armor. Her hand in the crook of his elbow was cold and immobile, like a cane hooked onto his sleeve. He watched the cartloads of men's clothes passing just beyond her profile, customers holding up nightshirts whose owners had gone to sleep in the earth, and imagined one of the missing men in town taking her by the arm, escorting her through a hole in the bright fall day into a world that had disappeared.

"You know, of course, that the only reason I don't despise you is because you're Jewish," she said, when they had finally left the square.

"A refreshing reversal of the attitude of nearly everyone else on the planet," he replied. "I'm much obliged."

She seemed surprised by this answer; it was clear that she was amused, though she didn't want to be. He watched as she tried hard to continue looking straight ahead. "Just promise me that you weren't at Shiloh," she said.

"I wasn't."

She turned to look at him now, scrutinizing him. Her hand slipped from his arm. "I don't believe you," she hissed. "I already heard your regiment was there."

"I'm new to the regiment," he said.

She considered this. He watched as one corner of her mouth curled. "I don't believe you," she repeated.

"It's true," he said. "I used to be in the 18th New York." He remembered telling this to Jeannie, how surprised she had been to hear it.

"A New York regiment?" Abigail asked. Now she was intrigued.

"I'm from New York City," he explained. "I've only fought in Virginia until now."

"That can't be," she said. "Really?"

"Yes," he answered. After months of lies, it felt odd to tell the truth, even if only a partial truth. "I was at Manassas, and other battles in Virginia," he said, sliding into vagueness as he bumped up against the time he spent in New Orleans and in the Levys' house. "I've actually never been in a battle that we've won." It had been such a long time since he had been in a battle that this particular pattern hadn't previously occurred to him, but now he noticed it with a sense of wonderment. "Every time I've been in a battle, we've retreated."

Abigail smiled. "Perhaps your own talents have contributed to that result," she said.

"Undoubtedly."

She took his arm again, and smirked. "The Union needs more men like you."

For the first time in what felt like an eternity, Jacob laughed.

They had walked down a few smaller streets, and now they were strolling on a public green, with a church on one end and the edge of the forest on the other. Even though the weather was cool, some women were out in the bright afternoon playing croquet on the lawn, while others sat on blankets in the grass, taking their knitting and sewing labors outdoors. It was strange to observe this alternate universe, a world without men. It occurred to him that this might well become a permanent situation, that a world had been created in which free men his age were becoming a species near extinction, the entire South populated only by slaves, children, and lonely women like Abigail. Some boys ran by with a ball, not forgetting to stick out their tongues at him as they passed. A world without fathers, too. Whatever men finally grew up here would be a generation coddled by grieving and indulgent women, raised fatherless, angry and damned.

"Tell me what New York is like," Abigail said. "I've never been to a city bigger than Jackson. Someone once told me that in New York there are so many horses that the streets are always flooded with manure, and nobody can even walk outside without wearing boots. Is it true?"

The idea of New York seemed utterly alien to him now. His entire life there—his parents, the company, the Jonases, the night when his father had sold him off—might as well have taken place on the other side of the moon. "When it rains, it's beyond disgusting," he finally said. "The dung flows like a river, and the garbage like a mighty stream."

Abigail laughed. "It sounds lovely."

"It is."

"I've heard there are thousands of Jews there," she said.

"Except for the ones who are busy losing battles in Virginia," he replied, and tried to make it sound like a joke.

"My mother was from Virginia," Abigail said, with a brightness that he wouldn't have expected. "She only came to Mississippi after she met my father. She didn't want to come here, but he succeeded in dragging her away. He was a very persuasive person. I still have an aunt and a few cousins there. Of course I haven't seen any of them in years."

The mention of her parents intrigued him. It reminded him vaguely of Jeannie, of his first real conversation with her, when she told him how her mother died. But everything in the entire world reminded him of Jeannie. "Is your mother living?" he asked.

Abigail looked across the green, at the women playing croquet, and shook her head. "There was a yellow fever epidemic a few years ago. As of this past spring I'm a full-fledged orphan. And a widow."

This astonished him. "A widow?"

Abigail sighed. "I know. I'm not wearing a veil, and the patrons call me Miss and I never correct them. But one makes choices. I just couldn't manage it, not with having to also manage the boys and the tavern alone. It was too difficult to compete with the other taverns in town. The only reason we aren't starving anymore is because I'm behind the bar."

She said this boldly, but as she understood what she had suggested, she blushed, turning away from him to look at the ground.

"My condolences for your loss," he said softly.

She shook her head again, brushing another loose curl back behind her ear, and moved to sit down on a bench next to the church. Jacob sat down beside her. There was only an inch of space between them. He didn't move closer, though he was surprised to find that he wanted to. "To be honest, I hardly knew him," she said. Jacob did not know whether to believe this. "He was a distant cousin, from Jackson. His name was David Solomon. Our name is Solomon too, so I never had to take a new name. I had been friendly with David and his brother, and David had made some money in the railroad. When the inn had a dry spell, he bought it from my father. But we were only married two months when he left. He and my father were in the same regiment. They both died at Shiloh."

There was something unspeakably sad about this, something no grief could even encompass. He thought of Jeannie again, and the baby, how two generations had been erased in an instant. He was grateful when Abigail interrupted his thoughts. "Now my brothers are the men of the house," she said. "Rather pathetic."

"The boys I saw at the tavern?" he asked.

She nodded. "The only thing that's saved their lives is that they had the sense to be born after 1845. Franklin is thirteen years old, and Jefferson is eleven."

He knew it was inappropriate, but he couldn't help but laugh. "A very patriotic family," he said.

Abigail smiled, a tired smile. "There was a Washington too, who was older than Frank and Jeff. But he died from the fever a few years ago, when our mother died. Though I suppose he'd be dead within a few years now anyway. And at this point it would only mean another brother for me to worry about."

Jacob pictured this parade of miniature founding fathers, three Jewish boys named after dead patriots and a girl named after a dead president's wife, all running a tavern in a Mississippi forest, raised to serve their neighbors and their country. "Do you have any other relatives here?" he asked.

"No. But there are about a dozen Jewish families in town. It's really like one family now." A dead leaf fell on her lap. She brushed it off. "My father's family is in Jackson. I wanted to take Frank and Jeff there, when we heard about our father and my husband. It was a few months before I managed to find someone who wanted to lease the inn from me, and by then the lines had moved and Jackson was in another country. I was a fool, I should have just abandoned the place. But I always hear my father's voice in my head, and I know he would have been devastated if I had lost it. I told you my father was persuasive. He still is. Sometimes I think that it doesn't matter that he's dead. I still speak with him all the time."

Jacob looked at the women on the green, and wondered if they did the same, communicating with their missing men. Most likely they only wished they did. At that moment he noticed that Abigail had been talking to him for quite a while, and much more intimately than any woman had ever spoken to him before, other than Jeannie. "It's a gift to be able to speak to the dead," he said.

For a few moments she said nothing. Then she breathed in, a long breath that faded into a sigh, and folded her arms against her chest. He looked at the thin inch of wooden bench between his legs and hers, and suddenly wanted to wrap his arms around her, to prove that they both were still alive.

"I still can't quite believe everything that's happened in the past two years. Or even in the past six months," she said. She was looking down at her lap now, tracing a circle on her knee with her finger. "It's as if the world we all thought was real was just an illusion. One expects life to be difficult, but I must admit that I never expected to be widowed at the age of nineteen."

"Neither did I," he said.

Abigail turned to him, astounded. "Dear God," she whispered. "Was she ill?"

"There was a hysterical episode," he said carefully.

Abigail considered this. "And you must have been at the front when it happened," she said, as if thinking aloud.

"I was," he replied. It was almost true, though of course the picture it conveyed could not have been more false. He began to feel the familiar poisonous shame leaching into his body. There was no way to stop it.

"Are there—do you have children?" she asked, her voice still.

He swallowed. *Yes,* he thought, *I am a murderer—not only of my uncle and my wife, but of my baby too.* It was invariably surprising how fresh the wound was, how it never improved. "There would have been one," he said.

Abigail looked at him. "I'm so sorry," she murmured, almost under her breath.

"Please don't pity me," he said. "Trust me, I don't deserve it."

He hoped that she would interpret this as a casual attempt at bravery, however pathetic, but to his dismay she didn't. She leaned toward him, intrigued. "Why don't you deserve it?" she asked.

He said nothing, staring in horror at his knees.

"I suppose that means you killed her yourself," she said. When he looked up, he saw she was half-grinning, the same smirk from the very first time he saw her, in her lair, behind the bar. He was awed by the sheer power of that smile, at how familiar she was with death, so intimate with it that she could make jokes with it and smirk in its face.

He paused for a moment, terrified, and then he was foolish enough to answer. "I suppose it does," he replied.

A gust of relief blew through his chest as she laughed out loud. "It's impossible to find a man who isn't a murderer anymore," she said, twisting a dark curl around her finger. "Personally I'd rather be with a murderer than be alone."

She turned her head to look behind her, glancing up at the clock on the steeple of the church, and stood up. Without thinking, he quickly stood up beside her, his gentleman's reflex oddly intact. He was still trying to interpret what she had just said. Was it an invitation?

"I must go home now, but I would like to see you again," she said.

This astonished him. Before he had time to consider what it meant, she was curtsying to him, turning away. "Please come by the inn on Monday night. We close at ten o'clock. Come at half past ten."

"I—I shall," he stammered, but she had already taken off, her dark dress hurrying across the green. He watched her vanish and could think of nothing but Jeannie running from the cemetery, promising that she would come back.

4

*I*T WAS PRECISELY TEN O'CLOCK ON MONDAY NIGHT AS JACOB approached Solomon's Inn—half an hour early, but he couldn't keep himself away. The night was cool, with a full moon and stars shivering in their places above the dirt road to the tavern on the edge of the woods. A few times along the way, he allowed himself to wonder what would happen, why she had invited him, what she might want from him, whether it really could be what he thought it might be. Trying to apply sense to anything in his life had become a useless exercise. Instead he trailed Abigail like an animal, following her scent.

When he came to the inn, he saw that the door was closed, and the few windows on the tavern level were shuttered and dark. The only light, other than the moon and the stars, came from two windows on the second floor, where lamps glowed behind drawn curtains. He took his watch out of his pocket and lit a match to check the time, hoping he wouldn't have to wait long. To his dismay, it was still only a few minutes after ten o'clock. He stood outside the front door for a time, afraid to knock. He quickly grew restless, and wandered around the side of the bramble-covered lair until he was standing at the edge of the forest that backed up against the property. On a whim, he stepped into the woods.

The last time he had walked alone in the woods was in Virginia, when he was fleeing from Lottie, but it had been daylight then, and the plants and trees had been familiar even to a city boy like him—ordinary maples, oaks and elms, occupied by ordinary chipmunks and squirrels. But these woods were enchanted. He was standing in a corridor of towering trees that he couldn't even identify, with heavy curtains of Spanish moss that hung down to his knees and swayed slightly in the cool night breeze, a shivering upside-down forest. The forest floor was a tangle of pale thorns and patches of black mud, and the air rattled with the voices of hidden crickets and croaking frogs. In the silver moonlight that seeped through

the branches and vines, he saw a path on the ground between the brambles, leading to the brightness of a clearing just beyond the first few rows
of trees. He followed it for about a dozen yards, and came upon a pond.

The pond was small, only about twenty yards wide, and surrounded
by curtains of heavy moss. The gleaming pool of water lay on the forest
floor like a mirror dropped by a giant, its surface gently rippled by the
breeze and the occasional fallen leaf. He had barely emerged into the
clearing when he heard a soft splash, and saw the water shiver as if shattered. He heard the frogs croaking; an animal must have jumped into the
water. Despite his time sleeping in tents, he was still a city boy, and the
suggestion of wild animals nearby unnerved him. He started to turn to
go back to the inn when he noticed a dark sheath of something dangling
from a low-hanging branch near the water's edge, about twenty feet from
where he was standing. As he squinted in the moonlight, he recognized
that it was a dress, hanging next to something rectangular and pale, perhaps a petticoat. He heard a burbling sound, and saw a dark head emerging from the surface of the pond. It was Abigail.

She had her back to him, and she didn't notice him at first. She rose
from the water slowly, tilting her head to the sky until he could almost see
the crown of her forehead, her dripping dark curls flowing into the water
in a ragged triangle against her naked moonlit back. Her shoulders were
bare and round above the water's surface. He watched as her pale silver
hands rose from the water into the air, her elbows framing her head as her
fingers trickled into her hair. His heart pounded, intoxicated. An animal
memory, the kind one feels in the body instead of recalling in the mind,
thrummed within him: a week after their wedding, Jeannie had surprised
him by pulling him into their bedroom in her dressing gown just after she
had emerged from a bath. Once he was inside, with the bedroom door
closed behind him, she had turned her back to him and let her robe fall
to the floor, so that he could see her dark hair dripping down her bare
body as she slowly slid a comb through it, while she grinned deliberately
at a small mirror on the wall that revealed only her face. When he asked
her to turn around, she had laughed at him, teasing him, until he had no
choice but to pounce.

Now he watched Abigail in the water and held his breath, praying that
she would turn to face him, his entire body stirring to life. But instead
she sank back down into the pool until she was submerged to her neck,

her hair floating around her head like swirls of dark ink on the surface of the water. She turned slightly, paddling her way back toward the edge of the pond where her dress was draped on the branch, her head parting the water into a thin channel of waves. Then she saw him, and screamed.

He jumped, and tripped into the shallow edge of the pond, catching himself with one boot submerged to his knee. He stumbled out of the water with a series of clumsy splashes, unable to right himself, as if the world were shifting under his feet. He stammered in the dark. "Miss—Miss Solomon, please pardon me, Miss, I—"

"Sergeant Samuels?" he heard her ask, with a note of relief.

He regained his footing, then tried not to continue watching her as she sank lower into the water, down to her chin. He saw the water rippling and could feel in his stomach how she was folding her arms across her breasts under the water, her naked legs curling together below the opaque surface of the pond. Her invisible movements left an imprint on his gut. He forced himself to look at the ground as his body burned. He began babbling, his tongue caught between his teeth.

"Please—please p—pardon me, Miss Solomon, I—I—I was—I wasn't—I—I didn't—please, Miss, I—"

"You are early," she said. "You were supposed to come at half past ten." To his astonishment, she laughed. "Did Frank tell you I was here? I'll murder him."

Her boldness astounded him almost more than her nakedness. When he allowed himself to look up again, he saw her head dipping back into the water, her face a small oval on the water's surface. Then she raised her head very slightly, and looked back at him. He watched her wet curls grazing the surface of the water and had to stop himself from panting.

"Turn around, you imbecile," she said.

He gulped at the cool air and turned to face the forest, agonized, watching the hanging moss in front of him as though it were a theater curtain. Then he listened to the hollow thunking of the water as she climbed out of it, the delicate swishing as she wrung out her hair and brushed the moisture from her legs, the almost inaudible rumpling of dry undergarments against damp skin, and then the louder rustling as she lifted her dress over her head, the fabric fluttering as it alighted on her body, falling into place like the beating wings of a bird. These noises were at once intimate and shockingly familiar: the audible, unnoticed landscape of the ordinary life of every married man. Each sound seeped into his body like a smell, overripe and saturated with an unspeakable sadness. He stood watching the moss, awed and alive, surprised by a sudden and electrifying grief.

"I really didn't intend for you to see me like that," he heard a voice say beside him.

He was still shuddering when he turned toward her. She had tied her hair back behind her head, but the errant curl still hung along the side of her face, dripping and glistening in the moonlight. Her dark dress clung tightly to her wet figure, the neck and bosom damp and stunning, a silhouetted version of the shape he had seen rising from the water. Her feet were bare and pale. As she seated herself on a fallen log, the hem of her dress rose until he could see her ankles, long, thin ankles that shimmered as he imagined the long living legs that flourished beneath her skirt. He looked at her bare toes, watching them sink like roots into the dark earth.

"I didn't intend for you to see me that way, but I did intend for you to see me alone," she said.

This was almost impossible to believe. For an instant he thought of glancing behind him, the adolescent's ingrained habit of checking for someone nearby who would forbid it. His body vibrated with the memory of his first evenings with Jeannie, of trying to control himself, waiting for Philip to walk in the door. But Abigail lived free of parents, fully liberated from anyone who might stop her. The world was an open gate. She motioned for him to sit down beside her, a slow wave of a thin pale hand. He felt something he hadn't felt since the first time he had met the three officers, when they told him to assassinate Harry Hyams: the strange and comforting sensation of the ebbing of his own will. He sank down onto the log beside her, hypnotized.

"I've never met a man this way before. On my own, I mean. There was always some sort of arrangement," she said. He tried to listen, mourning her covered skin. "It was always awful. Usually it was some peddler I was supposed to meet. Invariably he was twenty years older than me and spoke nothing but German."

He watched her in the dim moonlight, dazed. Clearly she wanted to have a conversation, but the memory of her naked body rising from the water was almost too much for him to bear. She was looking up at the sky, gray light illuminating her face and neck. Then she turned to him, waiting for him to speak. He tried to think, and largely failed. At last he thought of something to say. "My father always used to joke about how I was going to marry the daughter of one of his business associates," he said. "It was only when I turned eighteen that I understood he wasn't joking. That was why I enlisted." To his surprise, the words slipped out painlessly, freed from memory.

"She must have been rather awful for you to prefer risking death," Abigail said, smiling at him in the shadows. He winced at the implied insult to poor Emma, a vestigial shame left over from a lifetime of holiday meals full of pity. "Whom did you marry instead?" she asked.

He looked at Abigail's dark damp hair, then looked away. "The daughter of one of my father's business associates," he answered.

Abigail laughed out loud.

"A different one," he added.

Abigail's smile disappeared. He watched as she wound a dark wet curl around her finger. "One that you loved," she said.

It wasn't a question. Abigail leaned toward him, digging her pale toes deeper into the muddy earth. "Tell me something about your wife," she said.

He swallowed, tasting the cool night air. Again he felt that amazement that he had felt when he sat with her on the village green, the astonishment of her deep familiarity, her comfort and intimacy with the dead.

"What would you like to know?" he asked. He wondered what he could possibly say about Jeannie. That she was an actress? A magician? A liar? A spy?

"Oh, anything, really," Abigail said. "How old was she?"

"Nineteen," he answered. His reply was mechanical, as though he were filling out a census form.

"What did she look like?"

He glanced at the brambles beside his boots, trying to picture Jeannie, and was horrified to discover that he couldn't. At that moment her face had faded from his memory like a photograph left by a sunny window. Then he turned to Abigail, and saw her.

"She looked like you."

Abigail laughed again. He dug his fingernails into the soft damp bark of the log they were sitting on, his fingers inches from her skirt. He felt something warm move across his knuckles, the brush of Abigail's sleeve. Then she planted her palms against her knees, very unladylike, very Jeannie-like. She leaned toward him. "Close your eyes," she said.

"Why?" he asked. Suddenly he was afraid.

"Consider it an experiment," she answered, with a smile.

This was absurd, he knew. But he couldn't help himself. His will was ebbing away, as though he were being tugged toward a sweet, delicious dream. He closed his eyes. Blind, he sensed the entire forest closing in around him, the sounds of crickets rattling the cool wet air. He felt warm breath against his neck, and heard Abigail's voice.

"Imagine that I'm your wife," he heard her say softly in his ear. "What would you say to me?"

He imagined Jeannie emerging naked from a Mississippi pond, her dark hair rising in the moonlight as she turned to face him.

"Please come back," he said.

"I'm here," she whispered, and took his earlobe between her lips. For the rest of that evening, he drank in his beautiful dead wife.

5

*T*HAT MONTH PASSED IN A FEVER DREAM. NEARLY EVERY NIGHT Jacob met Abigail at the pond, even as the weather turned colder, arriving late and staying even later, creeping back to the camp past midnight and collapsing into a deep and dreamless sleep, waking at dawn to sleepwalk his way through endless drills in the woods, and then waiting for nighttime to arrive and return him to his imaginary life. The men in the regiment noticed his transformation, and mocked him at every opportunity for taking up with someone McAllister had described to them as "the lady sphinx." When they asked him for details, he didn't respond, though he couldn't have answered them truthfully even if he had wanted to. Because it wasn't Abigail in his arms at all, but Jeannie.

Jacob and Abigail spoke little. When they did, they talked only of their original families, their mothers and fathers, her brothers, childhood neighbors, childhood friends—children's memories, from lives over and done with. They never spoke about the war, or the future. It was better to pretend that neither existed. As soon as she was in his arms, the delusion was total. All he had to do was close his eyes and Jeannie was there, summoned before him, running her fingers along his skin, pushing him to the brink of euphoria. More than once he suspected that Abigail felt the same way, that for her, he too was someone else, a warm body that she could hold while she closed her eyes and imagined that he was another man. But he didn't care. He was delirious, hypnotized.

The walk from the camp to the inn each evening was part of the hypnosis, his slow, gradual passage from one realm into another, from public to private, male to female, north to south. The camp was always at its most disgusting at the hour when he left: men getting drunk on dirty tree stumps, those too tired to get drunk passed out in their blankets in the mud, the air thick with pipe smoke and the makeshift latrines reeking from the long dull day. When he left the camp, everything changed. The tall trees whose name he didn't know, the hanging moss, the brambles along the starlit path, the dim-windowed inn, the gleaming pond beyond it: all of it was a promise that a better world existed, a place where there was no future and no past, only a beautiful fantasy of the here and now, where he was someone he could never be. One night as he walked along the path, transporting himself between reality and dream, it occurred to him that six whole weeks had passed since he and Abigail had first met by the pond. If he were a wiser man, or a better man, he might have thought for a moment about Abigail, about whether there might be con-sequences to this age of delusion. But he was living in a world without consequences, and all he could think of was that six weeks was precisely how long he had been married to Jeannie before he ran away.

That night the air was cold, a Mississippi winter night. Abigail was sitting on the log where they had first kissed. On many nights he had found her seated there, waiting for him, but this time something subtle had changed. The moon was waning that night, and she had a lantern at her side. Usually she didn't bother with lanterns, preferring the dark-ness, as he did. He saw the lantern and immediately felt uneasy. The light illuminated her body in her dark cloak, and he saw how she was sitting with her back rigid, her feet, no longer bare, pressed together in the mud. She didn't greet him. Instead, she motioned for him to sit down, with the lamp resting between them. She wasn't smiling.

He was certain, then, that he knew what she was going to tell him — and he vowed to himself, in that instant, that he would do for Abigail everything that he had failed to do for Jeannie, that he would make her every promise that needed to be made in order to maintain the illusion forever. But when Abigail finally spoke, she took him by surprise.

"I can't love you, Jacob," she said.

He said nothing. For a moment she looked at him, and he avoided her eyes, leaning forward, pressing his elbows against his knees. It wasn't what he was expecting, and in every way it was worse. He was waking from a dream.

"I thought I could," she continued. Her words were slow, deliber-ate. It occurred to him that she had practiced this, that she had taken pains to find the gentlest possible way of destroying his imagined world. He listened to the rippling of the pond behind them, the gulp of a frog emerging from the water in the dark. "I thought I could make myself love you, make myself marry you, and then you would make everything easier for me and my brothers. But I can't." She paused, and he could hear her breathe. Then she said, "I'm in love with someone else."

In his delusional state, all he could think of was that he was in love with someone else too, and that she must have experienced the same thing that he had: a love affair with the dead. "With your husband?" he asked.

"No," she said.

Now he was frightened. The idea that someone existed beyond the fantasy that they had created was like a cannonball tearing through the woods.

"I told you I never cared for my husband," she said. "I meant that. But I was in love with his brother."

"His brother?" he repeated, like an imbecile.

"His younger brother, Michael. My father wanted me to marry David, because David had the money to buy the inn. I agreed to marry him in the end, because I knew that if I said no, I would never see Michael again." She paused, swallowed. "At the time it was a ridiculous choice, but now it isn't anymore. David died at Shiloh. Michael was there too, but he survived."

For a moment Jacob was stunned, and insanely envious. The best his dreams could conjure up was a dead woman, but here he had been lying in her arms, substituting for a living rival. If he were a different man, he would have exploded with rage. But in his deadened state, all he could do was curse the world, and wish the man dead.

Abigail was still talking, more and more animated. "I haven't seen him since my wedding. And I hadn't heard from him for the past three months. I was certain he was dead." So he had been a corpse in her arms too, he thought. "But I just learned this morning that he is still alive. Someone brought me a letter from him today. He's in the army with General Van Dorn. They will be coming up from Vicksburg to meet you. They expect to be here in less than a week, and then I shall see him again. And when he comes, he is going to marry me."

To marry her! Jacob thought of the past six weeks, of his imaginary affair with an imaginary woman, and felt as though the muddy earth were swallowing him whole.

But Abigail was ecstatic. He looked at her and was astonished to see something he had never seen in her face before: happiness. She was laughing, crying, unable to control herself. She grabbed him, startling him, giddily holding his hands, dancing in place. Her face was shining. "Jacob, I can scarcely believe it. I'm going to see Michael again!"

"I—I am very happy for you," he said slowly. All human relations, he was learning, were eased by lies. But he almost meant it. She deserved it, he thought, far more than he ever would.

"It's like a dream," she was saying, her eyes full of tears. "I'm only sorry that I have to say goodbye to you. You have been so kind to me."

He watched her, dumbfounded, as she stood. After a long time, he finally spoke. "Abigail, if anything should change—" he said, and hesitated, wondering if there was a way to express it. "If—if you should ever need me—for—for anything at all—please know that I am here for you," he stammered. "I promise you that."

"Thank you, Jacob," she said. She looked at him, but there was nothing left to say. He walked her back to the inn, and she let him kiss her on the doorstep. Then she closed the door, and he turned back to the dirt road that led to the camp.

The moss was still hanging from the high branches as it was before, the tall trees still glowing in starlight. Now all he could see were the brambles on the ground, the deep, thick mud as he returned to the wastes, the residue of a dream. The next day, General Grant expelled the Jews from the Department of the Tennessee.

NO ONE COULD KNOW then that the expulsion would last only three weeks—that a group of those expelled would make their way to Washington and win an audience with Lincoln, who had never heard of the order and who gladly overturned it, even though it meant spiting his best general. At the time when it was issued, there was no reason to believe that it wouldn't last four hundred years.

Jacob heard about it first through a memorandum from headquarters, posted and distributed to all officers in the camp. There had been talk, in the previous few weeks, of how something desperately needed to be done to control the endless stream of war profiteers who had overrun the Department. The other officers were likely less alarmed than Jacob was by the form the order actually took:

GENERAL ORDER NO. II

HOLLY SPRINGS, DECEMBER 17, 1862

THE JEWS, AS A CLASS VIOLATING EVERY REGULATION OF TRADE
ESTABLISHED BY THE TREASURY DEPARTMENT AND ALSO DEPART-
MENT ORDERS, ARE HEREBY EXPELLED FROM THE DEPARTMENT
WITHIN TWENTY-FOUR HOURS FROM RECEIPT OF THIS ORDER.
POST COMMANDERS WILL SEE THAT ALL OF THIS CLASS OF PEOPLE
BE FURNISHED WITH PASSES AND REQUIRED TO LEAVE, AND ANY-
ONE RETURNING AFTER SUCH NOTIFICATION WILL BE ARRESTED
AND HELD IN CONFINEMENT UNTIL AN OPPORTUNITY OCCURS
OF SENDING THEM OUT AS PRISONERS, UNLESS FURNISHED WITH
PERMITS FROM HEADQUARTERS. NO PASSES WILL BE GIVEN THESE
PEOPLE TO VISIT HEADQUARTERS FOR THE PURPOSE OF MAKING
PERSONAL APPLICATION FOR TRADE PERMITS.

> BY ORDER OF MAJ. GEN. U. S.
> GRANT:
> JNO. A. RAWLINS,
> ASSISTANT ADJUTANT GENERAL.

Nearly everything Jacob had read in the past few months had been difficult to believe. He read through the memorandum once, then twice, and was reminded of nothing more than the article in the copy of the *Washington Daily Chronicle* that he had idly picked up on the train to Tennessee—a decree that could not possibly be true, that reversed every hope one had ever had of what the world might be, but that somehow was nonetheless undeniable and even predictable, a jolting but inevitable waking from a deep, beautiful dream. As he read it for the third time, he understood that everything he had done in the past year, all the lives he had destroyed, including his own, had been for absolutely nothing, that there was nothing waiting for him at the end. Judah Benjamin had been rewarded in his own ostensible country, but that was only an imaginary country, a delusion. In his own real country, Jacob never would be.

The order didn't seem to apply to Union soldiers, because in the camp no one sought him out—though later he heard that Captain Trounstine, the only other Hebrew officer he knew of, chose to resign. He was a braver man than Jacob was. Instead, along with the order, Jacob was handed a particularly heavy schedule of drills to run in the camp during the next two days. The additional drills were gratuitous, he slowly understood, designed to keep him out of town. He ran the drills as though asleep, trying not to think of anything that mattered, and succeeding grandly at it. It was only when he saw McAllister the following day in the mess tent in the camp that he understood what he had lost.

"I was out enforcing the new order this morning, and you'll never guess who we arrested," he said to Jacob, spearing potatoes with a fork. "Your lady sphinx!"

Jacob had blocked out any thought of Abigail after reading the order, burying her in his mind beneath thick layers of shame. But now, midswallow, he choked. "What?"

McAllister jabbed his fork at the air. "The pastor and the mayor gave us the names we needed, and she and her brothers were on the list."

The absurdity of this was so vast as to defy any attempt to respond. McAllister swallowed a few more mouthfuls before speaking again. "We managed to clear out nearly everyone else in town without any problems. Especially the old people. I was surprised. We were afraid we would be dragging grandmothers out of their beds, but most of them were already packed when we came for them. It was as if they were expecting it."

Of course, Jacob thought, remembering old Isaacs. They would have been expecting it for fifty years. Their only surprise would have been that it had taken so long.

"Even that brat from the tavern must have had some sense knocked into him, because he went with his brother on the next train to Illinois," McAllister continued. "But it was different with your lady friend. She screamed and screamed, and then she started kicking us. She was like a lady possessed. She even bit Lieutenant Hicks." He wiped his mouth with his sleeve, wide-eyed and grinning. The whole affair was merely an entertaining episode to him, as though he were relating something improbable that Hoff had done while drunk. "I was guarding the jail just before I went off duty," he said. "By the time I left she was raving hysterical."

The image of Abigail hysterical in a prison cell was more than Jacob was willing to picture. "When she saw me leaving," McAllister added, "she started shouting about you."

"About me?"

"Yes, you."

For an instant he was ashamed, horrified of what she might have said. But as always, Abigail surprised him.

"She started screaming that you should guard the tavern, to make sure no one takes any of her parents' things," McAllister said. "Heaven knows how she expects you to manage that."

He smiled at Jacob, then turned and waved to someone. Jacob followed his eyes and saw Hoff, who had just appeared with his own rations, ready to join them. Without excusing himself, Jacob rose from his seat and ran out.

There was no point in trying to go to the jail; he knew that route would only lead him to an unwinnable argument with whoever was on guard. Instead he went to headquarters and made every plea he possibly could to be heard. At first he was told that no one was there to register his complaint; finally, on his ninth attempt, he managed to get a lieutenant there merely to record his concerns on paper and promise him further inquiry. He returned to the camp, defeated. He already knew that nothing would be done. But the following day, when the commanders requested additional guard duty for the new supply houses in town, he volunteered, and had himself stationed at Solomon's Inn.

6

*J*ACOB WAS ASSIGNED TO THE GRAVEYARD SHIFT, ALONE. IT WAS A perfunctory assignment, protecting the supplies not against any actual enemy raid—for which a single soldier would likely be useless—as much as against spiteful boys from town. It was really a job for a private, but apparently only petty officers could be trusted not to help themselves to the goodies stored in the place. He was provided with a key and instructed to stand guard, watching for imbeciles. At first he paced in front of the inn, trying not to think of Abigail lying sleepless in her prison cell, and resisted the temptation to enter. But after several long and lonely hours, he gave in to curiosity and went inside.

It was completely dark, of course. He took out a match and lit the two large lamps on either side of the door just inside the tavern. At first he was surprised by how long it took his eyes to focus. For a minute or more, he couldn't see anything but black shadows, as if new walls had been erected in the room. But his eyes had indeed adjusted. The tavern had been filled, floor to ceiling, with wooden crates.

The tavern was unrecognizable. The room had been stripped of its furniture; it was now packed with teetering towers of boxes. The supplies were pushed up against the windows, boxes lining the walls as if the room itself had shrunk. The center of the room was clear and empty; a kind of aisle had been built out of crates that widened after the doorway into an empty space that stretched all the way to the bar. He walked further into the room and lit another match, which he then used to light a lamp hanging overhead. Now he could see not only the crates lining the walls, but also the heaped sacks of flour and corn and potatoes, along with coils of rope and rolls of canvas. There was an enormous castle, taller than he was, built out of smaller jars, which upon closer inspection were labeled as full of marvels largely unknown to the noncommissioned soldier, including sugar, jam, real coffee, and even chocolate. He wondered how much of it had been taken right from the kitchen of Solomon's Inn. Piled on the bar itself were rifles and boxes upon boxes of ammunition; above the bar, on the rack that had held tin tankards, officers' uniforms were hanging in a row, like dangling men on a gallows. Behind the bar, where the drinks had been kept, were more crates, carefully labeled as brandy, ale, and whiskey. Apparently the inn's liquor supply would be accompanying the Union officers en route to Vicksburg. The door behind the bar was open, though the space behind it was dark. There was a clear path through the room to the open side of the bar; he followed it until he was standing behind the bar, and took down a lamp from the wall. He lit the lamp and passed through the doorway where he had seen Abigail for the first time.

The threshold of that door had become a Mason–Dixon line between order and chaos, dividing the carefully organized army supply house from the Solomons' ransacked home. Just past the threshold behind the bar, he came upon what apparently was once the pantry. As he raised the lamp higher, he saw that the floor was covered with broken jars, hardened puddles of honey and molasses, round stains of spilled milk, scraps of bread and potato peelings. Above the floor were wooden shelves that had been emptied, some of them partly pulled from the wall. Large smears of jam decorated a few of the dangling shelves, embedded with shards of the glass jars that had once contained them, and thoroughly colonized by ants.

He passed through the pantry to the narrow staircase beyond it, and followed the mud-encrusted stairs up to the family's apartment on the second floor. The parlor had been searched, and apparently looted. Every piece of furniture—a dining table, six ladderback chairs, a chest of drawers, and a desk—had been turned upside-down, as though the room itself had been inverted. A large rectangle of pale paint on the wall marked where a picture or a mirror must have been removed; the drawers from the chest and the desk were lying empty and scattered on the floor of the room. The floor was covered with papers, pen nibs, and feathers that must have fallen out of pillows. In places where the floorboards showed, there was a pair of thick dark scratch marks that ran toward the door like a railroad track; apparently something large and heavy—a sofa?— had been dragged out of the room. Next to an amputated drawer he saw a bundle of letters, some of which were falling loose from the string that held them. He picked them up, examining the envelope at the top of the stack.

His lamp had begun to run low, flickering a bit, and it was difficult to see the entire envelope at once. There was no stamp, and the return address was Abigail's. He shifted the lamp and glanced at the last line of the address; it was a letter to someone in Richmond. Presumably she had intended to send it more than a month ago, before Holly Springs had changed hands. He held the letter, amazed by the warmth of the paper against his skin, the soft beauty radiating from it that must have come from knowing that Abigail's hand had held it last. As he stood holding the envelope, the lamp shifted in his other hand, illuminating the whole address. It was addressed to Eugenia Rappaport.

He stood paralyzed in the upside-down parlor, looking at the name inscribed on the paper. For the first few moments he didn't think at all. Then, when he finally allowed himself to think, all he could think was that it was impossible. Clearly it was nothing more than a coincidence, another woman with the same name. Even the address was wrong; Jeannie had never lived in Richmond. And even if it had really been for her, this letter still couldn't possibly mean anything at all; it was surely written before Jeannie died, or at least before anyone had heard about her death. But even Jeannie's name on a piece of paper in his hand was something. In fact, it was everything. In that instant, the letters of Jeannie's name encompassed the entire world. He heard a noise downstairs, a wooden slapping sound like a door swinging shut. He had forgotten to close the door to the tavern behind him.

He stuffed the letter into his pocket, fighting hard against the urge to tear it open. Then he hurried back downstairs, barely able to breathe as he rushed through the pantry and stumbled around the bar into the room that used to be the tavern. And that was when Jacob saw a man in Confederate uniform standing in the doorway, pointing a rifle at his face.

JACOB REACHED FOR his own rifle, but it was too late. The other man's gun was already leveled right at him. He slowly raised his hands until he was reaching for the ceiling, unable to touch the sky.

"On your knees," the man ordered.

Jacob sank down slowly to the hard wooden floor in front of the bar, putting one palm down to balance himself against the floorboards before raising his hands again. He was sickened to notice how natural this posture felt to him, even comfortable. The man stepped over to Jacob, keeping his rifle pointed at Jacob's face until he was able to reach around and remove Jacob's rifle, slinging it over his shoulder, and then Jacob's pistol, which he tucked into his belt. Somewhere outside Jacob heard shots being fired in the distance, followed by an explosion. It was a real raid. As Jacob held his hands above his head, he saw that the man was looking around the room, peering around the towers of crates, checking to make sure Jacob was alone. Jacob looked down at the floor, wondering how it would end—until he decided not to spend his final moments looking at the floorboards, and instead looked back up at the other man.

He was about Jacob's age, and about Jacob's height, with sandy blond hair and blue eyes like Jacob's, and a thick blond mustache. His nose was like Jacob's, too, long and narrow, though his skin was rough and chapped, hardened from months of living outdoors. When he turned his head, Jacob saw a long red scar running from the middle of his cheek to the top of his right ear, part of which was missing. Jacob looked beyond him to the door of the tavern, where the lamps he had lit when he first came in were still burning. He listened for more people outside, but he could hear nothing but the other man's boots on the floorboards, and more guns firing in the distance. Even if the other man's regiment had successfully raided the town, the man had come to Solomon's Inn alone, at least for the moment.

Now the man was nosing his way through the boxes, taking inventory of the stacked supplies. He glanced behind the bar, at the liquor packed into labeled crates, and turned back to Jacob.

"How much have you stolen from this place?" he asked, glowering. From one side, he was quite handsome. But when he turned his head, Jacob winced at the sight of the disfigured ear.

"I haven't stolen anything," Jacob answered. Then he thought of the letter in his pocket, and felt himself blush.

The man noticed. "You're lying," he spat.

"It was looted, it's true," Jacob said. "But not by me."

The kick came suddenly, a swift hard crunch to Jacob's groin. The burn of his cheek against the floorboards preceded the pain by a long, languorous second, and then his entire body snapped into a tight ball like a spring recoiling. For a moment he was blinded, nauseated, listening to a long, low howl that he only gradually recognized as his own voice. The pressure of the other man's boot against his spine an instant later felt almost ethereal, a comforting pat on the back, until it forced Jacob's stomach against the floor. Jacob gagged on bile, retching, before opening his eyes to see the toe of the man's other boot, encrusted with mud, inches from his nose. Beyond it, a tower of cartons hovered sideways, floating on air. Jacob closed his eyes again and imagined William Wilhelm Williams the Third standing before him, Jeannie cowering at his side. But now there was no one to save him but himself.

The man's voice came through clearly over the rush of blood in Jacob's head. "This was my brother's business," he said, pushing his heel deep into Jacob's back. Jacob grimaced, still nauseous, his teeth pressed against the floor. "You have no reason to be here except as a thief."

A tight knot of thought suddenly loosened in Jacob's mind. His brother? But that meant—

"You have a choice. You can be captured, or you can be dead."

—that meant he was—

"Which would you prefer?"

Jacob opened his eyes, wincing as he twisted his neck so that he could see the man's face. The man's bristled eyebrows were taut with rage, his jaw clenched into some cruel equivalent of a smile. It was obvious to Jacob at that moment that he had been planning this for days, mentally performing it, fantasizing about how he would make whoever was here suffer. Jacob's mind raced, delirious, trying to choose the best way out.

"Perhaps you might consider a prisoner exchange," Jacob finally said, wheezing.

The second, third, and fourth kicks were harder than the first, directed at Jacob's ribs, knees, and face, and followed promptly by the man's boot on his back. Jacob gagged again, choking, fighting for air as the man laughed. "You aren't holding anyone here. Who on earth would I exchange you for?"

Jacob's left eye was swelling, and it was too difficult to open it. He opened his right eye, and with tremendous effort, he turned his head toward the man. "Abigail Solomon," he gasped.

The man's mouth opened in disbelief. He whispered, "Abigail?"

His face utterly changed, as if he had transformed into another person. Jacob watched him soften, his jaw slackening, his eyes widening as he looked down at Jacob's face. "I heard you expelled them," he said. "What have you done with her?" The man tried to keep the fury in his voice, but he failed to make it sound convincing. He was frightened.

Jacob's body was still throbbing, and it was difficult for him to speak. He huffed at the air, grimacing. "I didn't expel anyone," he wheezed. "It was an order from headquarters. If I had followed it, I would have had to expel myself."

Jacob watched as the man considered this. He removed his foot from Jacob's back and looked down at him, still holding his gun. Even after both his feet were resting on the floor beside Jacob's face, Jacob still felt his wooden heel digging into his spine. The man's face was pale and still, the way Abigail's had been when Jacob named the opposite of meat. "What's your name?" he asked.

"Jacob Rappaport," Jacob gasped. He had forgotten the alias, but it no longer mattered. He had returned from the dead. "And your name is Michael Solomon."

The man looked at Jacob for a moment. Then he stepped back, and stepped back again, and finally turned to face a column of cartons by the doorway. Jacob curled himself onto his better side, allowing the pain to wash over him, clutching his stomach and breathing hard. Between breaths, he could hear the man swallowing, clearing his throat. At last he turned back to Jacob, his face reddened with shame.

"Is Abigail—is she here?" he asked. His voice was meek, hesitant, like a child asking his father for permission.

It was easier for Jacob to breathe now, though still painful. "She refused to leave," he said, and pressed his fists against his gut. "She's being held in the jail in town. Her brothers went to Illinois. I promised I would guard her parents' things, but I didn't get here in time."

The man crouched down next to him, studying him as if he were a fascinating animal, some odd creature he had found in the yard. "Why would you promise that?" the man asked. "Are you in love with her?"

To Jacob's surprise, it wasn't a sarcastic question, but a real one. The man's voice was unsteady, shaken by fear.

"No," Jacob said, and was amazed that he meant it. "She's in love with you."

Michael Solomon stood up slowly, and buried his face in his hands.

The light in the room was fading, the lamps going dim as the pain in Jacob's body dulled. At last Michael raised his head, and looked down at Jacob. "I need to see her," he murmured. "How can I see her?"

Jacob looked at his face and recognized what was waiting for him, if he wanted it: redemption. "Take me prisoner," Jacob said, "and exchange me for her."

There was another explosion outside, louder than the earlier ones. Jacob was still in so much pain that he could barely move, but he found that it was a small relief to remain on the floor. He lay curled on his side and felt oddly comforted, as though the floorboards were a soft, warm mattress. He watched as Michael stepped over to the corner of the room and helped himself to a length of rope. Then he returned to Jacob, bending over him like a father putting a child to bed. He carefully pulled Jacob's arms around to his back, tying his wrists together with an almost gentle touch. Jacob didn't resist.

"Stand up," he said.

Jacob tried to move, but couldn't. "Help me."

Michael lifted Jacob from the floor as though Jacob were a small boy, hoisting him up with his hands beneath Jacob's armpits. Jacob's side was still burning, and he winced, recoiling as Michael touched it. He could feel how Michael tried to be gentle, leaning him against his own body as he escorted him to the door and out to the dirt road that led away from the inn. After a few steps Jacob was able to walk, though slowly, with Michael's hand gripping his bound elbow, as though they were a couple out for a stroll on the green.

The two of them walked on together through the gray predawn haze that hovered over the hanging moss. As Jacob struggled through each step, he glanced at Michael again. He was a good man, Jacob suddenly knew: devoted, loyal. All Jacob could think of at that moment was how fortunate it was—for Abigail, for Michael, for their future, in the event that delusions had consequences—that Michael Solomon looked so much like him.

7

*T*HE TOWN WAS ON FIRE. NOT ENTIRELY, OF COURSE, NOT YET. The buildings that the Union forces had commandeered as storehouses were being burned one by one, but only after being emptied by a kind of reverse bucket brigade of Confederate soldiers, who were tossing sacks and crates full of supplies straight out of windows and along lines of men onto waiting carts that were driven away as soon as they were filled. Once a building was emptied, it was set aflame. The only Union troops Jacob saw in town were kneeling at gunpoint outside the storehouses; apparently the masses hadn't yet mobilized, or more likely were engaged on the other side of town, in the woods by the camp. Every now and then a shell would explode, or a tree would catch fire.

Michael escorted Jacob through this scene almost casually, as though it were an ordinary morning in Holly Springs. They barely paused, even as they passed rows of cringing captured soldiers and burning buildings. For Michael, none of it mattered except for one place, and he began pulling Jacob along faster, hauling him along the streets lined with captives until they reached the jail.

The sun had risen by then, and the world was soaked in light, smoke, and thunder. But the street where the jail stood remained relatively undisturbed. Some captured soldiers knelt in clusters on the street, but nothing was on fire. The jail was a pathetic little building, nothing more than a police station with a cell or two inside. The front door was locked, but the constable's office facing the street had a glass window, which Michael promptly smashed with a loose cobblestone. He had just finished pulling both of them through it, mangling Jacob's uniform and skin in the process, when a Union soldier appeared in the office doorway.

It was a boy Jacob knew in passing from the camp, from one of the newest regiments. He couldn't have been older than fifteen. Assigned to guard the prisoner overnight, he had apparently locked himself inside the little jailhouse, too paralyzed by the call of duty to abandon his post when he had first heard the shelling, and now he was trapped.

Michael raised his gun at the boy, who was pointing a pistol at him in return. But the boy saw Jacob's bruised, swollen face, and recognized him. Suddenly the boy began quaking in horror. He dropped his gun and raised his hands in the air. To Jacob's astonishment, the boy started to cry uncontrollably, sobbing like a baby. "Please don't kill me," he begged.

Michael glanced at Jacob, and almost smiled. "This is a prisoner exchange," he announced, his voice a parody of gruffness. "Who are you holding here?"

The boy paused, gulping. "Only a lady," he said, his voice cracking.

"Give me the keys," Michael told the boy. The boy backed away, cowering toward the wall. "Now."

The boy glanced at Jacob, as if looking for approval. Jacob nodded at him, and watched as the boy's hands tugged at his belt until he had released a ring of keys, which he threw at Michael.

Michael grabbed them out of the air, then fumbled for a moment to put them in his pocket. In the meantime the boy quickly bent down, desperately reaching for his pistol. But Michael saw it. He straightened in a fraction of a second and fired a shot high at the wall, shattering a clock into a downpour of glass and brass numbers. The boy fell to his knees, wailing, "Jesus, save me, Jesus, save me!"

"Get out," Michael said.

The boy sobbed again and rose quickly, hurrying out the office door. Michael followed, taking the boy's pistol off the floor and then pulling Jacob with him until they were both in the little hallway, watching the boy unlock the front door and flee into the street.

"Michael?"

Michael dropped Jacob's elbow and rushed around the corner. By the time Jacob limped behind him, Abigail was already rising to her feet in her cell, rushing to where Michael was fitting key after key into the lock until one finally caught.

Abigail looked nothing like Jacob had ever seen her. Her hair was wild, tangled in thick clumps around her head. Her dress was stained with something—food, perhaps, or vomit. But when he saw her kissing

Michael through the bars, he recognized her, and Michael too, and he felt each kiss as though it were his. It was only when Michael finally opened the door that she saw Jacob, and drew in her breath.

"The sergeant generously agreed to a trade," Michael said. Jacob watched him as he checked her, hesitant, searching her expression. "We're leaving him here."

Abigail looked at Jacob, but her face betrayed nothing. "Thank you, sergeant," she said.

Fortunately Michael couldn't see Jacob's face after that; he had turned Jacob around, untying his hands. "The town is surrounded," he told Jacob as he pulled at the rope. "If you walk out that door, you'll be taken immediately." Jacob heard Abigail breathing behind him, and tried not to weep. "Stay here until it calms down. We're only burning the supply houses, and it doesn't seem like there are any on this street. If you wait here until we leave, you'll be safe."

In fact the shop right next to the jailhouse had been commandeered weeks ago as an ammunition dump. If Michael didn't know this, Jacob reasoned, then his fellow Rebels didn't either. And Jacob had seen the captives in the street and knew that what Michael said was true: walking out that door in a blue uniform, unarmed, would lead only to imprisonment or death. The boy had surely fled directly into a trap. Jacob had barely thought the matter through before he heard Abigail's soft breathing again. He closed his eyes and felt the hard ache in the side of his head, his left eye forced shut.

Finally his hands were freed, and Michael turned him around. His face was too bruised and swollen for Michael to notice the tears in his eyes.

"We owe you everything, sergeant," Abigail said to Jacob. "May God reward you, in the next world or in this one."

Before Jacob could think of anything to say in return, Michael had taken her by the hand and hurried her out the door. Jacob sank down to the cold floor in the corridor outside Abigail's cell, and accepted his reward.

THE WALK FROM the inn had been torture, though his body only registered it now in its fullest capacity. He panted, exhausted. For a time there was a strange quiet in the air; the shelling and gunshots paused, the eye of the battle's storm. He looked down at his uniform, torn and bloody from the trip through the shattered window, and felt his pockets to see if he had anything on his person that might be useful as he tried to make his way back. And that was when he remembered the letter.

He took it out of his pocket, looking at the front of the envelope for a moment before tearing it open to read the curled handwriting inside:

> *October 20, 1862*
>
> Dear Jeannie,
>
> We just received your letter of October 9 with your new address at Aunt Rachel's, which you sent us a full week after Yom Kippur, so it is to our great chagrin that we must now send you our belated best wishes for the new year, three weeks after you have surely been sealed in the Book of Life. Nevertheless, we hope that the holidays were happy for you, and that the year 5623 will bring everyone peace.
>
> We also hope you will accept our belated thanks for the $20 we received from you over the summer, which we direly needed. Your husband was so generous. We look forward to meeting him someday.
>
> *With great affection,*
> *Abigail, Frank, and Jeff*

With each line his good eye grew wider, his mouth hanging open as he slowly read and reread every word. "I have cousins in Virginia," he heard Abigail saying in his head. *Your new address at Aunt Rachel's . . .* He thought of his own wedding, of talking to Jeannie's aunt from Richmond just moments before William Williams burst through the door. Had that been her name? *Your husband was so generous . . .* Had his hundred-dollar bill from the command been divided, a portion of it sent to Holly Springs? . . . *which you sent us a full week after Yom Kippur . . .* A week after the day she had died in jail? But that meant—that meant—

And then he heard the thunderous roar as the earth opened its jaws and swallowed him whole.

PART SIX

THE CAUSE

I.

THE AMMUNITION DUMP ADJACENT TO THE JAIL IN HOLLY SPRINGS exploded just moments after Abigail and Michael fled. Later Jacob remembered the sound of the first detonation, so near that he felt it instead of hearing it—felt himself lifted and hurled through the air and then slammed and crushed against a wall, and then under a wall, a wall that caught fire. He remembered a pillar of fire rising before him, bowing down over his head as he kneeled beneath it, cowering lower and lower, prostrating himself deep into the earth. He didn't remember the rest.

The raid on Holly Springs mattered, in the end, to almost no one. The railway lines and roads that Jacob's regiment had been protecting were destroyed, along with vast stores of supplies. But Grant reconstructed the supply line within weeks and proceeded on to Vicksburg to great success, while Jacob lay in his bed in New York, useful as a soldier only for retreat and defeat. The only people for whom the attack made any difference at all, as it turned out, were the captured, the dead, Abigail and Michael Solomon, and Jacob.

His mother later read him the reports describing it all: how his mangled body was found, unconscious, by the burial detail, who assumed he was dead; how they noted his rank and loaded his body in with other officers' corpses to be transported home for an officer's burial; how someone, by the obscurest of miracles, happened to hear a moan emerge from the stack of dead bodies, and pulled him back into the land of the living. Both of his legs were shattered and he had lost his right eye, among other wounds, but for some idiotic reason, he was alive.

Five months passed before he could get out of bed. Pain was his constant companion, clasping him in bed night and day in a lover's torrid embrace, kissing his face with its burning lips and sinking deep into his seared and branded flesh. During most of that time his face was bandaged daily, and it was usually too painful to speak. When his parents first saw him, his mother had sobbed and wailed, doubled over, screaming to the skies, "My baby! My baby!" His father had examined him in utter revulsion, afraid to approach him. When his father finally deigned to touch him, he held him only gingerly, with the tips of his fingers, his skin radiating disgust. Jacob perceived through his remaining eye, as he proceeded through the long blank months of his convalescence, that things in the household had changed. Few visitors came by, and there seemed to be only two servants left. But it was his parents who had changed the most.

His father had aged. He seemed to have lost much of his hair in the year and a half since Jacob had left; what remained of it appeared less blond and more silver, and was combed carefully across the top of his bare head. His blue eyes appeared watery, red around the rims of his eyelids. He had become thinner, too, his belly no longer protruding beneath his vest. But what had changed about him most was that he no longer smiled at Jacob, not even condescendingly. He no longer spoke to Jacob at all. He came into Jacob's room only once a day, if that, and when he did he didn't open his mouth. Instead he sat watching Jacob as though Jacob couldn't see him, rendering judgment.

During those long months while he remained in bed, the only time Jacob heard his father speak was when he listened to his parents in the hall beyond his bedroom, when they both thought he was sleeping. One night outside his closed bedroom door, his mother's voice began as a whisper and grew into an unbearable wail. When he could finally make out her words, she was sobbing.

"You did this to him, Marcus," she cried. "You did this to him!" In his bed, Jacob cringed.

"Don't insult me." His father's voice was a hard black stone. "He did this to himself."

Jacob listened as his mother lost courage, and begged for his approval.

"Please, Marcus, I—I didn't mean—it's just that he's only a boy, Marcus. Please, he's just a boy, he's—"

He heard his father's foot pound the floor. "I won't accept responsibility for someone else's foolishness."

"Marcus, please, you're a generous man, a reasonable man. Please, be reasonable, please, be generous, please—" She was whimpering now, cowering before him, the way Jacob remembered her. It was oddly comforting to him. "Marcus, think of yourself when you were young. You ran away from your father too."

"Don't be ridiculous," his father spat. "My father wanted me to spend the rest of my life in the yeshiva. It was a life sentence to prison. What I gave Jacob was an opportunity."

"You gave him a life sentence," his mother said, with a quaver. "And he knew it."

"At his age I would have killed to have what he was offered."

His mother's voice retreated, as though her voice itself were kneeling on the floor. "Please, Marcus. At least be kind to him now, now that he's here. You ought to at least be pleased that he won't leave again. He—he can't." Jacob could hear her weeping. "Please, Marcus—"

"I'm being quite kind to him just by having him in my house," his father said. But Jacob was shocked to hear a slight crack in his father's voice. His father cleared his throat, and tried to speak firmly again. But his voice was a ghost of what it had been. "Another father would have rejected him, punished him. But I don't have to punish him. God is punishing him."

"No, Marcus." His mother's voice was cold now, and he could hear how much she had aged. "God is punishing you."

It occurred to Jacob, as their voices faded, that it was the first time he had ever heard his mother say no.

Most of the time it was Jacob's mother who stayed at his side, along with one of the remaining servants, whom his mother would direct to reapply his bandages, turn him in his bed, feed him, bathe him, and attend to his most unpleasant needs. Both he and his mother were ashamed of it. When the servant left the room, his mother held his hand and kissed the unburned side of his face. Yet even in those rare instances when the pain ebbed back, all he could see when he looked at her wide lips and her green eyes was the face of Elizabeth Hyams. And when his mother spoke

to him, she invariably delivered some sort of awful, damning utterance—
something which perhaps wasn't deliberately designed to extinguish the
last remaining embers of his soul, but which inevitably had precisely that
effect:

"Papa and I heard about what Grant did to the Jews in Tennessee,
right where you were found. It was in the Jewish newspaper here. An
American embarrassment, Papa says. How you could have possibly joined
the army of such a man is beyond him, he says. Papa didn't want to tell
you, but I thought you ought to know."

"I must tell you that it has been rather difficult at the firm since you
left. Papa could never find anyone to substitute for you, at least no one
who could handle the accounts the way you did. The firm lost half its
value in the past year alone. Papa didn't want to tell you, but I thought
you ought to know."

"David Jonas's company went bankrupt last summer, and the Jonases
put poor Emma in an asylum. David said that you would have been her
last chance at a decent existence, but now she's in the asylum for life. Papa
didn't want to tell you, but I thought you ought to know."

"Last year I had a letter from Aunt Elisheva—well, 'Elizabeth,' as
you'd say—after the Union took New Orleans and she could finally write
to us again. She's lost her mind, I'm afraid. Do you remember Uncle
Harry? He was always so fond of you. Well, he was murdered by one of
his own slaves. Poisoned, at the seder! Can you imagine? Otto Strauss has
a nephew in New Orleans and he told me it was true, but if I had only
heard it from Elizabeth I'm afraid I wouldn't have believed her, because
in her letter she was clearly hysterical. She wouldn't stop rambling on
about *you*, of all people. You can't imagine how upsetting it was for us.
She'd had some sort of elaborate delusion that you had come to their
house, and that you were in their army, and even that you had a dead wife
in Alabama or some other such nonsense. Really it was quite outrageous.
At the time we wondered if it might be true somehow, since we didn't
know where you'd gone off to, but once you came back we knew that it
made no sense at all, absolutely none. I'm afraid she's lost her mind completely after Harry's death. I've written to her many times, but I haven't
heard any more from her since then. To think that Harry was murdered!
By his own slave! Papa didn't want to tell you, but I thought you ought
to know."

Even after Jacob was able to speak again, he did not want to. There was simply nothing that he could say.

Instead he retreated into his own mind, developing imaginary photographs on the blank plate of the ceiling above his bed. During the day he envisioned Abigail and Michael as he had seen them just before they left him behind, kissing through the bars of her cell in the jail. It occurred to him that he had probably only survived the explosion because he had been in the corridor, farther away from the side of the building adjacent to the ammunition stockpile; if Abigail had remained trapped in her cell, she would surely have been crushed to death. But Abigail wasn't the one who haunted him at night. After his mother and the servants abandoned him each evening, the pain would wake him in the darkness—searing, unforgiving pain. Each time his mind would cower into delirium, and then he would see Jeannie appear on the black expanse of the ceiling, laughing.

After the wave of pain subsided, he would sometimes allow himself to remember Abigail's letter, the haunting possibility that it had illuminated for him in the instant before the world exploded. Sometimes, when the night was darkest and the momentary relief from the pain was greatest, he would even permit himself to believe it: that somewhere in the world Jeannie was alive, and waiting for him. In the rarest of such moments, he would fall asleep, freed into the realm of total fantasy, and discover Jeannie lying naked in his bed beside him. He would invariably wake up just before touching her, in sudden and excruciating pain. Abigail's letter, of course, had been incinerated in the fire, along with the rest of the world as he had once known it. By the end of the first year of his convalescence, he had at last managed to convince himself that the letter had never existed at all.

After he was finally able to rise from his bed, it took another four months to learn to walk again. Even once he had mastered it, he still could only manage short distances, with the help of a cane. Stairs were a special torture, possible at first only with his mother supporting him. But after what seemed like centuries of agony, a day came when he was able to get out of bed, walk through the house, lower himself down the stairs, and even limp out the front door with nothing but his cane at his side—without collapsing, and with only a deep, dull ache substituting for the searing embrace of pain. It was the eve of Yom Kippur, September 22, 1863, and he went with his father to the synagogue.

The synagogue, B'nai Jeshurun, was in a grand building on Greene Street which had been built when Jacob was six years old. In their prewar religious life, his parents generally preferred the more social events like the annual Purim parties and the Simchas Torah ball, and his father was more likely to be found at the Harmonie Club than in the synagogue. Jacob had even once heard him admit that on ordinary Sabbaths, he occasionally preferred to pay the members' fine rather than attend. But the synagogue was nonetheless a traditional one, its grandness not intended to outshine the churches in the manner of Temple Emanu-El—the "reformed" congregation that Jacob's parents enjoyed loathing—but rather simply to outshine the old Spanish-Portuguese synagogue farther downtown. Jacob's last memory of it was of the high holidays when he was eighteen years old, of listening to the rabbi, Dr. Morris Raphall, give a sermon defending slavery—a long and convoluted exegesis with the unspoken purpose of preserving the union, of preventing a war in which many would die. It sparked a conflagration: it was published in national newspapers, rabbis around the country wrote their own sermons against it, and congregants came close to blows. Jacob's father had lashed out at the rabbi for it, calling him a charlatan and a fraud, a pretentious British import whom the chief rabbi of London had been snide enough to ship off to the New World as some sort of patronizing joke, a man who knew nothing about liberty or about the country where he had so condescendingly deigned to reside, and now here he was making the whole congregation look like bigots at best and traitors at worst, they who could least afford to be either. His father was so enraged that he ought to have left the congregation for good, but that would have meant forfeiting the pleasure of remaining enraged. It shamed Jacob now to remember how irrelevant the subject had seemed to him when he was eighteen, as if they were arguing about whether people should be permitted to raise chickens on the moon without a kosher butcher. Most Jewish arguments seemed like that to him at the time. He had no idea, then, that those arguments were about how best to be human, about the most trivial and most horrifying obligations involved in repairing a broken world.

The sanctuary was crowded. Every seat was filled, and the air inside was uncomfortably warm, heavy and burdened by another year of regret. Every man in the room stared at Jacob as he entered the sanctuary, hobbling along at his father's side, and every last one of them looked away the instant his eyes met Jacob's, particularly the rich boys whose parents had paid the bounty and bought their way out of the war. Jacob was grateful that they arrived at their assigned seats at nearly the very last minute, so that no one was able to speak to them in the crowd. His father pulled him into a standing position as the congregation rose for the annual annulment of future vows between man and God.

It is meant to be the moment when lives are altered, when one declares one's failures before the Eternal and tries, by anticipating future failures, to renew a damaged trust. But Jacob knew that no future failures could outweigh what he had already destroyed. The rabbi stood on the platform with two men holding Torah scrolls beside him, and the ceremony began with the traditional announcement: "By the authority of the tribunal above, and by the authority of the tribunal below, we are permitted to pray with sinners." Jacob understood, as he glanced around the room and saw everyone avoiding his one good eye, that the words referred to him.

That evening and as the fast continued the following day, he chanted the public confession of sins along with the congregation, the alphabetical litany of crimes against God, and marveled at how many of them he had personally committed. His father didn't question him when he remained at his side for the memorial service for the dead, attended only by those who have lost parents, children, siblings, or wives. The names of the congregation's war dead were read aloud, and Jacob saw the dead boys' parents watching him, burning with envy as he burned with shame. For the entire twenty-five-hour fast, he recited the words in the prayer book, confessed his sins with the congregation again and again, privately begging God for forgiveness, just as he had done in that very same room on every Yom Kippur from when he was thirteen until the war began. But now, for the first time in his life, he felt no relief from it, no unburdening, no answer to his prayers. Usually the end of the fast is an exhilarating moment: an ancient trumpet is sounded, and everyone hurries home happily to food and family, washed clean of their sins. But when the day ended and the gates of repentance had swung shut, Jacob knew that God had not forgiven him, and worse, that he could not forgive himself. He and his father walked out together in a leaden silence. When they sat down to break the fast, Jacob had no appetite. He was twenty years old, and he was an old, old man. The following day he went back to work in his father's firm, at last admitting defeat.

During his second long, blank year—the bloody fall and winter and spring as the wretched 1863 turned into the abominable 1864, after he had returned to work, but not to life—he slowly came to understand that there is something perversely appealing about defeat. After one has been beaten enough, Jacob discovered, falling on one's knees is no longer humiliating. One simply makes a home for oneself groveling on the ground, thrilled to be left as a simpering shell of the person one might have been, relieved at last of the terrible burden of owning one's own life. Jacob had long accepted this state of affairs when his father came to him, in the autumn of 1864, and unwittingly offered him freedom.

2.

"Jacob, there's a client of ours in Philadelphia whom we ought to meet in person," his father said one morning in the firm's office, with a deliberate casualness in his voice.

Jacob looked up from his desk, where he had been sorting through account books, searching for ways to cut losses. It was the kind of work he had done for Philip Levy, and it felt oddly comforting. His life, if one could call it that, had resumed a sort of tedious routine, the tedium of which was his only source of solace. The fewer people he had to speak to, the calmer he became. With his father he barely spoke at all. His father, too, seemed to prefer it that way, and encouraged his isolation. Usually he even tried to keep Jacob away from the clients, and for that reason, his remark struck Jacob as strange. It was as though he suddenly wanted to include Jacob in the real work of the business, returning him to the person he had been years before. Impossible, Jacob thought. He looked at his father, waiting.

His father was looking right at him, something he rarely did anymore. "I'm sure the client would be pleased to come to New York, but—well, I wondered if you might be willing to go to Philadelphia to meet him instead," his father said. Then he winced, as he often did now when doing anything involving Jacob, hiding it by fidgeting with the chain of his watch.

Jacob watched him carefully as he looked away. Did he mean it? He listened as his father coughed, hesitant. The blond hair on his father's wrists bristled along his carefully pressed cuffs as his fingers twitched. His whole body seemed to sag, empty and tired. Jacob did not respond. Finally his father looked at him again.

"I thought it might be an opportunity for you to start developing your own clients," his father said, with the faintest hint of hope in his voice. His father spoke to him in German—or, as Jacob had been made aware in his occasional contact with "real" Germans, in something closer to the German-Jewish jargon, though Jacob could only vaguely tell the difference. "It would be a short trip, only a few days. Though you might stay longer if you found it necessary."

His father was getting rid of him. Jacob was more than ready. "Of course," he replied, in English. When he was a boy he used to answer his father in German, but he had stopped doing that when he was thirteen years old. Speaking English to his father was something he once associated with being someone different than his father—someone more intelligent, more sophisticated, more American. He had since learned that it was easier simply to meet expectations, to succumb to someone else's will. He added in German, "Tell me what to do."

"Wonderful," his father said, slapping the desk hard with his palm. It was a gesture he used with clients, usually, at the end of a deal. "I'll give you all the account information and the correspondence. They're restructuring their firm, and I would like for us to acquire them as a subsidiary. The head of the firm took on his brother as a partner recently, and I used to work with the brother before the war. He's the one I'd like you to meet."

His father stood, stepping over to the shelves by Jacob's desk and taking down some account books, rifling through the pages. He paused for a moment, and looked at Jacob. "You may even remember him, from before the war. He used to own P.M.L. Shipping in Virginia. Philip Levy. Do you remember him?"

Fortunately Jacob's injuries made it a fairly common occurrence for his father to hear him gasp. He bit his lip and watched as his father tried to hide his own wincing, mistaking Jacob's astonishment for agony.

Jacob tried to speak, then choked, and at last managed to relax his face into a bemused frown. "I don't—I don't think so," he stammered.

His father smiled, satisfied that Jacob's pain had subsided, and sat down in a chair across from Jacob's desk. "Levy was my age, but looked younger," he said. "Tall, dark hair, dark mustache, spectacles, very well-dressed, a bit of a drawl. You really don't remember him?"

"No," Jacob lied. He pictured Philip as he had last seen him, at the jail: stooped in his shackles, his clothes covered in mouse droppings, squinting without his spectacles. Philip was in Philadelphia? But how? He looked at his father, and noticed how his father had glanced away from him, unnerved by what he thought was Jacob's discomfort. Jacob was only beginning to appreciate how easily a cripple is able to hide.

"Well, he remembered you," his father said. "He asked after you in his last letter."

"Me?" Jacob nearly gagged on the word. "What did he say?"

"About you? Oh, nothing, really," his father replied. "He just said he remembered meeting you at the office a few years ago, and he wondered if you had enlisted. I told him you were wounded and had come home. He sends his condolences." Jacob's chest heaved, a sigh of relief that his father clearly assumed was related only to his physical pain. But there was more.

"In fact, he asked me if he might meet with you, rather than with me. It was his idea," he heard his father say. "His company in Virginia collapsed, and he's working with his brother in Philadelphia now. God knows how he managed to cross the lines. I was afraid to ask. That's another reason why I wanted you to meet him in person. There's a very small possibility that he and his brother are trying to set up a sham company, to funnel money south. That's something a person can't determine from correspondence. It's easier to detect lies in the flesh." His father looked at him carefully, with an expression that might have been an attempt at a grin. "I know you don't like to talk about your—well, your service, but I suspect that the army gave you a nose for detecting traitors."

Jacob's eye patch was large and distracting enough, along with the various scars on the right side of his face, that it was almost impossible for others to notice when he blushed. He nodded. "You may depend on me," he said.

"Wonderful. I shall send you down on the train tomorrow," his father replied, and left the room.

Jacob sat back in his seat, his body tingling with the first anticipation he had felt in almost two years: the gleaming possibility of redemption.

3

PHILADELPHIA WAS A POOR MAN'S NEW YORK, RICHER IN INTEGRITY and tradition, and poorer in everything else. The buildings were older and more stately in design, but also smaller and more decrepit; the people were better educated, but less fashionably dressed; the food was worse, but cheaper; the smell of manure in the streets was less intense, but the wait for an omnibus or hansom cab was at least three times as long. When one of the conductors helped Jacob off the train at the station on Broad Street, he looked around and felt strangely at ease, as though he had arrived in the countryside. On that afternoon in early November 1864, the breeze outside the station was chilly, but not yet cold; the trees on the streets, freshly denuded of their leaves, spread their gray branches gently alongside the old tilted brick row houses, and the air smelled of fresh possibilities. He hired a porter to carry his bags to a hotel near the station. After a long, exhausting wait outside the hotel's front door, during which he was too ashamed to lean against a tree or the hotel's façade for the support he desperately needed, he at last found a cab to take him to the Board of Brokers, the Philadelphia stock exchange, where he was to meet Philip Mordecai Levy by the entrance at half past three o'clock. He hadn't taken a cab alone since before the war; after his injury, he almost always had his parents or a servant accompanying him to the few places he might go. But the office hadn't been able to spare anyone to join him for his trip. Jacob suspected that this was intentional, his father's secret test for him. He was determined to pass.

The cab that finally stopped for him was an open-air type, with nothing dividing the driver from the passengers. The driver was older than Jacob's father, a wiry man with a sagging belly and thinning blond hair like his father's combed across his narrow head. Jacob had hoped to find a carriage with a younger driver, someone who would have less trouble helping him up to the running board and into his seat. But when the driver stopped the carriage and saw Jacob with his patch and cane, he immediately came down to assist him. Jacob tried to wave him away, but he was surprised by how strong the older man was. Without a word, and with utter dignity, he lifted Jacob's body up into the cab. As he returned to his perch, he smiled at Jacob, asked him where he was going, and told him the fare. Jacob settled back in his seat and was enjoying the ride on that bright afternoon, relieved and thrilled to have been treated as though he were merely another human being, when the driver turned to him and asked, apropos of nothing, "Where were you wounded?"

It occurred to Jacob that, for a driver picking him up at a hotel, the more normal question might have been "Where are you from?" But normalcy no longer applied to him; he had become a walking symbol of defeat. He grimaced, and answered.

"Mississippi," he said.

"Vicksburg?" the driver asked.

People always asked that, Jacob had noticed, if they ventured to ask at all. At least his disfigurement ought to have contributed to a battle the Union had won, they seemed to demand, so that they could count Jacob's missing eye and hobbled legs to be the worthy price of victory, and look at him without guilt. "No, I never made it that far," Jacob said, and reddened with shame.

The driver sighed, and in his sigh Jacob was alarmed to hear less pity than disgust. "Revolting, isn't it," the driver said.

"Pardon?" he asked. The few people who dared to speak to him since his injury had invariably congratulated him, praising his "service," his "valor," his "sacrifice." They used words like "heroic" and "courageous." Of course, "revolting" was what they were all actually thinking, he knew. But never before had he heard it said aloud. Perhaps he had imagined it.

"It's absolutely revolting," the driver repeated. "All you boys dead or mangled, and for what?"

It was the question that the entire country was afraid to ask. Jacob's remaining eye opened wide.

"I'll tell you for what," the driver said. His voice wasn't angry, or even harsh. To Jacob it sounded radiant, the outer edge of prophecy.

"I'm listening," Jacob said. He looked at the woolen scarf wound around the driver's narrow neck, and at last succeeded in ignoring the pain in his legs as the carriage bumped over loose cobblestones. It was exhilarating just to be sitting alone with this driver in this cab, far away from his parents and New York, independent again, and at last close to the truth. No one had ever even tried to answer that question for him before, and it was the only question he needed answered. "Tell me," he said.

"For niggers, abolitionists, Republicans, and Jews, that's for what," the driver announced. "Blame the Rebels all you want, but that's who did that to you, my friend. They're the only ones with something to gain. The niggers and the abolitionists got what they wanted, and now it's the Republicans and the Jews running the show. It always was, behind it all. The Seligmans are the ones making the uniforms. The more boys like you who are killed or mangled, the richer they get. Your blood is their gold."

Jacob thought of Rebecca Seligman—the daughter of the founder of the Seligman dry-goods empire, who was a client of his father's in New York. Once, at a luncheon at another family's house when he was six years old, Jacob had gone to the cloakroom to fetch an extra handkerchief and had come across seventeen-year-old Rebecca Seligman with her bodice and corset opened, panting in the arms of the son of one of her father's rivals. It was Jacob's first glimpse of breathing beauty. In the back of the hansom, he briefly engaged in a small mental fantasy in which he spat in the driver's face and jumped down to the street without paying the fare. But his crippling had consequences, and he was the driver's prisoner. He shifted his lame legs, and thought of another way to escape.

"Sir, you are absolutely right," he replied. "And I am so relieved to finally meet someone who isn't afraid to say it."

The carriage just in front of theirs had stopped, and now the driver turned to look at Jacob. He grinned, thrilled.

"Thank you!" he cried. "And what a relief for me, to finally meet someone who isn't afraid to look for a little dignity for himself." He offered Jacob his hand. "My name is Donaldson—Charles Hunt Donaldson. What is your name, young man?"

Jacob paused for an instant, and then smiled. "Edwin McAllister," he said.

The driver took his hand and squinted at him, examining his face. For an instant Jacob wondered if the man had somehow recognized him, if he knew who he really was. But then the driver spoke. "The McAllisters from Bucks County? You wouldn't be Chester McAllister's brother, would you?"

Jacob hesitated, before deciding he had nothing to lose. "I am," he said.

The driver's face turned grave. Adopting the liar's habit, Jacob adjusted his own face accordingly, glancing back down at his knees. "My profound condolences," the driver said, and clasped Jacob's hand in both of his. "I used to work up near Bucks, and I heard about it from one of my passengers last year. What happened to your brother was a crime, son. Executed for trying to desert! Absolutely obscene. It was murder, that's what it was."

Jacob looked up again, trying his best to keep his face severe, grateful for his scars and his eye patch. "I can't say I disagree," he said.

"My most profound condolences. May the Lord compensate him in heaven, and may his soul be avenged on earth," the driver said. He pumped Jacob's hand. "It is truly an honor to meet you, Mr. McAllister," he said. "I can't tell you what a pleasure it is to meet someone with some sense still left in his skull, in a country full of fools."

The carriage in front of them had moved, and now the driver whipped the horse into a brisk trot, leading them around a corner. On the right Jacob saw the tall white columns of the Board of Brokers rising above the street, recognizing it from his last visit, four years earlier. Tight knots of men in top hats gathered on the marble steps, just as they had four years before, as though this place were a tiny coin that had fallen through a hole in time's pocket. He scanned the crowd for Philip, but didn't see him. Then he slipped his watch out of his vest and saw that it was a quarter of an hour too soon.

"Of course, maybe this whole war is simply divine punishment for the fools, for being duped into electing a nigger president," the driver called to him over his shoulder. "Heaven help us all if he is elected again. Perhaps we will be blessed to see Providence make an end to him." The carriage slowed, and the driver pulled the horse to a stop. He turned his head toward Jacob. "Of course, Providence might well benefit from the assistance of mortals," he added.

The driver looked at Jacob with a strange elation in his features, his reddened face pinched with glee. He was a man who rejoiced in being infuriated, Jacob saw—drinking up rage like liquor, reveling in it, dependent on it, always eager for more. He had what Harry Hyams, for all his throttled fury, had lacked: the delight in anger that makes real evil possible, that makes destruction fun.

"I could think of no more worthy task than to serve Providence in that respect," Jacob said.

The driver paused, watching Jacob, judging. His smile vanished. Then he turned around completely in his seat, bending down until his face was nearly level with Jacob's. "I would like to know whether you really mean that," he said.

At that moment, anything was possible. For an instant Jacob felt his heart lurch toward fear and failure, felt himself about to laugh the whole thing off as an exaggerated joke. But in the last remaining second, he rallied, and looked the driver in the eyes.

"Yes," he said. He shifted his cane across his lap, pressing his fingers against his knees, trying not to wince. "And I'm not afraid to say it."

The driver glanced at the street. There were three cabs in the line ahead of theirs; no one was standing nearby. He leaned toward Jacob, and lowered his voice. "There are some men you might like to meet," he said. "Men who feel the way you do."

Jacob braced his cane against his legs. "Really," he replied. "Who?"

The driver glanced again at the street. This time a man was approaching the side of the carriage, starting to climb up onto the platform, waiting to board. The driver waved at him. "Sorry, sir," he called. "No more rides now. Horse's shoe is a bit loose. I've got to get him back to the stable." The man paused, and glanced at Jacob before quickly looking away, as nearly everyone who looked at Jacob did. Jacob watched as the man climbed down and waved away the few other men in top hats who had gathered beside the platform. Then the driver reached under his perch for a wooden sign, painted with the words OFF DUTY—WILL SOON RETURN. He hung it on the side of the carriage, and turned back to Jacob. He reached into his pocket and withdrew his hand, his fingers balled into a tight fist. Then he grasped Jacob's hand, and Jacob felt something small and metallic pressed into his palm. When the driver took his hand away, Jacob opened his fingers and was surprised to see a small gold-colored ring.

He held it between his thumb and index finger, examining it. He thought of how he had held Jeannie's mother's ring in the air at their wedding, and tried not to notice how his blood was draining down into his damaged legs. The world circled around him, fierce and dizzying. He clutched his cane, holding still.

"We are the Order of the Sons of Liberty, formerly the Knights of the Golden Circle," the driver said. Now his face was inches from Jacob's. Avoiding the driver's eyes, Jacob looked down again at the ring, weighing it in his palm. It clearly wasn't made of gold; brass perhaps. This time he noticed the engraved words circling the ring's inner surface: COME RET-RIBUTION. "Our responsibility is to protect American liberty when no one else will," the driver continued. "We have been attempting to recruit more men like you, men who know the Federal army well. You yourself can avenge your brother's death."

Jacob looked up at the driver, pressing his lips together. Without a word, he nodded.

"You have business to take care of this afternoon?" the driver asked, waving a hand at the columns on the right.

"Yes," Jacob said.

"The head of our Philadelphia group has a seat on the exchange. His name is John Clarke. You can introduce yourself to him with this ring. How long will you be here in town?"

"Not long," Jacob said. "I—I have a business obligation in New York."

"The Order exists in New York too. I'm not certain who the leaders are there, but you might contact Clarke's brother-in-law. Look for a man named Edwin Booth. He's a partner in Clarke's firm. Wherever you go, show them the ring. Tell them what happened to your brother. You have nothing to be ashamed of. Retribution shall be yours."

"Thank you," Jacob said. He reached into his pocket and pulled out his change purse. But when he presented the driver with the fare, the driver pushed back his hand.

"Please, you owe me nothing," the driver said. He came down from his perch and lifted Jacob bodily out of his seat, transporting him from the carriage to the platform to the sidewalk. As the driver carried him, Jacob closed his good eye, almost enjoying it. When he was standing upright again, the driver once more shook his hand, and then climbed back up to his perch. "Long live liberty!" he called, and flicked his whip against the horse's back.

Jacob watched as the carriage with its sign moved from the curb and drove away. Then he walked toward the exchange, and began waiting for Philip Mordecai Levy. It was a bright autumn afternoon, and for the first time in years, for reasons he did not quite understand, he felt a lightness and liberation that almost resembled happiness. He had been off duty, but he would soon return.

4

ONE CAN ALWAYS TELL THE STATE OF A NATION BY STANDING alongside the doors of a big city exchange and watching the faces of the men walking in and out. Jacob noticed this the very first time he ever went to the stock exchange in New York, when he was fourteen years old. His father had sent him there to bring someone a message, and he had waited just outside the doors on a hot, late summer afternoon. The '57 panic had begun, and as he watched the men coming through those doors, rivulets of sweat dripping down their cheeks and necks as they emerged into the heavy humid air, he saw how none of them looked at anyone else, even if they were involved in conversation with the men beside them. Each man's eyes were focused on the narrow strip of bare ground just in front of his own feet, and each man's brows were drawn together, a tight knot of worry lodged at the base of each man's forehead. Even at fourteen, Jacob had sensed the queasy dread of every man there, the seasick feeling of a ship's deck falling away beneath one's feet. Now Jacob saw the faces of the men outside the Philadelphia Board of Brokers and recognized once more that seasick fear. For a few moments he stood by the towering Greek columns and watched harried, worried bodies shuffling in and out, their eyes fixed on the ground, and he searched for Philip among them. But he couldn't stand up for long without pain, and he didn't want Philip to see him suffering. At last a group of men vacated a bench alongside the steps leading to the entrance. Jacob sank down onto it, overwhelmed with relief. And then he saw Philip coming down the stairs.

At first Jacob didn't recognize him. His hair was completely gray, and even with his overcoat Jacob could see that he had become rail-thin. His unbuttoned coat and dark suit hung on his gaunt frame like clothes on a scarecrow, and he held a battered top hat in his hands. His pince-nez looked new, smaller, and he squinted through the lenses in the bright sunlight. Jacob watched as he descended the marble stairs. His shoulders were hunched, as though the sky were pressing down on him, forcing him to bear its weight. The first time Jacob tried to call to him, his voice stuck in his throat. It was only after several tries that he finally managed to shout his name.

"Mr. Levy!"

Philip stopped and looked around. Despite his stoop, he seemed quite alert, almost anxious. But when he turned in Jacob's direction, he looked through him, his eyes passing right over the eye-patched cripple on the bench. "Mr. Levy!" Jacob called again.

Philip turned toward Jacob, and flinched. But Jacob had become accustomed to that. He stood, an effort that required all the time it took Philip to cover the distance between them. Then they were standing face to face.

For a moment they looked at each other in silence. Jacob had imagined, on the long anxious train ride that morning, that Philip would look at him with that same expression of contempt that Abigail's brother had given him in Holly Springs, or even that Philip would draw out a revolver and point it at his chest. Instead, Philip looked at him for a long time, taking in his eye patch, his scars, his cane, his hobbled legs. Then, very slowly, he extended his hand to Jacob.

Jacob raised his right hand to take Philip's, balancing himself with his left hand on his cane. It was a gesture that he had long perfected, but now he stumbled, and fell against Philip's chest. Locked in a grotesque parody of an embrace, Jacob felt Philip's damp cheek on his neck.

They sat down on the bench, side by side. Philip's eyes were sunken into his skull. He had become an old man. When he finally spoke, his voice was cold.

"My regards to your father," he said. "Please thank him for me, for sending you."

The words turned Jacob back into a child, one whose behavior the adults will no longer tolerate. He bit his lip, feeling himself sinking into the ground. He had never seen Philip's letter to his father—what had Philip written? His heart fluttered like a child's, afraid that his father knew what he had done.

"Did you tell him—" Jacob started to say.

"No," Philip said. Jacob breathed with relief. "I didn't want to endanger you," Philip added, "in case you were still working—well, in the field." In all the time Jacob knew him, he had never heard Philip use the word "spy." Philip coughed, and continued. "I merely inquired after your family. I wrote that I remembered you in passing, and asked if you had enlisted. He told me you were wounded and had come home. I hoped we might see each other."

Jacob wanted to ask him, then, why he didn't seem to despise him. But he couldn't bring himself to ask; perhaps Philip did. Instead he asked, "How did you come here?"

Philip looked down at his knees, avoiding Jacob's good eye. "I was exchanged for my daughter," he said. For an instant Jacob's soul ignited, flaring with hope. Philip added, "For Charlotte."

Jacob trembled, a reflex that lingered after two full years. "For Lottie?"

"It only happened three months ago," Philip said, his voice low. "No one explained it to me at the time. A military escort took me out of prison and brought me to the lines. Federal troops were waiting for me there. Later I was informed that it had been your idea."

Since his injury, Jacob was prone to headaches, a hard dull burn inside his skull behind where his right eye used to be. Now he felt the pain seeping in, deep within his head. He pressed the heel of his hand against his temple and tried to think. It was his idea? But his idea had been to exchange Philip for Jeannie, two years ago, when she was still alive!

At last Jacob spoke. "You were still in prison three months ago?" he asked. Months and years had melted away for him; he could no longer remember how much time had gone by.

Philip sighed, a deep defeated breath. "Jacob, my trial was a nightmare. The incident apparently didn't pass muster as a proper duel. The prosecutor came up with character witnesses, old clients, neighbors with grudges, people I hadn't spoken to in years. I didn't know it was possible to be that humiliated. I was sentenced to twenty years for murder of the second degree. I was probably lucky it wasn't more. The Union secret service saved me. I suppose I ought to thank you for that."

Jacob noticed that he stopped short of actually thanking him. But now Jacob was the prisoner in the dock. He was silent, awaiting judgment.

"I saw Charlotte when we were exchanged," Philip said.

Jacob watched as Philip swallowed, his heavy eyebrows drawing together, a knot of worry tightening at the base of his forehead. Jacob tried to think of something to say, but Philip continued before he could say a word. "I saw her, but I couldn't speak to her. We were both in chains, and surrounded by guards." The image sickened Jacob, but Philip forced him to listen. "She looked horrid. It was frightening. She was wearing rags, and she was so—so thin. Her skin was almost translucent. But what frightened me was the way she looked at everyone. She was so angry, so full of fury. I almost didn't recognize my own child. When you're a father, you always imagine them as children, you picture them running toward you, throwing their little arms around your legs. It's—"

He turned away from Jacob, looking at his fingers in his lap. Jacob tried to think of something to offer him, some way to begin begging him for absolution. But Philip had more to say. He had been planning it for years.

"There is something many women know instinctively, but few men ever understand," he said, "which is that raising children is one of the only things you can do with your life. My wife taught me that years ago. One can devote oneself to a cause, but what cause could be worth more than a child?" Now he was looking straight ahead, gazing at the white marble steps as they turned yellow in the late afternoon light. "Dying for a cause is the last resort of those too weak to live for one. That's something my daughters never understood."

Jacob heard, beneath his words, everything he hadn't said, everything he refused to say. Lottie was a proxy for another daughter, for an unnamable grief.

"I don't expect you to forgive me," Jacob said.

Jacob saw him blinking, and waited.

"For a long time I used to curse you," Philip said at last. "I cursed myself, too, for being foolish enough to let you in. I knew why you had come, almost from the beginning. But I—I saw how the girls changed in your presence, how happy you made them. It was so exhilarating, to see them that way. I had forgotten it was possible." Jacob pursed his lips, and felt his remaining eye watering as Philip continued. "As a result I became a bit delirious. I had the notion that you would be exceptional somehow, that you would give up whatever glory or respect you were after for something that mattered more. Of course there are no exceptions. You did what you were told to do. I suppose you had to. What sickens me is that I was naïve enough to expect something different from you."

Jacob looked down at his knees. For an instant he thought of defending himself, of explaining how he had tried to save Jeannie even if he had turned Lottie in, how he had at first even tried to save them both by keeping the evidence to himself, how Lottie had been the one who had wanted him dead—but he understood now that all his half-measures had been pointless. He rubbed at his scars.

"Eventually I forced myself to understand that all of it might have happened just as easily without you, or that without you it might have been even worse, if such a thing were conceivable," Philip said. "I know now that it was all the girls' fault, or my own fault—that I failed as a father, that I failed to protect them, or to prepare them. But I can't even tell you how many months I spent praying that God would exact revenge on you."

"He did," Jacob said.

Philip indulged a long glance at Jacob's eye patch, at his cane, at the distorting scars on the right side of his face and neck. Like all cripples, Jacob had become accustomed to people deliberately looking away from him. He was surprised by how much he relished having someone look, at last, at his damaged body. "How were you wounded?" Philip finally asked.

Jacob paused, reminded of the hansom driver. What could he say? "During a prisoner exchange," he replied.

Philip smiled, a cruel smile. "'The judgments of the Lord are true and righteous altogether,'" he quoted. He removed his spectacles, rubbing at the lenses with his handkerchief. It was intended to seem like a casual gesture, but Jacob saw how hard he was rubbing at nothing, trying to distract Jacob from his shuddering hands. At last he put them back on his nose, and glanced down at his lap.

"I haven't been able to find out anything about what's become of the girls. Not Charlotte, nor—nor any of them," Philip said slowly. Here it was, Jacob knew. He listened as Philip paused, gathering strength. "My brother told me that he read in the newspaper that Eugenia—" Philip paused, swallowed. "That Eugenia—that she—she—" He swallowed again, before adding, "—perished in prison."

He glanced at Jacob, registering his lack of surprise. Philip had expected him to know. For a long time Jacob said nothing, afraid of what he might say, and afraid that saying it would make it false. But Philip spoke first.

"Perhaps you are wondering why I am even speaking to you now, if I know that," he said, and glared at Jacob. "For that sort of retribution, I would need to ask God to remove your other eye too, along with your heart."

Jacob couldn't endure Philip's eyes. He bit his lip and blinked his own good eye, rubbing it with the back of his hand. Those who believe in a hell in the afterlife cannot possibly imagine what it means to be damned while still living, he thought, the unrelenting torture of the conscience. For eternal suffering, nothing more is necessary.

"The only reason is that I don't believe it," Philip announced. "I won't believe it. I haven't even said Kaddish for her. I won't until someone proves to me that it's true, even if I have to wait until this entire war is over. Even if I have to wait for the rest of my life. I know it's a delusion, but I—I indulge it. It's all I can do."

Jacob looked at him again, afraid to speak. Philip was crouching with his elbows on his knees, pressing the heels of his hands against his brow. He glanced at Jacob briefly, with a slight sneer. "I had an absurd thought when I wrote to your father. I foolishly believed that seeing you would ease my suffering somehow, or even put it to rest. I don't know why I thought such a thing. You are irrelevant to me, utterly irrelevant. I only want my daughters back, and that you cannot give me." Jacob cringed, but Philip's eyes were closed, pressed against his hands. He was in another world. "Foolish girls, all of them," he muttered. "But I only blame myself."

Jacob looked down at his own lap, which was now in the shadow of a tall oak tree behind them. Since the injury, his vision often failed him at odd moments, his single eye unable to take in the full revulsion of the world, and his mind would substitute memory for life. Now his hands in his lap blurred, and a bright pale space expanded between them. In that instant, seated outside the Philadelphia exchange, he suddenly held Abigail's letter before him, the paper stiff and certain in his hands, the words dark and crisp and clear in Abigail's handwriting: *three weeks after you have surely been sealed in the Book of Life*. At last he dared.

"I think Jeannie is alive," he said.

Philip raised his head, and turned to look at Jacob. For the briefest of instants, a light moved across his eyes. But it disappeared just as quickly as it had come. His face darkened, and he stared at Jacob, seething, barely able to contain his rage. "Don't do that to me," he said, his voice cold. "You have no right."

Jacob shook his head, panicked, suddenly believing it. "I have a reason to think so," he said. "I—"

"You have no right," Philip repeated.

Jacob could see how Philip was struggling to control himself, to keep himself from strangling him on the spot. Philip's hands were pressed against his thighs, his fingers clutching his knees. But Jacob couldn't help himself. He asked, breathless: "Do you have family in Mississippi?"

Philip's brow unknotted itself, his wrinkled face easing, as though Jacob had changed the subject. When he spoke, his voice was light, curious, puzzled. "My wife's sister Sarah. She died about five years ago." He looked at the air in front of him, as if searching for a face in a crowd. "Her husband was killed in a battle over there. I really pitied the children," he added, his voice distant. Then he turned back to Jacob. "Why do you ask?"

"I met them when I was with Grant," Jacob said.

"Really?" Philip asked. Then his face darkened again, the fury returning. "Why should I believe you," he muttered, without making it a question. "I have no reason to trust anything you say."

"Their name was Solomon. The children were Abigail, Franklin, and Jefferson," Jacob replied, his memory racing. "There was another son named Washington who had died. The father was killed at Shiloh. They owned a tavern in a town called Holly Springs. The daughter looked like yours."

Philip watched Jacob, alarmed and baffled, and mustered the courage to speak. When he did, he could barely form the words, releasing them under his breath. "Why are you telling me this?"

Jacob swallowed. What could he possibly say? That he had had an entire love affair with Philip's niece? "I saw a letter in their home," he finally said. "It was addressed to Jeannie, in Richmond. I shouldn't have read it, but I—I did, and it said she was living there with an aunt."

"Rachel Cardozo," Philip murmured, astounded. He was no longer speaking to Jacob, but rather to whatever phantasm was appearing before his eyes. "My wife's youngest sister."

"I suppose so. The letter said 'Aunt Rachel.' And it said that they had heard from Jeannie a week after Yom Kippur, with her new address in Richmond. That would have been a week after her arrest."

Philip hovered on the edge of his seat, his mouth hanging open.

"There's something else I ought to tell you," Jacob said slowly. "The last time I saw Jeannie, she—" He stopped, strangely embarrassed, until he remembered that he had no reason to be. "She told me she was expecting."

Philip turned to Jacob, stunned. Then he stared at his knees.

"Mr. Levy, I never should have accepted the mission that I took on against your family, and you should never forgive me for it," Jacob said. "But I shall forever be grateful to God that it brought me to Jeannie. I shall regret everything else I've done for the rest of my life, but I shall never regret marrying her. I love your daughter, Mr. Levy. I still do."

Philip pressed one eye with the heel of his hand. For a long time Jacob listened to him breathe. When he finally spoke, his voice was dark and cold.

"You think you know what devotion is," Philip said. "You think you understand what it means to dedicate your life to something. To risk absolutely everything for it."

Jacob looked at Philip and imagined him in prison during the last two years, stooped in a dark cell stained with mouse droppings, wearing irons on his legs. Then he imagined him in the front room of his house at his daughter's wedding, standing in his top hat and tails, raising his revolver in his hands as Jeannie crouched on her knees. He imagined him as he must have been during the years when he had known him only as a cheerful business client: presiding alone over a dinner table full of daughters, forever working, forever giving and forgiving, forever curbing their every foolishness, never once revealing his own grief. And then he imagined him in that same front room, years before, wrestling a shotgun out of the hands of a slave woman over the bleeding body of his wife, with Lottie and Jeannie and Phoebe and Rose as little children cowering on the floor.

"I do," Jacob replied.

Philip examined Jacob's scarred face, judging. Jacob submitted himself to his judgment, unafraid. And Philip sentenced him.

"Then go there, Jacob. Go down to Richmond and find them."

Jacob stared at him, condemned. Philip leaned forward and took hold of Jacob's knee, clutching it with an impossibly strong grip. Jacob winced, his whole body wrinkling into a tight cringe of agony. Philip did not notice, or did not care.

"I can't go back behind the lines," Philip said. His voice was heated, urgent. "There isn't any way for me to get there, and even if there were, someone would find me and put me back in prison. But you can go. You must go. I am ordering you to go."

Jacob was still reeling from the pain in his knee, unable to think through the implications of what Philip had said. When he did, he saw how absurd it was, impossible. "How could I ever do that?" he finally asked. "Even the army isn't desperate enough to want someone like me."

"The army isn't, but the secret service might be," Philip replied. He was animated now, revived and frantic. His eyebrows bristled as his spectacles slipped down his nose. "Surely you can find some way to make yourself indispensable to them again."

Jacob felt the pain beginning to dissipate, replaced by the dull ache of shame. "Look at me, Mr. Levy," he said at last. "Do I look like I would be indispensable to anyone?"

But Philip rejected his plea for pity. He was a man with a cause. "That is precisely what would make you indispensable," he said. For a fraction of an instant, the giddy eagerness in his voice reminded Jacob of Jeannie. "You appear utterly harmless. People avoid looking at you. With your face like that, no one will even recognize you, unless they really look." Now Philip was clutching Jacob's knee with both hands, knocking his cane off his lap. "You have to convince them to take you back."

Jacob looked at him, foundering in his seat without his cane to hold on to. "I don't have anything to offer them," he stammered.

"Don't make excuses," Philip spat. His hands were lighter on Jacob's knee now, but his eyes were hard and unrelenting, fixing Jacob in place. "You've been back at the firm for a year already. Half the people in this business are either scoundrels or traitors. Think. What have you heard that might be useful?"

"I don't—" Jacob began to say. Then he remembered the hansom driver. He looked back at Philip and asked, "Do you know a man at the exchange named John Clarke?"

Philip straightened, at last removing his hands from Jacob's knee. Jacob breathed, pure physical relief. "Everyone knows him," Philip said. "He owns a securities firm with his brother-in-law in New York. Why?"

Jacob was about to pull the ring from his pocket, but thought better of it. Suddenly he remembered what he had been trained to do, a lifetime ago: reveal nothing. "I would like to meet him," he said. "It would be in reference to—to what you are suggesting."

Philip peered at him, pushing his pince-nez back up on his nose. For a moment his brow wrinkled, as though he were about to ask Jacob a question. "He's in Maryland now," he said. "He's been there for the past month. His wife's family is there." He rubbed at his mustache, thinking. "But you don't need to meet him. His brother-in-law in New York owns half the firm. Speak to him instead. Assuming it's something about the firm, of course."

"Yes, about the firm," Jacob said.

"His brother-in-law in New York is Edwin Booth. Have you heard of him? He owns the firm with John Clarke, but he's mainly an actor."

"The name sounds familiar," Jacob said. "What else do you know about them?"

Philip eyed him, curious. "Only what everyone knows. Clarke's wife and brother-in-law are from Baltimore, but their father was from England. The father had a wife in London, but he ran off to Baltimore with a flower girl. It's an open secret that the children are all bastards. You've probably heard of the father. Junius Booth."

"Of course," Jacob said, startled. Junius Booth was a household name even for someone Jacob's age; he was the greatest Shakespearean actor of his generation. He had died years ago, but as a child Jacob had once seen him perform in New York, in the role he was most famous for, Richard the Third. The man himself was apparently a raging alcoholic, his personal life an advertisement for classical tragedy. But no one who had seen him perform could ever forget it.

"There's another son, too, who made a fortune in the theater, and he and another actor bought an oil drilling company here in Pennsylvania. But they sold off the entire company last month," Philip said. "If you ask me, it was a strange sale."

"Why?" Jacob asked.

"Because the drilling concern was very profitable, and it's foolish to liquidate assets like that when the market is as volatile as this one, unless one needs the capital for some kind of urgent opportunity. I don't need to explain this to you. His brother-in-law ought to have advised him against it." He drew his eyebrows together again as he pursed his lips. Jacob had often seen him in this pose in his office in Virginia, as he watched his own firm collapse. "I've heard that they send a lot of money to Canada," he added.

"Everyone keeps money in Canada," Jacob huffed. In his year of burial in his father's account books, he had noticed that this was true.

Philip shook his head. "I'm not talking about investments or promissory notes. I'm talking about gold." Philip leaned the side of his head against the palm of his hand, his elbow perched on his knee. Jacob had often seen his daughters in this same childish posture, thinking, planning. "There was a rumor on the exchange that the gold was coming from Richmond. I wouldn't have any idea how to corroborate that, though." He looked back at Jacob with his eyebrows raised, like a child hoping for approval. "Is any of this useful to you?" he asked. "I will tell you anything that's useful to you."

"You have often seemed remarkably eager to betray the place where you lived your entire life," Jacob said.

Philip glared at him, his eyes hard, unforgiving. "Jacob, surely by now you understand who I am," he said, his voice even. "I am an American, a Jew, a businessman, and a father of daughters. For all of those reasons, my worst enemy is lawlessness."

He removed a watch from his vest, glanced at it, and stood up. Jacob was surprised by how tall he seemed now, his stooped shoulders higher in the fading afternoon light. "Speak to my brother about the company," he said quickly, in the efficient business voice Jacob remembered him using years ago, in a world that had since disappeared. "He will expect you at the office tomorrow morning. But I would prefer not to see you again until you've done what I've asked of you."

He hadn't forgiven him, of course. Philip coughed, then blinked, unable to continue looking at Jacob's face. "I don't care how you do it," he said at last. "Find my daughters for me. Tell them that their father is waiting for them."

Jacob would have shaken his hand, but Philip turned around more quickly than Jacob was able to stand up. Instead, he watched in awe as

Philip walked away in the November afternoon shadows. And there Jacob saw what others claimed they saw when they looked at his own wounded body: devotion to a cause.

When he returned to New York later that week, Jacob reassured his father that Philip Mordecai Levy was an honorable man. Then he made some inquiries, and invented a reason to meet the actor Edwin Booth.

5.

*A*S A CHILD BEFORE THE WAR JACOB OFTEN WENT TO THE
theater with his parents. His parents' English was very good, but not
perfect, and even as a boy he could see that Shakespeare was far beyond
their ability. They went to the theater not to see the plays, but rather
to be seated in a box just two balconies above the Astors and the Bel-
monts, to point out other people to Jacob and (they dearly hoped) to be
pointed out by everyone else, to be part of a world that their own dead
parents in their Jewish town in Bavaria could never have imagined. For
Jacob's parents, the play itself was irrelevant. They were not spectators
but actors, appearing onstage before all of New York. Jacob had been an
essential part of their performance. His role, carefully scripted, was to
remain riveted to the action no matter how bored he might be—to sit
on the edge of his seat, enthralled, to show all of New York that even
though his parents spoke with accents, their child was being educated by
the best English tutors and could recite all of the Shakespearean solilo-
quies even more perfectly than the actors themselves, regardless of how
pointless such an education might ultimately prove to be for a destiny as
the future owner of Rappaport Mercantile Import–Export. Jacob had
played the role gladly for many years, until his escape. Now, crippled and
hideous, he bought a ticket and went to the theater, for the very first
time, alone. His ticket was for the opening night at the Arcadia Theater
of *Julius Caesar*, featuring the actor Edwin Booth in the role of Brutus, the
honorable man.

Edwin Booth was extremely attractive. After the war, Jacob read
somewhere that he was said to have "the most perfect physical head in
America." From his seat just two rows back from the stage, Jacob could
attest to it, particularly since his injury had left him with an acute awareness of the handsomeness of other men. Edwin Booth had deep brown
eyes, a glamorous wave in his dark brown hair, perfectly unblemished

and glowing skin, a profile worthy of a Roman god, and a stylish dark mustache that he must have refused to shave off for the role. The mustache left him looking like a modern stockbroker who had fallen through a trapdoor in time and landed in the Roman forum. Jacob listened as he declaimed his lines in a kind of deliberately vulgar vernacular, venting his hatred for Caesar as though he were spoiling for a fight in a saloon on the Bowery. As Jacob watched him outshine his more demure fellow actors onstage, he found the overall effect unnerving. It was as if Brutus were a man of modern times, invading the supposed glory of the past in order to shame and destroy it.

Julius Caesar had never been Jacob's favorite of Shakespeare's plays. Years earlier, when he first read them, he had loved *Romeo and Juliet* best, though now the thought of that particular drama disturbed him. But *Caesar* had always bored him. The assassination plot always seemed too obvious, the dramatic arc of honor, hypnotic evil, doubt, hesitation, conviction, sin, regret, dishonor, and retribution too predictable.

Yet this time he was startled when an ancient-looking Cassius announced, to the painfully modern Edwin Booth, that "The fault, dear Brutus, is not in our stars, / But in ourselves, that we are underlings." And when Edwin Booth took the stage for his soliloquy, Jacob listened to his barroom drawl with rapt attention:

> "Since Cassius first did whet me against Caesar,
> I have not slept.
> Between the acting of a dreadful thing
> And the first motion, all the interim is
> Like a phantasma, or a hideous dream:
> The genius and the mortal instruments
> Are then in council; and the state of man,
> Like to a little kingdom, suffers then
> The nature of an insurrection."

The space behind Jacob's missing eye throbbed as the words washed through his brain. The past three years, from the moment he first slipped into the barrel that brought him to New Orleans, had been a hideous dream, his entire being suffering from the nature of an internal insurrection. Jacob was surprised by how relieved he was when Brutus died. He was even more surprised at how emboldened he was when the play finally ended, when he rushed backstage to meet him.

BACKSTAGE, WHERE HE had been directed after telling one of the stage-hands that he had an appointment, Jacob wandered through a series of firetraps, tiny rooms and hallways crammed with costumes and wigs that were heaped up to within inches of the lamps mounted along the walls. The little corridors were crowded with the actors he had just seen onstage, smoking and laughing while still wearing their togas. It was odd to see these Roman senators taking up their pipes—even in the presence of Caesar's wife, whom Jacob saw laughing at something one of them had said, her dark hair flowing beautifully down her back for the role—and to watch as they stopped to stare at him when he appeared with his cane and his eye patch, invading their glamorous domain. He didn't care. He was fascinated by everything he saw, intoxicated by a thought that wouldn't leave him: once, a lifetime ago, this had been Jeannie's world. Surely she had stood just like this backstage, costumed and laughing, chatting boldly with her fellow performers, charming the men with whom real life would be impossible, thriving in a world that was nothing but illusion.

At last someone directed him to a narrow door, adorned with a wooden star. For a moment, standing before that door, he hesitated, a phantom image of William Williams the Third rising before him. He gathered his courage, and knocked.

"Mr. Booth?" he called.

He expected a servant or stagehand to open the door, but instead he heard a man's voice sing out, with great cheer, "Come in, come in, the door is unlocked!" Balancing one hand on his cane and the other on the doorknob, Jacob opened the door and entered Edwin Booth's private dressing room.

The actor was seated on a low stool in front of a mirror, the most perfect physical head in America scrutinizing itself above a dressing table littered with combs and bottles of cologne. Two tall gas lamps mounted on either side of the mirror illuminated his handsome face. Unlike his friends, Romans, and countrymen in the common areas outside, he was already wearing a very smart suit, as though preparing for a late evening party. His toga and laurels from the production were draped over a clothes tree to his left. When Jacob entered the room, the actor didn't turn around. Instead, he continued grinning at himself in the mirror, untying and retying his cravat.

"You're that chap Rappaport, aren't you, here to discuss something about the firm?" he asked. His eyes were still fixed on his reflection. He picked up an ivory comb from the dressing table and began running it through his perfect hair.

"Yes, I am," Jacob said. "I do so appreciate your meeting me here, Mr. Booth." He worked hard to sound ingratiating, sufficiently awed. "Your secretary informed me that this was the only way to see you this week before you depart for Cincinnati. I cannot thank you enough for your graciousness in accommodating me." He took a few steps into the room, trying his best to control the thumping of his cane against the floor.

"Not at all, not at all," Edwin Booth replied, his voice absurdly gallant. He was still speaking to his own reflection. He gave himself a smile and a wink, as though his reflection were a pretty young lady seeking his affections. At last he turned around toward Jacob, correcting his expression into a hardier, more manly grin. Then he noticed Jacob's cane, his eye patch, and his scars, and flinched.

"Oh, my—my apologies, Mr.—Mr. Rappaport," he stammered. People often apologized to him now, Jacob noticed, perhaps for their own two eyes and working legs. Edwin Booth had jumped up and was hiding his flinch with a rapid bow, gesturing toward the stool where he had been sitting. "Do have a seat."

When Jacob had first learned to walk again, he had made a point of never taking seats when they were offered. But a year and a half of physical torture had transformed him into a delicate lady, at the mercy of the chivalrous. "Thank you," he said, and lowered himself onto the stool. Edwin meanwhile jumped to a corner to retrieve an empty crate, seating himself on it across from Jacob. It was difficult for Jacob to look at his handsome face. There were mirrors on every wall, and lamps lit beside each one. Jacob glanced around the room and saw his scars multiplied thousands of times in every direction, his hideousness extending into eternity.

"You do know, good fellow, that I don't usually like to sully myself with financial matters, any more than is absolutely necessary," Edwin sang. He had turned away from Jacob's ugly face again, looking back in the mirror above the dressing table and dabbing cologne behind his ears. "The firm is half mine, of course, but as you can see, acting is my true métier." He said this with flourish, though he pronounced it "meatier."

Jacob glanced around at the thousand perfect physical heads in the mirrors around him and thought for an instant of the immense talent of Junius Booth, Edwin's father. A bastard is a man who forever has something to prove. "Indeed," Jacob said.

"So what sort of opportunity do you have for me?" Edwin asked. He stretched a hand past Jacob's shoulder to set the cologne down carefully on the dressing table, winked at himself one more time, and at last turned to his visitor again. Now he leaned toward Jacob, his hands on his knees. A thousand duplicated Edwin Booths leaned forward with him, their infinite handsomeness challenging Jacob's infinite ugliness to a duel.

Jacob thought of Jeannie in the alley behind the jail, how she had told him that he was a terrible actor. He looked at the mirrors around the room, at the endless scars and eye patches. Terrible acting was the best he had to offer now, and his future depended on it. "An opportunity to serve the cause of liberty," he said, summoning his actor's voice. He reached into his pocket and held up the ring.

Edwin Booth peered at the ring, and then took it between his thumb and index finger. He leaned back, the dark mustache on his upper lip twitching as he examined the inscription inside. Jacob watched as every last drop of pretense evaporated from the actor's handsome face.

"You got this from John, didn't you," Edwin Booth finally said, his voice low.

John Clarke, Jacob assumed. He had decided in advance to say as little as possible, to listen, to take the utmost care in determining the best approach. "Yes, from John," he replied. He no longer had to worry about concealing his expression; his scars and his eye patch did that for him.

Edwin Booth breathed in, a long, deep breath, and glanced at his own reflection in the mirrors around the room. Suddenly, he jumped to his feet and threw the ring to the floor. Jacob watched, startled, as it rolled on the ground, striking the end of his cane and landing beside it.

"Listen, my friend," Edwin hissed, in a fierce stage whisper. His whisper managed to inflict all the power and fury of a scream. Jacob winced, curling back against the dressing table behind him. Now Edwin was pacing the room, waving his arms in the air as though he were onstage. "I don't know what sorts of rumors you have heard, but I am not part of the Order, and I never was. I may have catered to your people before, but that was merely as a favor to my brother." His brother-in-law, he must have meant; clearly John Clarke was the one with the ring. His tone was rising, slowly approaching a roar. "And I won't do it anymore. I refuse. The fact that my brother has become an irreconcilable fanatic has absolutely nothing to do with me. I have indulged him in the past, I know. But I shall no longer bear responsibility for any idiocy on my brother's part."

Now he was enraged, his glamorous face burning bright red, his furious snarl closing in on Jacob from every angle in the room's thousands of reflections. He approached Jacob, thrusting his hands toward Jacob's face as he ranted. Jacob ducked.

"You want me to take your gold again? Send it along to Toronto for you, first-class courier, discount rate, no commission, no questions asked? Just one more time, is that it? Just one more goddamned time, like it was for the past three times?" he sneered. "Well, I won't do it. I won't take any more of it. I am a free man, and I refuse. I am out of this chain of imbeciles. Out!

"Go talk to my brother and tell him I'm finished," Edwin Booth raved. "I've told him myself, but he won't listen. Clearly he prefers to continue sending along new cronies like you." He paused for a moment, his brows pinched together, ready to explode. "No, don't bother even telling my brother," he said. "Tell Benjamin directly. Tell him to stop sending it. I'm finished."

Jacob held his palm against his jaw. Benjamin?

"And tell him he's never going to hear from me again," Edwin huffed, triumphant. "He can send me his card when he arrives in hell."

The most perfect physical head in America glistened in the lamplight. The actor folded his arms across his chest, caught his breath, and looked at Jacob, waiting.

Jacob exhaled slowly, observing Edwin Booth as his confident pose faltered. The actor had begun tapping his foot. Jacob was glad to make him wait, and enjoyed watching him as he became more and more nervous. He was avoiding Jacob's glance now, a bead of sweat rolling down one of his gorgeous cheeks. Jacob leaned back and took his time as he decided what to say.

"They are expecting your participation, Mr. Booth," Jacob told him, his tone calm and controlled. "I need to give them the receipt." Jacob had no idea what this meant, of course. But he was willing to hope that Edwin would.

Edwin did, it seemed. He cocked an eyebrow at Jacob, then tossed his head back, each perfect hair landing back in its perfect wave. "They may feel free to expect whatever they wish," he retorted, his arms still crossed against his chest. "It's of no concern to me."

"It will be of concern to you if I turn you in," Jacob said. "I doubt that the Union authorities will share your cavalier attitude about your contributions to the cause."

Jacob was surprised by how much he enjoyed watching Edwin's handsome face change color. His skin faded from red to a cold, pale white, draining into a death mask.

"You would never do that," he breathed.

"I have turned in people much closer to me, when it has been necessary," Jacob said, his voice utterly bland. "You cannot possibly imagine the sort of devotion I am capable of. Two years ago I assassinated my own uncle, and later I turned in my own wife." Jacob watched as Edwin shrank before him, his confident posture slouching down toward Jacob's crippled form. To Edwin, Jacob had become precisely what his disfigured face symbolized to everyone who saw him, the visceral element in his hideousness that made everyone flinch: pure evil. Jacob smiled. "You have to be careful with devoted men like me," he said. "I owe you nothing."

Edwin Booth's glamorous lips contorted into a sneer. "You disgust me," he spat. "All of you disgust me."

Jacob was quite accustomed to disgusting people. He laughed. "I have explicit instructions from Richmond to send everything through you," Jacob said. A bolt of brilliance flashed through his mind, and he seized it. "Unless," he added, "you are willing to appoint me as your substitute."

Edwin Booth steadied himself and nodded. His nodding continued so long that it became ridiculous, like a manic puppy unable to control his bobbing head. "A substitute. Yes. Yes indeed," he yelped. "That's a capital idea. Capital." He began pacing the room, waving his hands in the air again. "Tell them I've got consumption. Or yellow fever. Tell them I've had a stroke. Tell them I've gone mad. I don't care what you tell them. I'm through."

His ranting gave Jacob time to think. By the time Edwin had thrown his hands in the air for the last time, Jacob was ready. "I can't simply send everything along myself," Jacob told him. "There is a chain of command in place. Benjamin would need to be informed, and to approve it."

Had he bet right? Edwin Booth nodded again. He had. "So send him a telegram," Edwin said, with a wave of his hand.

Half of deception is condescension, making everyone assume that one's wisdom is above reproach. Jacob snorted, insulted. "You know that's impossible. And even if it weren't, he would never trust any message unless it were delivered in person."

Edwin Booth pulled at his own cravat, glancing again at the mirrors around the room. "Then go and tell him yourself," he said. "Surely you have a way to go back down to Richmond."

"Of course," Jacob said. "But I shall need you to put your appointment of me in writing, for Benjamin. Then I shall bring it to him in person, and we shall reestablish the route to Toronto." It was amazing how many assumptions were floating in the thick air between them, waiting to be pulled out and put to use. Meanwhile Jacob thought it through again. Could he be sure it was *that* Benjamin?

"I shall do it right now," Edwin Booth said, and jumped to where Jacob was sitting. Shoving Jacob aside, he tugged open a drawer in the dressing table and pulled out a sheet of paper, a pen, and a small pot of ink.

His shove caused Jacob great pain, though Jacob struggled mightily not to show it. Jacob rose from the stool, slowly, and limped over to the crate where Edwin had been sitting. Edwin Booth drew out the stool and planted himself on it. Then he opened the inkpot, set it down beside the paper and dipped his pen into it. He didn't risk dripping ink on the paper. Instead he bent away from the desk toward the clothes tree, and wiped the pen nib along the bottom of his toga. Jacob had just taken his new seat on the crate opposite, watching the actor's sweating face in the mirror, when Edwin began declaiming the words as he wrote them down.

"'For the Secretary,'" he announced, in a grand theatrical voice. "'Insofar as I have been incapacitated by sudden and grave illness, I am unable to render the services requested. I hereby humbly ask that you accept my appointment of the bearer of this notice, Mr.—er, Mr.—'"

"Jacob Rappaport."

Edwin glanced at Jacob, his eyes full of contempt. "Spell it," he hissed.

Jacob smiled, thinking of Rose. "R–A–P–P–A–P–O–R–T."

"'R–A–P–P–A–P–O–R–T,'" Edwin repeated, with a schoolboy's sneer. He looked at the paper, mouthing the letters as he wrote them, and glanced at Jacob. "What the devil sort of name is that?"

"Italian," Jacob replied. It was true. Porto di Mantova, his father had once told him, was the name of the town in Italy where their ancestors—a family by the name of Rappa, originally Rabba, descended directly from the biblical high priest—had set up their first merchant business before making their way over the Alps. They had arrived in Italy in the first Christian century against their will, as slaves brought from Jerusalem to Rome. Their fellow Hebrews had bought them and set them free, following the ancient law that still held Jacob in its grip: the obligation of every Hebrew to redeem Hebrew captives, no matter the cost.

"I'll be damned," Edwin Booth muttered. He paused to share a scowl with Jacob, one that multiplied thousands of times in the mirrors around him, before continuing. "'I hereby humbly ask that you accept my appointment of the bearer of this notice, Mr. Jacob R–A–P–P–A–P–O–R–T, a gentleman with a long and unimpeachable record of service, as my most honorable replacement,'" he read aloud as he scribbled. Once he had finished, he glanced up at Jacob. "I presume I am correct concerning your devotion to the cause."

Jacob thought of Philip Levy, and remembered why he had come. For the first time in years, he felt no shame. "You are hardly one to question my devotion," he said.

Edwin Booth spat at the ground, barely missing Jacob's foot, and slammed down his pen on the dressing table. The cologne bottles jumped, startled. "Well, then, you may have it," he concluded. He lifted the paper and began waving it in the air, flapping it back and forth in front of Jacob's face as the ink dried. "Is this sufficient for your needs, or do you expect cash payments as well?"

Jacob felt it unnecessary to push his luck. "Just sign and seal the note," he said. Edwin let out a loud puff of relief. But Jacob wasn't ready to relinquish control. "For now, that is. If it is necessary for you to fulfill any financial obligations to us in the future, I shall keep you informed," he added, and grinned.

"You bastard," Edwin muttered.

Jacob laughed. Edwin blushed, grumbling as he signed his name, with an absurd flourish. Then he pulled open the dressing table drawer and fished out an envelope, a red stick of sealing wax, and a brass seal. "You are scum, all of you," he announced, stuffing the letter into the envelope. He dipped the stick of wax into the flame of the lamp by the mirror and melted it onto the envelope flap, pressing his seal into it. "Pure scum," he repeated, and handed the letter to Jacob. "I shall take pains to avoid all of you upon my arrival in hell."

"Likewise, I'm sure," Jacob sang. He waited a moment for the seal to dry, touching the hardened raised monogram E.F.B. before putting the envelope into his vest pocket. Then, with considerable discomfort, he bent over and picked up the ring, which had been lying on the floor where Edwin Booth had flung it down, and slipped it into his pocket with the envelope. His future lay pressed against his chest.

He took up his cane and rose, slowly, taking his time and enjoying Edwin Booth's handsome defeated eyes as they observed his broken body. "Thank you for your time, Mr. Booth," he said. "It has been a pleasure doing business with you." He meant it.

"You are scum," Edwin repeated. "Now get out of my dressing room."

Jacob smiled. Edwin stood before him, his pitiful subject, and then turned back to the mirror, readjusting his cravat. He pursed his lips proudly at his reflection, but Jacob could see that he was beaten, humiliated. Jacob glanced around the room, at the thousands of dejected Edwin Booths with their backs turned to the thousands of triumphant cripples. He turned around and hobbled out of the star-studded door.

WHEN JACOB RETURNED HOME, his parents were still out for the evening. He didn't wait for them. Instead he wrote them a letter, thanking them for everything they had given him and vowing that he would see them again, though he could not promise when. After that, he lay in his childhood bed and allowed the familiar pain to keep him awake until daybreak, when everyone else was still asleep. He placed the letter on his own bed, left the house, and took the first train south, where the cause of his devotion was waiting for him.

PART SEVEN

NO ONE IS EVER FORGIVEN
FOR LOSING A WAR

I.

*T*HIS IS A LOVE STORY:

When Jefferson Davis, first and only president of the Confederate States of America, was a lieutenant in the army in the war against the Black Hawk Indians in 1833, he served under General Zachary Taylor, who would later become the twelfth president of the once and future United States. He fell in love with the general's daughter.

Her name was Sarah Knox Taylor, and by all accounts she was beautiful: blue-eyed and captivating, freezing every American man in his tracks. She was hard to please, too, always smirking at the men who tripped over each other to open doors for her and offer her seats as though she were a cripple. Like many women who see the advantages of being treated like a cripple, she was also clever, parrying every fawning compliment with remarks so witty that the recipient usually laughed out loud before noticing that he had been insulted. But the first and only future president of the Confederacy devoted himself to winning her affections, and—with the bewildering and unabating shock of anyone who has ever, while attempting to prove a point, stumbled upon a new world—he succeeded, and married her. His success was unfathomable to him. At night he would sometimes rise and light a lamp just to watch her sleeping: to behold, in awe, the curls of her hair as they rested on the pillow beside her impossibly soft cheeks, to watch how her face and breasts gently rose and fell with each unspeakably delicate breath, marveling at the bounty and beauty of this vast new continent of happiness. Surely it was just a dream, unearned and unreal. Three months after their wedding, at the bayou plantation where they had built the home of their dreams, Sarah died of malaria.

After her funeral, Jefferson Davis abandoned their home and retreated to his brother's plantation, where he locked himself into a single room. He spoke to almost no one for the next eight years. Eight years later, he met and married Varina Howell, the only First Lady of the Confederacy. At eighteen, she was barely more than half his age, and fully prepared for happiness. But while he was on the riverboat that would take him to their wedding in Natchez, Mississippi—as he stood on the deck breathing the wide open river air and noticing that the world had at last become bright and beautiful again—someone tapped him on the shoulder, another passenger who happened to be on the same boat on the same day. It was Zachary Taylor. When his former father-in-law congratulated him on his impending marriage, the world once more came to an end. As Zachary Taylor walked away, Jefferson Davis fell back down into the abyss of those eight dark years. One week later, on his honeymoon, he took his new bride to visit Sarah's grave. He was a man who knew what devotion was—no matter how cruel it might be to those who had to endure the future, and no matter how lost the cause.

THIS IS ALSO a love story:

Judah Benjamin was in love with America. Like Jefferson Davis's, his was a tortured and tormented love, one that left his passion forever unrequited and unfulfilled.

By all accounts, this country he loved was beautiful, more beautiful than any he or his ancestors had seen in centuries: more beautiful than his native St. Croix in the Caribbean, where hurricanes blew half the island to pieces every autumn; more beautiful than England, where his mother had grown up with Finsbury's cold rain and even colder neighbors; more beautiful than Holland, where his grandparents had lived in sagging homes on Amsterdam's man-made landfill; even more beautiful than Spain, where his ancestors had been chased to the sea in the wake of Columbus in 1492. Like all the rest of the country's immigrant suitors, Judah Benjamin would do anything to win his country's love. He tried to attract her, to make up for his lack of conventional beauty with his brilliance, his wits, and his charms. He tried to impress her, becoming an attorney who had mastered the very laws that made her who she was. He tried to marry her, acquiring a patrician American wife, though that failed spectacularly—not through death or even divorce, but abandonment, the most profound depth of indifference. He tried to serve her, taking his seat in the United States Senate, committing himself to her with absolute devotion. In her moment of greatest trial, when she suffered the nature of an internal insurrection, he stood at her side—on the side where he had lived his entire life—forever dedicated, willing to risk absolutely everything for her. But she was always hard to please. So he moved into Jefferson Davis's office, spending fourteen hours a day with the eternally brokenhearted Confederate president as they tried to save whatever could be saved, committing every last ounce of his soul to his beloved, devoting himself to what would become the grand lost cause.

AND THIS TOO is a love story:

Three months after his arrival in Richmond, through the providence of God, Jacob saw Jeannie on Main Street. She was standing just across the street from where he stood, facing an old vendor who was shouting at her over a sack of potatoes she was trying to buy. He nearly fainted.

She looked much thinner than he remembered her, and smaller too—shorter in simpler shoes, her face less full, her curls calmer against her thin face. Her threadbare cloak hung open on her shoulders, though the afternoon was cold, and he could see that she was wearing a plain dark dress that he remembered her wearing many times. But the dress looked shabby now, even from across the street, and in it her figure looked less womanly, her beautiful curves diminished. She had suffered, he could see: she winced in the face of the shouting vendor as though she were still a young girl, her old confidence shriveled. Jacob was captivated, and held his breath.

He almost yelled her name, but in the same instant he thought better of it. He was in the Confederate citadel, and the threat of capture and hanging awaited him on every corner. How could he be sure that she wouldn't turn him in? He watched her for a moment before deciding that he did not care, that he was prepared to risk everything. And so he called.

"Jeannie!" he shouted.

The street was busy, horses and carriages passing back and forth between them. She didn't hear him. He shouted her name again, and his heart quickened as she finally glanced in his direction. He would have waved both arms in the air, if it hadn't taken all he had just to remain balanced on his cane. But she didn't see him, or didn't recognize him, and turned back to the potato vendor. She returned the sack of potatoes to the vendor's cart and quickly walked away.

At that moment he would have given absolutely anything just to run after her, to dart through the traffic on the street and sprint behind her, to capture her at last, to seize her and never let her go. Instead, as she disappeared into the crowd, he sank down to the sidewalk, suddenly struck by the overwhelming force of everything he had lost. He buried his face in his hands, swallowing sobs.

"Don't do that," someone said in his ear. "The ladies will see you."

When he uncovered his good eye and turned around, he saw a man seated on the sidewalk just behind him. He must have been Jacob's age, but a haggard beard like an old man's covered his emaciated face. He was resting awkwardly on the ground, with a battered tin tankard in front of him. Jacob glanced down at him and saw that the man's right leg below his knee was missing.

"Believe me, you don't want the ladies to see you like that," the man said. "I made that mistake myself."

Jacob did not want to listen, but it would have been too painful for him to rise just then and walk away. The man coughed, and continued. "When I enlisted, there was a lady waiting for me at home," the man said. "I wrote to her after I was wounded, and she promised me over and over that she would love me forever no matter what. But when she finally came to see me in the hospital, the whiskey was wearing off, and I was weeping from the pain. She told me that she could never marry a man she had seen cry. Later I found out that she had taken up with another fellow while I was away. But I still think that everything might have been different if she hadn't seen me crying."

The man looked Jacob over in the way only cripples look at each other, free to admire one another's wounds. When he was done, he put his hand on Jacob's shoulder, briefly, and then took it away. "Once the men start crying, then the entire cause is lost," he said.

At that moment, Jacob looked past the man's bearded face and saw a young lady walking down the sidewalk, about to pass them by. It was Jeannie.

This time she looked right at Jacob, without recognizing him. To her, he was just another crippled veteran languishing in the streets. He would have said her name, but he could barely breathe. He watched, every part of his body pulsing with pain, as she bent down and dropped some sort of coin into the bearded man's cup.

"Thank you, miss," the man said. "May the Lord reward you with a long and happy life."

She was very close to Jacob now. Her face was too thin, almost gaunt, but even so he could see how fresh and beautiful she looked, even more so than when he had known her, as if time had not passed for her, but had rather moved in reverse. His wife was a young girl, innocent. She smiled, and in her smile he noticed a disturbing distortion in her features, as if she too had been disfigured. Then she spoke.

"No evil I did," she said, in a clipped and cryptic voice that didn't sound at all like Jacob remembered. "I live on."

As she hurried away, Jacob realized that it wasn't Jeannie at all. It was Rose.

2

*S*ERGEANT RAPPAPORT, YOU UNDERSTAND THE POTENTIAL CON-
sequences of this mission, don't you?"

On the day Jacob arrived in Washington, his old tribunal was in ses-
sion, just as it had been two years before. But things had changed. As Jacob
soon learned, the major had died in the battle at Wilderness. Jacob had
avoided reading the newspapers as much as possible during the past two
years, but Wilderness had been so horrifying that everyone had talked
about it for weeks, even in New York. The rains in the months before the
battle had washed out the soil in the woods before the regiments arrived,
uncovering the decomposing bodies of the men who had died there the
previous year. But the summer had been dry, and when the underbrush
caught fire, the living soldiers, running with their rifles over old and new
corpses, were quickly enveloped in flying curtains of flame that consumed
both the living and the dead. The major's replacement was scarcely older
than Jacob, a young man with an eye patch of his own.

"So you and Judas Benjamin shall at last have an opportunity to meet
again," the general said.

The reference to Judas was so commonplace by now that Jacob hardly
heard it. He was more surprised by how pleased they were to see him.
During the years since they had exiled him westward, everyone had
become increasingly desperate. Jacob may have been maimed, but within
the dwindling pool of potential agents, he at least had experience in the
field and a record of success. As a further cause for wonder, he had even
returned from the dead. The three Christian men at the table looked at
his wounded Hebrew body and saw salvation incarnate.

"Benjamin is their spymaster, or at least one of them. We're quite
aware of that now," the colonel announced.

"The longer you are able to stay with him, the more useful your services would be," the new major said. "Ideally you should remain there indefinitely."

"In your current condition, any emergency escape of the sort you undertook on your last mission would likely be impossible," the general added.

"Consider it in this fashion: we do not expect to see you again until the war ends."

"Unless someone smuggles out a photograph of your body on the gallows."

"You must to be prepared to stay there."

"Surely you are already aware that this sort of life can be mentally exhausting."

"Some agents have reported suffering from neuralgia."

"Consumption."

"Nervous attacks."

"Lunacy."

"Hysteria."

"That's not including the ones who are captured and hanged."

"Fifteen have been hanged, to date."

"It will require a great deal of dedication on your part."

"Unconditional fidelity."

"Absolute devotion."

"Are you prepared for it?"

He was.

If Edwin Booth had the most perfect physical head in America, Judah Benjamin had the most perfect mental one. He was widely regarded as one of the most intelligent men in America, North or South, and he was going to be harder to fool than Edwin Booth. Yet it had been done before. Three years earlier, Benjamin had made the colossal mistake of hiring Timothy Webster, a Union agent, as one of his own Confederate spies. For six months, Webster was the Union secret service's greatest hero. After that, Benjamin noticed his error and Webster went from hero to martyr, hanged in Richmond in 1862. Jacob was aware of this. But he believed that he had a very slight advantage. He knew that on Sunday mornings, all Hebrews let down their guard.

Every American Hebrew, including Jacob, knew the strange freedom of Sunday mornings. At first the streets would be crowded, the peals of church bells crowding the air as horses and carriages crammed the roads, one after another, loaded with families wearing their best clothes and their most serious faces, even the children chastened into little sorrowful adults. These sad children and their sad parents, along with their sad grandparents and sad uncles and aunts, would then all assemble on the steps of the churches, waiting for the doors to be thrown open. Then the owners of these sad faces would shuffle inside to devote the next hour of their lives to the praise of God. For that magical hour of every week, Hebrews in every American city were free to be themselves. On Sunday mornings they took to the empty streets, the empty courtyards, the empty squares, and breathed. Even as a child in New York, Jacob was aware of the paradise of that precious hour. It was the only time when Hebrew children were allowed to be children, released into the wilds of the gardens, streets and fields, talking as loudly as they wanted without their parents warning them to lower their voices, free to argue and rampage without the haunting fear of embarrassing their parents and thereby ruining their prospects for the lives of their dreams. The adults were more demure, but even they would at last raise their voices, amazed by the existence of an entire hour when absolutely nothing was required of them by either God or man, laughing loudly at the children and each other, talking about whatever they wanted in whatever language they wanted, casting their hands wildly through the air as they spoke, delirious with freedom, relieved, for an entire hour, of the everlasting burden of worrying what others would think. For that magical hour each week, America was theirs. And that was the time when Jacob chose to meet Judah Benjamin, Confederate Secretary of State.

BECAUSE IT WAS Sunday morning, Jacob was not surprised when he rang the bell at the Davenport house on West Main Street and saw Benjamin himself open the door. What surprised him was how awful he looked. When Jacob had last seen him, he had had a stylish cuff of a beard just along the edge of his jaw; now the whole of his chin, jowls, and cheeks was scraggly with dark hair, graying in places and thinning grotesquely in others, as though some sort of ailment had created irregular bald patches on his face. His dark eyes were sunken into his shadowed skin, and his complexion was even darker in the layered bags beneath his eyes. Jacob remembered him being short, but now he seemed even smaller than Jacob remembered. He was hunched like an old man, the weight of years pressing down on his low shoulders. He was in his shirtsleeves, though he still wore a dark vest, with a thick watch chain draped across his belly. His broad waist seemed to sag. But everything he had endured showed only in his body, not in his demeanor. His pose was steady as he stood in the doorway, and he peered at Jacob curiously, his expression cheerfully alert, as if he were anticipating some delightful surprise. He had a little piece of cake with him, and he was nibbling on it even as he looked at Jacob. Jacob had read that he was often mocked for his childish sweet tooth, for nibbling at every opportunity on the cakes and candies that always seemed to fill his pockets. The caricatures in the newspapers depicted him as grotesque, stuffing himself while his fellow Confederates starved. It was only many years later that Jacob learned that he suffered from diabetes.

"Good morning, Secretary," Jacob announced, with a slight bow. "My name is Jacob Rappaport. I had the honor of meeting you once several years ago, though I looked a bit better at the time."

Benjamin's dark eyes examined him, but Jacob soon saw that the Secretary was smiling—a warmer smile than Jacob remembered. It was Sunday morning, the hour of refuge from the assumptions of others. In a sense at once superficial and profound, he knew who Jacob was.

"Good morning to you, Mr. Rappaport," he replied, and clasped Jacob's hand in both of his as though they were old friends. He scrutinized Jacob as he grasped his fingers, still smiling, searching for clues before at last giving up. "I do apologize, but I am afraid you must remind me of our acquaintance," he finally said. "Where did we meet?"

Jacob swallowed, prepared. "On Passover in '62, at a seder in the home of Harry Hyams," he said, and added, with great effort, "may his memory be a blessing."

A dark shadow crossed Benjamin's face. For an instant Jacob's throat tightened as he sensed the noose around his neck. But Benjamin's eyes lit up, thrilled. "Ah, yes, you were the young Rebel private, the turncoat from New York!" he cried. Jacob breathed as Benjamin added, "Please, do come in."

He took Jacob's coat himself, hanging it carefully on a clothes tree beside the door as they entered. The house was silent. Jacob followed him down a short corridor and into a small study. The corridor was lined with books, but the study was positively vomiting them. Jacob looked around the room and saw nothing but books, hundreds of volumes in English, Latin, Greek, and French—almost all law books, though here and there a volume of Tennyson or Balzac peeked inauspiciously out from between the larger folios. The shelves were stuffed to bursting, additional volumes crammed into the spaces above the rows of books. If there was a rug on the floor, it had been rendered invisible by neatly organized piles of papers—newspapers, magazines, telegrams, printed documents, and personal letters, all meticulously arranged in enormous stacks, each carefully bundled, as if the papers were regenerating themselves back into trees. The room was a veritable firetrap, and clearly a realm where no lady had ever set foot: as Jacob glanced at the walls and shelves again, he noted that there were no portraits of any family members anywhere, not even a lady's cameo or silhouette. Jacob remembered that Benjamin was theoretically married and even had a daughter, though both wife and daughter lived in France; one of the more gratuitously vicious rumors Jacob had heard was that the daughter wasn't his. Their absence felt oddly irrelevant. Jacob later learned that Benjamin lived with his wife's brother, a dandyish man fifteen years his junior whom he treated as half companion, half ward. There was a pair of upholstered armchairs in front of the exceedingly neat desk, and the small table between the two chairs was occupied by a dish of cake, half-eaten, and a copper tea set, dregs of tea leaves already curling at the bottom of one of the cups. As Jacob glanced at the walls and shelves once more, he noted again that the man seemed to have no commitments in evidence beyond the books and papers that surrounded him, no signs of any more personal cause for devotion. At length Jacob noticed a bronze bust perched on the mantel above the fireplace. The bust was the only human likeness in the room, the closest thing to an image of a beloved. It was of Thomas Jefferson.

"It was tragic, what happened to Harry," Benjamin was saying as he gestured to Jacob to take a seat.

Jacob lowered himself carefully into a chair and nodded as he helped himself to a piece of cake. The cake was dry in his mouth, like the tasteless unleavened confections that Jewish women serve on Passover. His stomach swayed, black bile churning his gut. "It was terrible," he agreed.

"And also tragic in the literary sense," Benjamin said, sitting down across from him. "That runaway slave had a sickening sense of humor, to do that at the seder. One must give him credit for timing and wit." Jacob focused his attention on the cake, though he was puzzled. Benjamin's attachment to his dead cousin seemed minimal at best. "Of course, we ourselves are descendants of runaway slaves," Benjamin added, "and runaway slaves always ought to look over their shoulders. Harry's mistake was that he stopped looking."

Jacob glanced at Benjamin, feeling his heart pound as Benjamin poured him a cup of tea. He was surprised by how intimate it felt to have this familiar little man hovering over him, trying his best to make him feel at home. For a bizarre instant, as Jacob brought the tea to his lips, he did.

"So what brings you here?" Benjamin asked at last. He sat back, comfortable and expectant.

Jacob steeled himself before he spoke. "I've come with a message from New York," he announced, and withdrew the envelope from his pocket. "From Edwin Booth."

"Hmph," Benjamin grunted. "Edwin Booth." His tone imparted just the slightest touch of disgust. He still maintained his Sunday morning ease, taking the envelope from Jacob with delicate fingers, as if insulted that its contents might disturb the magic of the hour. Jacob watched as Benjamin inspected the seal and reached over to his desk for a letter opener, with which he dissected the envelope with a single graceful slice. He removed the note and took in its contents almost instantaneously, absorbing its few lines in a single glance. Benjamin looked back at him, and Jacob could see how he was weighing him in the balance of his mind.

"As you can see, I too have been somewhat incapacitated since we last saw each other, while serving in the line of duty," Jacob said.

Benjamin blushed, his face reflecting the shame of a man who had taken on God's task of determining who would live and who would die. His patchy beard hid it well, but not well enough. "So I surmised," he said. "We are eternally grateful for your service."

"I appreciate your gratitude," Jacob replied, and glanced down in a display of feigned humility before staring Benjamin in the eye. Successful lying requires full eye contact, with however many eyes one is privileged to own. Jacob had learned that from his wife. "I was able to spend much of my convalescence at my parents' home in New York, and for a time I was in a position to assist Mr. Booth in disbursing the Toronto funds, in connection with my work at my family's firm," he said, without hesitation. "Mr. Booth asked me to come here in person on his behalf, to ensure that you would trust me as his substitute. I apologize that so much time has passed since the date of his letter. I could not find safe passage through the lines, and had to come on a blockade runner via Bermuda." The real reason for the delay, of course, was that the command had insisted on retraining him; the code system had evolved considerably since the officers had last engaged his services, as had other protocols. He had also had to master everything he could about the resources available in Richmond, paltry though they were: which rooming houses wouldn't ask him questions; which segments of society to avoid at all costs; which neighborhoods were poor or rich or black or white; which bakery he would use to send his messages back over the lines. He held his breath and prayed that Benjamin would believe him.

"I see," Benjamin said. "Well, we have all come to expect that sort of delay." Benjamin examined him, again inspecting his eye patch and his scars, but Jacob could detect no suspicion in his glance. He was grateful that Benjamin didn't seem interested in the details of how he had been injured, or more importantly, how he had returned to New York thereafter; he had stories prepared to explain it all, but it was exhausting to keep track of them. Fortunately Benjamin had other things on his mind. He glanced at the note again before looking back at Jacob's disfigured face. "What's become of dear Edwin, then?" he asked. "He doesn't specify."

Lying with a purpose had become second nature to Jacob. What he was still learning to enjoy, however, was his newfound talent for lying purely for his own amusement. "The matter is a bit delicate, I'm afraid," he replied, his face somber. "Most men prefer not to advertise it when they've contracted syphilis."

"Oh dear," Benjamin sighed. Jacob stifled a smile. "Well, I must admit that I never did find him terribly reliable for our purposes," he said. "It seemed to me that he cared rather more for his brother than he did for us." Benjamin's perceptiveness was more than a rumor, Jacob noted. He would have to be careful, if he valued his life. He watched as Benjamin sipped his tea. "It's just as well, though," Benjamin added. "We are halting funds to Toronto at the moment, so as to concentrate resources on

Maryland and the signal corps line. The Canadian operations have been a bit cursed, it seems. The great challenge now is to convince a few more of those in Canada to return, so that we can use their services in Maryland and in the Northern Neck."

"Hm," Jacob said. On a Sunday morning between him and Benjamin, the air was redolent with trust, and ripe with low-hanging assumptions. Jacob tried to touch one, to see if he could. "Edwin did mention the Maryland plan. To him the arrangements appeared overly compromising, though perhaps that was merely due to his lack of commitment to the cause."

He was stretching, he knew, reaching far beyond his grasp. But luck was on his side, this time at least. Benjamin's eyes narrowed. At first Jacob's throat clenched, but soon he saw that Benjamin's anger was directed not at him, but at Edwin Booth. "In that case, let me be absolutely clear, to ensure that everyone understands this," Benjamin said, his voice firm. "This is not an assassination plot."

Jacob pursed his lips, fighting the impulse to gape. Benjamin's irritation, layered over the free air of Sunday morning, rendered the space between them electric. The Secretary buzzed like a fly trapped in a kerosene lamp. "In fact, if even one of them were to die, then the entire objective would be lost," he added.

One of them? One of whom? Benjamin had already settled back in his chair, at once aware of his indiscretion. He took another piece of cake and chewed it quickly, swallowing with barely disguised regret. Jacob worked hard to affect only the mildest of interest as he stirred his tea, trying to think of a way to change the subject. Benjamin changed it first, or nearly did.

"The problem at the moment is that too much of the capital is with our agents in Canada," he said. "We need some of these agents to return, but the funds have already been disbursed. There is some allotment to draw them back here, but there is very little room for waste, and it isn't clear to me how to use what we have most effectively. Despite the popular prejudice, I haven't much of a mind for finances."

Jacob struggled to look at him calmly. "Your talents in other areas are surely more than sufficient to compensate," he said.

"Well, I am more a man of letters than a man of numbers," Benjamin replied.

Jacob looked pointedly at the stacks of books and papers around the room. "One never would have guessed," he grinned.

Benjamin smiled, though he seemed barely to have heard him. He was watching Jacob, weighing his own thoughts. Then, suddenly, he leaned toward Jacob, planting his hands on his knees. "Rappaport, you were the bookkeeping wizard, weren't you? Harry mentioned that to me. Weren't you the one working in your father's import-export firm in Madison Square?"

"I was," Jacob replied, nervous. How had Benjamin remembered that?

"Harry said that your father had relied on you completely since you were sixteen years old," Benjamin said. "He couldn't believe that your father would have let you leave New York, given how valuable you were to him. He speculated that you must have run away."

Jacob's head ached, thinking of his father. His father had never told him how much he needed him. "I did run off, it's true," Jacob said. "And the firm did lose half its value while I was gone." Of course, the firm's losses had far more to do with the ostensible country Benjamin served than with Jacob's absence. But Jacob allowed the assumptions to dangle, ready for the taking.

Benjamin nodded, captivated, and took one. "So you are a sort of magician with funds, then," he said. "Brilliant with numbers."

Jacob thought of his father, and winced. "People have told me that," he replied.

Benjamin nodded again, and took a bite of his cake. As Benjamin chewed, Jacob could see him thinking, though he could not imagine what was on his mind. Benjamin swallowed, and spoke. "Tell me, Rappaport," he said. "From a purely financial perspective, how would you motivate these agents to return, without an exorbitant expenditure of capital, when most of them believe that they have already been paid in full? They are all quite committed, of course; nobody is doing this to become rich. But one needs to defray their expenses, at the least, and that is no small matter. As you can imagine, we hardly have unlimited resources at our disposal. I have been thinking this through for quite some time, but it seems to me that once one has paid someone out, there isn't really any going back."

"Not necessarily," Jacob told him. "One just has to offer future incentives on a sliding scale over time."

Benjamin leaned forward. "What do you mean?"

"I mean a schedule of payments, with choices to encourage loyalty," Jacob said, the space behind his missing eye aching. "First one offers a small sum, but with perhaps only fifteen percent of the payment available immediately, and arranged such that the person has to return to the desired location in order to draw it in liquid. Then one offers the recipient a choice as to how to collect the remaining eighty-five percent. First, he might receive it in a lump sum on a predetermined date. Or, as a second option, he might receive it in the form of installments to be collected at multiple predetermined dates further in the future—but the installments are paid out with compounded interest and, if necessary, with additional incentives attached to each payment at the later dates. Now if the initial cash outlay presents a hardship, one might be tempted to offer only the installment plan, but I believe that would be a mistake. One needs to offer a choice, so that the recipient believes himself to be personally invested in his own compensation. That makes a much larger difference than one might expect." Jacob's head throbbed as he continued. "In my experience, most men are rather shortsighted and prefer to be paid as soon as possible, even if it means being paid less. But the presentation of a choice creates an advantage for those making the payments, because it provides a sorting mechanism. The recipients who choose the more immediate payment have already proven that a continuing relationship is not their real priority. And those who choose the installment plan are precisely the sort of men one actually wishes to retain. The interest is money well spent to find those who are truly dedicated."

This was almost childishly simple, nothing that anyone who had ever engaged in the most rudimentary sort of business wouldn't know. But Benjamin had been immersed in quite a different world, with far more urgent problems, and at this point there was apparently little room available in his intellect to devote to this sort of minutiae. He drew his dark eyebrows together. "I see," he said, rubbing at his beard. "Rappaport, are you expected back in New York?"

Jacob saw his opportunity, and seized it. "Not particularly," he said. "My parents have quite given up on expecting me, I'm sorry to say. They—

they did not approve of my late wife, and even now there is considerable discord between us." The lies were becoming easier to tell, and harder to distinguish from the truth, even for Jacob himself. "I had intended to return only as Edwin's replacement."

"Well, that will no longer be necessary," Benjamin said. He clearly had no interest in Jacob's alleged personal troubles, and for that Jacob was grateful. Benjamin rubbed at his beard again, and Jacob wondered whether this sort of rubbing was precisely what had thinned it: a physical worrying, anxiety deflected from his demeanor onto his cheeks. "You would be far more useful to us in handling disbursements from here," Benjamin said. "Tell me honestly: would that be of interest to you? You would receive a commission for your services, of course."

This seemed almost too easy. Surely this was how Timothy Webster had felt after receiving an offer just as promising, unable to conceive of his own success. But he was hanged six months later. Was it possible that Benjamin was as gullible as he seemed? Or perhaps Jacob was the gullible one. But he remembered his promise to Philip, and understood how limited his options were. He had to risk everything.

"It would be a privilege to serve you, and the cause," he said.

Benjamin's bearded face parted into an enormous grin as he shook Jacob's hand. "Rappaport, I cannot even express to you how useful your services would be. These disbursements have generally been my sole responsibility, but I trust that you would be able to execute them with requisite discretion."

Jacob nodded, trying his best to smile. "I would."

"And I would be forever grateful for your assistance. I have far too many other matters occupying me, and I've already taken on too much. Mr. Davis is unavailable all too frequently, I'm sorry to say. He suffers from neuralgia, and lately he has had bouts where he has been incapacitated for days. I have had to extend myself quite beyond reasonable limits to compensate for his absences." This was new information to Jacob. He wondered how many people in Washington were aware of it. "The new plan's odds of success may not be terribly high, but the reward would be priceless. It is calculated to end the war, on favorable terms."

This was almost inconceivable. What sort of plan? He knew Benjamin would tell him nothing further, at least not yet. But he couldn't help prodding him. "I must say that the common perception from New York is that our prospects are rather bleak," he said.

Benjamin pressed his palms against his knees, his face animated with sudden energy. "The naysayers are fond of telling me that we are doomed. But Mr. Davis and I believe that if we were as doomed as they claim, then we would surely have met our demise long ago. Think of the resources at the Union's disposal. The fact that our country still exists at all ought to boggle the mind. They should have beaten us in '61, and easily at that. They haven't the slightest notion of what we are capable of enduring."

This hardly seemed optimistic to Jacob. He was reminded of the witticism that his father claimed his grandfather had coined during a string of anti-Semitic riots he had survived in the German states: "God forbid that this should last as long as we are capable of enduring it."

Benjamin took another bite of cake, swallowing before he continued. "Our prospects may appear a bit grim at this point, but we are by no means exhausted. Many more strategies are possible, most of which I cannot share with you. Be assured that the current plan is merely one of many. I have also been working on an emancipation proclamation."

Jacob gagged on a piece of cake, which he only succeeded in dislodging from his gullet after an embarrassingly long series of coughs. Benjamin, ever the master of equanimity, dabbed at his mouth and glanced away.

"Pardon?" Jacob asked.

"It's a very innovative plan," Benjamin said cheerfully. "The idea is that we shall offer freedom to any slave who agrees to join the army."

Surely this was some sort of joke. Jacob smiled, waiting for Benjamin to laugh.

"The Yankees appear to have endless manpower," Benjamin said, launching into a speech. "But the truth is that whenever we kill too many of them, they simply import more Irishmen to send down into the trenches. They actually pay the Irish five hundred dollars a head for the privilege of dying. Those are the slaves the Union has bought for itself." He drummed his stubby fingers once on the arm of his chair. "I've tried to lure the Irish here the same way, but Britain has not been particularly cooperative. It's quite a complicated situation, you see." He smiled at Jacob, his eternally inappropriate smile, and continued. "We appear to suffer from a shortage of means, but it is a false shortage. We simply haven't been using all of the means at our disposal. This emancipation plan ought to increase our ranks by fifteen percent or more."

The absurdity of this suggestion caught Jacob off guard. He thought of the slave woman who murdered Jeannie's mother, and of Caleb Johnson and his laundry-hanging wife in General Longstreet's headquarters, and of the entire Legal League, and marveled. The idea was so idiotic that only a genius could have thought of it.

"You want to arm the slaves," Jacob said carefully.

"Well, they wouldn't be slaves anymore, you understand," Benjamin retorted. "They would simply be free Rebels." The man was a lawyer through and through.

"Does this—does this idea have any support?"

"The men in the trenches are practically begging us for it," he replied. This did not impress Jacob; it seemed clear to him that men in the trenches would beg for just about anything that might delay their inevitable deaths. But Benjamin was undeterred. "Mr. Davis agrees with me in theory, but not in his heart. It's going to be a hard battle to convince the Congress that I'm right."

Jacob tried his best to summon his acting skills, but he was at a loss. Wasn't this, at the end of all the arguments, the reason everyone had gone to war? If the Rebels were to free the slaves themselves, then what cause had there been for Jacob murdering his uncle, or for Jacob's crippling, or for the deaths of hundreds of thousands on either side? Was any of it necessary? Later Jacob would be able to think of many answers, many explanations, many comforts to aid him through the wreckage left behind. But now he could think of only one cause, the smallest and most private. Both Jacob and Benjamin were preoccupied, haunted by the desperation of their loves.

"There are few people to whom I can say this frankly, Rappaport, but perhaps you are one of them," Benjamin said, his hands on his knees. "I shall say it directly: These men are fools. They would honestly prefer to lose the entire war, as long as they can lose 'honorably.' Their idea of 'honor' is absurd, but they won't hear it. They would rather keep their slaves, maintain the principle—even though, if they lose this war, they will become slaves themselves. But Rappaport, you understand this. You may be young, you may have been born in America, but you are still a Hebrew. You know what it means to lose."

Benjamin ate the last remaining bite of cake. "All Hebrews know that there is nothing honorable about subjugation and defeat," he said. "History does not care whether one had the foresight to lose with style. No one is ever forgiven for losing a war."

They sat for a moment in silence, each contemplating the other, the weight of thousands of years of losses burdening the air between them. Then the room reverberated as the deafening peals of church bells flowed through the walls, the happy triumphant music of those accustomed to victory. The magical hour was up.

Benjamin rose from his seat. "I am sorry to end our conversation, but I am expected at the Davises' for Sunday dinner," he said, with unmistakable pride. "I shall see you in my office tomorrow morning at nine. It's the building just across from the Capitol. First floor, the last door on the left. Thank you, Rappaport."

"And thank you, Secretary," Jacob said.

He left Benjamin's home in a daze, with the sound of church bells around the city resonating through his damaged head, wondering whether he would win.

3.

BENJAMIN'S OFFICE, IN A LARGE STONE GOVERNMENT BUILDING on Capitol Square, was even more neatly organized than the study in his home, and even more impersonal. Two walls of the room were occupied by bookshelves, full of bound volumes and bundled papers. The mantel above the fireplace held another bronze bust, this time of George Washington. The last wall, behind his desk, was occupied by a large window looking out onto Capitol Square. Beside the window hung a floor-to-ceiling map of the Confederacy, with thousands of blue and gray painted pins stuck into it. Jacob had never before seen the war laid out in such a large format, and it was impossible not to notice how unforgiving the Northern stranglehold had become: blue pins ran along all the coasts and half the rivers, up and down the Mississippi and the Atlantic and the Potomac and the Gulf, and now more blue pins had encroached inland, a long deadly parade of them all across the country, straight through Georgia and now progressing up into South Carolina. The entire South dangled over Benjamin's desk like a tortured voodoo doll, pricked by blue pins everywhere it bled. This bleak image hovered just over his shoulder as he sat at his impeccable desk, which had nothing on it but a single sheet of paper. Benjamin, as always, was smiling.

"I am quite grateful to have you here, Rappaport," he said. "As you must be aware, the age for impressments has been lowered to seventeen and raised to sixty-five. It is almost impossible to find men to fulfill even the most basic duties in the office, let alone men of competence. We are forced to make do with old men and boys, or the occasional wounded soldier, most of whom are considerably less literate than you. I do have a clerk of my own, but he is quite ill this week. Thus I apologize if some purely clerical work is involved in the tasks I assign to you today."

Jacob nodded as his remaining eye burned. "No apologies are necessary," he announced, trying to keep his voice cheerful, nonchalant.

"You may use the clerk's room immediately to the left of this one. There is an empty desk there for you," Benjamin said. "But first let me give you everything you will need." He stood and turned to his left, scanning the shelves. "Here are the account books with records of the available funds for this project," he told him, pulling two ledger books off a shelf along the wall. "And here are the names of the six agents whom we would like to engage at present," he said. He lifted the single page on his desk, and handed it to Jacob. Jacob took it in his free hand as he leaned on his cane. It couldn't possibly be this simple, could it? Benjamin turned to another shelf and removed a large bundle of papers. "This file has their current addresses and other information that the courier will require for each of them in order to deliver the funds. Some are still in Canada, but some are already in Maryland and Washington. They move quite frequently, as you can imagine, and unfortunately I haven't had time to sort out their current addresses on my own, but I assure you that they are all here in these papers. You must look through them yourself to ascertain each person's whereabouts, I'm afraid."

"I would be pleased to do so," Jacob said. He meant it. It was all he could do to stop himself from drooling.

"Your first task shall be to devise the payment schedule as you proposed to me, based on the finances recorded in these books. You will see in the records that we have some credit pending from private sources in Europe, so you will have to calibrate at least some of the payments based on when the funds become available to us here. And keep in mind that there will be perhaps two score more agents whose services we may need to engage in the future." Two score? "So do be certain to reserve resources accordingly." Jacob eyed the documents and ledger books in his arms. How many lives could be saved by the briefest glance at the contents of those papers, with his single eye?

"Once you have devised the payment schedule, I would like you to draw up a letter for each agent describing the payment options, along with indications of where he will be able to draw future payments in liquid. You may sign the letters yourself, on my behalf. There is also information in these papers about which banks and other locations can be used for deposits. Those currently in Canada will draw from the Washington banks when they arrive. For those already in Maryland, you can correlate the deposit points to their addresses, based on these maps," he said, and removed some rolled-up maps from a drawer before turning back to Jacob, the little smile still lingering on his lips. "At five o'clock, the courier will come by for the gold. The gold is in this safe."

Benjamin opened a wooden cabinet below the window to reveal a thick iron strongbox, padlocked shut. Jacob knew, somewhere deep in his addled brain, that it was impossible that Benjamin was doing this, that something must be horribly wrong. But he was enraptured, hypnotized. Without intending to, he returned Benjamin's smile.

"I shall only be here in my office today at intervals, I'm afraid," Benjamin said. "I must meet with Mr. Davis upstairs, and we must not be disturbed. Should I be absent when the courier arrives, I shall entrust the key to the safe beneath the bosom of our founding father," he said, pointing to the bust on the mantel. Jacob nodded, his head bobbling as though he were drunk. "I've sent the courier a note to expect you, in the event that I am otherwise engaged. I trust that you will handle this additional responsibility with equal discretion."

"Of—of course," Jacob stammered. It occurred to him that someone else might have immediately begun planning a robbery. But now he had just one reason for living, and that reason might be in this city somewhere, if he could stay long enough to find her. The only way he could possibly hope to stay was to do exactly what Judah Benjamin told him to do. Benjamin kept smiling at him as he pressed the cabinet closed.

"The courier's name is Little Johnny. He should receive fifteen dollars gold for his services. Give him his fee along with the letters and the gold for each agent, and send him on his way. For today, that ought to be all. Is everything clear?"

"Yes," Jacob replied.

"Good, then. Here is your desk."

He took Jacob by the elbow, steering him out of his impeccable office and into a rather ramshackle clerk's room down the corridor. The room consisted of two bare, scratched desks with nothing but inkwells and empty ledger books on them, and many bundles of documents stacked on shelves around the room. Benjamin placed the books and bundled papers on the desk, then turned back to Jacob. "Thank you for all of your assistance, Rappaport. I greatly appreciate it," he said. "And now I must be off to Mr. Davis upstairs. If I do not see you earlier, I shall stop by before the end of the day. Until then." And with that, he patted Jacob's shoulder as if Jacob were his young son, ambled delicately around Jacob's crippled body, and hurried out the door.

Alone at last, Jacob breathed, dropping down into the chair of the closer desk. The officers were right; he was exhausted, and not merely from standing for so long as Benjamin delivered his instructions. His heart was pounding, a cloud of anxiety hovering above his head. But now some of his anxiety took the form of excitement, a terrifying thrill at what he held in his hands. Surely it couldn't be this simple. Or could it?

He touched the papers on the desk. First he examined the handwritten list of names. These, he knew, he had to report immediately, whoever they might be. He was too frightened to write them down, aware that Benjamin might return unannounced at any moment. Instead he committed them to memory, reading them again and again: *Sgt. Thomas Harney, Rev. Kensey Stewart, Chaplain Thomas Conrad, Mr. David Herold, Mr. Lewis Powell, Mr. T. F. Macduff*. None of these names meant anything to him.

Then he untied the bundle of papers that Benjamin had given him and began to look through it. It was a large packet stuffed with hundreds of pages' worth of documents. He could see why Benjamin hadn't bothered to find the agents' addresses himself. If they were indeed buried in this packet of papers, it was going to take a great deal of time to find them. The documents inside were assorted: a group of messages from Canada, a list of banks in Maryland, a topographic map of a hilly area that Jacob couldn't identify, an unlabeled photograph of an old man. Many of the papers were receipts for laughably small shipments of quinine, which was apparently being smuggled into the Confederacy from Canada. The thought of it unexpectedly moved Jacob, a swell of sympathy rising in his chest for those poor boys whose suffering could easily be cured but for the stubbornness of others. As for the letters in the file, they were mostly requests for money, some for astonishingly large sums, and written in language that suggested the correspondents' confidence in receiving them—though perhaps that was merely a symptom of the quintessential Southern illness, delusional optimism. The messages that didn't deal with money were maddeningly unrevealing: "Secretary: Dr. Blackburn is in place in New York with materials from Bermuda," or "Secretary: A farmhouse has been secured in Dent's Meadow, with assist. of Rev. Stewart," or "Secretary: I have arrived in Washington, and have placed a classified advertisement in the *Washington Daily Chronicle* informing J. Wilkes of same." Many times he resisted the temptation to copy anything down. Instead he read each page several times as he worked for his two masters, memorizing what he could for the command, and recording addresses and bank information for each of the names on the list for Benjamin. It took hours. But as he reached the end of the packet for the sixth time, he looked down at the list of addresses he had compiled and could no longer deny what had become obvious. No matter how many times he read through the documents, he could not find a single mention of a Mr. T. F. Macduff.

The fireplace across from his desk provided inadequate heat in the winter chill, yet he was sweating. He flipped through the papers one more time, but there was no question that the name hadn't been there. Was it a mistake? If so, whose? He considered his options. If he went to Benjamin to inquire about it and he had simply missed the name somehow, then he would be dismissed as incompetent. But if the name truly wasn't there— and as he turned the pages again, it seemed clear that this was the case— then it would be incompetent not to inquire. He had to ask. Biting his lip, he rose from his seat and limped down the hall to Benjamin's office.

Benjamin wasn't there. Jacob waited for a time, but Benjamin did not return. Once more Jacob considered his choices. Was it worth going upstairs, to interrupt his meeting with Davis? Fascinating though that would be, it was surely a poor gambit for one trying to prove himself as an able assistant. He decided that he would continue checking for Benjamin, and in the meantime take care of the mindless task of putting together the payment plan.

But it was far from mindless. As Jacob discovered to his great dismay upon opening the ledger books, the finances were vastly more complicated than he had anticipated. Benjamin may not have been a man of numbers, but one would have to be a man of advanced calculus to extricate any sense from the tangle of digits knotted in the ledgers. Jacob perused the figures, probing the barely decipherable mess of gold specie, tobacco reserves, promissory notes, unsold cotton bales warehoused in an apparently endless wait for higher prices, a complicated series of loans from the house of Baron Erlanger in Paris (a bank he knew from his work at his father's firm), credit, more credit, even more credit—and debt, debt, debt. It would take days to translate it all into an even slightly more realistic sense of what was actually there. But a cursory glance suggested that the prognosis was indeed bleak. He found it staggering that Baron Erlanger had been foolish enough to risk his own capital on an enterprise that appeared, to Jacob at least, to show all the signs of financial disaster. He later learned that Baron Erlanger was married to the Confederate ambassador's daughter.

Jacob barely had time to think. Devising even a basic payment plan took the remainder of the afternoon. Over several hours, he made three more trips down the hall to Benjamin's office, each one a physical and mental agony. Each time Benjamin's office was empty. Jacob set aside the problem of the missing agent and composed the letters quickly, trying his best to sound as much like Benjamin as possible. He had just finished the fifth one when someone knocked on the open door.

Jacob looked up to see a lanky man his age loitering in the doorway, a dark stylish mustache bridging the narrows of his face. "Pardon me, sir," the man said, with an adolescent swagger. "Is the Secretary here?"

Jacob swallowed. "No, I'm afraid he isn't available at the moment," he replied. "May I be of assistance?"

The man smiled. "You must be the new fellow. Rappaport, was it?"

Jacob smiled back, surprised by how pleased he was that the man didn't flinch at his wounds. It was as though he had found a friend. "Yes, it was. And is."

"Pleased to meet you. I'm Little Johnny."

Jacob stifled a laugh. Little Johnny was over six feet tall. He had to take off his hat in order to fit through the low door to the room. Once he entered, Jacob could see that his height was matched by his slimness, as though a man of Judah Benjamin's build had been grasped at both ends and stretched. He had long fingers, deep-set brown eyes, and a chest so narrow that it was almost indented beneath his vest. Jacob imagined him thirty years older, and could picture no one but Abraham Lincoln.

"So where are the goods?" Little Johnny asked. His pronunciation was almost comically distinct, but his diction was slightly vulgar, like a man with little education and much talent for mimicry. "Show me what you've got."

"Here," Jacob said, fanning out the unsealed letters on the desk. "These are the messages for each of the agents on the list I was given, with addresses indicated," he told him, passing him the envelopes. "We shall have to draw the payments from the safe. The Secretary left me the key."

"Bully for us," Little Johnny said, as though Jacob had just offered him a free tankard of beer. His grin reminded Jacob of the men in the camp when he had first enlisted—of how he and his fellow soldiers would speak to each other when the officers weren't present, finally free to reveal to one another that they were nothing more than boys. Little Johnny rubbed his hands together. "Let's get that gold."

But Jacob was no longer a boy. "Before we do, I must ask you something," he said. Little Johnny looked at him with deep suspicion as he turned the list around on the desk. "The Secretary requested that I include a message and payment for this gentleman," Jacob told him, pointing to the final name on the list. "But I couldn't seem to find his address."

Little Johnny looked at the name, and shrugged. "Can't say I've heard of the fellow," he said, with casual cheer. "What else have you got on him?"

"Nothing, I'm afraid," Jacob said. "Only the name."

"Well, a name isn't worth much, now, is it," Little Johnny replied. It wasn't a question. His cheerful tone had dissipated; there was something sinister in his voice.

"Nothing is worth more than a good name," Jacob parried, attempting a joke. Little Johnny grimaced at him. Jacob retreated. "Might there be some way for you to find him?" he asked.

Suddenly Little Johnny flared with temper, slamming his fists onto Jacob's desk before throwing his arms in the air, his eyes burning with fury. "What am I expected to do, knock on the door of every farmhouse between here and Washington, just to see who will turn me in first? Do you have any idea of just how impossible my work already is?" His face turned purple, making Jacob shrink into his seat as he raged. "I go out before dawn to pay off some drunken boatman to break the godforsaken ice on the godforsaken river for me; I get shot at by Yankee gunboats; I pass myself off as a country doctor and have to look down sick old men's throats just to get into their houses; I dress up as a French ambassador until someone notices that I don't speak a word of French; I pose as a preacher and walk around quoting the Gospels until some farmer's wife hears me quote something wrong and runs after me with a shotgun; I barely make it to my mother's boarding house alive—and despite all that, *despite* all that, I have never missed a single delivery, never lost a single word of a message or a single ingot of gold. But that isn't enough for you, is it? It's never enough! Now I need to find some bloody Scotsman's *address*, somewhere behind enemy lines, simply because you can't be bothered to dig it up yourself? Am I expected to get myself hanged just because you can't find something in your goddamned *papers?* Forgive me, but I thought I was doing this for my country. I didn't know that I was risking my backside merely for a bunch of sniveling, condescending, conniving little—"

Jacob cut him off. "Just pay these five agents, then, please," he told him.

"How very gracious of you," Little Johnny replied, his voice a parody of haughtiness. Jacob watched Little Johnny's face return to its original color, and felt sweat beading on his own temples. The courier was one of those secretly volatile men, Jacob saw—the sort who seem like models of propriety and discretion just up until they burst. William Williams the Third had been like that too. So had Edwin Booth. Was there a way to provoke him again?

Little Johnny watched with utter disdain as Jacob struggled to his feet. "Please come with me to the Secretary's office," Jacob said. "The Secretary gave me the authority to open the safe."

The courier sniffed. Provocation was unnecessary, Jacob saw: Little Johnny resumed his tirade with gleeful resentment, loping and lambasting beside him as he limped down the corridor. "He gave *you* the authority to open the safe," he sneered. "And all he gave *me* the authority to do was to risk my goddamned hide, to dress up like a circus clown or a goddamned French mime, to show up half-dead on my mother's doorstep in Washington, to leave a trail of cash like breadcrumbs all the way through Maryland, to run from the Yankees with my tail between my legs every time someone notices that I'm not a goddamned French mime—"

Jacob entered Benjamin's office for the fifth time that afternoon. Benjamin wasn't in. Dusk had already fallen outside; Jacob took a match from his own pocket and lit the room's lamps in the fading twilight from the window. He made his way to the mantel and tipped back the bust of

George Washington. A little brass key was lodged beneath its base. Jacob blushed as he returned the former president to his regal pose, wincing under his honorable eyes while Little Johnny continued to babble. His hands were sweating as he opened the safe. He half expected to find it empty. Instead he was temporarily blinded, his good eye blinking at the tall columns of coins, carefully arranged and stamped with their denominations. He held his breath and began counting, reminding himself of the cause.

Little Johnny was still rambling. "No, all *I* have the authority to do is to make sure all of these goons get paid, to measure the currents in the goddamned river myself as though I'm some kind of goddamned ancient mariner, to find every godforsaken barn within ninety miles where someone could be hogtied with no one noticing, to figure out how in hell to hide a hostage in the bottom of a goddamned canoe—"

A hostage?

"—and *I'm* the one who needs to ask *you* for the key to the safe!"

Jacob had lost count of the coins. He took several piles of them in various denominations and placed them on Benjamin's desk before sinking into Benjamin's chair. As he crouched down beneath Little Johnny's gaze, he was suddenly aware of the picture he made: he was reduced to a living version of the ancient caricature, a hideous man counting out gold. "These are for the agents, and this is for you," he said, grimacing as he separated out fifteen dollars from the pile and added it to the columns he had made for the five agents on the list.

Little Johnny swept his hand across the desk, dumping the coins into his satchel in a huff. "I suppose I'm meant to kneel down before you in endless gratitude," he sneered.

The courier was playing a part, too; everyone was. "That won't be necessary," Jacob said. "Just sign a receipt for the Secretary, please."

Little Johnny snorted, taking a piece of paper from a shelf and helping himself to the pen in the inkwell. Jacob watched as the courier scratched out a few words, printing them in the childlike hand of someone for whom schooling was a very minor part of youth: *I got the gold and left. John Surratt.*

Without saying goodbye, he did exactly that. Jacob quickly locked up the safe and put away the key. He had just lowered himself again into the large chair behind Benjamin's desk when a knock on the open door startled him. It was Benjamin. He began to struggle to his feet, but Benjamin quickly waved at him to sit down.

"I'm so sorry not to have come by earlier," Benjamin said, the perpetual smile still on his lips. "I trust you were able to complete your tasks."

Jacob felt his scars throbbing. "Yes. I—I hope you will forgive me for taking your seat momentarily. It is difficult for me to remain standing for long." Benjamin nodded, indifferent. "The courier just departed with the gold a moment ago," Jacob added. "In fact, you might even still see him yourself if you hurry to the door."

Benjamin pursed his lips, rubbing at his beard. "That ought to be unnecessary," he announced. "Assuming everything went as expected, of course."

Jacob breathed as he steadied himself, fighting hard to keep the unease out of his voice. "In fact, there was one difficulty," he replied.

"What was that?" Benjamin asked. He seemed genuinely curious, rather than critical—as if he, rather than Jacob, were the young apprentice trying to determine the facts.

"There was a name on the list that I couldn't locate," Jacob said. He leaned over the desk, looking at the names again before placing his finger under the last one. "This gentleman, Mr. Macduff. There was no information about him in any of the files you provided. I assure you that I was quite thorough, and I was still unable to find him."

"Hm," Benjamin said. The half-smile lingered on his lips, making Jacob even more uneasy. "So did you give the funds for Mr. Macduff to the courier?"

For a moment Jacob considered lying. Perhaps it had been a mistake not to send the money along? But surely there was a way that he could cast his failure as prudence. "No, I did not," he said. "The courier didn't know any more about the gentleman, and it seemed unwise to me to disburse further funds without confirmation of an accurate address," he continued and ingratiated himself. "I had been intending to speak with you about it, but I visited your office several times in the hopes of finding you, and never succeeded. And I did not think it important enough to merit interrupting your work with Mr. Davis, though perhaps I misjudged on that point. I apologize if I was insufficiently vigilant."

"Hm," Benjamin replied, his voice utterly blank.

It was becoming hard for Jacob to control his unease. He wiped his remaining eye. Benjamin placed his hands on the desk, and leaned forward. Jacob was caught between Benjamin's elbows, the paper framed between the Secretary's thick hands.

"Rappaport, I must say that your difficulty in locating Mr. Macduff does not surprise me," he said.

His words terrified Jacob. Jacob breathed in, and for an instant he felt his entire soul being sucked out of his body, drawn into the poisoned air between them. Benjamin added, with a smile, "Because the poor gentleman doesn't exist."

"He—he doesn't exist?"

"Not outside of Shakespeare's Scottish play," Benjamin said, still grinning. "You might recall that in Shakespeare's version, the murderer is warned to beware of him."

Jacob's scars tingled along his cheek. Benjamin stood up straight, still looking at Jacob. "Another man might have adjusted the account books to reflect Mr. Macduff's payment, particularly during my anticipated absence, and helped himself to the gold," Benjamin said. "Surely for the unscrupulous, that would have been the obvious course." He paused, and finally leaned down on the desk again. "There are two possible explanations for your failure to do so. Either you are not as bright as I was led to believe, or you are truly devoted to the cause."

There were, of course, several more explanations beyond these two, though if Benjamin were aware of them, he chose not to share. Jacob's head throbbed. "I should hope to claim the latter, Secretary," he replied.

Benjamin smiled—the same perpetual smile, the mask. "That remains to be seen," he said. Jacob swallowed, frightened. He had become Benjamin's captive. "I would like you to be here every morning at nine o'clock. As you have surely noticed today, our finances would benefit from your organizational skills. Tomorrow you may proceed with sorting through the accounts."

"Gladly, sir," Jacob murmured.

"Until tomorrow, then," Benjamin said.

"Thank you, sir," Jacob replied, and struggled to his feet. "I wish you a pleasant evening."

Benjamin didn't say goodbye. Instead, he simply nodded and stepped back toward his desk. In awkward silence, Jacob turned and began limping out. Just as he reached the door, he heard Benjamin say to the back of his head, "Rappaport, I am watching you."

Jacob looked back, but Benjamin was already seated at his desk in front of a new stack of papers, immersed in his work. Jacob hobbled out the door and into the suffering city, shivering in the cold winter air, looking over his shoulder like a runaway slave.

PART EIGHT

THE ESCAPE ARTIST

I.

*A*s WINTER FADED INTO MARCH, JACOB BEGAN TO DISCERN, IN almost imperceptible outline, the workings of the plan.

Nearly all of the funds were being directed toward Maryland and northern Virginia—most of them toward small plantations and farms, though some went to other establishments too, like a tavern or a boarding house or a doctor's home. Many of these were so isolated that the closest towns were miles away. At first Jacob could perceive no pattern to the payments, nor to the sorts of people who appeared to be receiving them. The recipients were both men and women, soldiers and civilians, landowners and laborers, planters and tavernkeepers, officers and privates, elderly widows and adolescent boys, with no apparent rhyme or reason to any of it. But over time a thought occurred to him. Among the papers he had been given was a detailed map of Maryland and Virginia. One morning when he knew that Benjamin would be giving a speech to the Congress, he spread the map out on his desk. Afraid to mark it, he began plotting points with scraps of paper, labeling each recipient's most recent location with little removable flags. A picture unfurled before his remaining eye as he connected the dots: a clear, solid advance marching in perfect formation, the farmhouses and taverns and post offices and boathouses and barns assembling single file in an uninterrupted line from Richmond to Washington—or, perhaps, in the other direction.

They were building a road. But was the road being built for invasion, or for escape?

Then there was the matter of the munitions. Another series of payments—at first it appeared to be the same project, but soon it was clear that none of the names overlapped—went toward the delivery of gunpowder and the like to the Northern Neck, a no-man's-land in northern Virginia where the only soldiers were supposed to be those on furlough. A very active furlough, it seemed. Then there were the boatmen, the river current and tide measurements, the schedules for the Union gunboat patrols on the Potomac. It was a raid of some sort, clearly. But what kind of raid?

Reporting the situation back to the command was becoming more and more difficult. Jacob avoided the bakery entirely during his first week, too terrified of who might be following him. He moved through the teeming city as though he were being watched. When he finally did go to the bakery, the messages he sent back to Washington were cautious, reticent, listing only facts. In exchange he received cash baked into rolls, along with the occasional request for specific information that he could never manage to provide. Each time he went to deliver a message, he was frightened. At one point he arrived at the bakery to find it closed. A sign on the door explained that the baker was ill, but Jacob had seen the man the day before, in perfect health. The next message he received from the command, delivered by a private courier who demanded an exorbitant sum, informed him that he could no longer use the bakery for communications. Instead he was asked to deliver his messages to a certain grocer, but only on Thursdays. Then the grocery was shut down. Jacob pictured the grocer and the baker sharing a prison cell, awaiting hanging. After that he had to send messages through a cobbler, a free Negro who mainly occupied himself with passing along messages between slaves, and who could only send Jacob's coded letters when he had enough leather to make an extra pair of shoes in which to hide them—far too infrequently for comfort. Each time Jacob went to him, he wondered how many days either of them had left. The weather was cold, but Jacob's clothing was soaked with sweat. He wandered the streets of the city like a rat in a dark cellar full of traps, waiting to be caught. And when he found the courage, he started searching for his wife.

———

THE CITY HAD SWELLED to over a hundred thousand people, with refugees of every description filling every attic and basement and street corner. The city registries were unreliable; he managed to locate an address for a Mrs. Cardozo who might have been Jeannie's aunt, but when he knocked on the door one evening, another family was living there. He decided he would ask at the synagogues. Surely someone there would know of the Levys, he hoped, even if the Levys were rarely in attendance themselves. His first instinct was to go to the German synagogue—the larger one, and the more familiar to him. But he was unlikely to find anyone there named Cardozo. So he went to the Spanish synagogue, Beth Shalome.

The congregation was sparse. When Jacob walked in on a cold Saturday morning, he was counted as the tenth man, the one whose presence made it possible to continue the prayers. The other nine men present were all quite old, and those who arrived later were mostly elderly as well, with a few his father's age among them. There were almost no younger men, save a few boys. He looked up to the women's balcony behind him and noticed some young ladies—all strangers to him, of course. Each saw his blond hair, along with his scars, and quickly turned away. They were an aristocracy among the Hebrews, above the likes of him. His own ancestors in Germany had been fools, refusing conversion during the Crusades and dying by the sword, but the Spanish Jews during their own Inquisition had been smart enough to feign conversion, pretending to serve one master while actually serving another—an entire community of secret agents. But now even the old aristocrats suffered. He listened as every single person in the room recited the mourner's prayer.

When the service ended, the old man beside him greeted him gruffly, tipping his hat without offering his hand. "I don't believe we've met before. Are you new to the city?" he asked.

This was Jacob's chance, and he embraced it. "Yes, and perhaps you can help me," he said, before the man could ask his name. "I would like to inquire after a family named Levy."

"Levy," the man repeated, as the congregants began to file out of their seats. Jacob followed him to the aisle, limping at his side. "Which Levys?"

"The Levys from New Babylon. Relations of the Cardozos."

He drew his eyebrows together. "The ones who had the shipping company?"

He knew them! Jacob stumbled, then regained his footing, overwhelmed by sudden joy. "Yes. I—" He searched for the right words, afraid to say too much. "I was acquainted with the family some time ago, but I haven't heard any word of them in more than two years. I was concerned about one of the daughters. I had heard a dreadful rumor that—"

The man cut him off, and saved his life. "Oh, of course. You want to know about Miss Charlotte," he said. "She's safe here in Richmond now, thank God."

"Miss Charlotte?" Jacob stuttered.

"She was in a Union prison for two years. They accused her of espionage! Can you imagine? If you know her yourself, then you know just how outrageous that is. I've never met a more honest, forthright young lady in my entire life." The room blurred in Jacob's half-vision, shifting its shape until it had become the front room of the Levys' house, the walls rattling with Lottie's Rebel yell. "She was only released when the beasts finally admitted they had no evidence against her," he heard the man say. Lottie's lies were apparently being disseminated, and accepted. Who knew what anyone here might have heard about him? "But I assure you she is quite well, and with her family. Thank God."

"Thank God," Jacob repeated, mindlessly. *With her family?* With whom? But he couldn't ask anything more; he saw now that the danger was too great. He began edging his way toward the door.

"So are you from New Babylon too? It must be difficult being away from home. Please, won't you join us for dinner?"

The women had begun descending from the balcony. Once the women were involved, Jacob knew, there would be no way out. "Oh, thank you, but I can't," he answered, thinking quickly. "I am staying with a family from the German congregation, and they are expecting me."

The man smiled, though Jacob could see he was insulted. "All right, then. But I hope we shall see you again soon. What is your name?"

"Sergeant Samuels," Jacob said. He tipped his hat to the man and hobbled out the door.

It was clear that each of his two missions was fatal to the other: there was no way to ask anyone about Jeannie without risking his life. Now he knew that he could find her. The question was whether he should.

THE PUZZLE PIECES in the office were accumulating far too slowly. Benjamin had bogged Jacob down with sorting out the accounts; it was a tedious, endless task which left precious little time for further explorations. He was able to gather a few more names of agents, and at one point he even managed to identify Edwin Booth's brother—not his brother-in-law, as Jacob had originally thought, but his actual flesh-and-blood brother, the actor Philip had mentioned, who had sold off the oil drilling company. As an actor he was apparently quite well known outside of New York, though he spent most of his time offstage smuggling quinine over enemy lines. But the nagging problem was that the nature of the larger project still eluded him. Thus far, he could not even discern any activity with which to accuse these people, other than their fondness for accepting small sums of Confederate gold. One afternoon when he knew Benjamin wouldn't be in, he was immersed in documents that he had no right to see when someone knocked at his door.

At first he panicked, but when he looked up, he saw that it was only the Negro girl. She was holding a mop and a bucket, and wearing a stained dress beneath an apron stuffed with rags. Her hair was covered with a kerchief, but Jacob could see dark pigtails bristling beneath it. She was very short, and thin as a rail—a child. She couldn't have been older than twelve.

He had seen her before, of course. She came to the office several times a week to clean the soot from the fireplaces, and each time Jacob resented how awkward he felt in her presence. He had grown up in a home with paid servants, but this was different: this girl was a slave, and worse, a child. Usually he chose the moment she entered to hobble out into the hallway on some imaginary errand, too ashamed to watch this scrap of human property scrubbing his office floor. But this time he needed to keep reading, while he still could. He swallowed, and waved a hand.

"Come in," he muttered. Then he averted his good eye, trying to ignore her as he flipped through the papers. She interrupted him.

"Sir, you packin' up?"

He looked at her. It was odd to hear her voice. "What?"

"You packin' up? Upstairs, they all tyin' up papers, rearrangin' everythin'. I need to know if you gonna be packin' up too. 'Cause if you gonna be packin' up, then I ain't gonna mop this floor." She looked at him, waiting.

Was it true? If it was, then why? And what else might this girl know?

"Why are they packing upstairs?" he asked.

The girl shrugged. "No idea, sir. That ain't my business," she said. Her dark eyes were vacant, tired, bored.

"Well, don't mop the floor, then," he said.

"Yes, sir."

She left the mop in the doorway and carried the bucket with her as she entered the room. Her bare feet slapped the floorboards as she carefully hauled the bucket, struggling to keep the soapy water from sloshing out. Now he was watching her, suddenly unable to look away, as she plunked the bucket down beside the mantel and fished a thick scrub brush out of the water. Then she got down on her knees beside the unlit fireplace and began scrubbing out the soot from the previous day, when the weather had been cold. As he watched, he was captivated by the revolting ease of how she knelt on the floor. The torn collar of her dress hung open, revealing too much of her childlike chest as she pushed the scrub brush back and forth. The pale bottoms of her bare toes, encrusted with calluses and dirt, peeked out from beneath the skirt of her soot-smeared dress. It occurred to Jacob that even his parents' scullery maid had worn shoes. He saw that row of little toes and felt a surge of unexpected pity rising within him. *What cause*, he heard Philip Levy say in his head, *could be worth more than a child?* Ignoring her made him feel filthier than her filthy feet.

"What is your name?" he asked.

She looked up, startled. "Sally, sir."

He examined her, noticing her tiny, callused child's hands, and wondered what more he could say to her. What do children care about? "Sally, do your mother and father work here too?" he asked.

Sally looked back down at her scrub brush. "I ain't seen them in a long time, sir. They got sold some years ago."

He glanced at the papers on his desk, ashamed to look her in the eye. But then he looked back at her, watching her as she knelt before him.

"Sally, there's a Negro cobbler on Thompson Street," he said, surpris-

ing even himself. The cobbler was his contact, but now Jacob was thinking of his other trade. "I'll write you a pass to go there. I would like you to
go to him and tell him to make you a pair of shoes. I'll pay for them."

She stopped scrubbing and looked up at him, speechless.

"I shall give you the money for it now, and the pass," he said. He
scribbled out a few words on printed stationery, aware of the risk, but
no longer caring. The girl was still gaping at him. He reached into his
pocket and took out a silver dollar. This was much more than the shoes
would actually cost her, but the shoes were not the point. "This cobbler,
he—he knows many people, and he sends messages between—between
servants," he stammered. ("Servants," he had long noticed, was what
polite Southerners called their slaves.) "I would like you to ask him about
your parents. Perhaps he could find them for you." With great effort, he
stood up and leaned over his desk toward her, offering her the paper and
the coin.

For a moment she did not move. She stared at the pass and the coin,
her mouth hanging open. Then, gingerly, as though he were some sort of
dangerous animal, she straightened, reached out with her little hands and
snatched them both from him, her eyes wide as she quickly stuffed them
into the pocket of her apron. She kept her hand pressed against her apron
pocket for another long moment, as if he might take them back.

"Thank you, sir," she finally said, her voice low as she looked back
down at the floor. He watched as her eyes filled with tears.

"You're welcome," he replied.

He ought to have felt self-righteous, he supposed, but the entire
exchange only left him more ashamed. He sat down quickly and returned
to the papers on his desk, crouching back over them. His head was throbbing. He tried to begin reading again, but he couldn't, not while she was
there. He listened as she scrubbed, hoping that she would soon be gone.

But a moment later the scrubbing paused, and he heard her voice
again. "Sir, you's one of them who's tryin' to kidnap Lincoln, ain't you?"

The space behind his missing eye was pulsing again, currents of pain
coursing through his head. "Pardon me?"

The girl still knelt on the floor, scrubbing the sides of the fireplace as
she spoke. "I heard 'em talkin' about it upstairs, just like they was talkin'
about it last fall, before you came," she continued. "That ain't Christian,
you know. Lord Jesus ain't forgivin' nobody for that."

He sat back in his seat, astounded. Could it be? *This is not an assassination plot*, he heard Benjamin repeat in his head. He thought of everything he had collected so far—the line of agents from Washington to Richmond, the notices of farmhouses that had been "secured" along the way, the boats and measurements across the Potomac, Little Johnny's ramblings about hogtying people in barns—and held his breath.

The girl was still talking as his head reeled. "If you wanna whup me for sayin' so, go right ahead," she told him. "But you seem like a good Christian, so I know I oughta try an' save your soul. You ain't makin' it to heaven if you do that. Oh no. If you do that, you gonna be cussed for all time."

He couldn't hold back his smile. He was elated, flying on air. "Unfortunately, I am already cursed for all time," he said.

The girl frowned at him. "Don't you smile like that. You still got time to repent."

He kept smiling. He was knee-deep in repentance already, gathering up the pieces of a broken world. "And you've still got time to get your new pair of shoes," he said. "Go now, and save your own soles." Rose might have laughed, but Sally failed to appreciate his poor attempt at humor. She frowned again. "If anyone misses you," he added, "I shall tell them you were here the whole time, mopping the floor."

She looked doubtful, but all her life she had followed orders. She rose quickly and scurried to the doorway, leaving both mop and bucket behind. "Lord bless you," she murmured, and rushed out the door.

He sat in silence, seeing, with his remaining eye closed, how life and death had been set before him, the blessing and the curse. The glimmering possibility unfurled once more before his missing eye: redemption.

It took all of his strength just to limp back to the rooming house that evening to cipher his message in privacy. When he went to the cobbler's to deliver it, Jacob found him cutting out a leather sole for a foot about Sally's size, and smiling. Sally never returned to the office, and Jacob never saw her again. But one week later on Main Street, the Lord blessed him, and that was when he saw Rose.

2

*T*HE PART OF MAIN STREET WHERE JACOB HAD FIRST SEEN ROSE had been nicknamed the Trenches, as a tribute to all the crippled begging veterans languishing on its cobblestones. As the only fool who didn't thrust a cup in the faces of passersby, he was easily overlooked. The vendors were almost as desperate as the beggars, and Jacob watched every morning as they pulled at their customers' sleeves and pleaded with them for the price. The customers were beggars too; nearly every transaction began with a long speech from the potential buyer about how there wasn't anything left to eat and how many children in the household needed to be fed. The entire city was on its knees.

Jacob had been waiting there each morning for weeks, hoping to see Rose again. But when he actually saw her, it was late afternoon, on a day when he had taken advantage of Benjamin's absence to leave a bit early, to clear his head. He had just passed through to a quieter part of the street, leaving the largest cluster of beggars about half a block behind him. Across the street, he saw her.

It was astonishing to him how much she had changed. When he had last seen her at her father's house, she had been a little girl, not even twelve years old. But the two years that he had spent in hell had been, for her, the two years during which she had grown into a young woman. It was apparent now that she was the sort of girl who matures quickly; at fourteen, her body was already equal to any woman's. She was too thin, but nearly everyone in Richmond was. He watched her as she began negotiating with the same potato vendor, turning red with humiliation as he shouted in her face. Today, he noticed, she was wearing an apron tied around her waist, over what was once Jeannie's dress. He could barely imagine what her life was like now. Was she working somewhere?

He observed her, holding his breath as she left the vendor's stand with a bulging burlap sack. He waited, unable to chase after her, praying that she would cross the street as she had the first time he had seen her. She didn't. Instead she walked toward the end of the block, and he watched, devastated, as she entered a store on the corner. Only a few moments passed before she came out again and crossed to his side of the street. Soon she was approaching him.

The begging veterans farther down the block heralded her arrival with wolf whistles. In the Trenches, apparently, the rules of chivalry did not apply. It seemed she was used to this. She began walking faster, with her dark eyes fixed right in front of her, not even blushing as she ignored the catcalls of the crippled men on the sidewalks. But she was slowed somewhat by the sack of potatoes she was hauling along, and it was easy for Jacob to intercept her. When she reached the spot where he was standing, he stepped into her path, and extended his hand.

"Pardon me, miss," he said.

She was about to brush by, but he thrust one arm in front of her, blocking her path, and angled his cane in front of her feet. She stopped.

His heart pounded, but she didn't look at him. Of course not; no one ever did. He watched as she reached into the pocket of the apron tied around her waist and fished something out. Without looking at him, she pressed it into his palm. When he glanced down at his hand, he was surprised to see that it was a ten-dollar Rebel bill, until he remembered that the money had become almost worthless. "Now, sir, a war is won," she said with a smile, and began to walk away.

For an instant he gazed at her, enjoying the strange and delectable taste of a memory long forgotten. He marveled at how an old routine could be recalled so physically, so unthinkingly: he heard Rose's little palindrome as though it were a smell. He couldn't let his life pass by again. He balanced himself on his cane with one hand and seized her by the arm.

She stopped, caught. Her thin arm felt fragile in his grip, like the wing of a little bird. His heart fluttered; he hadn't touched a woman in over two years, other than his mother. And how close he was to Jeannie now, how agonizingly close!

Rose turned and glanced at him, then quickly looked away, watching his hand clutching the worn sleeve of Jeannie's old dress. Jacob felt that familiar sleeve against his fingers and almost took her whole body in his arms, swooning from mere memory. But he held himself steady, clutch-ing her, a slow ache seeping into his locked knees. Rose looked at him again, and then fixed her gaze on the ground. All she had seen was his eye patch.

"I don't have any more money, sir," she said. Her voice was higher than it had been before, weaker. He could hear how she tried to keep her words firm, and failed. "Really, it's true. I have nothing more to give you. I'm—I'm—I'm sorry, sir. Please—please let me go."

The sidewalk where they were standing was becoming too crowded, with too many people jostling them; he couldn't speak to her there. He glanced to his left and saw a narrow alley. With agonizing pain pulsing through his legs, he moved as quickly as he could. He clutched her arm in one hand and his cane in the other, and then pulled her around the cor-ner until she was facing him, her back to the alley's brick wall. She gasped, of course, a cry smothered by shock, but no one heard her. If any of the chivalrous gentlemen on the street saw a disfigured cripple accosting a pretty young lady and dragging her into an alley, they gave no notice.

Now Rose was standing before him, her whole narrow body trapped, braced against the brick wall between his left hand and his cane. He looked at her face and saw the absolute terror in her eyes. He recognized that fear from every place he had seen it, imagined it, and lived it—from Dorrie at the slave auction, from Jeannie on the floor at their wedding, from old Isaacs telling him about his first wife, from the moment he was ordered to his knees at Solomon's Inn, and the moment he first stood before the tribunal in Washington: the frightening instant when you realize that your life depends entirely on someone else's whim.

"Please, sir, please," she begged, and looked down at the bag of pota-toes that she was still clutching in her hands. "Take the potatoes. You may have them all," she said, her words a desperate blur as she dropped the bag on the ground at his feet. "Please, only let me go."

"I don't want your money or your food," he said.

She looked up at him, judging. In the light of her dark brown eyes he recognized a depth of beauty that he hadn't even remembered, Jeannie's beauty. He smiled at her, startled to find himself on the verge of tears. But his face was a hideous mask, and she misunderstood his smile. She panicked, and tried to duck, nearly slipping out from under his arms.

He panicked in turn, and braced his cane against her waist, pushing her back against the wall. Just as she began to open her mouth to scream, he touched her shoulder with his hand, and to his shock she didn't flinch.

"Rose Levy," he said. "Don't you recognize me?"

She started at her name, and shuddered in horror. At length she looked at the scars on his cheek below his eye patch. She began to shake her head. But then he perceived the precise moment when she looked at the unscarred side of his face, stared into his remaining eye, and knew.

"A parrot's pappy," she breathed. *RAPPAPORT, A SPY.*

Now Jacob was the one who was frightened. Suddenly he felt the full weight of where they were, of what it meant: a fourteen-year-old girl in the enemy's capital knew precisely who he was, and could give him away to absolutely anyone. There was no longer any way to return. But he had to risk everything. "Rose, please, tell me," he said, swallowing his own desperation whole. "Is Jeannie still alive?"

Rose stood still. Finally she spoke.

"I won't tell you anything," she said, glaring at his remaining eye. Her face was a mask, revealing no emotion. "You destroyed us."

This reply electrified him, leaving him pulsing both with thundering despair and lightning bolts of irrational hope. He gathered his strength.

"Rose, listen to me," he said. He glanced behind him. The street was still crowded; at any moment his unchivalrous position might be noticed, or Rose might suddenly call for help. "I have a message for you, from your father."

Her stoic mask seemed to fall to the ground, revealing the little girl he had known, long ago. "From Papa?"

He nodded. "He asked me to find you."

She bit her lip, her eyes wide. She was on the brink of tears. He looked at her dark eyes, Jeannie's eyes, and knew how close he was. He saw his chance and seized it.

"I want to help you, Rose," he told her. "I know that your family needs help. But I need you to tell me about Jeannie."

"Doom an evil deed, liven a mood," she intoned.

This was excruciating, both mentally and physically. His legs were beginning to buckle. He lowered his cane to the ground and pressed his other arm against the wall, putting his weight on his hands. "Rose, I'm begging you," he pleaded. "I can give you anything you want. I have money, I have food. I can contact your father for you. Only speak to me."

She blushed, looking down at the ground. "Never, even," she said.

The maddening word puzzles continued even now. In the time he had known the Levy girls, he had never thought about Rose's motivation for her odd obsession. He had simply considered it yet another Levy eccentricity, on a par with Lottie's broken engagements or Phoebe's boyish whittling or Jeannie's sleight of hand. It was only now that he saw how clearly it served a purpose, the same purpose that all of the girls' idiosyncrasies served. It was a way of digging an impassable ditch between themselves and others, a mined trench of protection for those who had seen the wreckage that could be inflicted upon the heart.

"Rose, I know you loved your mother, even if you hardly knew her," he said slowly. "I know you love your father. I know you love your sisters. And I know what you think I did to your family." She was watching him now, a knot of anger loosening between her dark eyebrows. "But I haven't stopped thinking of your family for the past two years," he said. "I freed your father from prison. I even freed your cousin Abigail from jail in Mississippi, when the army detained her." These claims were too simple to be precisely true, but they were the only deeds he had—his feeble, best attempts at redeeming captives. He watched Rose, wondering how much of this she knew. Very little, it seemed.

"Look at me, Rose," he said. "You can't be afraid of me anymore. You can run away, and I can't run after you. Look where we are. Think of who I am. You are safe here. I am not. You can send me off to the gallows any time you'd like. But I came here for you and your sisters, because I promised your father that I would find you." He paused, a dull lump of pain throbbing behind his missing eye. Rose was examining him now, inspecting his eye patch, his legs, his cane. "I don't expect your forgiveness, Rose," he said at last. "All I can ask for is your mercy. I love your sister, and I always will. Please just tell me if she's alive."

He watched as little Rose, Philip's treasure, cracked before his eyes. She didn't weep, of course. She was Philip's daughter, too smart and too proud. Instead he saw how her face softened, her breath slowing as she began to think.

"Could you send my father a letter for me?" she whispered.

"Yes," he said.

For the first time in two years, Jacob saw Rose smile, a Levy smile, like her sister's. The beauty in that smile was unfathomable, almost unreal.

"I shall write it this evening and bring it to you," she said, her voice full of joy. "Shall I find you here tomorrow morning?"

"Yes," he said. "But only if you tell me—"

But she was wriggling now, edging her way out of where he had braced her against the wall. He tried to stop her, but he had been standing too long; he no longer had the strength. He held her wrist, and she looked at him. "Please let me go," she finally said. "I shall come back tomorrow, I promise. But I must go now. I'm expected."

Should he believe her? "Where are you going?" he asked.

She shrank down into herself, her shoulders rising as she bowed her head. She looked back at him, and he saw that she had caved in completely, that he had succeeded in breaching the deep trench of distrust. "I have to go home. My aunt isn't well, and I have to stay with Deborah."

The name was familiar to him, though at first he couldn't place it. It was someone in the Levy family—a cousin he had met at the wedding, in that hour before William Williams arrived? Then he remembered where he had seen the name Deborah: on the gravestone in the cemetery, where he had held Jeannie for the last time. Now he was confused, absurdly imagining Rose guarding their mother's grave.

"Who is Deborah?" he asked.

Rose swallowed, and looked down at her own feet. "Jeannie's daughter," she said.

Jacob stood still, stunned. The beauty of the world lay revealed before him, a tantalizing glimpse at a vast continent of happiness just beyond reach. He couldn't even begin to imagine her—*her*, a daughter!

"Rose," he gasped. "I need to meet her." He gripped her thin arm. "And I need to see Jeannie." *To see Jeannie!* The words washed through his shameful life like a cleansing rain. "Please, Rose, take me home with you."

Rose shook her head. "I can't," she said.

For an instant he thought this was her defiance again, and he wondered why she hadn't used some sort of word puzzle to express it. He saw how her face was tightening, her little-girl eyebrows furrowing back into worry and grief.

"Why not?" he demanded.

"Because of Lottie," Rose said. "If she sees you, she'll have you killed. She said she would, if she ever sees you again."

He thought of what Philip had said about how Lottie had looked when they were exchanged: *She was so angry, so full of fury. I almost didn't recognize my own child.* But now he was the one who wouldn't recognize his own child.

"I don't care," he said. "I need to meet—I need to meet Deborah." He tasted the name in his mouth, imagining a little dark-eyed, dark-haired, miniature Levy girl. Jeannie's daughter. "And I need to see Jeannie." He allowed himself to think the words: *My wife. My daughter. My family.*

"I can't," Rose repeated. "I won't."

It occurred to Jacob that it wasn't his fate that Rose cared about, but rather her own. If Lottie discovered him and had him hanged, then Rose wouldn't be able to write to her father—and the war might continue for another thirty years, and she might never hear from him again. Rose was in Lottie's thrall now, her prisoner. Their home was a citadel within a citadel, and he would have to find his own way in.

He noticed an almost imperceptible crack in the fortress wall. "Why are you watching the baby?" he asked. "Where is Jeannie?"

Rose pursed her lips, looking down. As he waited for Rose to answer, he imagined that his joy had been misplaced, that he had been terribly mistaken, that Jeannie—

At last Rose spoke. "A few months ago Jeannie found a—a position. She's supporting all of us now. Even Phoebe and her mother-in-law."

Phoebe was married? He remembered Phoebe too as more girl than woman, engrossed in her whittling, laughing with the guests at his wedding. But he couldn't think of Phoebe now; all he could think of was Jeannie. And Deborah.

"A 'position'?" he asked. "What sort of 'position'?"

Rose wouldn't look back up at him. "She works in the evenings, and I look after Deborah," she said.

This was a childish evasion, and he wouldn't accept it. He stared at Rose, suddenly nauseated. Had Jeannie become some sort of—some kind of—

"Where does she work?" he demanded. "How can I see her?"

Rose shook her head. "She doesn't want to see you."

He stood still, stricken. With a gravity that pulled at his weakened knees, he suddenly understood that this must be true. But he could not let it matter to him, not now. "Tell me where she works," he demanded again.

"She doesn't want to see you. She hates you."

He flinched, cringing from the blow. *She hates you.* It was entirely possible. Probable, even. But he had come too far. "I don't care. I want to see her. Tell me where she works."

"No."

He clutched Rose's wrist, his tight grip brushing the edge of cruelty. "Rose, do you want me to send that letter to your father? If you ever want to hear from your father again—"

Rose finally looked up, and he saw in her eyes the flaw in the fortress wall, the crack widening. "She wouldn't want you to know," she said.

"Why?" he asked, though he was afraid of the answer. "Is it—is it something shameful?"

"No," Rose said simply. He breathed with relief. Rose added, with a Levy smile, "It would only be shameful for you."

He looked at her, baffled. "Shameful for me?"

Rose couldn't help herself anymore; the citadel was breached. She grinned as she pulled a folded piece of paper out of her apron pocket, which she then passed to him.

He unfolded it, expecting some sort of letter. But he soon saw that it was a printed advertisement—or, rather, an invitation. The ink had blurred along the creases where Rose had folded it, but the text was still eminently clear:

You are Cordially Invited to Attend

The Cary Sisters' Starvation Ball

WITH ENTERTAINMENTS BY

The One-Legged Orchestra

AND

The Acclaimed

Miss Eugenia Van Damme,

PERFORMING AS

"The Escape Artist."

Prepare to be ASTOUNDED!!

30 MARCH, EIGHT O'CLOCK
AT THE CARY RESIDENCE, 23 CLAY STREET
"REFRESHMENTS" WILL BE SERVED!

Donations accepted at the door
for Chimborazo Hospital

He read the words on the page, utterly bewildered. At last he spoke. "Van Damme?" he asked.

Rose smiled. "It's the name she used in the theater, before the war." Of course. He had wondered, a lifetime ago, how she had managed to have such a successful theater career with a name like Levy. "She was famous here," Rose added. "People remember her."

He looked at the invitation again. "What is a starvation ball?" he asked.

"It's the fashion here. The society people hold grand parties just like before the war, but with empty plates instead of food. Everyone thinks it's great fun."

He thought of the Passover seder in New Orleans, of the drunken cheering for the cause. It was a land of delusion, a glorious, ridiculous dream. He read the advertisement once more, hypnotized. "*The Escape Artist.*" Of course, of course! He would have laughed, if he hadn't been so stunned. Rose was right: it was only shameful for him.

"She performs everywhere now. This week she is occupied with rehearsals for another performance, but this one is next Thursday night," Rose said through the haze of his thoughts, pointing to the date. "No one will stop you from going in, if you are dressed appropriately enough," she told him. "They are always eager for more gentlemen. Stay in the back of the room. She won't recognize you from a distance. But you must not let her see you there."

She plucked the paper out of his hand. He tried to grab it back from her, until he saw that she was tucking it into his own vest pocket. "I shall come back tomorrow morning at eight o'clock, with a letter for Papa," she said, and smiled. "If you aren't here, you may expect to be hanged."

With that, she bent down, picked up her sack of potatoes, and darted away. He would have followed her, but she was much too fast for him. He watched her as she disappeared around a corner, and then he sank down to the ground, his legs buckling under the weight of newfound wonder. He read the invitation once more, and marveled at the revival of the dead.

3

*T*HE NEXT MORNING, ROSE GAVE HIM HER LETTER FOR PHILIP, without a word. Once she had left, he opened it, in case it was some sort of trick. Inside he found pages of scenes, some rendered in anagrams, but most in painfully direct prose, describing everything the sisters had endured in the past two years: the death of Phoebe's husband in the battle at Spotsylvania; how the baby Phoebe had been expecting was born too soon and died; their aunt's illness; Rose's job as a hospital orderly; Phoebe's promotion to hospital matron; Lottie's raving fury since her release. *She breaks things*, Rose wrote. Of Jeannie, out of fear, she offered only one cryptic sentence: *Miss Van Damme has returned to the stage, and thanks to her efforts we are no longer hungry.* A single line toward the end of the letter made him unable to read any more: *Deborah will be two years old at the end of May, and I regret to say that she looks exactly like her father.* He returned the letter to the envelope, blinking his remaining eye. That evening, he brought it, with special delivery instructions, to the cobbler.

When he arrived at the cobbler's, he discovered that there was already a message waiting for him from the command—a response, he knew, to Sally's revelation. He hobbled back to his rented room to open it, amazed by how elated he felt. It was as if the leather harness he had just purchased was itself the medal they planned to pin to his chest. But when he pried open the seams of the doubled leather and excavated the message, he deciphered it four times, each time unable to believe what he read:

REGARDING YOUR LAST MEMORANDUM: PINKERTON IS SKEPTI-
CAL OF YOUR INFORMANT, WHOSE INTELLIGENCE WE CANNOT
CONSIDER RELIABLE. WE REQUEST CONFIRMATION FROM A MORE
REPUTABLE SOURCE. UNTIL THEN WE SHALL HOLD OFF FURTHER
PURSUIT.

He read it again and again. *Hold off further pursuit?* But what if the plot were already in motion, the deed about to be done, and no one prevented it— merely because no one would believe a twelve-year-old Negro girl?

Over the next few days, he wrote back urgently, each time explaining how Sally's remarks corroborated what he had found before, insisting that they believe him. In each response he received, he was addressed like a child: gently reprimanded, scolded for his naïveté in accepting an unknown Negro girl's ramblings as fact, accused of concealing his own failures behind a child's fantasies (or, one message insinuated, perhaps even inventing the story himself), instructed not to panic, reminded that he needed to be more thorough, more dependable, more certain. His own certainty was driving him mad. At length they reassured him that Lincoln was about to embark on a riverboat for a conference, where he would be guarded very closely for several days; at the least, this would give Jacob time to try to gather more reputable evidence. In the meantime, the following Thursday arrived, and Jacob waited for evening, when he at last would see his wife.

"RAPPAPORT, I HAVE an important task for you."

It was late Thursday afternoon, and Jacob could not have been more agitated when Benjamin walked in the door and planted himself across from his desk. Since Sally's revelation, no further details had emerged about the potential kidnapping. Jacob couldn't stop denigrating himself for allowing her to escape, or thinking of all the ways he might have used her to his advantage. Of course, everyone had always used Sally to their advantage; for her entire life, she had been nothing more than an advantage, to everyone but herself. He felt like a fool for setting her free.

He tried to concentrate on corroborating the evidence, but with each passing day he became more and more frustrated. To distract himself, he often took out the invitation Rose had given him, counting down the hours until he would finally see Miss Eugenia Van Damme. But now, just as he was preparing to leave the office, Benjamin had walked in, ready to assign him yet another "important task." He held back a groan.

Benjamin stood in front of him with a pile of papers under his arm. Jacob looked up at him as he always did, summoning his most obsequi-ous expression. He noticed that something seemed different about Benjamin, though at first he could not determine what. The Secretary was dressed as impeccably as ever, his suit perfectly pressed; his face was as haggard and weary as it always was, with its usual perpetual smile. Then Jacob saw that Benjamin's hands were trembling.

"There is a small possibility," Benjamin said, "that we may need to briefly relocate certain government offices to Danville."

"Danville?"

Benjamin coughed, taking the papers out from under his arm. "Danville, Virginia. It's about a hundred and fifty miles south of here. It would simply be a precaution."

Jacob paused, wondering what this might mean. "Which offices?" he asked.

For the first time, he saw Benjamin's perfect equanimity falter. His smile vanished as he cleared his throat, his careful gaze averted to his feet. He replied, under his breath, "All of them."

Jacob bit his lip, unable to believe it. The information he had been receiving from the command had been severely limited; all he knew about the front was what he read in the Richmond papers, various delusions recorded on newsprint. But now it was clear that the Union army was at the door. He saw Benjamin blush, his sallow skin taking on an almost purplish tone. "Davis's clerk has left instructions for the local militia in the event of our departure. I am entrusting a copy to you as well," he said, and handed Jacob the sheaf of documents. His hands fluttered quickly to his sides as Jacob took the papers, as though he were relieved to be rid of them. "Should circumstances require our relocation, I expect you to remain here, to address any problems that may arise in our absence."

Suddenly Jacob understood. The government officials would escape, and leave him behind to take the fall.

"I expect that I can trust you to handle any contacts with our agents in the event of our temporary displacement," Benjamin said. "If our displacement is even required, that is. Most likely it will prove unnecessary, but I think it wise to be prepared."

"Certainly," Jacob said. He was hardly able to keep the cheer from his voice. But then, almost by accident, he glanced down at the first few paragraphs of the instructions on the pages Benjamin had handed him. *In the event of a governmental evacuation, all supplies are to be burned . . . all manufactories are to be burned . . . all river vessels are to be burned . . . all bridges are to be burned . . . all warehouses are to be burned . . .* Jacob turned one page, then the next, his vision faltering. They had arranged for the end of the world. He looked down at his shattered legs and wondered how he could ever save himself from a fire, when he could no longer run.

Benjamin was still speaking as Jacob turned pale before him. "Little Johnny is scheduled to depart for Washington this coming Sunday evening at midnight," he said. Now his voice was bland again, as if all of this were perfectly routine. "He will meet his transport at the old burial ground on Shockoe Hill. I selected this meeting point myself. It's not as frequented as the newer cemeteries, and the hill makes it a good lookout point." Benjamin was digressing now. "It's both a Christian and a Hebrew burial ground, you may be interested to know," he added. "The two grave-yards are distinct, but they sit side by side. Perhaps that is another reason why I selected it. The dead have achieved an equivalence to which the living only aspire." Jacob nodded as Benjamin stiffened, as if waking from a dream. "In the event that we are obliged to relocate the government before Sunday, I would like you to deliver this message to him prior to his departure," Benjamin said. He held up an envelope, already closed with his own seal. "Under those circumstances, this message would become rather urgent. If we depart, I shall leave it for you in the safe."

"You—you may depend on me," Jacob stammered, looking at the envelope. Benjamin was already putting it into his own vest pocket, changing the subject.

"There is one more very minor favor I would like to request of you, Rappaport, should this relocation occur," he said.

"I am at your service," Jacob replied.

Benjamin's eyes were wide, almost childlike. He looked toward the window beyond Jacob's desk, as if speaking to someone who wasn't in the room. "My older sister is in New Orleans," he said. "Her name is Rebecca Kruttschnitt, but the family calls her Penny. I haven't seen her since '62, before the city fell. If—if all seems lost, please notify her that I shall find my way to England. She will want to know that I am safe."

"England?" Jacob asked.

He smiled. "I was born in St. Croix in the West Indies, so I am a British subject. My family came here when I was two years old."

Jacob waited for Benjamin to return to the matter at hand. But Benjamin preferred to evade the inevitable, and continued his retreat into the certainty of the past. "I grew up in South Carolina, in Charleston. My parents owned a fruit store near the harbor," Benjamin said brightly, as though Jacob had asked. "Penny and I used to go swimming in the harbor's older section whenever there weren't too many boats, off the abandoned docks."

Jacob wondered why Benjamin was telling him this. For a moment he tried to think of an innocuous reply. But Benjamin kept talking, his words flowing one after another until their happy irrelevance filled the doomed and quiet room. "Our parents didn't allow us to swim there, and of course that was precisely why I always wanted to do it. And Penny always agreed to come along, just to indulge me, even though she knew how foolish it was," he said, apropos of nothing. Jacob had never seen Benjamin like this before; perhaps no one had. He listened, captivated, as Benjamin continued.

"One afternoon we were swimming there when a storm broke," he said. "It came very suddenly. I remember that I was swimming rather far from the docks, and I was floating on my back when I noticed that the sky had turned into a slab of slate, right above my head. The rain broke through it and started pouring down in torrents, with the wind whipping the waves into hideous squalls. The water churned quite violently, and soon it was pulling down on my arms and legs. I was sure I was about to die. I was on the verge of sinking when I felt someone dragging me back to the dock. Penny was always a stronger swimmer than me, and always better at judging risks. I was lying on the dock beside her like a living shipwreck when I saw our father running toward us. I was more afraid of him than I was of the storm. He brought us both back to the store, and when I saw his face I knew he was ready to beat the life out of me. And then Penny told him that she had been the one who swam out in the storm and nearly drowned, and that I had saved her. My father always admired me after that. Two years later, when I was fourteen, I had the opportunity to attend the law school at Yale. My mother was always very ambitious on my behalf, but she hesitated. She thought that I would leave the family forever. But my father told my mother that he trusted me, that anyone who risked his own life to save his sister was a person who knew the meaning of devotion."

Benjamin was blushing now, his eyes cast down at the floor. Jacob lowered his scarred face before him. The only thing that made either of them matter was the presence of someone else's love.

"I shall tell your sister where to find you," Jacob said.

"Thank you," Benjamin replied, and at last raised his eyes. "Tell me, Rappaport, do you have a family?" he suddenly asked. "Besides your parents, I mean. Harry Hyams's wife had mentioned that you were widowed, that night in '62." Jacob winced, remembering the lies. But Benjamin was looking at him with curiosity, empathy. "Are you—are you married now?"

For a moment Jacob held his breath, before deciding to tell the truth. "Yes," he said.

"Do you have children?" Benjamin asked.

Jacob swallowed. "A daughter," he answered.

"I made a grave mistake with my own daughter," Benjamin said. "I hope you will never make one like it." His candor was strange, disarming, a fortress of pretense suddenly dissolving into sand. Now he was leaning over Jacob, his melancholy clouding the air between them. "One night many years ago, my wife asked me if she could take our daughter away with her, to Paris. We had a long argument about it. I am very good at winning arguments; my entire career has been built on winning arguments. But that night I gave in. I suppose I thought that I had merely lost the battle that night, and that on some other night in the future, everything would be different. I have since learned that there are no exceptions. What you allow to happen one night will happen on all other nights as well. The person you are tonight is the person you will always be."

Benjamin stepped back from Jacob's desk, suddenly embarrassed. He coughed, and pulled a watch out of his vest pocket. "Excuse me, but I am expected upstairs," he said. "I wish you a pleasant evening."

With that, he walked away, leaving Jacob drowning in wonder.

When the day faded, Jacob limped out the door. As the invitation warned, he was prepared to be astounded. But, as he knew when he rang the bell at 23 Clay Street that evening, no one is ever really prepared.

4

*J*ACOB HAD WORRIED, AS HE RETURNED TO HIS CHEAP ROOMING house and changed his suit in preparation for a society evening, that he would attract more attention than he might want at the Cary sisters' ball. Except for his own wedding, he hadn't been to any sort of party since before the war, and his wedding had hardly been a society event. He peered into the dirty mirror on the wall of his rented room, observing the long red scars that radiated from the patch that covered his missing eye, examining how deeply his shoulders hunched as he leaned onto his cane. How could he make any kind of society appearance, looking the way he looked now?

He arrived at half past eight, both out of fear of being the first guest and out of adherence to the Manhattan society stricture instilled in him before the war—that only persons of no consequence have the naïveté to arrive on time. He didn't know, then, that the New York custom of arriving "fashionably late" was actually the sole invention of August Belmont, the Rothschilds' New York agent and the great playboy of the circles to which his parents aspired. If Belmont had remained, as he was initially destined, a rabbinical student in Bavaria named Schoenberg, then no one in New York would have ever felt that appearing on time was a sign of social weakness. Richmond society, Jacob immediately discovered, had remained untouched by his influence. At half past eight, he entered the Cary sisters' home to find the party well underway, the enormous front hall crowded with people dancing and laughing as musicians played the most upbeat tunes. As he looked around the room, he saw that all of his fears about high society were entirely misplaced.

He had nothing to be ashamed of with his eye patch and cane at the Cary sisters' starvation ball, because there was barely a man there who had all of his limbs. As he entered the room, bumping his elbows into arms that stopped at the elbow or higher, he saw that the One-Legged

Orchestra—a lively string quartet, exhibited on the exceedingly grand and wide staircase landing that served as a dramatic stage in the enormous marble-tiled front hall—was, as advertised, composed entirely of one-legged musicians, performing proudly in their Rebel army caps. There were a few able-bodied men here and there, most of them either old or dressed in officers' uniforms. But the hobbled and the crippled ruled the room, perching on stools and chairs that were scattered around the dance floor. The one-armed men were dancing with ladies who grace-fully endured their flapping sleeves, while the men with crutches each attracted their own share of ladies who gathered at their sides. Everyone was in the highest of spirits; if anyone knew of the horrifying possibility Benjamin had mentioned to Jacob that afternoon, no one let on. A slave approached him, holding out a platter of wineglasses full of white wine. He took one and had already brought it to his lips before he noticed that what he thought was wine was nothing but water, dyed a slight golden color by filth. He discreetly poured it into a houseplant. But when he looked around the room, he saw that the other guests were holding their glasses full of dirty water, toasting one another with them. It was all an elaborate game, a dream. He was still distracted by this delirious scene when two blond young ladies, one tall and one short, approached him, smiling. At first Jacob looked behind him, unable to believe that they could be smiling at him.

"Good evening, sir," the taller one said. Both of them, he noticed, were the sort of women who reminded him of pieces of straw: flat blond hair, pale pink complexions, blank smiles, and figures straighter than his own. But he was hardly in a position to be critical of anyone's looks. "I do hope you won't mind if we take the liberty of introducing ourselves. It's always a pleasure to see new faces. My name is Antonia, and this is my sis-ter Imogene," she said. Imogene curtsied, and blushed. "We're cousins of the Carys," Antonia added. Face powder, it seemed, had become a luxury item; the two sisters had made up for it by scrubbing their skin so brightly that they almost shone. They looked at him, smiling, anxious.

Never in his life had Jacob been approached so directly by women; it had always been his burden to chase after them himself, and it seemed to him that the ladies had always been trained to be pursued, not the reverse. But here only the women were able-bodied enough to follow anyone around a room. He adjusted his cane, and bowed. "A pleasure, ladies. My name is Jacob." He had thought for an instant of using an alias, but decided against it. Perhaps Benjamin was part of these circles as well. But he hoped they wouldn't ask for his surname, in case he needed to reserve a way out.

They didn't. "Jacob, you said?" Imogene asked. The orchestra had stopped playing, but it was still quite noisy in the room.

"Yes, Jacob. Like the patriarch," he replied, injecting as much drawl as he could into his voice. He had become a master at the accent, if nothing else.

Antonia smiled as she and Imogene curtsied again. Their faces were almost painfully strained by the scrubbing and the smiles; being this carefree with nothing but dirty water at one's disposal required the utmost effort. "And I see you've also been wrestling with angels," she said.

"Only with the better angels of my nature," he replied. The sisters laughed. Jacob was flattered, and cheered. It had been years since he had heard a woman laugh.

"Where were you wounded?" Antonia asked.

This, it seemed, had become the latest and most fashionable version of "Where are you from?" He was relieved to have a neutral answer. The command had been right; the constant lying was exhausting. "Mississippi," he said. "At Holly Springs."

"Holly Springs!" Antonia cried, and gestured to her sister, whose mouth was hanging open. "Imogene's husband was captured there! Major Rufus Halliday. Did you know him? She's quite anxious for any word of him, anything at all." The two women gaped at him, eager, and suddenly he understood why they had cornered him. Every new face was an excuse for fresh hope, a renewal of delusion.

"No," he said.

He watched as Imogene's face fell, her gaze fixed to the floor. "Do— do excuse me, please," she murmured. She turned and quickly crossed the room, escaping into a corridor. Jacob watched as her fingers fluttered up to her eyes, and felt the space behind his own missing eye throb with someone else's pain.

Antonia had been scrubbed clean of all empathy. She turned back to him and grinned. "It was worth asking," she said cheerfully, and turned toward the stage. "Oh, look, there's Miss Cary." The one-legged musicians, he saw, were putting away their instruments; some slaves were helping them down from the landing, while others busied themselves with hanging a sort of makeshift velvet curtain over the ordinary doorway at the landing's back wall. Once the landing was vacated, a thin young woman with a severe blond bun of hair proceeded up to it, where she banged a spoon against her dirty-water-filled wineglass.

"Ladies and gentlemen," she announced, "welcome, and thank you all for your generous contributions to Chimborazo Hospital." The room quieted. "Please make yourselves comfortable. In just a moment, our main performance will begin."

Glasses clinked as people set them down around the room, the men on crutches settling into their seats. "Miss Van Damme is next," Antonia whispered to Jacob. "Have you ever seen her perform?"

Sweat beaded underneath his eye patch. But he couldn't help himself. "Yes," he said.

"Really!" Antonia gushed. "Everyone says she's sensational. Is it true?"

"It is," he said.

Antonia had him by the elbow now, trying to steer him toward the stage. He remembered what Rose had said, and stopped. "Please, go ahead. I would prefer to stay back here," he said, gesturing toward a row of seats along the side of the room.

"Nonsense," Antonia said. "I shall stay with you." Apparently he was now Antonia's escort for the evening. The prospect revolted him, but his legs gave him no choice. She pulled up a chair and offered it to him, as she herself sat down on a stool beside it. He made his best attempt at a bow to her as he accepted, swallowing his shame at how the roles had been reversed. All the men were ladies now.

"Of course, her reputation precedes her," Miss Cary was saying as he took his seat. "Many of us are privileged to remember her performances before the war, from her debut in Washington as Ophelia in *Hamlet* when she was only fourteen years old, to her appearance as 'The Illusionist's Assistant' here in Richmond. Since her return to the stage, her audiences have only become more devoted as she delights us in our darkest hour, performing as actress, illusionist, and conjurer. We are particularly honored to have her with us for tonight's special performance, where she will provide us with a demonstration of some of the tricks of the escape artist's trade—a trade which Miss Van Damme is known to have mastered, both onstage and elsewhere." A laugh and a cheer rose among the guests.

Miss Cary waited patiently, smiling, attempting to speak and finally giving up as the cheer spread. At last she threw out her arms, a broad gesture of welcome to the guests. "Without further ado, it's my pleasure to present to you this evening's 'Escape Artist'—the exceedingly talented Miss Eugenia Van Damme!"

Miss Cary stepped aside, proceeding down the stairs and into the crowd. The newly hung curtain behind the landing stirred, and everyone with at least one leg rose as Jacob's wife stepped onto the makeshift stage.

She was vastly more beautiful than he had remembered her. Time and suffering had left their impressions on her face, but the effect was to deepen her dark eyes and soften her mouth, broadening her disarming smile. Her hair hung in dark wild curls around her shadowed throat. She was wearing a red dress with a low décolletage; the pregnancy and birth had apparently protected her from the gauntness he had noticed in Rose. If the baby had changed her figure, it was only to render her body more spectacular than before, less like a girl's and more like a woman's, her hips more emphatic, her breasts more pronounced. Jacob sat captivated, barely breathing. Every moment that he had ever spent with her flooded back over him as though the past two years had never been. He could feel her hair between his fingers, taste her skin against his tongue, sense his hands shaking as he struggled to untie her corset, remembering the last time he touched her naked body, his last night in their married bed, the night before he fled. To think she had been his! But now he was nothing but a spectator, no different from any other man in the room, drooling over an unattainable star. It would be impossible even to catch her eye. He watched as she walked with grace toward the edge of the landing. She raised her arms out toward the guests, and he squinted his remaining eye and saw that she wasn't wearing her wedding ring. She made a sweeping curtsy before the audience, her arrival alone warranting the crowd's applause. It was fortunate that Jacob was crippled, because if he weren't, he would have leapt onto the stage and carried her away.

"I was told that she was stunning," Antonia whispered in his ear. "But I rather think she looks a bit Oriental; wouldn't you agree?"

It was a euphemism he hadn't heard since his old society days in New York. He would have laughed, but he was too enchanted. "A bit," he whispered back, relieved when Antonia finally turned away from him, scrutinizing the figure on stage. He stared at Jeannie, his living wife, and held his breath, suddenly overwhelmed by gratitude to God. It was all he could do to keep himself from weeping as she began to speak.

"Ladies and gentlemen, thank you for welcoming me here tonight."

He heard her actress's voice, the voice she had used the moment they first met: *Gladly, Mr. Rappaport. But only if you will allow me to repay you.* For an instant it was as if time had not passed, as if he had just stepped into the front room of the Levys' house—seeing, for the very first time, Jeannie and her three sisters curtsying before him, standing on the precipice of their family's destruction. But now he watched, and began to imagine, for the first time, how Jeannie had managed to escape.

"LADIES AND GENTLEMEN, the art of escape is quite complex, involving many different skills which I hope to demonstrate for you this evening. But once one masters it, it is possible to find one's way out of almost any situation. And perhaps some of you will even take from my demonstration a measure of hope for these dark times." The audience began to cheer again, and Jeannie waited patiently until they had stopped before she continued, producing a fan almost out of thin air and waving it gently at her side. "Now the phrase 'escape artist' tends to suggest a rather pedestrian set of skills. Most of you are probably expecting me to tuck myself into a barrel or a steamer trunk and simply pop out of it—as if every smuggler on the Potomac hasn't been doing precisely that for the past four years." The crowd laughed as Jacob remembered folding himself into the barrel that took him on his first journey to hell. He listened as Antonia giggled, aware of how his scars made it difficult for anyone to notice how he blushed. "Of course I wouldn't dream of disappointing you, and I do promise to pop out of a barrel at least once during this performance." The guests laughed again, and he could feel how they were warming to her, leaning toward her, eager to see where she might lead them. "But the technique that any escape artist must master first isn't the art of escaping from physical constraints, but of escaping from mental ones—that is, liberating oneself from the expectations of others." The guests were silent now, captivated. Jacob could barely breathe.

Jeannie smiled, waving her fan. She had taken ownership of the landing, pacing across it and sweeping her wide skirts along its worn carpet. "I see that we are privileged to have many soldiers and veterans with us this evening," she announced, leaning forward as she gazed out at the crowd. "Perhaps some of you might be able to assist me in my demonstration of the escape artist's trade. Please tell me, gentlemen, if you will: are any of you experienced at guarding prisoners?"

A man at the front of the room raised his hand. Jacob couldn't see him well from where he was seated, but when Jeannie gestured to him, Jacob heard him clear his throat, his voice tight with pride. "Yes, miss," the man announced. "I was serving at Andersonville down in Georgia until last Easter." Jacob held his breath. Even in New York, the rumors about the prison camp at Andersonville had been widespread, and frightening. Apparently those who returned from there had come back as living skeletons, if they returned at all.

Jeannie leaned toward the man, her face pure confidence. "What is your name, sir?" she asked.

"Captain Strathmore, miss."

"Captain Strathmore, would you do me the honor of joining me onstage?"

The crowd clapped as a man in an elegant officer's uniform made his way up the grand staircase to the landing. Now Jacob could see that unlike most men in the room, Captain Strathmore was entirely able-bodied, a genuine active-duty officer, his uniform's cloak bulging from the holsters at his hips and his chest decorated with medals. He was about Jacob's height, with blond hair, a blond mustache, a tall forehead, and an unmistakably smug expression on his face. As he took his place onstage at Jeannie's side, he reminded Jacob of William Williams.

"Welcome, Captain Strathmore," Jeannie said, and curtsied. "Thank you for your generous contribution to Chimborazo Hospital. And thank you also for your service to the cause at Andersonville."

"My pleasure," the man said.

This struck Jacob as a rather inappropriate reply, but the audience applauded as Jeannie offered him her hand. Jacob watched as the officer brightened, initiating a deep bow to her and kissing her fingers—far too warmly, and for far too long. Jacob burned with jealousy as Jeannie smiled.

"Now would it be correct, Captain, to say that escapes from Andersonville were few and far between?" she asked, fluttering the fan in his direction as she spoke.

"That would be correct, miss," the officer answered. "And none of them were on my watch."

"I see," she said, as though thinking aloud. "So it is quite unlikely that even an experienced escape artist, if imprisoned there, would have been able to liberate herself from beneath your watchful eyes."

The officer grinned at her, relishing his moment beside her onstage. "Well, it would have been rather difficult, since the guards were each armed with at least two pistols. But Miss Van Damme, I wouldn't dream of underestimating you," he added, his voice gallant. The old William Williams queasiness returned to Jacob's stomach. He shook his head, fighting it as he listened.

"How gracious of you. I do appreciate it," Jeannie said. She stepped closer to him, which clearly cheered him, and flicked her fan in his direction. "What sort of persons were you guarding at Andersonville, Captain Strathmore?"

"Mostly Yankee privates, miss. Many in rather sickly condition."

"Tell us, Captain: were there any ladies among your prisoners?"

Now he laughed, blushing, as the audience laughed along with him. "No, unfortunately. I expect I would have enjoyed my responsibilities quite a bit more if that had been the case."

Jeannie laughed too, standing right at his side. "I expect you would have. But as the situation stood, those sickly Yankee privates had your full attention," she said, waving her fan softly back and forth.

"I should hope so," he said, with a chuckle. His eyes were glued to Jacob's wife. Jacob watched as the officer's gaze traveled along her body, down to her dress's generous neckline and her breasts beneath it.

"Captain Strathmore, I take it that you are armed this evening, as is customary," Jeannie said.

"Indeed," the officer nodded. His eyes, Jacob noticed, were still on her breasts.

"Do you truly find it necessary to be armed at a ball?"

Captain Strathmore paused, surprised by the question. "Well, it is customary, as you say," he said. "It seems a poor idea to leave valuable weapons unattended at the barracks, what with all the deserters and the like. And one prefers to have protection of some kind, if one appears in uniform."

"I see. And how many pistols are you carrying at the moment?"

"Two, miss."

Jacob immediately knew what was about to happen, because it had happened to him. He smiled to himself, relishing the moment, immeasurably proud of his brilliant wife.

"Are you certain, sir?" she asked. Then she raised one foot, letting her skirt fall so that her leg was revealed halfway to the knee. The eyes of every man in the room bulged, including Jacob's remaining eye, as Jeannie reached up along the outside of her own leg, her hand hidden beneath the skirt of her dress. "Because I only found one," she announced. Her leg returned to the floor, and the audience gasped as she raised a revolver high in the air.

The officer's jaw dropped. He looked down at his hip and hopelessly pulled his cloak aside to reveal his own right holster, which was empty. He stared at his own raised pistol in Jeannie's hand, flabbergasted.

She smiled at him. The guests, recovering from shock, at last burst into applause. Jeannie stooped down, placing the gun on the wide flat surface of the banister before straightening up again suddenly, as if she had forgotten something. "Oh, I'm so sorry, I was mistaken," she said loudly, cutting the applause short. "You did indeed have two." Then she reached behind her back and pulled out another revolver, which she pointed straight at the ceiling. But this time, before the audience could even regain its breath, she pulled the trigger—causing Captain Strathmore to drop by reflex to the floor. The gun only clicked.

"I couldn't help but notice that it wasn't loaded," Jeannie said with another smile, as Antonia gasped at Jacob's side. Jeannie reached out to hand the gun to the officer. Captain Strathmore jumped back up to his feet, visibly shaken, taking the gun back from Jeannie like an obedient child. She then took the other revolver from the railing, holding it in the air again as she turned to the audience.

"As you can see, the mental constraints of expectations are what the escape artist must first overcome, after which she may help herself to whatever she finds useful for a physical escape," she said to the crowd. "In fact, if I wished, I should find it quite simple to rob Captain Strathmore at gunpoint." She paused, her eyes narrowing as though she were trying to decide what to do, before adding, "Except that that would be—" She looked back at the shocked Captain Strathmore and smiled, waiting until he regained his senses enough to smile back at her. Then she reached into her décolletage, pulled out a billfold, and concluded, "entirely unnecessary."

The crowd was silent for a moment, astonished, before finally cheering as she handed the money and the second gun back to the bewildered officer onstage.

"She's a witch!" Antonia said to Jacob over the crowd's applause. "Truly a witch! Heaven help whichever man she marries!" Jacob looked at his wife, resplendent with brilliant beauty, and glowed with unearned pride.

"I thank you for your sportsmanship during this demonstration, Captain Strathmore," Jeannie said, and kissed his limp hand. "And I hope that you will never again make the mistake of underestimating the ladies. Fellow Rebels, please join me in a round of applause for the captain!" The officer descended the stairs quickly, chagrined as the audience cheered. Jacob clapped his hands as hard as everyone else, fighting to keep himself from weeping.

For the rest of that evening, Jacob watched as his wife liberated herself from handcuffs, wriggled free from a ladderback chair onto which she had been tied by another audience volunteer, and concealed herself completely in a bale of cotton—from which she emerged wearing a different dress. As promised, she popped out of a barrel that had been nailed shut, and out of a steamer trunk bound with chains. During the course of her performance, she also "borrowed" numerous items from people in the audience, all without their knowledge, and all returned to their great surprise—personal effects ranging from handkerchiefs to daggers. The audience was amazed, amused, laughing at each trick's finale, wondering what might happen next. But to Jacob, the tricks were almost irrelevant. The very fact that she was alive was the most astounding feat of all. As Jeannie made yet another demonstration of the escape artist's trade, he suddenly understood what had happened on that Yom Kippur two and a half years before.

"Borrowing weapons and breaking free from shackles, of course, are often convenient ways to escape from an unpleasant situation," she was telling her audience. "But occasionally one finds oneself under certain constraints—in a prison cell, for example—in which more dramatic means are necessary for redirecting the attention of one's guards. In those sorts of circumstances, I have found that the most effective way to distract people is by suffering an apoplectic stroke."

The guests leaned toward her, their applause from her previous act still fading as they eagerly awaited whatever was coming next. But Jacob thought of the newspaper article that had destroyed his life. Could it possibly be? "Now, I know what many of you are thinking," Jeannie said. "Even an amateur performer might be able to feign certain ailments with relative ease, but simulating something as severe as an apoplexy must surely be impossible. Inconceivable, isn't it?" Some of the guests nodded, though most simply watched her in silence—prepared, as the invitation had warned them, to be astounded. "Well, then," she said, with a wide smile, "why don't we see just how inconceivable it is?"

Of course, *of course*; why hadn't he thought of it before? Jacob watched, for the second time in his life, as Jeannie Levy voluntarily dislocated her jaw.

It was even more appalling than the first time he saw it. The entire lower half of her face appeared to fall right off of her head, her mouth distended beyond recognition, her jaw dangling by one corner in an unimaginably ghastly way. It was like watching a botched decapitation, just before the spurting of blood. The men in the room had surely all seen their share of gruesomely wounded soldiers, but witnessing a beautiful young woman becoming instantly and catastrophically disfigured onstage was something altogether different, and atrocious. Every person in the room gasped. But this was not enough for Jeannie. She let out a long, loud moan, a dark rattle of pure animal suffering, and collapsed on the landing, her body lying in a heap on the Cary sisters' carpet as her eyes rolled back into her head.

Once the guests overcame their astonishment, they waited, still leaning forward, for Jeannie to rise and conclude the trick. But Jeannie offered them no such relief. Instead she languished in her awful pose for one endless minute after another, as the audience's anticipation gradually faded into animated terror. A whisper rushed through the crowd.

"My word!" Antonia exclaimed, her scrubbed face turning pale as she pressed her fingers to her lips. "She must be—she must be—" Jacob pressed his own lips together, struggling not to laugh out loud.

Jeannie lay on the landing, immobile and deformed, for a very long time. Even Jacob worried for an instant, before reminding himself of who she was. But the guests had never seen anything like this before. The stillness of her body was lasting too long, the wait for her next move becoming indefinite, frightening. The audience rustled, the guests' confusion bordering on panic. At length, a one-armed man from the front row hastened up the stairs, pushed forward by the people around him. The man stooped down, standing just above Jeannie's head so that her body and disfigured face were still within the audience's view. He winced as he inspected her distorted features. "Miss Van Damme?" he asked meekly.

Jeannie did not move. The man scrutinized her, and hesitantly placed his remaining hand on the bare skin just above her dress's low neckline, inches from her corset. The crowd held its breath, but Jacob wondered, as he saw the man pressing his palm against her bosom, whether he was secretly enjoying it. The man looked back at the audience, his face flushed. "The lady isn't breathing," he announced.

At that moment, Jeannie raised her hand and slapped the man's wrist. He jumped up, startled, and then quickly lost his balance and tripped backward down the stairs, his fall broken only by three ladies who caught him by his remaining arm. The audience was still gasping when Jeannie sat up, took hold of her own jaw, and set it back into place with a loud, repulsive snap.

"Sir, even a dead lady deserves more respect than that," she said, adjusting her décolletage and smiling at the man in the front row. "But as you all can see, it is quite possible, when the situation calls for it, to feign an apoplectic stroke."

The crowd cheered as Antonia scowled at Jacob's side. "The lady is a witch, an actual witch," she repeated, with open disgust. "It's all some sort of Oriental witchcraft. I'm sure of it."

Jacob nodded, bewitched. Onstage, Jeannie was already moving on to her final act—demonstrating how, once dead, one could hypothetically proceed directly to the morgue, in order to conveniently escape just prior to one's own funeral. A long pinewood box was brought up to the landing, and now Jeannie was climbing into it with great flourish, lying down dramatically in her own coffin after inviting several volunteers up to the stage to nail it shut. As his wife was hammered into her casket, Jacob began to add up the pieces in his head. He thought of the hysterical attack that the newspaper had reported, and suddenly he understood precisely how she had done it: her feigned stroke must have gotten her carried out of the prison and into a hospital, and then from there she had continued to the great beyond. Some pieces were missing, to be sure, leaving him raging with curiosity. It was one thing to fool people at a ball, for instance, but how could she have convinced doctors in a hospital of her supposed death? How could anyone have reported her death to the newspapers, with no body to show for it? How had she made it out of the hospital, or out of the morgue? After she escaped, how had she managed to cross the lines and return home? But he already knew that for Jeannie, these were mere details, the predictable limits of other people's expectations. She would have transcended them all.

The volunteers left the stage, their task completed. The coffin on the landing rattled, and then it was still.

The silence lasted quite a while. Everyone in the room watched the casket, waiting. It occurred to Jacob that for the other guests, the scene must have been familiar, even if not consciously so: they had all been trained since childhood to expect a body to rise up from its coffin, to anticipate a resurrection. But Jacob saw the casket and thought of a different story, one his Hebrew tutor had taught him long ago: that when the Romans conquered Jerusalem, a certain rabbi saw the danger and had himself smuggled out of the city in a coffin, so that he could find a refuge for his students where they could reconstruct the edifice of life. He knew that Jeannie would never do something as predictable as rising from a coffin; her imagination was far too large to be contained within it. And so Jacob was the first person to notice when Jeannie emerged like an apparition, wrapped in a gauzy white robe—at the top of the staircase, looking down on them all.

"These shrouds are so unbecoming," she announced.

Everyone looked up, flabbergasted. How had she gotten there? Jacob didn't know either, but it didn't matter. She was proceeding down the stairs now; soon she was standing on the landing again, next to her own coffin. She cast the shroud aside, revealing, yet again, an entirely different dress. It was a plain white gown that was strangely inappropriate—too poor for this sort of society ball, even under the circumstances. Despite his compromised vision, even Jacob could see where the skirt had been torn and patched. The audience, still amazed, burst once more into

applause. But Jacob kept watching her, his one eye watering as he struggled not to weep. She was wearing her wedding gown.

"Thank you all so much for indulging me this evening," she declared,
with a sweeping curtsy. "I hope to see you all again soon, well above
ground."

Miss Cary had ascended to the landing, a wide grin on her face as she
took Jeannie by the hand and announced, "Ladies and gentlemen, please
join me in a round of applause for Miss Eugenia Van Damme!"

The cheering was loud and long, almost endless. Jacob watched as
Jeannie wearied of it and began to retreat, gradually edging toward the
curtained door at the back of the landing. And that was when a man near
the front of the room, with officer's epaulets, raised his one remaining
arm and shouted over the crowd's applause, "Miss Van Damme, will you
marry me?"

Jacob assumed that this was simply an offhand joke, crude but unre-
markable. But the other guests made no such assumptions. To Jacob's
astonishment, the guests stopped clapping and leaned forward with genuine curiosity, waiting to hear the celebrity's reply. Every person in the
room was drunk on dirty water and dreams.

In her wedding dress, Jeannie was perfectly poised. "Of course," she
replied.

The guests gazed at her, unsure of whether to believe her. Jacob sat
motionless. Then Jeannie smiled, and everyone laughed. "But yours is
a rather popular request, and I'm afraid it would be cruel to the other
gentlemen in the room not to acknowledge their interests as well," she
said. "So I must try to be fair." Jacob swallowed. Had she seen him? No,
she was still grinning, still Miss Eugenia Van Damme. It was all a joke to
her. Even her own wedding gown was nothing more than a disguise.

"Hold a lottery!" someone shouted.

"Why don't we hold an auction?" Jeannie suggested, eyeing Miss
Cary. "For the benefit of the hospital, of course. Miss Cary can be the
auctioneer."

Antonia nudged Jacob, gasping. "Can you imagine?" she huffed. "How
utterly revolting. I've heard she's had dozens of paramours."

Had she? He thought of his affair with her cousin, and was surprised
to discover that he did not care if she had. He only cared—and cared
desperately—whether she had one now.

But now Miss Cary was holding a wooden spoon that someone in the audience had passed to her, her angular face grinning wildly. "An excellent idea, Miss Van Damme. Let's begin!"

Jeannie jumped up onto the coffin, standing on it as if it were an auction block. Miss Cary banged the spoon against the end of the banister, and affected her best attempt at a baritone drawl. "Gentlemen, next on the block is Eugenia Van Damme, age twenty-one, in the prime of her breeding years. She has proven herself to be exceptionally industrious in the fields, and her former masters have lauded her for her unimpeachable servitude. I am, however, obliged to admit that she does have one demerit—her attempts at escape."

Everyone laughed, but Jacob was sickened. He watched as Jeannie paced back and forth on the wooden coffin and thought of Dorrie, naked on the block, down the street from Philip's old office. What had so nauseated him on that long-ago afternoon was, to everyone here, simply routine, ripe for parody only because it was so familiar. He glanced at the glasses of dirty water that were littered about the hall, and realized something. The secret service had been sending him gold coinage to defray his expenses, much of which he was obliged to keep on his person, out of fear of burglary in his inconspicuously poor lodgings. But even his commanders did not appreciate how starved the city was. He suddenly understood that he was the richest person in the room.

"Shall we start the bidding at twenty dollars for Eugenia Van Damme?" Miss Cary called. "In gold only, gentlemen." Confederate cash was worthless, of course; even the otherwise deluded knew that. "Do I hear twenty dollars for Eugenia Van Damme?"

"Twenty-five," a man in the back of the room yelled.

"Thirty," countered another, near the front.

"Thirty-five."

"Forty."

Miss Cary held the spoon high. "Forty dollars. Do I hear fifty?"

Rose had warned him to stay back, to avoid being noticed. *She hates you*, he heard Rose say in his head. Surely it was true. But how could he simply watch?

"Fifty," a man just past Antonia called.

"Sixty."

"Sixty-five."

"Seventy."

If Jeannie saw him, she would turn him in. It wasn't even a question. Perhaps she would even expose him onstage, in front of everyone. But what if he were to wait, and someone else were to take her? The auction was just a game, of course, but to Jacob it represented something larger: at any moment, she might fall in love with someone else, and forget him forever. Every man in Richmond was clearly drooling over her; it was surely only a matter of time before she attached herself to someone else, if she hadn't already. But if he at least made the attempt, then there was some small possibility that he might stand beside her again, even if only for a moment. And even if he were caught and hanged tomorrow, she would at least know that he had never forgotten her—that he had made a promise to her father and kept it, that he had wanted to see the baby, that he knew the meaning of devotion, that he had tried.

"One hundred," Captain Strathmore shouted, to cheers.

Jacob raised his hand. "One hundred fifty," he called, with as much drawl as he could summon.

"Jacob!" Antonia gasped.

Her idle jealousy made him smile. The other hands in the room had gone down by now; only Captain Strathmore remained. "One hundred fifty-five," he announced.

It was a transparent tactic, one Jacob recognized immediately as a businessman. He was finished. "Two hundred," Jacob said. Dorrie had sold for more than six times that.

"Two hundred," Miss Cary repeated. "Two hundred. Going once. Going twice." The room was silent. Miss Cary banged the spoon on the banister. "Sold, for two hundred dollars gold, to the gentleman with the eye patch. Please, sir, come up to the block and claim your property." The crowd cheered.

Jacob stood up, slowly, with the eyes of the guests on him. Jeannie squinted in his direction and quickly looked away, granting her beautiful smile to the crowd. She didn't recognize him.

Miss Cary helped him up the steps to the landing. He stood in front of Jeannie, displayed on the platform in her wedding dress, and tried not to stare. She looked at him again, but only briefly. She still had barely glanced at his face. Instead, she watched as he pulled out his change purse, leaning on his cane as he dropped gold coins into Miss Cary's open hands, to the applause of the guests. "What is your name, sir?" Miss Cary asked with a smile.

"Sergeant Samuels," he replied, employing the accent to full effect. It was a name he was used to.

"Sergeant Samuels, we cannot thank you enough for your generous contribution to Chimborazo Hospital," she said, to further applause. Then she glanced at Jeannie, who fell immediately into character. Jeannie swooped down in a deep curtsy, dropping almost to her knees before him on the coffin. He could barely breathe. "As there are no priests on the premises this evening to perform the sacrament," Miss Cary continued, "I'm afraid you will have to consider this merely a betrothal, rather than a wedding ceremony. I trust that will be acceptable."

"Quite acceptable," he said in his artificial drawl. The guests tittered. But he couldn't take his eye off Jeannie, groveling before him for the benefit of the crowd.

At last she rose, shimmering in her wedding gown. "Thank you for your purchase, Sergeant Samuels. I shall look forward to loving, honoring, and obeying you for the remainder of my days," she said, winning laughs from the guests. But before he could even catch her eye, she turned to Miss Cary, silently urging her. Miss Cary nodded quickly, and turned back to the crowd.

"I'm afraid we must say goodnight to Miss Van Damme now and allow her to return home, so that she may continue to raise the morale of her adoring public in the future," Miss Cary announced, and turned to Jacob. "Sir, if you would like to meet your betrothed outside, a servant shall escort you," she said, and then eyed Jeannie. "If that is all right with Miss Van Damme."

"Don't worry, Miss Cary," Jeannie grandly announced. "If he attempts anything ungentlemanly, I can outrun him."

Jacob smiled. She always could. The crowd laughed as a slave took him by the elbow, helping him down the stairs and back into the audience, around the edges of the room, and toward the front door. But no one was looking at him now; once again, all eyes were on Jeannie.

"Ladies and gentlemen, please join me in one more round of applause for Miss Eugenia Van Damme!" he heard Miss Cary announce behind him. He glanced over his shoulder and saw Jeannie curtsying one more time, and then hastening down from the coffin and through the curtain behind the landing, as two slaves hurried up behind her to begin moving the coffin through the same curtain. The audience was still cheering when the slave deposited Jacob at the entrance to the Carys' home. The door closed behind him. He stood leaning on his cane in the cold evening air, wondering if the person he was tonight was the person he would always be.

JACOB WOULD HAVE expected a carriage to be waiting for Jeannie after her performance, but he was surprised to find nothing outside but the empty road, lit by the grand lamps beside the Carys' front door. He had forgotten that Jeannie wasn't actually part of high society here any more than he was. She was merely their entertainment, work for hire. A quarter of an hour later, when his legs were on the verge of collapse, he saw her rounding the corner of the house, emerging from a servants' entrance. She wore a thin dark cloak over her white wedding dress, with a satchel slung over her shoulder, her hair pulled back, unadorned, behind her head. She saw him standing by the door and squinted, hesitating for an instant before continuing to approach. He saw her coming toward him in her wedding gown, walking with unassuming steps, her grandiosity dissolved, and he could not believe that he was not dreaming. His remaining eye filled with tears.

Now she stood before him, and looked down at her feet. She still did not look at him. "Sergeant Samuels, I am quite appreciative of your generosity toward the hospital," she said. She spoke in her real voice this time, drained of all pretense. "But I trust you recognize that the tone of the evening was in jest. I would be pleased to become better acquainted with you at another time, I truly would. But I must hurry home now. I hope you will understand."

"I do," he said, in his own real voice. "But I would very much like to become better acquainted with you, Jeannie. With you, and with our baby."

Now Jeannie looked up, and stared at him. She stared and stared, her beautiful dark eyes taking in his eye patch, his cane, his scarred face, his smile. The world opened up between them. Before he could say anything more, his wife fainted—this time for real.

PART NINE

ALL OTHER NIGHTS

I.

"I WILL KILL YOU, I WILL, IF YOU SO MUCH AS COME NEAR ME OR MY baby, I will kill you, I will—oh God, Jacob, what happened to you?"

Jacob leaned over Jeannie as she opened her eyes, crouched painfully on his cane as she rose up from the ground. At first she backed away from him, frightened, shaking as she threatened him. When she stopped speaking, she stood watching him for a very long time, motionless in her wedding gown. She stepped toward him and squinted at him, absorbing his eye patch, his disfigured skin. He stood in silence as her eyes moved along the scars on his face.

"I thought you had died," he finally said.

She remained motionless. He watched her, still amazed that it was really she, and tried to imagine what she was thinking. Did she hate him? Was he a beast to her now, inside and out? What reason could she ever have to forgive him?

At last she said, "Our daughter looks like you."

The sound of horses' hooves clopped toward them as a carriage rounded a corner in the distance, coming toward the house. "The guests will start leaving soon," Jeannie said, under her breath. "Come this way."

She began hurrying toward the back of the Cary sisters' home, where he had seen her come out of the servants' door. But he couldn't walk as fast as she could, and it took her a moment to adjust to his pace. He saw where she was taking him—to a large wooden tool shed on the far side of the house.

She pulled open the door of the shed and stepped into it. Jacob followed. As she vanished into the shadows, he leaned against the wall inside the shed for balance, reached into his pocket and struck a match. When the match ignited, he looked around and saw that the shed was full of Jeannie's props: the trick handcuffs, the slip-knotted ropes, the barrel nailed shut with too-short nails, and even her red dress, its skirts rumpled inside-out and its dozens of secret pockets revealed. Opposite the door, Jeannie's coffin was standing upright, the trap door in its side hanging open on its hinges. In the flickering light of Jacob's match, Jeannie stepped back toward him. He watched as she took a half-burned candle out of the satchel on her shoulder and touched it to the match's flame between them, a tiny quiet kiss of heat and light. She dipped its other end into the flame and planted it on the lid of the trunk, before closing the door behind them.

The air in the little shed was still. Jacob shook out the match and waited, his gentleman's reflex strangely intact, as Jeannie sat down on the cotton bale, her wedding gown spread across it as though she were seated on a cloud. He settled down beside her, startled when the cotton didn't give beneath him but instead remained as firm as a wooden bench, as if there were some sort of support inside it. Of course there was. She was examining him now in the candlelight, wincing as her eyes scanned and then avoided his disfigured face. She looked away from him, and he saw the slight revulsion in her expression. He was hideous, and he always would be. He looked at the dripping candle, watching each teardrop of wax harden as it slid away from the little flame. At last he found the strength to speak.

"I didn't turn you in, Jeannie. I turned in your sister, because I was afraid, but I never turned you in. I—I'm so sorry."

She was silent. He looked back up at her and saw that she was stealing glances at his scars, blinking her eyes. At close range in the candlelight, it was clear how much she had aged in these few long years—how her eyes had grown tired, her forehead and cheeks creased by worry and fear. But her sadness only made her more beautiful, making her face more mysterious, more captivating. The curve of her body in her wedding gown still enchanted him. Everything about her enchanted him. He could hardly bear sitting beside her; it took all of his strength not to take her in his arms. But he could not tell whether she wanted to be taken. He held back, afraid, as she remained silent.

He rubbed at his remaining eye, blinded. A moment passed in darkness before his vision adjusted again, as he waited for her to speak. But she said nothing. "I waited for you that night," he said, when he could wait no longer. "I would have waited for days, if I could have."

Still she was silent. Her silence horrified him. He made one more attempt to speak, no longer able to keep the pleading out of his voice. "When I reached Washington, I tried to convince them to release you," he said. It was weak, feeble, but it was all that he had. She hadn't even needed him; she had released herself. "I asked them to exchange you for your father," he added. "I—" But he didn't know what else to say.

She was silent for another long moment, a small eternity. Finally she spoke. "Lottie said she saw our father at the border when she—when they—" She stopped, holding her breath, and at last looked back at him. "You arranged that?"

Jacob's head was throbbing. He tried to ignore it. He was half-seeing and half-imagining the woman in front of him; the gleam of the light on her lips was so glorious that it could not possibly belong to the same world as this dirty tool shed full of broken chains. He pictured her standing with her sisters in the front room of Philip Levy's house, the mirror behind her reflecting her ribbon in his hair. He still could not believe that it was really she. "I meant for them to release you, not your sister," he said softly, too terrified to lie. "And I didn't intend it to take two years."

"You don't know what a gift you gave us, just to know that he was freed," she said. "No one told us that it was because of you." The shed was cold, but the air between them was warm with her breath. "Have you seen him?" she asked.

Her father was the one who mattered to her, he understood. "A few months ago, in Philadelphia," he answered. "He was living with his brother."

Jeannie leaned toward him. He could smell her now, an unexpected smell that he had long forgotten—a sweet scent of ripe longing in the hollow of her neck, like fresh fruit. "Really?" she gasped. "Oh God, how—was he well?"

Jacob thought of everything he hadn't told her and her sisters while Philip was in jail, the familiar lies welling up in his mind. He pushed them away. "He's aged twenty years," he said. "He had heard that you were dead. He asked me to come here, to try to find you and your sisters. It was all that mattered to him."

Now she was watching him, her face skeptical. "You came here for him?"

Jacob perceived the doubt in her eyes, and started thinking quickly—the liar's reflex, planning the best approach. But then he stopped planning, and told the truth. "No," he said. "I came here for you."

Her eyes returned to his scars, and she cringed, a visceral disgust. He turned away from her to spare her his ugliness. But as he turned away, he felt her hand curl around his, her fingers warm and alive against his cold hard palm. He held his breath. In two and a half years of dreams, he had forgotten the specific beauty of her hands, the firm enveloping power of her magician's fingers around his mortal palm. He saw her looking down at his hand in hers, and he knew she was imagining how he used to be. The pity in her expression was unbearable. But he couldn't release her hand.

"When I heard you were captured, I—I—" he stammered after a moment, when at last he was sure she wouldn't let go. *I was devastated*, he would have said, but he couldn't bring himself to say it. He was still too ashamed to ask her about anything that had happened since—too ashamed, even, to ask about the child. "I wanted to go to see you in the prison, but no one would allow it."

Her hair had fallen loose from where she had tied it behind her head, a dark curl hanging over her eye. It reminded him of her cousin Abigail. He flinched, oppressed by every mistake he had ever made, every unforgiven sin. She brushed the loose curl behind her ear. To his surprise, she smiled. Her smile unnerved him, as though he were once again sitting beside her in the front room of the house after her sisters had gone upstairs, alone with her for the first time. "You wouldn't have found me there in any case," she said. "I was sent to the hospital within hours, and then I was gone."

"I guessed as much, when I saw your show this evening," he said, watching her as she enjoyed his bewilderment. Her hand was still wrapped around his. "But I don't understand how you were able to convince the doctors in the hospital that you were dead."

Now her smile was even wider, as though she were trying not to laugh. It was the way she had looked at him the first time they met, when she had helped herself to his wallet, before he understood who she was. He still wasn't sure whether she was laughing at him. "The ward of the hospital in Washington didn't have any other lady patients, so the nurses put up a curtain around my bed when I was carried in," she began. He listened, mesmerized. "After my supposed collapse, I borrowed a pistol from the guard, which I kept under my dress. When the doctor came behind the curtain to examine me, he put his ear against my chest to listen to my heart. I pressed the pistol against his head and whispered to him, 'Pardon me, Doctor, but I must inform you that a guerrilla force of Rebels has infiltrated this hospital. Four of your fellow doctors are our agents, as are twelve of the nurses and twenty-seven of the patients. All of us are armed. The only way you can survive this situation is if you succeed in releasing me alive. If you sign my death certificate, declare me dead, and send my body promptly to the morgue, you will spare yourself and your true patients from further retribution. If you fail to do this, or if you tell anyone about this exchange, I will kill you immediately, and the shot will signal the others to begin the revolt. Doctor, am I being perfectly clear?'" She added with a grin, "The next thing I saw was a sheet being drawn over my face, and I heard the doctor telling the guards from the prison that the Lord would surely have mercy upon my sinful soul."

Jacob laughed out loud, and Jeannie laughed with him. For a moment it was as if nothing had been lost, as if they were laughing together in the front room of her father's house, as if she had forgotten how he had disfigured himself in every possible way. But he remembered.

"How did you get out of Washington?" he asked.

Her smile faded. She shook her head, drawing her feet up onto the cotton bale and pulling her knees against her chest, huddled in her wedding dress against the wall of the shed like a child. Her hand slipped from his. "I won't tell you," she said. "What I did was unforgivable. Even you wouldn't have done anything like it."

He considered her, diminished in the shadows against the wall of the shed, and remembered his own smallness, how he was nothing more than dust and ashes. "I'm quite certain that I would have," he said, and at last decided to confess. "Before I met you, I murdered my own uncle."

She stared at him, incredulous, then suddenly smiled. "Jacob, you're an awful liar," she said.

He forced himself to look at her. "No, Jeannie, it's true. That was my first mission. My uncle was plotting to kill Lincoln, so I was assigned to kill my uncle first." He thought of adding the gruesome details—how it had happened at the Passover seder, how Harry Hyams had poured out his wrath onto the table before him, how Elizabeth had doubled over screaming, how easily he had become the angel of death. But he was not that brave. Instead he added, "He really would have killed Lincoln, Jeannie. I heard him planning it. It was beyond doubt. I saved Lincoln's life." As he said it, he could hear how false it sounded, how little he believed it even now, how certain he still was that Harry Hyams would never have gone through with it.

He watched as her smile disappeared, her mouth slowly falling open. "Jacob," she breathed. "How could you have agreed to do that?"

"How could I have said no?"

Her beautiful face was pale. "He was your uncle," she said, her voice still. "You could have said no."

He tried to think of a reply, but there was none. Suddenly he understood that she was right. He could have said no. And he hung his head in shame.

She shifted in her place, lowering her legs back to the floor as a loose chain clanked somewhere against a wall. The coffin cast a flickering shadow over her face. Jacob looked at the seam sewn across the lap of her wedding gown, wishing there were some way he could atone. He thought of what Benjamin had warned: that the person he was that night was the person he would always be. But didn't that make repentance impossible?

"After I escaped from the hospital, there was a Federal army captain whom I—whom I—befriended," Jeannie finally said.

He was grateful to hear her voice, until he realized what she meant. Now he looked up at her, but she was looking away, her fingers tracing patterns on the patched skirt of her dress. "And he helped you to come home?" he asked, with forced innocence.

"He did," she said, then stopped, still looking at the seam on her skirt. "I was frightened, and desperate, and already expecting." He watched her, refusing to understand, until he did. She brushed a curl behind her reddened ear, and added, "I could have said no."

He looked at the candle, afraid that she would think he was judging her. He was, of course, just as she was judging him. She lowered her head, blinking her eyes in the dim room. He waited a long time, sitting beside her, until he sensed the shame slowly dissipating, the residue of all their deeds staining the ground beneath their feet.

"Jeannie, what is our daughter like?" he asked.

She looked up at him, and he saw how her face illuminated, suddenly brightened by something close to happiness. "Her name is Deborah, and she is always smiling," she answered. "Most children her age are afraid of strangers, but she runs up to people in the streets to say hello. She smiles at everyone, even the crippled beggars and the slaves. We joke that she could be a society hostess, except that her tastes are a bit too democratic." It was impossible to imagine this, though he struggled mightily to try. "I named her after my mother," Jeannie said, "but she looks exactly like you. It's almost frightening. Every time I look at her, I think of you, whether I want to or not," She looked down at her knees. "For most of the past two years I haven't particularly wanted to think of you," she said. "To say that I hated you would be too generous. I wanted you to suffer."

He imagined her prayers for retribution mingling with her father's, rising up from their mouths to God's ears. In the dim light, she examined his eye patch and his cane. He saw that her disgust had faded somewhat; she was becoming accustomed to his ugliness, able to look at him without complete revulsion. She didn't ask him how it had happened. In her own way, she knew.

"But everything changed when Lottie came back," she continued. "Because then I remembered all the things she had done to me."

He wasn't expecting this. "What—what do you mean?"

"When the cavalry captured me and Lottie, they gagged us and locked us into the back of a wagon together," she said. "At one point Lottie's gag fell off and she started shouting at me, unforgivable insults." Her cheeks were flushed as she spoke. "She screamed that I had sold her off like a slave, and then that I was a whore, that I had sold myself to you, that I—that I—" She bit her lip, looking at the candle. "At the time I was shocked to hear her say those things. But later I understood that it was no different from everything she had done before I met you. She was the one who convinced me to go back to William, so that he could become our contact."

"What do you mean, to go back to William?"

She bit her lip again in the dim light, her face darkening. "William had proposed to me the previous year, and I had refused him," she said. Jacob hadn't known this, though he could hardly be surprised that she had never told him. "It was beyond humiliating for me to crawl back to him like that. But Lottie told me that it ought to mean nothing to me, that I was being selfish, that I was betraying our mother—and I believed it all. I didn't know at the time that I could have said no." Jeannie was watching him now, taking in his whole mangled form before her. "Later I understood that you had been my escape."

Jacob's eye began to water, his vision blurring. Suddenly, with painful, unforgiving clarity, he understood that he would never be worthy of her.

"How did you manage to come to Richmond?" she asked, with strained cheer, after he had been silent for too long. "I hope you weren't smuggled down in a coffin."

She meant to lighten the air between them, he knew. But he shook his head. "I can't tell you," he said.

A shadow crossed her face. "Oh no. No. Don't say that."

"I haven't said anything."

"Jacob, it isn't like it was before. They hang everyone now. You can't continue."

He remembered what he needed to tell her. The space behind his missing eye throbbed as he understood what it meant: that this was not only his first time seeing her again, but likely his last. "No one is continuing, Jeannie."

"What do you mean?"

"The government is preparing to evacuate. They're abandoning the city."

She leaned back, alarmed. Then she laughed, as though she had just understood a clever joke. "That's an old rumor, Jacob," she said. "People were talking about that months ago, but it's not true. Everyone is still laughing at the rich people who left."

"No, Jeannie, it's true. I work in the State Department. The government has already distributed the evacuation plans. Even Judah Benjamin is going to escape to England somehow. He told me that himself." She leaned back against the wall, bewildered. "Jeannie, you have to leave. As soon as possible. Go with your whole family. Tomorrow morning, if you can. Is there somewhere you can go?"

Her eyebrows pulled together, a knot of worry lodging itself at the base of her forehead. He recognized her expression, from Philip's face. "My uncle once had a cousin in Lynchburg," she said. "But we haven't heard from him in years. I'm not even certain that he—"

"Good. Go to him. Get on the first train you can find. All of you. Leave tomorrow morning. Bring everything with you."

She was still shocked. "What about you?"

"I have to meet a courier at the old cemetery on Sunday evening, at midnight," he said. "I'm meant to bring him a message, but I plan to ask him to take me back to Washington with him."

Jeannie's eyes narrowed. "Why don't you just wait for the Yankees to come and save you?" she asked, and he heard in her voice the slightest edge of a sneer. "Someone always saves you. You never save yourself."

Was that what she thought of him? Surely it was, and rightly so. But it no longer mattered. "It's more difficult than that, Jeannie. I've seen the instructions for the militia when the government evacuates. They're going to burn down the city. I doubt I'd survive it."

"Burn down the city?" Her voice was strange, childlike, stricken with wonder. But she quickly recovered. "Jacob, that's absurd. Why on earth—"

"Oh, they only intend to destroy a few resources, of course, so the enemy won't be able to use them. They merely want to burn all the tobacco warehouses, and burn all the food, and scuttle all the ships, and blow up all the ordnance, and . . . well, if their only intention was to destroy the supplies, then why didn't anyone suggest simply dumping the supplies in the river?"

"Surely there must be some reason behind it," Jeannie said.

"The reason is irrelevant. Almost every building in this city is made of wood."

He saw her glancing around the tool shed, at the coffin and the barrel and the chains. He couldn't begin to imagine what she was thinking. But he had seen how impossible everything had become, and how impossible it would remain. Whatever was left of her love for him was poisoned by pity, and his for her was poisoned by regret. "Promise me you'll leave," he said.

She sat motionless, still astonished, as he struggled to form the words for what he now knew he had to tell her.

"Jeannie, I don't know when I will see you again, but it may be a very long time, or never," he said. *Because I have become too ugly*, he meant, *and you have become too beautiful, and mercy and longing are only corrupt cousins of love, and neither of us can ever return to the people we once were.* But he did not need to say it. She knew. "Please don't wait for me," he finally told her. "I—I release you, Jeannie. If people ask, tell them I've died. Find another father for Deborah."

For a moment she was silent. She lowered her head, bowing before him. Perhaps she knew that he was right. Then she spoke, and her eyes gleamed with tears. "Deborah started speaking clearly a few months ago," she said. "She isn't even two years old, but she understands much more than one might expect. I told her about you. She knows how to say 'Papa.'"

He was too small for this, he saw, too damned to deserve it. Suddenly she sat up, straightening in the shadows. "What time is it?" she asked.

He might have thought the question odd, but he was barely present, his mind awash with regret. Without thinking, he slipped his watch out of his pocket, as though he had been asked for the time by a stranger on the street. "A quarter past midnight," he answered. It was later than he expected, though he cared not in the least.

Jeannie was fidgeting, anxious, as if he had broken a magic spell. "I have to go home to Deborah," she said.

It was strange to hear her say these words, as though Deborah were an actual child rather than an impossible fantasy. For Jacob, the very idea was inconceivable. But Jeannie had given her life, sustained her, and enabled her to reach this very moment—and now somewhere in this doomed city, an almost-two-year-old child who looked exactly like him was lying in bed asleep, waiting for her mother. To Jacob it was nothing but a dream, unearned and unreal.

"I have to go home," Jeannie repeated, when he didn't reply. "My sisters will be frantic. They may even send Lottie to fetch me. It isn't safe for you if I stay here any longer." It was true, he knew, though he wondered if it were also an excuse, a way for her to take leave of him without guilt. She didn't invite him to join her; they both already knew that he never could. But she also didn't rise from her seat. Instead she leaned toward him, her face hovering over his scars, and he felt her breath against his cheek. "Forgive me, Jacob, but it's difficult to look at you," she said.

He said nothing as she stood up. Her cloak narrowed her dress and her body beneath it into a thin column before him, a pillar of white smoke. Before he could struggle to his feet beside her, she bent down and blew the candle out.

Darkness enveloped them, and suddenly he felt her arms around him, her lips against his fingers, his neck, his mouth, as she drew him to his feet. Her tongue against his skin was so electric that he became delirious: he tried to stand on his own, and forgot that he no longer could. In an instant he crashed to his knees on the hard dirt floor.

Pain shot through his legs, but he ignored it, overwhelmed by a sweet new agony. He groped in the darkness until he felt her shoes, and then her legs beneath her dress, the unbearable curve of her flesh rising beneath his fingers as he reached up to her, pulling her down until she was kissing him again. Then his hands were slipping beneath her corset, trembling against her breasts, and he felt how stunningly strange they were, reshaped by the baby, large and unfamiliar and beautiful in his hands. But she straightened, vanishing beyond his reach, kissing the top of his head like a child as he knelt before her in the dark, and his shattered legs failed him: he could not rise up again.

"I have to go home to Deborah," she repeated in his ear as she pulled him back to his feet. "They've surely missed me by now. I don't want my sister to—" She couldn't support his weight. He sank down on the cotton bale, drowning in regret. "I'm so sorry, Jacob. I shall come back to you, I promise. I'll come back with Deborah, when you leave the city. I shall wait for you," he heard her whisper in the dark, as he panted for air. He could detect the pity in her voice, and he knew she said it only to comfort him. She kissed him again, but now her comfort compounded his pain. She had always been a liar.

From his slouch on the cotton bale, he saw a tall gray rectangle of light appear as the door to the shed creaked open, dim lamps from the house and the street illuminating the room. The silhouette of her body was painted in black against the light. He took his cane from the ground and struggled to his feet. "Jeannie," he called, but she was already turned toward the door.

"I'll come back," she said. He knew better than to believe her; he had heard her say it before. She vanished, leaving him staring at the coffin with its open trapdoor. Three days later, the end of the world arrived.

2

*T*HE WORLD HAS ENDED MANY TIMES BEFORE, AS MEN LIKE OLD Isaacs of the Old World know. But when it is your first war, no matter how often you were warned, you are invariably surprised.

The Jews of Richmond were the last to hear. It happened during the magical hour, on a bright Sunday morning when everyone else was in church. Jefferson Davis was the first to be surprised, approached in his pew at St. Paul's with a telegram. When he read it, his face turned gray, and he rose in the middle of the sermon and hurried out of the sanctuary. The rest of the congregation soon followed, talebearers dispatched from church to church, and shortly thereafter every preacher in the city was announcing the news to the faithful. The Hebrews were still taking their Sunday walks when the Christians returned home early, rushing to pack their bags and running to the railroad depot. Jacob had remained in his rented room, but when he heard the shouting outside, he immediately loaded all the gold he still had into the various pockets of his suit and made his way to the office, where he expected Benjamin's letter to be waiting for him.

He usually took an omnibus between his lodgings and the government offices—a distance he would have happily walked, if he were able—but the combination of the Christian Sabbath and the Confederate apocalypse had eliminated that option. It would have been impossible regardless: the streets were jammed with every imaginable type of carriage, coach, and wagon, those already loaded unable to move because of all the furniture and belongings being carried into the streets. He made his way through the city slowly, forced to stop every thirty yards or so both by his legs and by the traffic on the sidewalks, and he grew increasingly nervous. Had Jeannie listened to him? He prayed that she had, that she and her family were long gone, though he still stared at every young woman he saw in the streets. It took him hours to traverse the distance to Capitol Square. By the time he arrived, the sidewalks were already on fire.

Small fires, this time: pyres had been lit in front of the government offices, and soldiers were burning large bundles of documents in the street. Jacob made his way around them, glancing at the piles of papers and wondering if there might be anything in them that he ought to rescue. But it had all become moot; his very presence had become unnecessary, redundant. The only paper he needed was the one in Benjamin's safe. He made his way into the building and limped toward Benjamin's office. He was about to knock on Benjamin's half-closed door when he heard Benjamin's voice inside, speaking in French. "I have nothing in particular to say to you, but I wanted to be sure that I shook your hand before we left," he heard Benjamin say, remembering what he had learned in French lessons years ago, in his rich boy's life. "We shall return in three weeks. Four at the most. I appreciate your services, Monsieur." Then the door opened, and the French consul emerged, looking utterly bewildered as he hurried down the hallway. Few people are ever prepared for the end of the world.

Judah Benjamin was. Jacob found him seated at his desk, arranging papers in neat stacks. As Jacob entered, Benjamin slid one of the stacks into the fireplace, as routinely as though he were inserting it into a drawer. "I have been waiting for you, Rappaport," he said, slipping another stack into the fire. "I expected you hours ago. We shall be leaving for the depot in an hour and a half."

"I do apologize," Jacob replied. "There was a bit of traffic on the way."

The perpetual smile emerged again, Benjamin's private shield against contempt. Jacob saw it and felt almost nostalgic. Benjamin may have been the enemy, but Jacob knew how much he had suffered, how he had borne his entire life as a burden of proof.

"I trust that you recall the assignment I mentioned to you," Benjamin said, and crossed the room to open the safe. The safe was empty now, Jacob saw, except for the little envelope with Benjamin's seal. The gold was finished; everything was finished. Benjamin handed the envelope to Jacob. "It is exceedingly urgent that this message be delivered to the courier without fail. He will be at the burial ground at Shockoe Hill at midnight. I know that I may depend on you."

"Of course," Jacob said as he tucked the letter into his vest pocket—

though at that very moment he was remembering the evacuation orders, thinking of how difficult it had been simply to walk across town in the crowds, and considering whether he ought instead to be heading to the depot himself. Wasn't his work here finished too?

It was, as far as Benjamin was concerned. Benjamin stood and reached out to shake Jacob's hand. "I'm sorry, but I must take leave of you now. I have a great deal to accomplish in the brief time remaining," he said. More documents to burn, Jacob assumed. "I hope we shall meet again someday, under kinder circumstances," he added. Then, to Jacob's surprise, Benjamin bowed to him. "I am grateful for your loyalty, Rappaport. It has been a great comfort to me to have someone here whom I could trust."

Jacob was speechless, but Benjamin was already ushering him to the door. "Remember me to my sister," he said. Before Jacob could reply, he had closed the door behind him, the scent of burning paper wafting into the hallway.

Jacob hobbled down the corridor, his last trip back to his shabby clerk's room, and wondered what he might be able to salvage from the papers there. But the room had already been thoroughly stripped, the shelves and drawers completely emptied, the papers presumably already incinerated in the street. Nothing remained except a few unused stationery supplies. Jacob took an envelope the same size as Benjamin's letter and slid it into his pocket. He wouldn't be able to reseal it, but it would have to do.

He left the building, passed the burning documents in Capitol Square, and retreated into an alley by a horses' stable. Then he tore open the letter and began to read.

TO BE RELEASED TO ALL AGENTS:

INSOFAR AS THE GOVERNMENT IS CURRENTLY UNABLE TO OVERSEE THE ACTIONS OF ITS AGENTS BEHIND ENEMY LINES, IT IS HEREBY ORDERED THAT <u>ALL OPERATIONS BE CANCELED</u>, AND THAT <u>NO ACTION BE TAKEN BY ANY AGENTS AGAINST THE ENEMY, UNDER ANY CIRCUMSTANCES</u>. ANY DEVIATION FROM THIS ORDER WILL BE SUBJECT TO CAPITAL CHARGES OF TREASON AGAINST THE C.S.A.

BY ORDER OF
J.P. BENJAMIN,
SECRETARY OF STATE.

The message startled him. Were there really people in the field who were still planning to kidnap Lincoln, despite it all? Or was Benjamin afraid that the agents would become rogues, that their rage couldn't be contained without specific instructions? The latter, Jacob decided. But if the agents couldn't be trusted to refrain from acting on their own—from going through with the kidnapping, or something even more dire—then how on earth would this mere message succeed in restraining them? The letter's final line was painfully poignant: to what defunct court would such charges be brought? What reason would these agents have to obey such an order at all? Only loyalty, Jacob understood: delusional devotion to a lost cause. That they surely had. He slipped the letter into the new envelope, and knew that he had to deliver it.

3

*T*HE PLAGUES THAT NIGHT BEGAN IN THE GUTTERS, WITH A STREAM of spirits washing down a drain.

Just before dusk, Jacob had had a brief and shameful change of heart: watching the people panicking in the streets, he was suddenly moved by the disgustingly human urge to save nothing but his own skin. He went to the depot in a fit of cowardice, paying fifty dollars' gold for a ride in an overcrowded carriage. But as soon as he arrived he saw that it was hopeless. The last train, the one for the government, was already loaded past capacity, its cars labeled with makeshift placards reading STATE DEPARTMENT, TREASURY DEPARTMENT, QUARTERMAS-TER DEPARTMENT, and on and on. The crowds around the train were so thick that Jacob was afraid of being crushed. He considered it a sign. His last remaining hope was to make it to the burial ground before the destruction commenced, but Shockoe Hill was on the opposite side of town. He had foolishly expected to hire a coach of some sort to take him there, but when he emerged from the depot, he saw that nothing with wheels remained in the city: the desperate refugees had commandeered every vehicle left. Night had fallen, the air dark and fresh on the cool spring night. If he were to make it to the graveyard on foot by midnight, he had to set out now.

As Jacob limped back from the depot to the center of town, he saw a Confederate soldier smash a case of whiskey and dump it onto the side-walk. At first Jacob assumed the man was drunk. Then he noticed dozens of other men in uniform up and down the street, each doing the same thing. It was part of the evacuation orders, an attempt to keep the enemy invaders sober. Unable to keep walking without stopping to rest, Jacob sat on a stoop at the corner of Carey and 12th Streets and watched as first bottles and then barrels were carried out of various taverns and saloons and unceremoniously smashed on the street. Soon the gutters were overflowing with whiskey, brandy, and beer, the streets rimmed with rivers of liquor. It was a remarkable sight. The sight that was even more remarkable was the horde of people—at first it was only a trickle of aimless soldiers, but then the stream swelled into a crowd of men of all ages—who swarmed into the streets with pots, cups, hats, and even boots, scooping up the liquor and pouring it directly into their own mouths, even lying down on the sidewalk to slurp the elixir straight from the sewers. Jacob saw the danger coming and stood up, eager to move out of the way of the crowd. But the crowd was growing, and also growing more drunk. In minutes Jacob was being swept along 12th Street and then onto Main, struggling with his aching legs to keep himself from being trampled. Then the madness began.

The first businesses to be robbed were the jewelry stores, followed by, of all things, the candy stores. Jacob watched as old men smashed windows, little boys screaming with glee as everyone helped themselves, throwing candy and gold out to the crowd. The dry-goods stores went next, followed by the saloons, and then the millineries. A few men broke windows at the banks, but they were disappointed: the Treasury Department had emptied them hours earlier. Jacob saw women rolling barrels of meat out of saloons, girls loading wheelbarrows with boots and hats. The government storehouses were opened, and the screams of joy and rage were deafening—in the middle of a starving city, there were immense hoards of food, entire warehouses full of flour and sugar and meat. Jacob tried to fight his way to the side as he saw men his father's age nearly clawing the guards to death, children taking soldiers' guns and attacking the unarmed men like animals, scratching and biting and beating them in unmatched fury while their parents pillaged the goods. He thought of the plans he had read and knew he had to hurry, but the mob had grown so thick that it was almost impossible to walk without being carried by the crowd. He spent over an hour trapped in the horde, progressing along Main Street, unable to move except by the whims of those around him. Along the edges of the throng he spotted several Union soldiers in chains, freed from the prisons when their drunken captors abandoned them; he watched as they took axes from the plundered stores and tried to chop open each other's shackles, before giving up and descending upon the gutters themselves. He smelled smoke, and knew the fires had been lit.

At first Jacob looked around, wondering what rampaging thief had stepped out of the mob to enjoy a cigar. The smell of burning tobacco is an intimate one. The scent alone suggests an easing of tension, a quiet moment in a saloon, in a drawing room, in a railroad car, in a barracks—a conversation replacing an argument, a secret unburdened to a friend, a comforting acknowledgment of desire and weakness: the thin wisp of tobacco smoke rising between two people is a quiet celebration of civilization over savagery. At least that was what it had always suggested to Jacob until that night, when he inhaled the overwhelming stench of entire warehouses full of tobacco bushels set aflame. The taste coated his tongue until he gagged. He looked up and saw the first flames encroaching on the night sky, even though the closest tobacco warehouse was several blocks away. And then he felt the wind begin to blow.

Fortunately the crowd was too drunk to run out of the way immediately; Jacob would have been trampled in an instant. But he had hardly progressed three blocks through the screaming, inebriated throngs on Main Street before he could see the fires spreading, the light of the blaze jumping from one building to another in the streets between the depot and where he now stood. He heard the clanging of bells, saw the fire brigades running, but the crowds blocked the streets; there was no way for anyone to get through, and the inferno had in any case grown too large to be contained. The city was lit like daylight; he could see the flames emerging onto 11th Street, and then onto 10th, and then onto 9th. Suddenly everyone ran.

Jacob was grateful at first; the rush of people carried him several blocks at a pace he couldn't have sustained on his own. Then the mob attempted to turn a corner, and he was nearly crushed. By the providence of God he found a clear path leading up 8th Street, where the drunks roamed loose, and tried to hasten his way toward Shockoe Hill, which was still several miles away. But he had been on his feet for so long that he could stay on them no longer. He found a doorway out of the reach of the throng and sank down on the threshold, leaning his back against the door. He panted for air, coughing and choking on the thick tobacco fumes until his lungs finally settled. He rested against the doorway for a long time, relishing the small blessing of that little wooden sanctuary, until he saw the building across the street from him ignite. He had not yet succeeded in struggling to his feet when the building groaned, an audible rumbling like an old man waking from a deep sleep, and exploded into a spectacular fountain of ash and flame.

Jacob clung to the buildings on his side of the street and tried to progress, but burning debris was falling all around him now, children screaming above his head and climbing out of second-story windows. He raised his hand in front of his face and saw that he was coated with a thick layer of ash. He hobbled along the buildings until he found an alley, cutting away from the flaming street to one that was filled merely with smoke—until an ember fell into a sewer and ignited the alcohol in the gutters. Walls of flame raced along the sides of the street. Jacob stayed along the edges of the houses that hadn't yet burned until he found another outlet, a back lane that led to an emptier road. He hobbled along it as fast as he could. This street was still full of drunks and thieves, for whom the light of the approaching fires was merely a convenient way to illuminate the stores that had yet to be pillaged. The ground was covered with shattered glass and broken crates. The plunderers, men and women and children, were covered with ashes. By the time he reached the bottom of Shockoe Hill, the people in the streets—soldiers and slaves and girls, black and white, little boys and old women, many of them drunk, all of them raving—were walking about dazed, their clothing and faces and hands and hair painted with a layer of gray soot. The effect was to erase the races, making the white people look like Negroes and the Negroes look like whites. The raging fires were mostly behind him now, though he didn't know when the winds might change direction. He stopped to rest every ten feet or so, collapsing on stoops and doorsteps as he proceeded uphill, but he soon found that it was faster going if he crawled, arm over arm. It took an eternity. At long last, half-dead, he crawled into the cemetery.

The old burial ground was an island of silence and solitude rising above the burning city, the blaze enveloping only mortal habitations, and the ever-growing mob committed to terrorizing only the living. By now the sky glowed as though it were sunrise; the flames from the fires spread and grew brighter by the minute in the city below. Jacob clutched a tree and rose to his feet, grateful to have retained his cane. With his back to the inferno, he saw Judah Benjamin's selected meeting point rising before him: he had arrived at the graveyard's Hebrew half. It was stately, well-kept, with its monuments elaborately engraved in both Hebrew and English. In the light from the fires below, Jacob glanced about at the graves and saw the dates going back over a century. Here were the first

Jewish families of Virginia, peacefully awaiting the messianic age as their city burned to the ground.

Just beyond the Hebrew graves, Jacob could see the tall crosses looming from the grand tombstones in the Christian cemetery, less than thirty yards away. Perhaps the two burial grounds had once been further apart, but now they were separated from each other by little more than a few wide patches of grass and a worn dirt path. Jacob limped past the Hebrew graves and across the dirt and grass divide until he was standing among the first Christian families of Virginia, peacefully awaiting the messianic age as their city burned to the ground. As he contemplated the crosses rising out of the earth, he noticed something—someone—stirring beside one of the gravestones. Jacob looked again, squinting as he breathed in ash. There, slouched like a living corpse against one of the tombstones, was his last remaining chance at American glory: John Surratt.

4

"RAPPAPORT! JUST WHO I WAS HOPING TO MEET ON THE NIGHT of Armageddon. Good evening, sir. Lovely weather, isn't it?"

Tall Little Johnny was lounging on the ground with his head and shoulders against a gravestone, observing the bright orange sky above the burning city while he smoked a corncob pipe. He had been spared the rain of ash and soot, it seemed; his worn coat looked perfectly clean. Surely he had been there for hours already, taking in the flames from a comfortable distance. Jacob watched as he twirled the pipe's mouthpiece around the end of his mustache, calm and relaxed, as though he were lounging in his own drawing room. He looked up at Jacob and grinned.

Jacob tried to smile back, but he was too exhausted even for the minimal performance that such a smile would require. The familiar pain burned in his knees, and he couldn't keep his footing anymore. He staggered toward Little Johnny and stumbled, his cane flailing before him. Just before falling, he caught himself on the gravestone of EZEKIEL HANAVEE, JR., 1748–1807, FATHER AND VISIONARY, and stabbed at the grave with his cane until the dirt yielded beneath it, balancing him on solid ground.

"So what brings you here tonight, Rappaport?" Little Johnny asked, still grinning. "Have you come to pay your respects? How thoughtful of you. I'm sure the honored dead are delighted to have your company."

Jacob tried to speak, but he had to breathe hard for a moment before he succeeded. He panted, each painful breath reminding him of his many weaknesses before he replied. "I was told you would be leaving from here this evening," he gasped. At last he turned and sank down to the ground, collapsing on Ezekiel Hanavee's dry bones. As he leaned his head against the tombstone, he could still smell the city burning, the perverse fumes mingling with the intimate scent of the tobacco from Little Johnny's corncob pipe.

Jacob continued panting as he observed Little Johnny seated on the grave beside him. On the ground next to the courier's legs was the same dirty old satchel Jacob had seen him carrying the first time they met. Surely it was full of gold. Now Jacob noticed that Little Johnny reeked slightly of liquor, perhaps fresh from the gutters. But it seemed not to have affected his senses. He took another puff on his pipe and scrutinized Jacob's face, his features twisting into a scowl. Suddenly he asked, "Who told you I was leaving tonight?"

Jacob looked around, glancing at the orange sky above the flaming city below. "The Secretary, of course," he said, though in the light of the burning capital this seemed utterly irrelevant.

Little Johnny blew a ring of smoke, his boyish lips forming a perfect circle behind it. Jacob watched as the courier took the pipe and tapped out the ashes onto the gravestone behind him. Each gesture was smooth, slow, almost comically controlled. Then he looked at Jacob, and Jacob noticed the incipient fury creeping into his face. "You've always had it easy, haven't you? The easy job in the office, the keys to the safe, the access to the gold. And of course he told *you* that I was supposed to leave tonight—tonight, of all the nights in the history of the world!"

Jacob braced his cane against his legs as he stretched them out on the grave, flinching from the pain. "I wasn't aware that it was a secret," he said, as his breathing calmed. "Mr. Benjamin simply said that—"

But Little Johnny was enraged. "Did you know that I slept here last night?"

Jacob looked at him, bewildered. Why should he know, or even care, where Little Johnny had slept last night? Tonight was the sort of night that wiped away every night that had ever come before it: last night no longer mattered; the last four years no longer mattered; the last four hundred years mattered not at all. To appease him, Jacob asked, "You slept in the cemetery?"

Little Johnny sneered. "No, in the Spotswood Hotel." He spat on the grave he was sitting on, and resumed his screech. "Yes, in the cemetery! I slept in this graveyard, right here on this dumping ground for every god-damned dead patriot since Jamestown, and right next to a pile of dead Jews!" He waved a hand at the Hebrew cemetery just over the dirt path, its old tilted gravestones glowing from the light of the fires in the city below. "Of course, I stayed up for hours before that, waiting for a carriage that never came. Even a horse didn't show up for me. Eventually I just fell asleep, like an abandoned corpse! 'Sunday at midnight,' everyone kept telling me, over and over and over again. 'Sunday at midnight.' 'Sunday at midnight.' 'Sunday at midnight.' Well, 'Sunday at midnight' was *last night*, you goddamned imbeciles! Tonight is *Monday*!"

One can become used to anything, Jacob was learning. The thick smell of burning tobacco, burning cotton, burning leather, burning meat and burning buildings was slowly becoming normal, no longer oppressing the space behind his missing eye. His head cleared as Little Johnny thrust the corncob pipe in his scarred and filthy face. "Now you had better be here to tell me when I ought to expect the transport going to Washington tonight," Little Johnny snarled. "Because otherwise I'm going to carry you back to town myself and throw your crippled backside directly into the fires of hell."

Jacob paused, waiting for him to calm down. Before, Jacob might have been nervous, but now he exuded patience, like a burned corpse who had all the time in the world and nothing left to fear. "I'm here to deliver a message for you, from the Secretary," Jacob said at last, after the color had drained from Little Johnny's narrow cheeks. "He told me that it was urgent."

Jacob was prepared for the courier to punch him in the face, but apparently this reply intrigued him. Little Johnny watched, his rage dissolving in the smoky air, as Jacob opened the jacket of his ash-coated suit and reached into the pocket of his vest. "Urgent, is it?" Little Johnny sneered. "It seems a bit late for that."

"I couldn't say," Jacob replied, and handed the open envelope to him. "I was merely told to deliver it to you before your departure, in the event of an evacuation. It would appear that the appropriate occasion has arrived."

"Indeed," Little Johnny conceded, and snatched the envelope from Jacob's hands. He opened it, removing the single folded page inside. Without unfolding the letter, he peered again into the envelope before looking back at Jacob with a frown. "This message was not accompanied by any *remuneration*, was it?" he asked. He pronounced the word like a man who had never said it aloud before, proud to have it pass through his pouting lips.

Jacob grimaced. He had been afraid that he would ask. But he was prepared to pay him out of his own pocket, for the cause. "No, it was not,"

Jacob told him. "If its dissemination should prove onerous, I would be pleased to assist in defraying your expenses until the government reimburses you."

Little Johnny snorted. "Or until pigs and cows start to fly." He proceeded to unfold the note, and Jacob held his breath as he began to read.

The courier clutched the paper in his hand for a long time, struggling as he mouthed each word. For Jacob, waiting for Little Johnny to work his way through the few lines on the page proved agonizing. Jacob watched him follow the writing with a finger—moving his lips, stumbling, returning to a word again, stuttering under his breath. After what seemed like hours, Jacob registered the moment when the written letters at last resolved in Little Johnny's brain from cipher into sense. He looked back at Jacob, and pursed his lips.

"Who wrote this?" he asked.

The question was absurd, unless he were unable to read the signature. "The Secretary, of course," Jacob replied, struggling to keep the condescension out of his voice.

Little Johnny looked down at the paper. "Ha!" he spat. His eyes traced through it again before he looked back at Jacob, his face locked in a terrifying scowl. "You, Rappaport, are the world's worst liar. Any fool can see that you wrote this yourself."

Jacob coughed, choking on ash. "Pardon me?"

"You wrote it yourself. It's as clear as day."

Of all the fears Jacob had in delivering this letter, he had never anticipated that it wouldn't be believed. He swallowed, stricken. Every innocent man accused of lying secretly imagines that there must be some tribunal somewhere where provable facts are being stored and catalogued, where every right and wrong is being inscribed in a massive ledger book so that true judgment may be rendered and all slander wiped away. Jacob had no way to prove anything anymore. Nothing was left but him and Little Johnny, facing each other over the bodies of those already judged: the courier's devotion against his.

"That's absurd," Jacob said.

"No, Rappaport. *This* is absurd," Little Johnny declared, planting his finger on Benjamin's script. "Why the devil would Benjamin 'cancel all operations'? After everything we've arranged all these months? And after

I've distributed thousands of dollars in gold? *Thousands* of dollars, Rappaport! 'Take no action against the enemy'? What kind of sense does that make? Why on earth would he ever write that?"

It wasn't a ridiculous question, though the answer was clear enough to Jacob: that unlike nearly everyone else in his doomed and deluded land, Judah Benjamin knew the consequences of losing a war. But that was an insight Jacob felt no need to share. "I don't know why he wrote it," Jacob lied. "All I know is that he did."

"Well, all I know is that *you* did, Rappaport," Little Johnny seethed. "And that you think I'm enough of an imbecile to believe you."

Jacob leaned away from Little Johnny's reddened face. Little Johnny stood up, stamping his boots on the grave. Jacob struggled to stand beside him, to avoid cowering at his feet. He hoisted himself up on Ezekiel Hanavee's tombstone, clutching his cane and leaning back against the stone as Little Johnny railed in his face.

"I don't know who you're working for, or why," Little Johnny declared. "But I wouldn't be surprised if you were just working for whoever offered you the highest price." Jacob saw now that Little Johnny was not only a volatile man, but also an imaginative one, the most dangerous combination. Did he know who Jacob was? Or was he merely spiteful—unmanned and enraged, like every white person in the burning city below, by the fact that he had lost? "You're a goddamned traitor, and you always were. Benjamin only listened to you because you're another Jew like him." Mere spite. Jacob felt slightly reassured. He would have wondered how the courier had known, if the air weren't quite so thick with ash. Little Johnny continued ranting. "You and him both, all of you—you'd hire yourselves out to just about anyone if the price were right. You'd sell out the whole country if the price were right, just like you've done in every place you've ever lived. You infest the whole damned world like a race of leeches. I've always wanted to know: what the devil is the point of you people? Are you here simply as bloodsucking parasites, or is there some greater purpose to your existence?"

Answers raced through Jacob's mind, every answer he had ever heard: to fulfill a contract with God; to recall the pain of slavery and the shock of liberation; to accept forever the gift of free will; to sense, in every living moment, the presence and the power of the law. But for Little Johnny, he only had one answer—a simpler, less glorious version of all the others, yet a true one. "To serve our country," he said. "Just like you."

"Is this your idea of serving your country? By tying everyone's hands behind their backs?"

The pain behind Jacob's missing eye had returned. "This is Mr. Benjamin's order," he replied, struggling to keep his voice level. "I am merely the messenger."

Little Johnny laughed, then spat at the ground. "That is horseshit, Rappaport. This envelope doesn't even have his seal."

This was true, of course. Jacob clutched his cane and steadied himself against the earth. "But the message has the Secretary's signature," he pointed out. "It's in his handwriting. You ought to recognize it yourself."

Little Johnny looked again at the letter, holding it up to the light of the eerily bright sky. Then Jacob remembered Little Johnny's childlike print on the receipt he had asked him to write for Benjamin. Perhaps the subtleties of orthography were beyond him. As the courier squinted at the paper, Jacob detected the embarrassment in his expression, accompanied by the slightest hint of doubt. Jacob had won.

Little Johnny turned to Jacob, his eyebrows furrowed into an exaggerated sternness. "All right, Rappaport, I've got a proposition for you," he announced. "If my carriage ever arrives, I'm going to take it straight to the Potomac, and from there I'm going to continue on through to Washington. Now if you really are a patriot, and Benjamin really did write this letter, then I propose that you come with me to Washington—and I shall leave it to you to convince all the agents of its veracity yourself. They've all received your correspondence before, so they can judge for themselves whether to believe you. But if you won't come with me, no matter what pathetic excuse you use, then I will know who you really are. And in that case you may feel free to secure your own transportation to hell."

It was precisely what Jacob was looking for, though, as it turned out, several hours later than he might have preferred. "Agreed," Jacob said. "Take me with you."

Little Johnny looked at Jacob, skeptical. Then he grinned. "All right, then," he replied. Jacob watched as the courier folded the note and returned it to the envelope, tucking it into the inside pocket of his vest. "When the carriage arrives, you—"

Suddenly he stopped speaking. For a moment Jacob was confused, watching as his eyes searched the sky. But in the same split second, Jacob heard what Little Johnny heard: a piercing whistle, and then a strange, suffocating silence, as if the whole world had stopped.

"Holy Mother of God," Little Johnny whispered.

And then they were both blown off the graves, as the wrath of God shook them free from the foundations of the earth.

The explosion was so deafening that it surpassed the realm of sound and became tangible, visible, as if they were clutched in a fist of thunder. For that instant, nothing existed but the awesome power of that sound. It released them from the ground, casting them both through the air before dropping them in an angry heap on a pile of soft earth just past the path dividing the Christian from the Hebrew burial grounds. Jacob cowered on the dirt, blinded by shock. When he at last pulled his head up and opened his eye, the first thing he saw in the glowing light from the fires below was an old tombstone carved with an image of two hands held together with their fingertips touching, the fingers separated into pairs—the mark for the grave of a descendant of the biblical high priest. As he regained his senses, his first conscious, illogical, and irrelevant thought was to remember that he should never have been in a cemetery to begin with.

"What the devil was that?" Little Johnny screamed.

To Jacob's astonishment as he shifted his legs, he felt almost no pain—or perhaps he had suffered so much that night that he could no longer sense it. He pulled himself up into a sitting position, righting himself on the earth. He glanced around and saw that his cane had been blown over with him; he moved a bit along the ground and grabbed it from where it lay on a patch of grass.

"It was the powder magazine," Jacob said. "The arsenal, by the river. The militia was told to blow it up."

Little Johnny looked at him with wide eyes, then narrowed them. The sky was lit like daylight. The courier's head was badly bruised, a red welt rising on one side of his forehead. "You've got all the answers, don't you?" he sneered, pressing his hand to his temple. "You're a goddamned Hebrew prophet."

"I saw the evacuation orders," Jacob spat back. "They were instructed to detonate the powder magazine. In fact they were told to blow up all the ordnance in the whole—" The battery of explosions began.

None was as violent as the first, but each was a rumbling, deafening crack that broke open the sky until the stars rained down over their heads, showering them with leaves, soot, pebbles from the tombstones, and once even a hailstorm of shattered glass from the single window of the morgue fifty yards away. Jacob clung to the granite slab with the priestly hands, trying to bend it over his own head as he buried himself in the ground beside it, his head rattling as though the pebbles from the tombstones had been deposited inside his skull. After what seemed like an endless volley of blasts, the silence that followed felt otherworldly, as if he were being ushered into the antechamber of death. For a long time he lay on the grave, dwelling in that dark and silent room. Then he heard the clop of horses' hooves, and a high voice calling out, "Little Johnny? Is that you?"

Jacob might have been able to stand, with the help of his cane, but he was afraid to try. Instead he pulled himself up until he was sitting on the dirt, his head high enough to see Little Johnny crouching by the grave beside him and, a few yards past him, a boy of about thirteen. The boy was skinny, and might have had blond hair, though it was hard to tell with the layer of soot coating his head. He was wearing a ragged jacket that was dyed gray with ash, and his thin face and hands were streaked with soot and dirt. The boy was leading a horse by the reins—a large, magnificent animal that Jacob first thought was gray in color. But it was only the ash.

Jacob watched as Little Johnny hustled to his feet. For a moment Jacob envied the quick movements of the uninjured, the unappreciated talent for instant motion, for ease, for sudden escape.

"Yes!" Little Johnny shouted, as if the boy were about to offer him salvation. "Are you—are you—"

"I'm your ride to Washington," the boy announced, and smiled "I brought a horse for you."

Little Johnny looked at the boy, then at the ash-covered horse. His face turned pale. "A *horse*?" he shrieked. "I've been sitting here for two whole nights, expecting a proper carriage, and all this time I've been waiting for a goddamned *horse*?" The boy said nothing, clutching the reins as Little Johnny continued shouting. "If I had known it was only going to be a horse, I could have managed on my own, without having to sit through the apocalypse in a goddamned graveyard!"

The boy scowled, his sooty face crinkling. "I started the night with a carriage, when I first set out," he said. "And a second horse, too." His voice was like a girl's. "But that was hours ago. Some drunken soldiers took them."

Little Johnny looked at him in despair. "You lost the carriage to a couple of drunks?"

The boy stamped a foot. "It wasn't a couple of drunks. There were ten of them, maybe more. There was nothing I could do." He rubbed the flank of the horse beside him, dusting ash off the horse's hide. "But the Lord was on our side, and saved us a horse. He was awful spooked by the blasts, though."

Little Johnny spat at the ground, clearly disgusted. "Well, bully for that," he said.

Jacob looked at the boy and marveled at the pull of duty, how a thirteen-year-old had traversed a burning city—with the cause, to all appearances, already lost—just to complete this errand, as though it were more important than his own life. The boy patted the horse on the side of its neck, releasing a small cloud of ash, and quickly passed the reins to Little Johnny. Then he jutted his chin at Jacob. "Is the cripple going too?" he asked.

Before Jacob could answer, Little Johnny did. "Unfortunately, yes," he replied, and glanced at Jacob with disdain. "But I'm a decent rider, so I'll manage it. He'll ride right behind me until we get to the next stop, even if I have to tie him to my waist. That horse looks like he can handle us. It's only twenty miles or so." Jacob flinched, anticipating the pain of such a ride, but it would hardly be the worst he had endured that night. Little Johnny was already looping the horse's reins around a tall narrow monument, next to a raised flat gravestone that was wide and tall enough for them both to stand on. Mounting the horse would be painful too, but Little Johnny was big enough to help him, and Jacob was small enough to know how to suffer. "It would have been a hell of a lot more comfortable with a carriage," Little Johnny muttered.

"'The Lord giveth, and the Lord taketh away,'" the boy quoted. He looked at Little Johnny, and smiled again. Then he held out a hand.

Little Johnny glared at him. "I suppose you are expecting full payment," he said.

The boy stood firm, narrowing his eyes at Little Johnny as though he were the adult and Little Johnny the child. "After everything I did to get here, I ought to be paid triple," he answered. He was almost two full heads shorter than Little Johnny, and had to strain to look up at him. His voice was comically high. "I risked my life just to keep that horse."

Little Johnny opened his satchel and pulled out a change purse. "I won't pay you more than you are owed," he declared. "You're lucky to get anything, frankly. You didn't bring the carriage. You ought not to be paid at all."

The boy smiled. Jacob thought of Rose, and of Abigail's brothers, and remembered again how the world had been destroyed for these children, how nothing at all was left for them. He looked at the boy's smile and imagined that he saw forgiveness in it, some expectation that the destruction the adults had wrought might not be in vain. But that was only Jacob's imagination. The boy was still smiling as he reached under his jacket, pulled out a pistol, and leveled it at Little Johnny's face. "I'll take whatever you've got," he said.

Jacob was surprised by how quickly Little Johnny complied. He turned purple, to be sure, but he didn't resist. Instead he opened the bag and held it out for the boy, dropping his change purse back into it. "On your knees," the boy ordered as he took the bag from Little Johnny's hands. Little Johnny dropped to the ground, eye to eye with the boy as the boy helped himself to the purse, still pointing the gun at Little Johnny. *Savagery is a way of life,* Jacob heard Philip Levy say in his head. *My worst enemy is lawlessness.* The boy rummaged through Little Johnny's satchel and pulled out a small Deringer pistol, which he slipped into his own jacket pocket, but apparently he found nothing else of interest. He dropped the bag in front of Little Johnny, without lowering his gun. Then he turned to Jacob. Jacob raised his hands above his head, but the boy merely smiled.

"Wounded in the line of duty, were you?" the boy asked, pointing at Jacob's eye patch.

"Yes," Jacob said.

"Don't worry, sir, I won't take anything from you. You've given plenty already," he said. "Any fool can see that you're a real patriot." He saluted Jacob, a gesture that sent a little cloud of soot flying off his unruly hair. Then he turned and ran into the woods beyond the graves.

When the boy was out of sight, Little Johnny jumped to his feet, threw his hands up in the air and slammed them down on the gravestone in front of him. "Damn it!" he shouted. "That was two hundred dollars in gold. Two hundred dollars! How in hell am I supposed to get to Washington now?"

"At least he left us the horse," Jacob said. He tried to make his voice nonchalant, as if he had seen thirteen-year-old boys holding up grown men at gunpoint every night of his life. *There was no king in Israel*, he heard Philip Levy quoting in his head, *and everyone did as he pleased*. Now he at least had the chance to stop the savagery in its tracks, his very last prospect for glory.

Little Johnny looked at Jacob where he was sitting on the dirt. "Well, Rappaport, this is your opportunity," he grandly announced. "Are you coming with me?"

He asked the question almost sincerely, as though Jacob had a choice. "Of course," Jacob said.

"First you'll have to give me two hundred dollars, or neither of us are going anywhere," Little Johnny replied. "You had better have it."

Jacob did, though it was all he had. Little Johnny held open his satchel, and Jacob emptied gold pieces out of his pockets as Little Johnny grinned. "I knew I could rely on you for the gold," the courier sneered as Jacob counted out the last piece. "Now let's get your lame backside onto this goddamned horse."

Jacob breathed in, a long, ash-laden breath, and exhaled, his whole life evaporating into the reeking tobacco-scented air. It was more difficult than he anticipated to bring himself to his feet. He struggled in his place on the ground for quite a while, fumbling with his cane. Little Johnny did nothing to help him. Instead he stepped away to fuss with the horse. Jacob turned around to balance himself on the tombstone and rose, with his back to John Surratt. And there he saw the little girl.

She was wearing a filthy soot-stained nightgown beneath a filthy soot-stained cloak, toddling toward him with uncertain steps in her battered buckled shoes. She was coated with gray ash. When she came closer, he squinted his remaining eye and saw her face—blue eyes, soot-smeared cheeks, a red gash on one side of her forehead, and ash-coated curls, her wet lips gleaming in the light of the fires from the burning city. She was standing before him now, shorter than his cane, looking up at his face. He trembled, unable to breathe. But she smiled at him, and wrapped her sooty arms around his crippled legs. He sank down to his knees and buried his lips in the ashes on her hair. Her mother was standing behind her.

"Sorry, miss. This livery service is already oversubscribed. You'll have to book your passage elsewhere."

Jacob turned, still on his knees, and saw Little Johnny watching him, his dark eyes bright and expectant in the unearthly light. "Rappaport, let's leave," he said.

Deborah had taken a step back from him now. She raised her hand to his face, reaching up to touch his eye patch and his scars. He took her fingers in his, gently, enveloping her whole hand until it was sealed within his fist, protected from ugliness and shame. He glanced at his wife, and looked back at Little Johnny.

"No," he said.

A long slow grin spread across Little Johnny's face. Jacob watched as Little Johnny reached into his vest pocket and removed Benjamin's letter, holding it carefully in the air before him. "Well, now I know it," he said, with a satisfaction Jacob had never heard before. "I always knew." And then Little Johnny ripped the letter to shreds, releasing the pieces to the winds. Before Jacob could rise to his feet, Little Johnny had jumped up onto the tombstone, untied the reins, and mounted the horse. The horse reared and whinnied with Little Johnny on his back, the man's figure tall and triumphant above the burning city.

"I know who you are, Rappaport!" he shouted at Jacob as he rode off into the woods beyond the graves.

For the first time in his life, as he held his daughter's hand, Jacob Rappaport knew too.

AUTHOR'S NOTE

WHEN I WAS NINETEEN, I HAD THE PRIVILEGE OF SPENDING a summer working as a fact-checker at the history magazine *American Heritage*. Part of my task was to protect the magazine from receiving angry letters from those readers most likely to be incensed by factual inaccuracies—railroad enthusiasts, military veterans, and dog lovers, among others. But I was warned that, among all irate readers, "Civil War buffs are to be feared the most."

Although this novel is a work of fiction, I appreciate the impulse. As a scholar in another field with a profound appreciation of the lifelong commitment required to truly understand any place and time other than one's own, I must admit that there are many people, living and dead, from whom I would be deeply honored to receive angry letters challenging the many liberties I have taken in this book.

First among these are the historical figures who appear in the novel, particularly Judah P. Benjamin—the first Jewish Cabinet member in American history, the author and orator of the address proposing the emancipation of the Confederacy's slaves toward the end of the war, one of the greatest American orators of all time, and a talented statesman who served a justly doomed cause, yet proved his devotion to the last. His service to his country, despite the extensive abuse he endured from every side, made it possible to imagine the broadening of opportunities for all Americans. Prior to the Civil War, Benjamin was the second Jew to serve in the United States Senate, where he represented Louisiana, and he was considered a contender for a seat on the United States Supreme Court. When the Southern states seceded from the Union, Benjamin was briefly made the Confederacy's attorney-general; he then became Secretary of War and finally Secretary of State, a position he held from 1862 to 1865. During the Civil War he was Confederate president Jefferson Davis's closest adviser and confidant, and he also served as spymaster for operations initially organized in Canada, where many Confederate agents were based.

The episode in this book involving the assassination plot in New Orleans, as well as the plot itself, is entirely fictitious, though Lincoln was threatened by assassins at several points during the Civil War (and though Judah Benjamin did have a first cousin in New Orleans named Hyams—Henry Hyams, who served as lieutenant governor of Louisiana). There is a great deal of debate surrounding Lincoln's assassination even nearly a century and a half later. Government investigations in the 1860s succeeded in proving only a "simple" conspiracy of locally organized assassins and collaborators (who also stabbed William Seward, the Union Secretary of State, on the same night), but it is now clear that many of these conspirators, including assassin John Wilkes Booth, had served for much of the war as agents on the Confederate government payroll, and that several of them, again including Booth, had also been engaged in a rather desperate plot to kidnap Lincoln and perhaps other Northern officials—a plot which circumstantial evidence has linked to the Confederate government. Given current research, one would have to stretch (as certain historians admittedly have) to claim any connection between the ultimate assassination and the by-then-defunct Confederate government, but it is reasonable to speculate that those involved in Lincoln's assassination were Confederate agents who acted as rogues in the wake of the Confederate government's flight.

In the months following Lincoln's death, the only potential link that the Union investigation could find between the known conspirators and the Confederate government was Judah Benjamin's hiring of John Surratt as a Confederate courier. Surratt's mother, Mary Surratt, owned the boardinghouse in which the conspirators met, and later became the first woman ever executed by the United States government for her role in the conspiracy. Some contemporary observers, as well as some historians, believed that her death sentence was in part an attempt to draw out the then fugitive John Surratt. Years after his own capture in Egypt in 1867 and his subsequent trial, which ended in a hung jury, John Surratt publicly claimed that he had been given two hundred dollars in gold by Judah Benjamin the day before the evacuation of Richmond to defray his expenses while delivering messages to agents in Canada, and that this was the extent of his service to the Confederate government. He also stated that neither Jefferson Davis nor Judah Benjamin had any knowledge of Booth's assassination plot. After the fall of Richmond and the collapse of the Confederacy, Judah Benjamin managed a fabulous escape, involving everything from disguising himself as a Frenchman to traversing the swamps of Florida on foot to following a talking parrot to the home of a Confederate sympathizer to surviving the sinking of one boat in the Caribbean and a fire on another. He ultimately succeeded in reaching England, where he had citizenship due to his birth in the British West Indies. In England he began an entirely new life as a barrister, rising to the level of Queen's Counsel and authoring an important legal treatise used to this day. He never returned to the United States.

Among the many other historical figures, spies, and citizens who served as inspiration for the characters in this book, I must first mention Eugenia Levy Phillips, a Southern Jewish woman and mother of nine who was imprisoned twice by the Union army: once, with two of her daughters, for espionage along with the Confederate spy Rose Greenhow (whose father had been murdered by one of his own slaves), and later, for insubordination against the occupying Union army in New Orleans, for three months in a boxcar on Ship's Island in the Gulf of Mexico. Mrs. Phillips was the wife of Philip Phillips, a Jewish congressman from Alabama who was a moderate and opposed the South's secession from the Union. Eugenia's sister, Phoebe Pember, was the head nurse of Chimborazo Hospital in Richmond, the largest hospital in the South. On the Northern side, I was intrigued by Dr. Issachar Zacharie, a Jewish Union spy from New York City who served on missions in New Orleans in 1862 and then in Richmond in 1863—the latter a covert peace mission authorized by Lincoln, during which he conferred with Judah Benjamin and other members of the Confederate Cabinet on a potential peace treaty. I was further inspired by Timothy Webster, a Union spy who succeeded in being hired by the Confederate secret service in Richmond, and by the Confederate spy sisters Ginnie and Lottie Moon, who worked in tandem under various identities. In addition to becoming engaged to sixteen men at the same time (one of whom, a Union soldier, she dismissed at the altar with the words "Nosiree, Bob!"), Lottie Moon had several unusual talents which she frequently used to her advantage—including the ability to dislocate her jaw at will and convincingly pretend to be suffering great physical pain. Others whose personalities contributed elements to this novel include Adah Isaacs Menken, a flamboyant Jewish actress and Confederate sympathizer in Baltimore whose gentleman caller was arrested as a Rebel spy; Pauline Cushman, an actress who used her performance skills as a Union spy herself; John Scobell, a fugitive slave and Union spy who worked with several white Union agents, including Hattie Lawton, who transferred her messages using hollowed-out handles of riding crops; Mary Bowser, a freed slave and Union spy who worked as a maid in Jefferson Davis's house and sent her messages through the bakery that supplied the executive mansion; Nancy Hart, age eighteen, a Confederate woman who, when captured by Union soldiers, tricked one of them into giving her his gun in order to escape; Antonia Ford, age twenty-three, who arranged for the capture of Union officers as they left a party at her father's Virginia boarding house; an anonymous female Union agent who posed as a refugee from New Orleans in Miss Ford's boarding house in order to "befriend" Miss Ford and ultimately turn her over to Union authorities; and an anonymous African American couple—the wife enslaved at the headquarters of Confederate General Longstreet—who relayed messages concerning troop movements through the arrangement of clothes on a laundry line. The renowned actor Edwin Booth, brother of Lincoln's assassin and the owner of the "most perfect physical head in America" according to an 1865 article in the *New York World*, would be most justified in objecting to this novel: by his own account, he was always loyal to the Union, and cast the only vote of his life for Lincoln in 1864.

There were approximately 130,000 Jews living in the United States in 1860, a significant portion of whom were of Spanish-Jewish descent and had come to North America from the Caribbean and Latin America as early as the mid-seventeenth century, and a larger portion of whom were of German-Jewish descent and had arrived in the United States in the early nineteenth century. By 1860 they were dispersed throughout the nation, with the largest Jewish community in New York and the second largest in New Orleans. These Americans were as divided as the rest of the country over the issues surrounding the Civil War, usually but not always along geographic lines. At Congregation B'nai Jeshurun, the oldest German-Jewish congregation in New York City, the nationally prominent rabbi at the time of the Civil War, Dr. Morris Raphall, was known for his pro-slavery stance. His Jewish opponents on the national level included, among many others, Rabbi David Einhorn, an outspoken abolitionist in the pro-Southern city of Baltimore. (New York's B'nai Jeshurun is a large and vibrant congregation today—and known for its progressive politics.)

Many scenes in this novel are drawn directly from historical events. Perhaps the least well known of these is the expulsion of the Jews from conquered areas of the South. Northern general Ulysses S. Grant issued General Order Number 11 from his headquarters in Holly Springs, Mississippi, on December 17, 1862, the text of which is reproduced verbatim in the novel. This order expelled the Jews from the Department of the Tennessee, an administrative territory covering areas of Tennessee, Kentucky, and Mississippi, for the ostensible reason that the Jews "as a class" were war profiteers. It resulted not only in the forced evacuation of Jewish families within twenty-four hours, but also in the imprisonment of those who refused to comply, as well as instances of property seizure. The order was overturned by President Lincoln three weeks later, when a delegation representing thirty-five Jewish families expelled from Paducah, Kentucky, visited the White House to plead to return to their homes.

Other incidents in the novel drawn from historical sources include the description of the slave auction, whose details come from interviews with ex-slaves that were collected by the Works Progress Administration during the Great Depression. The dialogue involving Dorrie and Dabney in the aforementioned scene is taken almost verbatim (along with its dialect) from an 1859 article in the *New York Herald*, written by an undercover correspondent who attended the auction of Pierce Butler's slaves in Savannah, Georgia. The details of espionage in the novel, such as the types of codes used by the North and the South, are also well documented, as is the Legal League, a network of African-American spies who worked for the North by providing information on Southern troop movements and also by maintaining an ancillary underground railroad used by Northern spies (both white and black) to move between North and South.

I am most grateful to the many writers and scholars, living and dead, whose works provided me with the historical background for this book. First among these are Bertram Korn, author of the pioneering study *American Jewry and the Civil War*; Eli Evans, author of the masterful biography *Judah Benjamin: The Jewish Confederate*; and Robert Rosen, author of the comprehensive and fascinating *The Jewish Confederates*, from all of which I drew extensively. I also used Jacob Rader Marcus's *Memoirs of American Jews*, itself an indispensable resource, and occasionally consulted American Jewish newspapers from the period, including the *Jewish Messenger* and the *Israelite*. Concerning espionage, I drew from sources including Edwin C. Fishel's *The Secret War for the Union*, Alan Axelrod's *The War Between the Spies*, Larry Eggleston's *Women of the Civil War*, David Kahn's *The Codebreakers*, which offers very technical explanations of certain Civil War ciphers, and *Come Retribution: The Confederate Secret Service and the Assasination of Lincoln* by William Tidwell and James O. Hall. The last of these is quite controversial for its unabashedly speculative probing of potential links between the Confederate spy network and the murder of Abraham Lincoln. (For a viewpoint quite opposite Tidwell and Hall's, see *Beware the People Weeping* and other works by Thomas Turner.) For general information on the war and the period I have relied upon works such as Shelby Foote's *The Civil War: A Narrative*, as well as the U. S. government's compendium of war documentation, *Official Records of the War of the Rebellion*. For the fall of Richmond I drew from Jay Winik's *April 1865*, in addition to several contemporaneous articles from the *Richmond Whig*, the only local newspaper whose offices were not destroyed during the city's self-destruction; for the December 1862 raid on Holly Springs, I relied on the memoirs of Ulysses S. Grant. On the culture of German-Jewish immigrants and their children, I used *Studies in Judaica Americana*, a volume of academic essays on the subject, as well as the less academic (and less informed on Jewish cultural matters) *"Our Crowd": The Great Jewish Families of New York* by Steven Birmingham, a book best enjoyed as American business history. I also drew from *A Century of Judaism in New York*, the celebratory 1925 volume published on the occasion of the centennial of Congregation B'nai Jeshurun in New York City.

These citations represent only the tiniest fraction of the vast resources available to any reader interested in this period. While I have tried to remain loyal to my fact-checking past, I can only hope that true Civil War buffs will do me the great honor of respecting my imagination as well.

MY MORE PERSONAL DEBTS in this book are both small and large. I am grateful to the editors of *Granta*, in whose Spring 2007 issue I was privi-

·leged to publish an early version of part of this book, and to former *Granta* editor Matt Weiland for his generous comments at that time. Dr. Nathan Winter, my family's teacher of generations, has continued to inspire me from the world to come through his extensive library, in which I first came across Bertram Korn's book and many other relevant works of history. I owe my initial interest in Jewish history in New Orleans to those who welcomed me to the New Orleans Jewish Community Center's book fair in 2002 and directed me to the old Jewish cemetery. I owe the riddle concerning the opposite of meat to Benjamin Lebwohl, and I also acknowledge the inspiration of my cousin Ross Linker, who, at our Passover seder when he was five years old, offered a memorably literal interpretation of the biblical phrase "Pour out Thy wrath."

As always, I owe tremendous debts to my agent, Gary Morris, and my editor, Alane Salierno Mason, for their immense generosity, sensitive criticism, and enthusiasm toward my work. And as always, I am even more grateful to my "in-house" editors: my siblings, Jordana, Zachary, and Ariel, all three of whom are professional writers or artists, and particularly Ariel and her husband, Donny, who allowed me to write this book in their apartment; my parents, Susan and Matthew Horn, who patiently awaited each serially published chapter with comments and encouragement; and my husband, Brendan Schulman, whose work as a careful reader inspired many elements of the story, and who knows the meaning of devotion.

And last, I am honored to thank those who have served as the greatest impediments to the completion of this novel: Maya and Ari, my dark-haired girl and my blond-haired boy. As I finish this book, I have had the privilege of hearing Maya recite the traditional Four Questions at the Passover seder, beginning with the Hebrew words "How is this night different from all other nights?" I hope her father and I will be blessed to hear our children asking these and many other questions on many Passovers to come—and, someday, to know that they understand the answers. This book is for them.

ALL OTHER NIGHTS

Dara Horn

ALL OTHER NIGHTS

Dara Horn

AN INTERVIEW WITH DARA HORN

What attracted you to the idea of setting a book in the Civil War?

I think that every historical novel is really much more about the time in which it is written than the time in which it takes place, and that is very true for this book. The Civil War attracted me because of how polarized America has become in the past decade, and because of how impossible it has become even to have a conversation about current events without knowing in advance what the other person believes. The divide between conservatives and liberals, or "red states" and "blue states," really does go back to the Civil War in so many ways; the "red states" and "blue states" tend to follow the Mason-Dixon line and its legacies.

In 2002, after my first novel was published, I was invited to speak in New Orleans, and while I was there, I came across an old Jewish cemetery. I was surprised to see that the graves went back to the early 1800s. When I read more about it, I discovered that New Orleans in the nineteenth century had the largest American Jewish population after New York. I began reading about Jewish communities during the Civil War and discovered a wealth of material, and what most intrigued me was how these communities responded to the war. Generally they did so with a passionate patriotism, regardless of which side they lived on. But as a national community, their response was a bit unusual. Many American religious denominations split at the time of the Civil War, which is why to this day there are "Southern" Baptists or "Southern" Methodists. But while there were already national Jewish organizations in America by then, such as B'nai Brith, none of them split during the Civil War. One could claim that this was due to the Jewish community's small size (about 130,000

Jews lived in America in 1860), but I think there was also a more profound reason. Today it is common for Americans to have relatives around the country, but in the nineteenth century this was comparably rare—except among American Jews, who, because they were more often running businesses than running farms, were more likely to live mobile lives and to have relatives and business contacts in other parts of the country. This made them somewhat more likely than other Americans to appreciate the other side's point of view.

It was this tension between the need to prove one's loyalty to one's home and a sense of closeness to people on the other side that I found fascinating. Civil War fiction is usually written from an uncompromising point of view—most often sympathetic to the South. I wanted to write something that showed the cruelty and the humanity of both sides, and in the Jewish community of the time I found a way to express it.

Do you think of yourself as someone with strong political views?

I am a political moderate, which makes me an endangered species. I am generally able to disagree with someone's point of view without also believing that they are the incarnation of evil. For this reason I'm particularly fascinated by situations where two sides demonize each other—especially when there is a certain legitimacy to each side.

To me, one of the most intriguing aspects of the Civil War is that most people who fought and died for the South didn't own slaves. Instead they saw themselves as defending their homes and defending an agrarian, traditionalist, independence-minded culture that they rightly saw as threatened by the way industry and technology had already changed the North. Most novels about the Civil War take a very particular approach to who the "good guys" and the "bad guys" are, whether they are novels nostalgic for the old South or novels that explore the evils of slavery. In my writing, I am more drawn to situations where the boundaries between good and evil don't run between people, but within them.

Your previous novels were quite openly engaged with the theological dimension of religion. Does that have any role in this book?

It's true that the supernatural is explicit in my previous books in a way that isn't apparent in this novel. But I do feel that there is a theological dimension to the book in the ethical dilemmas the characters confront and in the ways the characters change. The story of Jacob Rappaport, the Union spy who is the book's main character, was inspired by several actual spies from the period, but I also modeled him on the patriarch Jacob from the book of Genesis. Many of the events in Jacob Rappaport's life (his flight from his father's house to his uncle's house, his involvement with a set of deceptive sisters, and his life-altering injury, to name just a few) are taken from the biblical Jacob's story, following that figure's development from a liar, pushover, and all-around moral degenerate into a fully formed moral human being worthy of the title of father. The book's title, *All Other Nights*, refers to the Passover liturgy, when the youngest person present asks the question "How is this night different from all other nights?" But the question behind that question is more difficult to answer: Are we—or do we have to be—the same people from one night to the next? Do people ever really change? Or, to put it in religious terms, is repentance possible?

Nineteenth-century Americans often referred to God as "Providence," suggesting not only a provider but also an arbiter of destiny. There are a number of places in this book where characters see the events around them as directed by "Providence"—and in more than one instance, they turn out to be demonstrably wrong about the impact of those events. To me, the most powerful theological notion is the idea of human free will, the awesome responsibility that people have for their own choices. The crimes and betrayals committed by the characters in this novel are unforgivable, but these characters cannot continue their lives without finding some way to atone for what they have done. The characters often have opportunities to revisit these crimes, when they find themselves confronted once more with similar choices to make. Then they have to decide whether they are capable of being different people tonight than they were in the past.

What lies behind your decision to mix genuine historical figures and fictional characters in your work, rather than writing "pure" history or "pure" fiction?

The kind of fiction I tend to like best is usually the kind rooted in reality, allowing the reader to imagine his or her way into a life lived by someone else. One particularly voyeuristic way to achieve this is to write about someone who actually existed. In some ways, these real-life characters become a kind of historical detail in the book, like riding crops and gas lamps, with the effect of making the story's setting more vivid and making the invented characters seem all the more real in the process.

But as an academic with a tremendous respect for the unanswerable questions in historical research, I am also terribly cautious about the way I include real people in fiction. I've usually avoided writing from the point of view of a historical figure, for instance, because I think it would be very arrogant to pretend to know the thoughts of someone who really did once have his own thoughts and consciousness. Instead I introduce these people through the fictional characters who encounter them, and much of what comes through of these figures' personalities is filtered through a fictional character's point of view—just as our view of these real people is colored by our own perspectives when we try to learn about their lives from historical sources. The challenge of trying to bring these people to life in fiction, in ways that would be impossible if I were writing conventional history, is to serve the story while trying to be fair to the reality of their lives.

While many of the characters in the book are inspired by real historical figures, only three are "borrowed" from history with the known details of their real lives left intact: Judah Benjamin (the Confederate secretary of state), Edwin Booth (a renowned New York actor who was the brother of Lincoln's assassin), and John Surratt (a Confederate courier who was arrested for his alleged involvement in Lincoln's murder, though he avoided conviction). There is some security in depicting people long dead, but less than you'd expect. My previous novel, *The World to Come*, also featured real-life figures: the painter Marc Chagall and the Yiddish writer Der Nister, both safely dead. But that is when I discovered the phenomenon of the Angry Heir. (Chagall's granddaughter liked the book, though I did hear from others who were less thrilled.) I look forward to hearing from more enraged descendants this time, especially those who have had more than a century for their grievances to fester. I hope they'll believe me that I meant no disrespect.

There is a lot of emphasis in the novel on the ability or inability to say no. What got you thinking about that?

I was interested in exploring the ways in which freedom is a mental rather than a physical state. One character in the book, Caleb Johnson, is a slave who secretly works for the North as an agent for the Legal League, a network of African American spies that maintained an ancillary underground railroad for both black and white agents employed by the Northern government. (The Legal League really did exist, and I based Caleb's character in part on John Scobell, a renowned African American spy who posed as a slave, as well as on other African American agents from the period.) When Caleb takes Jacob in at one point in the novel, it becomes clear that Caleb has made his own choices about what to devote himself to, and as a result he is far more of a free person than Jacob is. Throughout the book, Jacob makes choices without realizing that all along he had the freedom to do otherwise.

People frequently give up their mental liberty in exchange for any number of things—pride, status, ambition, love, or any other desire—or simply to fulfill the expectations of others, often without being aware of what they have lost. Freedom isn't about having no obligations, but about the ability to choose one's obligations.

You wrote your dedication to your children as "the cause." Given that this novel has strong political themes and for each side the cause is political, it raises the question: If our children are the only cause, or a given cause is held as emotionally close as our children, can anything ever be achieved, or resolved, in politics?

In the book, one of the characters claims that "raising children is one of the only things one can do with one's life" because, as he puts it, "You can devote yourself to a cause, but what cause could be worth more than a child?" I do think that devotion to a cause is something that only people without children usually have the luxury of expressing. People who are parents have something else in their lives that will almost always matter more to them. But people with children are also more likely to have something else that people without children are somewhat less likely to have, which is empathy for other people's children. Large social changes tend to happen only when enough people see the problem at hand as something that affects their own children—or when enough people are motivated to care about other people's children.

What were the particular satisfactions (or frustrations) of writing this novel?

My two previous novels were written from many different perspectives, with scenes taking place at various points in history and never in chronological order. For me this was always an easier way to write a book—to follow whichever character's point of view was most intriguing or use whatever historical period seemed most relevant to the themes of the story that emerged. As I began writing this book, though, I wondered if it would be possible for me to write a more traditionally structured novel: to write from just one character's point of view, with the events happening chronologically. That is, with no tricks.

Many contemporary novels (aspects of my previous books included) tend to rely on tricks—on jumping around in time or perspective, or telling stories in a manner far more complicated than is necessary. This can be valuable, but only to a point. Ultimately the reader needs a story and characters worth caring about for their own sake, and not merely for the styles or techniques used to present them. It was very refreshing for me to write this book almost as a nineteenth-century novel, complete with all the shameless action-adventure plot twists that nineteenth-century readers would have expected—the book includes a shoot-out at a wedding, a kidnapping plot, a prison break (or three), and so on. It was a lot of fun, but it also forced me to focus on what matters most in writing a novel: making the plot and the characters compelling.

There are several different kinds of codes and puzzles in the book—is that a particular fascination for you?

The great thing about Civil War ciphers and codes, for the general reader, is that they are on a human scale. After the 1930s, military codes became machine-generated, but ciphers prior to that were really just created by clever people, and were breakable by clever people too. That makes them a lot more fun for readers who don't have a supercomputer in their garage.

The codes used by the North and the South are especially fun in this way. The Northern ciphers changed continuously but were always based on a word-reordering system, where the words of a message were restructured according to particular patterns and then certain crucial words were replaced with substitutes. This makes the coded messages seem easy to translate, but they are actually quite difficult to crack. The main Southern cipher was based on a two-layered alphabet substitution system—which makes the coded messages look completely indecipherable, but which is actually quite easy to break once you know how the letters are being substituted. (There are more detailed explanations of both ciphers given in this guide.)

Some of the codes in the book are simply there for nonhistorical fun. Rose, the youngest of the spy sisters, speaks in palindromes and anagrams, a talent she uses when ciphering real messages. These codes and puzzles interest me because people almost always speak in some sort of code. In the novel and in real life, an enormous percentage of daily conversation consists of both outward and hidden meanings, and the way something is said is almost always more important that the words themselves.

Your first two books ranged around the world, from suburban New Jersey to Holland to the Soviet Union to Vietnam. This one is set purely in the

United States. Do you have an itch to travel again? If so, where might you take us in your next novel?

I've been fortunate to travel a lot in my life; I've been to about fifty countries around the world, and that is something that has deeply influenced my novels. Now that I have three children aged three and under, I spend a lot more time closer to home. But I feel lucky to be able to draw from my experiences in other countries and cultures, even while writing a book set in my native country—because while this book takes place in America, it is a very different America from the one that anyone alive today has ever lived in. I don't know where my next book might go—at the moment I've only written the first fifty pages, which I'm sure to throw away—but it will likely involve another country, even if it's only this country in the past.

A NOTE ON CODES AND CIPHERS

The Union Cipher System

WISE ASSASSINATE IN ORDERED HIM HIS CIVIL IN FOR TONIGHT IS NIGHTS YOKE THE QUESTION FOR IS UNCLE TO ASIA MINT TO ON COMMANDERS WAR THE JACOB DIFFERENT FROM RAPPAPORT WHISKEY IT HAVE PASSOVER MURDER WHO DARA PLOTTING OWN HE ANSWERED A DURING JEWISH OTHER HOW ALL A WALNUT IS ALREADY 1862 HIS IS HORN
    —First two sentences of book description, in Union cipher

The cipher used by the Union during the Civil War worked through a system of routing columns. The code went through several evolutions between 1861 and 1865. In the cipher's most developed state, the first word of a ciphered message was a key word, indicating the number of columns and lines into which the subsequent words needed to be arranged as well as the route for reading them correctly. Meaningless words were used to complete columns or rows. Substitute words were used for terms such as state, city, and river names, names of officers or leaders on either side, hours of the day, military expressions, and later for common phrases. The key words and substitute words were initially few enough in number to fit on a small card or to be committed to memory. As the war progressed and the cipher became more complicated, twelve pages' worth of key words were used, along with more than sixteen hundred substitute words. The cipher was contained in a booklet whose listings were themselves rather convoluted and obscure, and the absence of instructions in the booklet made it useless to any enemy who might find it. The example here uses Cipher Number 9, the version used starting in January 1863.

The first word in the ciphered message, "WISE," indicates that the words have been arranged in six columns of nine lines each, and that the route for reading them correctly is up the third column, down the second, up the fourth, down the fifth, up the first, and then down the sixth. Here are the words rearranged according to this route, with substitute words decoded. (The last two words, "Dara" and "Horn," are of course meaningless.)

1	2	3	4	5	6
How	is	tonight	different	from	all
other	nights?	For	Jacob	Rappaport,	a
Jewish	[YOKE] soldier	in	[WHISKEY] the	[WALNUT] Union	Army
during	the	Civil	War,	it	is
a	question	his	commanders	have	already
answered	for	him:	on	Passover,	1862,
he	is	ordered	to	murder	his
own	uncle	in	[MINT] New Orleans,	who	is
plotting	to	assassinate	Lincoln.	[ASIA] Dara	Horn

While the use of normal words makes this code seem easier to crack than the alphabetically based Confederate code, it was in fact far more difficult to decipher and far more efficient than the Southern one. Although the cipher's coding booklet fell into enemy hands on several occasions, and although many message were intercepted, the Confederates never managed to decipher any version of this code. In fact, Southern desperation to decode this cipher was so intense that intercepted Northern messages were published in Southern newspapers, with an appeal to the public to try to crack the code. No one ever did.

The Confederate Cipher System

JCI MJ XHEQHBM LWSHSDIEX YIWN UET CGJSD RZKAKA GIK ROPQP
DEGTTGWSN T RSJKGT WFPWZMS CG BVR WBUSE EKDG EOKQBT
VVQ GZZBC EBL BB WF C EGI JXBFV ICL KCZO OZHVVL YIWY
TTFRCRK EEWPVZFX YWF UKA AR GELJWWYK 1862 PS VU CDHVVXU
BP GNZRRT VUW FAG LVDFX QB AGK AVCITEA XBH QG CNCFXZRZ
KW BMLIGFKBMXV PBEKPFG
    —First two sentences of book description, in Confederate cipher

While several local ciphers were used on a small scale in the South, the primary cipher used by the Confederacy during the Civil War was the Vigenère Tableau, also called the Vicksburg Square. It was a polyalphabetic substitution system, with a key phrase providing an additional layer of encryption. Messages were ciphered and deciphered using the "square," a table that arranged the English alphabet horizontally and vertically along the top and left-hand side, with alphabets listed after each letter like this:

```
  a b c d e f g h i j k l m n o p q r s t u v w x y z

a a b c d e f g h i j k l m n o p q r s t u v w x y z
b b c d e f g h i j k l m n o p q r s t u v w x y z a
c c d e f g h i j k l m n o p q r s t u v w x y z a b
d d e f g h i j k l m n o p q r s t u v w x y z a b c
e e f g h i j k l m n o p q r s t u v w x y z a b c d
f f g h i j k l m n o p q r s t u v w x y z a b c d e
g g h i j k l m n o p q r s t u v w x y z a b c d e f
h h i j k l m n o p q r s t u v w x y z a b c d e f g
i i j k l m n o p q r s t u v w x y z a b c d e f g h
j j k l m n o p q r s t u v w x y z a b c d e f g h i
k k l m n o p q r s t u v w x y z a b c d e f g h i j
l l m n o p q r s t u v w x y z a b c d e f g h i j k
m m n o p q r s t u v w x y z a b c d e f g h i j k l
n n o p q r s t u v w x y z a b c d e f g h i j k l m
o o p q r s t u v w x y z a b c d e f g h i j k l m n
p p q r s t u v w x y z a b c d e f g h i j k l m n o
q q r s t u v w x y z a b c d e f g h i j k l m n o p
r r s t u v w x y z a b c d e f g h i j k l m n o p q
s s t u v w x y z a b c d e f g h i j k l m n o p q r
t t u v w x y z a b c d e f g h i j k l m n o p q r s
u u v w x y z a b c d e f g h i j k l m n o p q r s t
v v w x y z a b c d e f g h i j k l m n o p q r s t u
w w x y z a b c d e f g h i j k l m n o p q r s t u v
x x y z a b c d e f g h i j k l m n o p q r s t u v w
y y z a b c d e f g h i j k l m n o p q r s t u v w x
z z a b c d e f g h i j k l m n o p q r s t u v w x y
```

Much to the South's detriment, only three key phrases were used with this square throughout the war: "complete victory," "Manchester Bluff," and "come retribution." (The last of these was in fact not used until the final months of the war, though it appears earlier in the novel.) Messages were ciphered by lining up the letters of each word with the letters of the key phrase. One then finds the junction between the message's letter and the key phrase's letter on the square, and records the letter at their junction, as follows:

Message: how,is,tonight,different,from,all,other,nights
Key: com,er,etribut,ioncomere,trib,uti,oncom,eretri
Cipher: jci,mj,xheqhbm,lwshsdiex,yiwn,uet,cgjsd,rzkaka

Deciphering the message entailed finding the letter of the key phrase on the top of the square, tracing down the column to reach the cipher letter, and then tracing along the row to the left-most column to find the message letter. Some agents eased this process by separating words with commas or other punctuation—a choice that ultimately made the code much easier to crack when such messages fell into enemy hands.

Despite the South's distinct advantage in many matters of espionage during the Civil War, this cipher system proved to be inefficient and often ineffective, since the slightest error (which anyone trying it will find difficult to avoid) can render a message illegible. One Confederate major, after trying for twelve hours to decipher a message containing an error, actually rode his horse around the Union formations on the battlefield to reach the general who had sent the message and ask him in person what he was trying to say. Meanwhile, the Union had assembled a team of three very young and very talented young men—known in Washington as the "Sacred Three" for the value of their service—who managed through pure brainpower to crack the South's three key phrases and thereby decipher Southern messages.

Sources: William R. Plum, *The Military Telegraph During the Civil War in the United States* (1882); David Kahn, *The Codebreakers: The Story of Secret Writing* (1967).

1. The title of this novel, *All Other Nights*, is in the author's view also a question: Are we the same people from one night to the next? If not, how are we accountable for our actions in the past? If so, how is it possible to change?

2. Jacob is twice presented with opportunities to potentially save President Lincoln's life, each involving great personal cost. Does he do the right thing?

3. How do the themes of escape and freedom from bondage (as celebrated in the Passover feast) play out in the book?

4. What is the role of deception in the novel? What are the different motivations for deception, and can any of them be good? What are the consequences, both for the deceiver and for the deceived?

5. Palindromes have a playful role in the book among the spy sisters' secret codes, but do they also play a serious one? Many events in the book are repeated (an encounter in a cemetery, a prisoner's unexpected release, a choice regarding a spouse), but with different outcomes. Is there a way in which the book itself can be read as a palindrome? What might this pattern suggest about the characters' control over their circumstances?

6. Theater and performance come up many times in the novel, including Jeannie's stage acts, Edwin Booth's portrayal of Brutus in *Julius Caesar*, and Jacob's role as a secret agent. There is also an element of performance in Judah Benjamin's detachment and courier John Surratt's swagger, among many other characters' traits. Are there any characters in the book whose motivations are completely pure? What is the price of honesty for the people in this novel? Is it possible to be true to oneself when one is forced to choose a side?

7. Slavery plays an important thematic role in the novel, explicitly in the circumstances of African Americans at the time of the Civil War as well as in other forms of interpersonal exploitation. How

are people bought and sold in the book, and what form does freedom take?

8. Relationships between parents and children are pivotal to the story in *All Other Nights*, particularly for the fathers of Jacob and Jeannie. What do these two fathers—one an immigrant and the other the son of one—reveal about their priorities and dreams for their children?

9. What is ultimately more important in this novel: family values or a search for self?

10. The author has suggested that historical fiction tends to address the time in which it is written much more than it addresses the past. Do you see parallels between the conflicts presented in this book and conflicts in American life today? How would you describe them? Which side are you on, and can you say anything good about the other side?

11. What makes someone an American in this novel? Is it birth? Ancestry? Ownership of property? Personal freedoms? The respect of others? What is patriotism for these characters?

12. Where do Jacob's loyalties lie, and is it possible to rank them in order? Where are your own deepest loyalties? Is there a difference between your loyalties as an individual and your loyalties as a member of an ethnic, religious, regional, national, or other kind of group? What do you do when they clash?

13. What do you think most deserves our personal loyalty? Our collective loyalty?

14. What does it mean to be able to say no?

ABOUT THE AUTHOR

Dara Horn was born in New Jersey in 1977 and received her PhD in comparative literature from Harvard University in 2006, studying Hebrew and Yiddish. In 2007 Horn was chosen by *Granta* magazine as one of the "Best Young American Novelists." Her first novel, *In the Image*, published by W. W. Norton & Company, received a 2003 National Jewish Book Award, the 2002 Edward Lewis Wallant Award, and the 2003 Reform Judaism Fiction Prize. Her second novel, *The World to Come*, published by Norton in January 2006, received the 2006 National Jewish Book Award for Fiction and the 2007 Harold U. Ribalow Prize, was selected as an Editors' Choice in the *New York Times Book Review* and as one of the Best Books of 2006 by the *San Francisco Chronicle*, and has been translated into eleven languages. Horn has taught courses in Jewish literature and Israeli history at Harvard and Sarah Lawrence College, and has lectured at universities and cultural institutions throughout the United States and Canada. *All Other Nights* was published by Norton in 2009. Horn lives with her husband, daughter, and two sons in New Jersey.

Wayne Johnston	*The Custodian of Paradise*
Erica Jong	*Sappho's Leap*
Peg Kingman	*Not Yet Drown'd*
Nicole Krauss	*The History of Love**
Don Lee	*Country of Origin*
Ellen Litman	*The Last Chicken in America*
Vyvyane Loh	*Breaking the Tongue*
Benjamin Markovits	*A Quiet Adjustment*
Emily Mitchell	*The Last Summer of the World*
Honor Moore	*The Bishop's Daughter*
	The White Blackbird
Donna Morrissey	*Sylvanus Now**
Daniyal Mueenuddin	*In Other Rooms, Other Wonders*
Patrick O'Brian	*The Yellow Admiral**
Heidi Pitlor	*The Birthdays*
Jean Rhys	*Wide Sargasso Sea*
Mary Roach	*Bonk*
	*Spook**
	Stiff
Gay Salisbury and	
Laney Salisbury	*The Cruelest Miles*
Susan Fromberg Schaeffer	*The Snow Fox*
Laura Schenone	*The Lost Ravioli Recipes of Hoboken*
Jessica Shattuck	*The Hazards of Good Breeding*
Frances Sherwood	*The Book of Splendor*
Joan Silber	*Ideas of Heaven*
	The Size of the World
Dorothy Allred Solomon	*Daughter of the Saints*
Mark Strand and	
Eavan Boland	*The Making of a Poem**
Ellen Sussman (editor)	*Bad Girls*
Barry Unsworth	*Land of Marvels*
	Sacred Hunger
Brad Watson	*The Heaven of Mercury**
Jenny White	*The Abyssinian Proof*

*Available only on the Norton Web site: www.wwnorton.com/guides